A WICKED KISS

Forcing himself to look up from her lush mouth, Julian met Chloe's gaze and felt himself become lost in the rich depths of her inky blue eyes. He began to lower his mouth to hers, ignoring the loud warnings in his mind. For too long he had wondered what she would taste like and he could no longer resist the temptation she presented. The way her eyes widened told him that she knew what he was about to do, but she made no move to stop him.

Chloe knew Julian was about to kiss her. She also knew she ought to push him away. Instead, she leaned toward him, hungry for the touch of his mouth.

The moment his lips touched hers, Chloe knew she was in trouble. As he brushed his mouth over hers, he slid the fingers of one hand into her hair and she shivered from the strength of the desire that roared to life within her.

Her senses reeled as he nipped her bottom lip and, when she gasped from the heat that roused, he slipped his tongue into her mouth. Chloe was startled by the invasion for barely a heartbeat before the stroking seduction of his tongue robbed her of the last of her resistance. She wrapped her arms around his neck and gave herself over to the heady delight of his kiss. She didn't think anything had ever felt as good or tasted as sweet . . .

Books by Hannah Howell

ONLY FOR YOU
MY VALIANT KNIGHT
UNCONQUERED
WILD ROSES
A TASTE OF FIRE
HIGHLAND DESTINY
HIGHLAND HONOR
HIGHLAND PROMISE
A STOCKINGFUL OF JOY
HIGHLAND VOW
HIGHLAND KNIGHT
HIGHLAND HEARTS
HIGHLAND BRIDE
HIGHLAND ANGEL
HIGHLAND GROOM
HIGHLAND WARRIOR
RECKLESS
HIGHLAND CONQUEROR
HIGHLAND CHAMPION
HIGHLAND LOVER
HIGHLAND VAMPIRE
CONQUEROR'S KISS
HIGHLAND BARBARIAN
BEAUTY AND THE BEAST
HIGHLAND SAVAGE
HIGHLAND THIRST
HIGHLAND WEDDING
HIGHLAND WOLF
SILVER FLAME
HIGHLAND FIRE
NATURE OF THE BEAST
HIGHLAND CAPTIVE
HIGHLAND SINNER
MY LADY CAPTOR
IF HE'S WICKED

Published by Zebra Books

IF HE'S WICKED

HANNAH HOWELL

ZEBRA BOOKS
Kensington Publishing Corp.
http://www.kensingtonbooks.com

ZEBRA BOOKS are published by

Kensington Publishing Corp.
119 West 40th Street
New York, NY 10018

All Kensington titles, imprints, and distributed lines are
available at special quantity discounts for bulk purchases for
sales promotion, premiums, fund-raising, educational, or
institutional use.

Special book excerpts or customized printings can also be
created to fit specific needs. For details, write or phone the
office of the Kensington Special Sales Manager: Attn. Special
Sales Department. Kensington Publishing Corp., 119 West 40th
Street, New York, NY 10018. Phone: 1-800-221-2647.

Zebra and the Z logo Reg. U.S. Pat. & TM Off.

ISBN-13: 978-1-4201-0460-8
ISBN-10: 1-4201-0460-8

First Printing: June 2009
10 9 8 7 6 5 4 3 2 1

Printed in the United States of America

To Evelyn Rose and Jennifer,
the two best granddaughters
anyone could hope for.

When you decide what you want to be,
don't let anyone tell you that you can't
or shouldn't
or won't.

Go for it, girls.
Be happy,
stay healthy,
be kind,
and always remember
that you are loved.

Prologue

England—fall, 1785

"Damn it, Tom, the woman is dying."

Tom scowled down at the pale woman lying so still on the tiny bed. "She is still breathing."

"Barely."

"Just worn thin from birthing is all, Jake." Tom picked up the swaddled child that rested in the woman's limp arm. "Poor wee mite. Throttled by the cord, it looks like. Well, come on then, Jake, set that lad in this one's place."

"I hate this, Tom." Jake gently settled the peacefully sleeping newborn he held next to the woman. "T'ain't right. T'ain't right at all. The poor lass has no strength to care for the mite. He will be dying right along with her. Mayhap we could—"

"You just stop right there, Jake Potter," Tom snapped. "You be forgetting what happened to old Melvin when he tried to say nay to that bitch? You want your bones tangled up with his in that pit? 'Course this ain't right, but we got no choice. No choice at all. Better the wee lad dies than gets reared up by that woman, I says. Or e'en murdered by his own mam."

"His lordship'd take good care of the lad."

"His lordship is blind to what that woman is and you be knowing that. Now, let us be gone from here. The bitch wants this poor dead babe in her arms ere his lordship returns, and that could be soon as he was sent word that his wife had been brought to the birthing bed hours ago. The fool who did that will be fair sorry, I can tell ye," Tom muttered and shook his head.

Jake started to follow Tom out of the tiny, crude cottage, but then hesitated. "I will come with you in a blinking, Tom. I just—"

"Just what? We *have* to go now!"

"I just want to make 'em warm and comfortable, give 'em a fighting chance, or I will ne'er rest easy."

"Hurry, then, or soon we be both resting easy right alongside old Melvin."

After making a fire and covering the woman and child with another thin blanket, Jake looked around to make certain Tom was not watching him. He took a sheaf of papers from inside his old coat and hastily tucked them beneath the blankets. When he looked at the woman again, he started in surprise. She was watching him.

"Your babe will have a fine resting place," he whispered. "I hate doing this, I surely do, but I got me a wife and five wee ones. Aye, and I be a coward when all be said and done. That vile woman would ne'er hesitate to kill me if I ruined her evil plans. If ye can, take them papers and hide them well. If his lordship survives all his wife's plots, he will be wanting his son and them papers will be all the proof he will be aneeding from you. 'Tis as much as I and a few others dared to do, sorry poor help that it is. I will pray for you, missy. You and the lad here. Aye, and I will pray for meself as well, for I have surely blackened my soul this day." He hurried out of the cottage.

After waiting a few moments to be certain the men were gone, Chloe Wherlocke crept out of the niche by the fireplace where she had hidden herself when the men had ridden up to the door. She moved to kneel by her sister Laurel's bed and stared at the child she held, the living, breathing child. Touching the baby's soft, warm cheek, she looked at her sister, grief forming a tight knot in her throat. Laurel was dying. They both knew it. Yet her sister smiled at her.

"'Tis just as you foresaw it, Chloe," Laurel whispered, weakness and not a need for secrecy robbing her of her voice. "Life appearing in the midst of death is what you said."

Chloe nodded, not at all happy to be proven right. "I am so sorry about your child."

"Do not be. I will join him soon."

"Oh, Laurel," Chloe began, her voice thick with tears.

"Do not weep for me. I am ready. In truth, I ache to be with my love and our child. My soul cries out for them." Laurel lifted one trembling, pale hand and brushed a tear from Chloe's cheek. "This is why I lingered on this earth, why I did not die soon after my dear Henry did. This child needed us to be here, needed my son's body to be here. I recovered from that deadly fever because fate required it of me. My little Charles Henry will have a proper burial. A blessing, too, mayhaps."

"He should not be placed in the wrong grave."

"It matters little, Chloe. He is already with his father, waiting for me. Now, remember, you must make it look as if this child died. Be sure to mark the cross with both names. Wrap the bones we collected most carefully. Ah, do not look so aggrieved, sister. Instead of being tossed upon a pile as so many others dug out of the London graveyards are, that poor child we gathered will have a fine resting place, too. Here in the country we are not so callous with our dead, do not have to keep moving the old out of the ground to make room for the new. 'Tis a fine gift we give that long-dead babe."

"I know. Yet throughout all our careful preparations I kept praying that we were wrong."

"I always knew we were right, that this was a fate that could not be changed by any amount of forewarning. I will miss you, but, truly, do not grieve o'er me. I will be happy."

"How could a mother do this to her only child?" Chloe lightly touched the baby's surprisingly abundant hair.

"She cannot bear his lordship a healthy heir, can she? That would ruin all of her plans."

When Laurel said nothing more for several moments, Chloe murmured, "Rest now. There is no need to speak now."

"There is every need," whispered Laurel. "My time draws nigh. As soon as I am gone, see to the burial, and then go straight to our cousin Leopold. He will be waiting, ready to begin the game. He will help you watch over this child and his father, and he will help you know when the time is right to act against that evil woman and her lover." Laurel turned her head and pressed a kiss upon the baby's head. "This child needs you. He and his poor love-blind father. We both know that this boy will do great things some day. It gives me peace to know that my sorrows are not completely in vain, that some good will come out of all this grief."

Chloe kissed her sister's ice-cold cheek and then wept as she felt the last flicker of life flee Laurel's bone-thin body. Pushing aside the grief weighing upon her heart like a stone, she prepared Laurel for burial. The sun was barely rising on a new day when she stood by her sister's grave, her sturdy little mare packed with her meager belongings, a goat tethered to the patient mount, and the baby settled snugly against her chest in a crude blanket sling. One wind-contorted tree was all that marked Laurel's grave upon the desolate moors. Chloe doubted the wooden cross she had made would last long, and the rocks she had piled upon Laurel's grave to deter scavengers would soon be indistinguishable from many another one dotted about the moors.

"I *will* come back for you, Laurel," Chloe swore. "I *will* see you and little Charles Henry buried properly. And this wee pauper child you hold will also have a proper burial right beside you. It deserves such an honor." She said a silent prayer for her sister and then turned away, fixing her mind upon the long journey ahead of her.

When, a few hours later, Chloe had to pause in her journey to tend to the baby's needs, she looked across the rutted road at the huge stone pillars that marked the road to Colinsmoor, the home of the child she held. She was tempted to go there to try to find out exactly what was happening. The village had been rife with rumors. Chloe knew it would be foolish, however, and remained where she was, sheltered among the thick grove of trees on the opposite side of the road that would lead her to London and her cousin Leopold.

Just as she was ready to resume her journey, she heard the sound of a horse rapidly approaching. She watched as a man recklessly galloped down the London road and then turned up the road to Colinsmoor to continue his headlong race. He made quite a show, she mused. Tall and lean, dressed all in black, and riding a huge black gelding, he was an imposing sight. The only color showing was that of his long, golden brown hair, his queue having obviously come undone during his wild ride. His lean aristocratic face had been pale, his features set in the harsh lines of deep concern. He was the perfect portrait of the doting husband rushing to join his wife and welcome their child. Chloe thought of the grief the man would soon suffer believing that his child was dead and the grief yet to come when he discovered the ugly truth about the woman he loved. She wondered how it might change the man.

She looked down at the infant in her arms. "That was your papa, laddie. He looked to be a fine man. And up the road lies your heritage. Soon you will be able to lay claim to both. On that I do swear."

With one last look toward Colinsmoor, she mounted her horse and started to ride toward

London. She fought the strange compelling urge to follow that man and save him from the pain he faced. That, she knew, would be utter folly. Fate demanded that the man go through this trial. Until his lordship saw the truth, until he saw his lady wife for exactly what she was, Chloe knew that her duty, her *only* duty, was to keep this child alive.

A fortnight later she knocked upon the door of her cousin Leopold's elegant London home, not really surprised when he opened the door himself. He looked down at the baby in her arms.

"Welcome, Anthony," he said.

"A good name," Chloe murmured.

"'Tis but one of many. The notice of his death was in the papers."

Chloe sighed and entered the house. "And so it begins."

"Aye, child. And so it begins."

Chapter 1

London—three years later

Struggling to remain upright, Julian Anthony Charles Kenwood, ninth earl of Colinsmoor, walked out of the brothel into the damp, foul London night. Reminding himself of who he was was not having its usual stabilizing effect, however. His consequence did not stiffen his spine, steady his legs, or clear the thick fog of too much drink from his mind. He prayed he could make it to his carriage parked a discreet distance away. While it was true that he had been too drunk to indulge himself with any of Mrs. Button's fillies, he had felt that he could at least manage the walk to his carriage. He was not so confident of that anymore.

Step by careful step he began to walk toward where his carriage awaited him. A noise to his right drew his attention, but even as he turned to peer into the shadows, he felt a sharp pain in his side. Blindly, he struck out, gratified to hear a cry of pain and a curse. Julian struggled to pull his pistol from his pocket as he caught sight of a hulking shadowy form moving toward him. He saw the glint of a blade sweeping down toward his chest and stumbled to the left, crying out as the knife cut deep into his right shoulder. A stack of rotting barrels that smelled strongly of fish painfully halted his fall backward.

Just as he thought that this time whoever sought to kill him would actually succeed, another shadowy form appeared. This one was much smaller. It leapt out of the thick dark to land squarely upon his attacker's back. As Julian felt himself grow weaker, he finally got his pistol out of his pocket only to realize that he could not see clearly enough to shoot the man who had stabbed him. Even now the pistol was proving too heavy for him to hold. If this was a rescue, he feared it had come too late.

Chloe held on tight as the man who had stabbed the earl did his best to shake her off his back. She punched him in the head again and again, ignoring his attempts to grab hold of her, as she waited for Todd and Wynn to catch up with her. The moment they arrived she flung herself from the man's back and let Leo's burly men take over the fight. She winced at the sounds of fists hitting flesh, something that sounded a lot more painful than her fist hitting a very hard head, and hurried to the earl's side.

He did not look much like the elegant gentleman she had seen from time to time over the last three years. Not only were his fine clothes a mess, but also he stank of cheap liquor, cheap women, fish, and blood. Chloe took his pistol from his limp hand, set it aside, and then, with strips torn from her petticoats and his cravat, bound his wounds as best she could. She prayed she could slow his bleeding until she could get him to Leo's house and tend to his injuries properly.

"Need him alive," Julian said, his voice weak and hoarse with pain. "Need to ask questions."

Glancing behind her, Chloe saw the man sprawled on the ground, Todd and Wynn looking satisfied as they idly rubbed their knuckles. "Did you kill him?"

"Nay, lass, just put him in a deep sleep," replied Wynn.

"Good. His lordship wants to ask him a few questions."

"Well enough, then. We will tie him up and take him with us."

"My carriage—" began Julian.

"Gone, m'lord," replied Chloe. "Your coachman still lives and we have him safe."

"Wynn's got the other man," said Todd as he stepped up to Chloe. "I will be toting his lordship."

Julian tried to protest as he was picked up and carried like a child by the big man, but no one heeded him. He looked at the small figure leading them out of the alley and suddenly realized that one of his rescuers was a woman. *This has to be some delusion brought on by too much drink*, he thought.

When he was settled on a plush carriage seat, he looked across at his coachman. Danny's head was bloody but his chest rose and fell evenly proving that he still lived. The small woman climbed into the carriage and knelt on the floor between the seats, placing a hand on him and the other on Danny to hold them steady as the carriage began to move.

"Who are you?" he asked, struggling to remain conscious and wondering why he even bothered.

"Hold your questions for now, m'lord," she replied. "Best they wait until we can sew you up and some of that foul brew you wallowed in tonight is cleared out of your head and belly."

His rescuer obviously had little respect for his consequence, Julian thought as he finally gave in to the blackness that had been pulling at him.

Chloe sat in a chair by the bed and sipped her coffee as she studied the earl of Colinsmoor. He smelled better now that he had been cleaned up but his elegant features held signs of the deep dissipation he had sunk himself in for the last year. She had been disappointed in him and a little disgusted when he had begun to wallow in drink and whores, but Leopold had told her that men tended to do such things when they had suffered a betrayal at a woman's hands. Chloe supposed that if her heart had been shattered so brutally, she too might have done something foolish. Yet, rutting like a goat and drinking oneself blind seemed a little excessive.

Even so, she had to wonder if the earl was lacking in wits. Three times before this he had nearly been killed, yet he had continued to do things that left him vulnerable, just as he had done two nights ago. Did he think he was simply a very unlucky man? She had hoped he knew he was marked for death and at least had some idea of the who and the why. Chloe did not look forward to trying to get the man to heed her warnings, but Leopold felt they could no longer just keep watch over the man, that it was time to act.

For little Anthony's sake she had agreed. The boy saw her and Leo as his family. The longer that was allowed to continue, the harder it would be to reunite him with his father. Her heart would break when that happened, but she was determined to see that Anthony did not suffer unduly. The boy also needed his father alive to help him claim his heritage and hold fast to it. Between the earl's increasingly dissipated ways and his mother's greed, Anthony would not have much heritage left to claim unless this game was ended very soon. That was unacceptable to her. Anthony was innocent in all of this and did not deserve to suffer for the follies of his parents.

She smiled at her cousin Leopold when he ambled into the room. Leopold never seemed to move fast, appeared permanently languid in his every action, but it suited his tall, almost lanky, body. Those who did not know him well thought him an amiable but useless fellow living off the wealth of his forefathers. Appearances could be deceptive, however. Leopold had been indefatigable in his surveillance of the Kenwoods, had gathered up reams of information, had assembled a large group of associates who were all dedicated to keeping the earl alive and getting proof of who was trying to kill him, and was himself responsible for saving the man's life three times. England also benefited from dear Leopold's many skills, for he was one of their most dedicated and successful agents. Chloe wondered at times if there was something about the earl's enemies that made Leopold think they might be a threat to England as well, but she never asked. Leopold held fast to the country's secrets.

"He will live," Leopold said after carefully examining Lord Kenwood's wounds.

"Again. The man has more lives than a cat," Chloe drawled.

"His enemies are certainly persistent." Leopold lounged at the end of the bed, his back against the thick ornately carved post. "Clever, too. If not for us they would have won this game long ago, even after his lordship discovered the ugly truth about his wife."

"Ah, but not *all* the ugly truth."

"I think he suspects most of it. He already strongly suspects that that babe was not his get. And that his wife was never faithful to him, never much cared for him at all."

"How do you know all that?"

"His best friend has become mine. Do not look so uneasy, love. I truly like the fellow. Met him the first time I saved this poor sot's hide. Thought he could be useful, but quickly saw that he was a man I could call friend. Even more important—he was a man I could trust."

Chloe nodded and set aside her empty cup. "How much does this friend know?"

"Nearly all. Guessed most of it himself. Since I was already disinclined to lie to the man, I *implied* that I had begun to look into the business after the second attempt on the earl's life. He told me that was exactly when Lord Kenwood himself had begun to believe that his wife wanted him dead, that she was no longer happy just cuckolding him."

"Who is this friend?"

"The honorable Sir Edgar Dramfield."

"Oh, I know him. I have met him at Lady Millicent's on occasion. She is his godmother. A very good fellow. He is kinder to Lady Millicent than her own daughter is."

"He *is* a good man and he is very concerned about his friend. That is why I sent word to him this morning about Lord Kenwood's injuries, asking him to keep it quiet. Very quiet. He will undoubtedly arrive soon."

"Are you sure that is wise? Lord Kenwood may not wish others to hear what we have to tell him."

Leopold sighed. "It was a hard decision. Yet the earl does not know us at all, does he? He has, however, known Edgar all his life, trusts him, and has bared his soul to the man on a few occasions."

"Whilst deep in his cups, I suspect."

"That is usually when a man bares his soul," Leopold drawled and then smiled at Chloe when she rolled her eyes. "I felt the earl would need a friend, Chloe, and Edgar is the only close one he has. We will be telling his lordship some very ugly truths, and he needs to believe us."

"You said he already has his own suspicions," Chloe began.

"Suspicions do not carry the same weight, or wield the same blow to one's heart. We will be filling in a lot of holes he may have concerning his suspicions and giving him proof. There is also one hard, cold fact we must present to him, one that would bring many a man to his knees. It would certainly cut me more deeply than I care to think about. We may also need Edgar to help us keep this fool from going off half-cocked and to convince him to allow us to stay in the game."

"What game?"

Chloe joined Leopold in staring at Lord Kenwood in surprise. There had been no warning that he was about to wake up, no movements, not even a faint sound. When he attempted to sit up, he gasped with pain and grew alarmingly pale. Chloe quickly moved to plump up the pillows behind him even as Leopold helped the man sit up and drink some cider doctored with herbs meant to stave off infection and strengthen the blood.

"I know you," Julian said after taking several slow, deep breaths to push aside his pain. "Lord Sir Leopold Wherlocke of Starkley." He looked at Chloe. "I do not know you."

"Chloe Wherlocke. Leo's cousin," Chloe said.

There was definitely a similarity in looks, Julian decided. Chloe was also slender, although a great deal shorter than her cousin. Julian doubted Chloe stood much higher than five feet, if that. She had the same color hair, a brown so dark it was nearly black, but her hair appeared to be bone straight whereas Leopold's was an unruly mass of thick curls and waves. Chloe was also cute more than pretty with her wide inky blue eyes. Julian nearly started in surprise when he suddenly realized where he had heard that low, faintly lilting voice before.

"You were there," he said. "When I was attacked."

"Ah, aye, I was." Chloe decided it would be best not to tell the man just how she had known he needed her help. People often found her visions a little difficult to understand, or tolerate. "Me and Leo's men Todd and Wynn."

With his left hand Julian touched the bandages at his waist and shoulder. "How bad?"

"You will live. The wounds were deep enough to need stitching but are not mortal. They also cleaned up well, the bleeding was stopped fair quickly, and you continue to reveal no sign of a fever or an infection. You have also slept most peacefully for nearly two full days. All good."

He nodded faintly. "I should go home. I can have my man care for me and relieve you of this burden."

"That might not be wise," said Leopold. "This is the fourth time someone has tried to murder you, m'lord. The ones who want you dead nearly succeeded this time. Indeed, they came closer than ever before. I think you might wish to consider letting them think that they *have* succeeded. The rumors of your sad fate have already begun to slip through the ranks of the ton."

Before Julian could ask just how Lord Sir Leopold knew this was the fourth attack on him, he was surprised by the arrival of Edgar Dramfield. He watched his old friend greet Lord Leopold with obvious warmth and wondered when the two men had become such good friends. It surprised Julian even more when Edgar greeted Miss Wherlocke as if he had known her for quite a while as well. Finally Edgar stepped up to the side of the bed and studied him.

"Either the ones trying to kill you are completely inept or you are one very lucky man, Julian," said Edgar.

"'Tis a bit of both, I think," replied Julian. "Have

you come to take me home?" He frowned when Edgar looked at Leopold before answering and that man slowly shook his head.

"Nay," replied Edgar.

"What is going on here?"

Edgar sat in the chair Leopold brought to the edge of the bed. "We have decided that it is time this deadly game was ended, Julian. You have been attacked four times. Four times someone has tried to kill you. Your luck simply cannot hold. Do you really wish to continue to give them the chance to succeed? To win?"

Julian closed his eyes and softly cursed. He was in pain, although he wondered what had been in that drink he had been given, for his pain was definitely less sharp than it had been when he had first woken up. Nevertheless, he was not in the mood to discuss this matter. And yet, Edgar was right. He had been lucky so far but this time, if not for the Wherlockes, he would be lying dead in a foul alley outside a brothel. And what the Wherlockes had to do with his troubles, he did not know. He looked at Edgar again.

"No, I do not want them to win, whoever they are," he said.

"I think you know exactly who is behind it all, Julian," Edgar said quietly, his eyes soft with sympathy.

Not ready to say the name, Julian turned his attention to the Wherlockes and frowned. "Just what do you have to do with all of this?"

Chloe felt a pang of sympathy for the man. She knew the pain in his jade green eyes was not all due to his injuries. Even if he had lost all love for his wife, the betrayal still had to cut deep, and she was soon to add to his wounds. As her cousin retook his seat at the foot of the bed, she clasped her hands in her lap and tried to think of just what to say and how best to say it.

"I believe we can leave the explanations as to *how* we stumbled into this until later," Leopold said.

"That might be best," Chloe agreed and then smiled faintly at Julian. "We have been involved in your difficulties for quite some time, m'lord."

Edgar nodded. "Leopold was the one who brought you to my house the last time you were attacked."

"But did not stay until I could offer my gratitude for his aid?" Julian asked.

"Nay," Leopold replied. "You were not as sorely injured as you were this time and I felt we still had time."

"Time for what?"

"To gather the proof you will need to end this deadly game." Leopold cursed softly. "It is time to be blunt, m'lord. You know who wants you dead. Edgar knows. We know. I can understand your reluctance to speak the ugly truth aloud."

"Can you?"

"Oh, aye, most assuredly. Our family is no stranger to betrayal."

"Fine," Julian said between tightly gritted teeth. "My wife wants me dead."

"Your wife and her lover."

"Which one?" The bitterness in his voice was so sharp Julian nearly winced, embarrassed by the display of emotion.

"The only one who could possibly gain from your death—your uncle Arthur Kenwood."

Chloe clenched her hands together tightly as she fought the urge to touch Lord Julian, to try to soothe the anger and hurt he felt. She was relieved when Wynn arrived with tea and food, including a bowl of hearty broth for his lordship. It was best if the harsh truth was allowed to settle in a little before they continued. She proceeded to feed Lord Julian the broth, oddly relieved by the way he grimaced over such weak fare in the normal manner of most patients. Edgar and Leopold moved to the table set near the fireplace to sip tea, eat a little food, and talk quietly while she tended to Lord Julian.

"What are they talking about?" Julian asked between mouthfuls of the surprisingly tasty broth.

"You, I suppose," Chloe replied. "They are probably making plans to keep you alive and bring down your enemies."

"Edgar's interest I can understand, but I still have to wonder what you and your cousin have to do with this."

"What sort of people would we be if, upon knowing someone was in danger, we just turned our backs simply because we did not know him?"

"Quite normal people."

"Ah, well, very few people have ever accused the Wherlockes of being normal." After feeding him the last of the broth, Chloe set the bowl aside and retook her seat by the bed. "Perhaps we just feel that one cannot allow people to dispose of the gentry whenever the mood takes them. Tsk, think of the chaos that would result."

"Enough of your sauce," said Leopold as he and Edgar rejoined them. "Shall we plot our plots, m'lord?" he asked Lord Julian as he sat down at the end of the bed again. "Unless, of course, you enjoy indulging in a slow, catch-me-if-you-can sort of suicide."

"And you reprimand *me* for sauce," Chloe muttered but everyone ignored her.

"No, curse you, I do not enjoy this game," snapped Lord Julian, and then he sighed. "I but wished to ignore the harsh truth staring me in the face. It is bad enough knowing one's wife is cuckolding one— repeatedly. To think one's own uncle is not only doing the cuckolding but that he and said wife want one dead is a bitter draught to swallow. I am not a complete idiot, however. You are all right. They nearly succeeded this time. I am just not certain what can be done about it. Did the man you caught say anything useful?"

"Nay, I fear not," Leopold replied. "He says the man who hired him was well hidden in a large coat, a hat, and a scarf. All he is certain of is that the man was gentry. Fine clothes, fine speech, smelled clean. All the usual clues. He also said that he was paid a crown to follow you about until an opportunity to kill you arose and then grasp that opportunity."

"A crown? Is that all?" Julian felt strangely insulted by that. "An earl's life ought to be worth more than that."

"To that man a crown is a small fortune, and he was promised more if he could prove that you were dead. And, nay, there is no hope of catching anyone red-handed. A very convoluted way was set up to deliver the extra payment. One that easily allows your enemy every chance to slip free of any trap set for him. Also, proof of your death must be shown, and we cannot feign that. I am assuming that you are rather fond of your right hand."

"You could say that." Julian frowned at his right hand, at the scar that ran raggedly over the back of it. "It was a near miracle that I did not lose it to this wound. A duel," he said when he noticed the curiosity the Wherlockes could not hide. "The first and last I fought in the name of my wife's honor."

Julian was beginning to feel very tired and he knew it was not just because of his wounds. It was his own emotional turmoil that stole his strength, a heaviness of the spirit and the heart. Not only had his pride been lacerated by his wife's betrayal, but his confidence in himself and his own judgment. However, he had wallowed in self-pity long enough. Painful though it was to face the truth, he could no longer try to ignore it, not if he wished to stay alive. Soaking himself in drink and whores might have looked like a slow suicide to others, but that had never been his intent. He was certainly miserable, but not so much that he was ready to welcome the cold oblivion of the grave.

"Edgar and I think you should play dead for a while," said Leopold. "Aside from us, the only one who knows you are alive is the man who attacked you. He will very soon be too far away to tell anyone the truth."

"Your servants—"

"Will keep the secret." Leopold smiled faintly at Julian's look of doubt. "You must accept my word on that, m'lord. Our family and our cousins the Vaughns have servants whose loyalty and silence is absolute."

"Something many would pay a fortune for. So, I remain dead. Do I hide here then?"

"Do you trust *your* servants to be silent?"

"Not all of them, no." Julian sighed. "I still do not understand how you became involved in this mess."

"We have been involved from the beginning, m'lord," said Chloe. "From the night your wife gave birth—"

"To someone else's child," he snapped. "That was *not* my child."

"I know, m'lord. It was my sister's."

Julian was shocked speechless. As he slowly recovered his wits enough to start asking a few questions, he became acutely aware of a new, very pressing need. He tried to will it away, but reluctantly accepted that his body was not willing to wait until he got the answers he needed.

"Damnation," he muttered. "We need to talk about that, but, right now," he hesitated, then said, "I need some privacy."

"Ah, I understand." Chloe stood up, quickly guessing what he needed, and moved toward the door. "I will have the answers to your questions when I return."

"How can she know what my questions will even be?" he asked Leopold the moment Chloe was gone and Edgar quickly moved to help him tend to his personal needs.

"Oh, she can easily guess," replied Leopold.

Julian fought down a sense of humiliation as the two men helped him, washed him down, and put him in a clean nightshirt. He hated being so weak and helpless but had to accept that he was both at the moment and that he needed all the help he could get. Once settled back in his bed, he needed a few moments to still the trembling in his body and will his pain to recede. When he finally opened his eyes again, he gave the two men watching him with concern a weak smile. Then he recalled what Chloe had said and frowned. Julian decided he must have misheard her.

"Did she really say that the child was her sister's?" he asked. "That I have interred her sister's child in my family crypt?"

Leopold sighed and nodded. "Her sister Laurel's child. Laurel married a poor man who died whilst out fishing. She knew she would not survive the birth of her child, that she was too weakened by a recurring fever and grief. Two men came whilst Laurel lay dying on her childbed, her babe born dead, and they took the child away."

"But why? Was Beatrice feigning that she was with child? Was it *all* a lie?"

"Oh, nay, not all," said Chloe as she entered the room and walked to the side of his bed, allowing little Anthony to remain hidden behind her skirts for the moment. "Your wife was indeed with child. She and Laurel took to their birthing beds at the same time, something your wife was well aware of as she held the midwife in her power. S'truth, I think the midwife made certain that both women birthed their children at the same moment."

"That makes no sense," Julian muttered. "If

Beatrice *was* with child, what happened to it? Where is it buried?"

"It is not buried, m'lord, although Laurel and I worked very hard to make your wife believe the child lies in a grave with Laurel. A trade was made. Lady Beatrice's live child for my sister's dead one."

"Again—why? To what purpose?"

"Why? Because the very last thing your wife and uncle wanted was for you to have an heir."

"If the child was even mine. That woman was never faithful."

Chloe stared at him for a moment and then smiled. "Then it seems you won the luck of the draw, m'lord. The child *is* yours."

"You have seen the child? You know what happened to the baby?"

"The baby has been well cared for." Chloe tugged Anthony out from behind her until he stood in front of her. "The child is the very image of his father. My lord, meet Anthony Peter Chadwick Kenwood—your son and heir."

Julian stared into eyes the same verdant green as his own. Thick golden curls topped the boy's head, sharply reminding Julian of his own boyish curls. Julian looked at the three adults all watching him intently and then looked into those eyes that marked the child as his own. Even as he opened his mouth to speak, he felt himself tumble into blackness.

Chapter 2

"What happened?"

Chloe turned from tending the fire the instant she heard those softly croaked words and walked back to stand by the bed. "You swooned, m'lord," she replied.

It took Julian a moment to recall where he was and who this delicate woman was. "I never swoon."

"I fear you have blotted your copy book this time. You have been out cold for three hours."

"Where is Edgar? And Lord Sir Leopold?"

She noticed he did not ask after little Anthony. "They are in the parlor playing with your son."

Lord Julian turned so pale that Chloe reached for him. It startled her when he grabbed her hand in a tight hold and looked around the room a little frantically. When he finally looked at her again it was a struggle to keep her own expression one of gentle concern. For the moment, he was not the earl, or even that lecherous debaucher of the last year. He was simply a man trying desperately to cope with the pain of an enormous betrayal. She cautiously returned his tight grasp.

"Tell me exactly how you came to have the boy?" Julian asked, thinking it odd that holding her small hand should bring him a measure of comfort, but reluctant to give that up.

"If you will be patient, I shall begin at the very beginning," Chloe said. "When my sister's husband died, she grew ill with grief. She was already several months gone with child, and that also sapped her strength. We both knew she would not survive the birthing and soon doubted that her child would, either. We knew your wife was also carrying a child and soon knew her plans for it."

"How?"

"Let me explain that later, please. So, knowing what was to come, we gathered the bones of an infant. As is custom, London graveyards are often cleared of the long dead to make room for the newly dead. During one of the times that Laurel felt somewhat stronger, we went to London and gathered the bones we needed. We then returned to our cottage on the moors that stretch between Colinsmoor and the baron of Darkvale's property. And then we waited. My sister grew weaker and the birthing was hard, the bleeding—" Chloe took a deep breath to push aside a lingering grief. "Two men arrived and so I hid myself away. They took poor little Charles Henry, who was stillborn, and set Anthony in my sister's arms. One man, Jake Potter, could not just walk away. He tried to make my dying sister and the baby comfortable and warm, even building a fire. Then he slipped some papers beneath her covers, telling her that he and a few others had gathered what proof they could for the boy so that, if he survived, he could prove who he was."

"But he did no more? He just left her and the child alone and helpless?"

"He was afraid. They are all afraid at Colinsmoor. People who disobey do not live long. Jake's partner reminded him of that sad truth. Something about a man named Melvin and a pit. Leopold knows more about all that than I do. The moment Jake left, I rejoined my sister. She soon died, but she was at peace with it. I buried her and that poor babe's bones near the cottage. Then I took Anthony and headed for London to join Leopold, who was expecting me. For the last three years we have waited for you to learn the truth about your wife."

"I have known most of it for a year now."

"True, but you did not take it well, did you? The way you behaved made Leopold feel that you were not really prepared to hear *all* the truth. We cannot wait any longer. You came too close to being murdered this time and, even now, Anthony sees Leopold and me as his family. And to be blunt, his heritage needs protecting—now."

Julian let go of her hand and covered his eyes, softly reciting every curse he knew. He sought to stir up anger and resolve, to overcome the urge to weep like some brokenhearted child. The crimes against him were almost too great to comprehend, especially since his wife and his uncle had committed them. Yet he did believe and the grief, the pain, he fought to control formed a hard knot in his chest. Worse, this wide-eyed innocent miss knew it all, even knew of the depths he had sunk into over the last year.

As he began to regain control of his emotions, he realized something else. This small, delicate woman and her dying sister had planned, very cleverly, a way to save *his* child. This stranger had buried her sister and, despite the grief she must have been suffering, had taken his child out of danger. She had made her way to London and cared for his child for three years as she waited for him to be able to take on the responsibility. What he owed this woman and Lord Sir Leopold was beyond calculating, and the debt was bound to grow as they helped him defeat his enemies. It humbled him and he found that an uncomfortable feeling. When he took his hand from his eyes, he stared at the bedclothes as he tried to conquer that feeling as well.

"I still do not understand *how* you knew to do all you did," he finally said.

"Ah, well, I suspect you have heard a few rumors about the Wherlockes and our cousins the Vaughns," she said.

"Foolish things about spirits and gifts. Even sorcery and witchcraft. There have always been such rumors about your family. One should pay no heed to rumors."

"Nay? Not even when those same rumors have been whispered throughout the ton for generations? True, many rumors are to be doubted, but I believe one should at least listen to them. In our case, these *rumors* have caused wives to leave our men and husbands to leave our women. And most leave the children they have bred together as well. Time and time again. In the past, those *rumors* have caused Vaughns and Wherlockes to be burned at the stake or hanged or hunted down like wild beasts."

He frowned at her. "Are you claiming to be a witch?"

"Nay, m'lord," she replied as she plumped up his pillows again and helped him sit up more comfortably. "Oh, there have been some of us who have dabbled in what many call the *dark arts* but, nay, we are not evil witches or warlocks or worshippers of Satan." She held out a goblet of cider enriched with healing herbs. "Drink."

After sniffing the drink she held under his nose, Julian asked, "What is in this?"

"A few herbs to gentle the pain you feel and to enrich your blood, build up your strength, and hasten your healing. No eye of newt or even a pinch of magic."

Ignoring that, he drank it down with a little assistance from her. "Why remind me of what is whispered about your family?" he asked as she set the goblet aside.

"Because of how Laurel and I, and even Leo, knew what was to come and what needed to be done. I had a dream, or vision if you will." She held up her hand when he started to speak. "Hear me out first, if you would be so kind." When he pressed his lips together and curtly nodded, she continued, "Laurel married beneath her as far as my mother and society was concerned, a good but very common man. My mother cast her out. Laurel and I had kept in touch through

letters I smuggled out to her and which my aunt
smuggled to me. That is how I knew when Laurel
suspected she was with child. Shortly after learning
that, I had a dream. In that dream I saw poor Henry,
her husband, swallowed by the sea. I saw Laurel
upon a bed, her body swollen with child, but there
was little life there and it was rapidly fading."

Chloe sat down in the chair by the bed and
tightly gripped the arms as she continued, "Lurking about outside the small cottage where my sister
lay dying was a beautiful woman, also great with
child. She wore flowing white robes decorated with
bleeding hearts and skulls. The dream quickly grew
very dark and frightening. The woman turned
frightening as well and yet remained beautiful. She
tore the dead child from my sister's womb and then
fled toward a mist-shrouded castle. Other figures,
shadowy ones, flitted about and all the while the
glow of life within Laurel continued to fade. I saw
Henry weeping and reaching out for his wife and
child. Then, suddenly, life appeared again, settling
itself in the crook of Laurel's arm."

"And you could make sense of that?" Julian asked
when Chloe fell silent for a moment, intrigued despite his lingering doubts.

"Some. I did know that I had to get to Laurel. My
mother said that if I left, I was not to return." She
shrugged. "I have not. When I reached Laurel, she
had just received news of Henry's death. I had to
help her bury him and then nurse her. She recovered a little, enough to give me false hope. I also
discovered who the beautiful woman was and gathered all the information on her that I could. Laurel

did as well. Soon the plot was clear and we began to spin our own plots, to prepare ourselves to thwart the woman. It all transpired as my dream foretold," she whispered. "Anthony was the life brought into the midst of death and grief."

Although Julian was still not sure he believed any of the talk about visions, he asked, "You discovered the plot so quickly?"

Chloe smiled faintly. "I was but the sister of a poor widow. People would say things to me or near me that they would never even whisper within a mile of you. Also, mayhaps, I had a natural, feminine tendency to immediately distrust such a beautiful woman. It matters not. When I first had the dream I thought I was needed to save Laurel. It did not take me so very long to see that I was drawn into that tragedy to save Anthony."

She watched him struggle with the tale she told. There was the hint of belief in his expression, but reluctance as well, and Chloe understood that. Few people wanted to believe in such gifts. She was pleased to see no fear. Doubts were something she could deal with, but for reasons she could not fully comprehend, she knew it would hurt if he feared her.

"It is difficult to accept that a dream was what saved my"—Julian hesitated—"the boy."

"He *is* your son, m'lord. I have the papers to prove it if you wish to see them."

"Later." He sighed. "He has my eyes," he whispered and then scowled at her. "Why did you not come to me immediately?"

"I doubted that you would believe me. So did

Leo. She was your wife, your love, and we were strangers to you. The cost of trusting in you too soon would have been Anthony's life. We dared not risk it. We *had* to wait until we felt certain you had seen the truth about her or, at the very least, knew enough to heed what we had to tell you."

Julian nodded in reluctant agreement, accepting the distasteful fact that he had been so enthralled with Beatrice he probably would have believed her over the Wherlockes. "I knew the child she showed me was not mine. In my heart, I knew, but I told myself many a lie until that doubt receded. The child did not have the Kenwood birthmark."

"Ah, aye, the little strawberry-colored mark upon the right buttock."

"Exactly. It was not there, but I convinced myself that its absence meant nothing. Told myself that it would have shown itself later, if he had lived. The boy has it?"

"He does." Lord Julian closed his eyes and Chloe knew he was feeling swamped with emotion again. "Anthony is such a pretty boy," she said. "Leo keeps sneaking about and cutting the child's hair. It grows into the most beautiful fat curls, you see. Just perfect for a bow or two. Green bows, of course, to match his lovely eyes." She tsked and shook her head. "Leo even had his valet make some little manly clothes for Anthony, even though the child looked adorable in his child's petticoats. Leo claims that, if I had my way, everyone would soon be calling the child Antonia. Quite silly, of course. Truly, most women would kill for curls such as

Anthony has. I see no harm in showing them off just a little."

Chloe babbled on about the exquisite lace adorning the child's little gowns, ones Leo adamantly refused to allow her to put on the boy. All the while she talked, she watched Lord Julian. His rather beautiful mouth soon lost the faint tremor afflicting it and firmed into a frown. By the time she began to complain about how Leo would not allow her to wash the child or his clothing in rose-scented soap, the man was glaring at her.

"Enough," Julian snapped. "Your ploy has worked. I am no longer feeling missish. B'God, I bloody well hope that was all nonsense."

"Some of it," she said and grinned. "He really does have beautiful curls."

Julian grunted and then frowned at the door. "I think I would like to see him again now that I have composed myself."

"No fear of swooning again?"

"I did not swoon. I merely succumbed, momentarily, to a lingering weakness due to my wounds."

"Of course you did. Actually, I believe Leo will be bringing Anthony by in a moment or two. He has brought the child here each hour on the hour since you, er, succumbed. Poor child thought you had died. Leo allows him to watch you breathe for a moment just to reassure him. Also, Leo hopes to find you awake again for Anthony's sake and so that you may begin to make further plans. The clock has just struck the hour." She listened for a moment. "Indeed, I believe I hear the pitter-patter of little feet coming up the stairs. Anthony's, of course. Leo has rather large feet."

"You are a very strange woman," Julian drawled, feeling an inexplicable urge to smile at her.

"I know. 'Tis a gift."

Before he could reply to that nonsense, the door opened and Leo entered with Anthony, followed by Edgar, who looked uncertain. Julian stared at the child, who skipped up to the side of the bed. He stared into those eyes that matched his to a shade and knew, without a doubt, that this boy was his son. A quick study of the boy's features, his hair, and even his long-fingered hands reminded Julian strongly of the portrait of himself at that age.

The depth of the betrayal he had suffered, still suffered, was almost overwhelming. Beatrice had denied him his own child, and had fully intended that the boy die. She had obviously not dared to kill the child herself, but leaving a newly born baby with a dying woman, not knowing that Chloe was at hand, was murder nonetheless. To know that his uncle had been part of that crime was even harder to bear. Now this bright-eyed child looked at him as he would any stranger, and that hurt.

"You all bedda?" asked Anthony.

"Yes." Julian hastily cleared his throat, a little embarrassed by the hoarse emotion in it. "I am all better, or nearly so."

"Good. Leo and Cohee said you would be. Leo says you are my papa."

"Yes, I am."

"You gonna live with us now?"

"For a while." He frowned when the child began to look a little distressed.

"I stay here. I live here. Leo and Cohee are my fambly."

"Ah, I see. Well, they always will be, for they are your godparents." Julian ignored the looks of surprise the Wherlockes hastily hid.

"Why did you go away?"

It took Julian a moment to understand the question, to realize that the child had obviously been told some tale to explain his lack of parents. "I fear I was lost for a while."

Anthony nodded. "And Cohee founded you."

"Yes, she did. She is also working very hard to make me better."

"She cannot find Mama. Cohee said Mama was swallowed by the Pitahell Monster."

Julian heard Edgar choke back a laugh. He saw Leo scowl at Chloe. Chancing a peek at her himself, Julian found her looking ridiculously innocent. Yet again, he felt the oddest urge to laugh, something he had not felt like doing for a very long time. The Pitahell Monster, indeed, he mused. Chloe Wherlocke obviously did not temper her opinions much.

"It made me sad for Mama," Anthony said, "but I gots Cohee and that makes me happy."

"I am sure it does." The bond between his son and Chloe was going to cause a problem or two, Julian decided. "She has taken very good care of you."

Anthony nodded. "She lubs me e'en when I am naughty. But I am a good boy. I have pretty hair."

Chloe ignored the way all three men frowned at her and she smiled at Anthony. "Very pretty hair indeed."

"Yes, well, I think this has been a long enough visit for now, young man," Leo said. "Your father needs his rest."

"I will take the boy to his nurse," Edgar said.

"I have to kiss Papa first," Anthony said.

"Careful." Leo quickly stopped the child from scrambling onto the bed, holding him up so that he could give Julian a kiss on the cheek. "Very good."

The moment Leopold set Anthony back down, the boy hurried around the bed to Chloe. He climbed up onto her lap, kissed her cheek, and wrapped his arms around her neck to hug her. Julian caught the child looking at him and recognized a surprisingly adult look of challenge. His pleasure over how easily Anthony had accepted him as his father dimmed just a little. Anthony might not call Chloe Mother, but it was very clear that the bond was there and set hard.

"Godparents?" both Wherlockes said the moment the door shut behind Anthony and Edgar.

"Why not? You have certainly fulfilled the role for these past three years," Julian said. "I might as well make it official." He scowled at Chloe. "Of course, all this pretty hair nonsense must cease."

Chloe rolled her eyes. "He is just a little boy. Time enough to turn him into a manly man." She looked toward the fireplace and mumbled, "A manly man with pretty hair."

"Does she practice how to be irritating?" Julian asked Leopold.

"Nay," replied Leopold. "It comes quite naturally, I fear."

Chloe gave both men a look of disgust and then asked, "Are we to plot our plots now?"

"Ah, well, the foremost plot had already been set in motion," said Leopold. "His lordship remains hidden, giving rise to the belief that he is dead. He needs to heal and regain his strength."

"A bit thin, but what about his coachman?"

"He was unconscious, if you recall, and too far away to see the attack. We found the carriage, and put it and the coachman out on the heath. My men stood watch to make sure no harm came to the man until he was discovered. We scattered enough blood in the carriage to cause the ones who found it to cry murder."

"A cry Beatrice and Arthur took up?" Julian asked even though he already knew the answer.

"I fear so, and quite loudly as well," replied Leopold. "The first cast of the die has been made. Now you must do your best to heal and get strong."

"I am not really capable of doing much else right now, am I."

"Do not sound so disgusted with yourself. It was but three days ago that you were attacked and stabbed—twice. You are capable of thinking, however, m'lord. After another day or two of rest, I will put your mind to work on all the information I have gathered."

"Information but no proof?"

"Proof has been a little difficult to grasp. I have not been able to get too close or to search any of your properties." Leo made himself comfortable at the foot of the bed just as Edgar returned. "Your servants provide only a rumor or two. The most telling thing is that it is not loyalty that stills their tongues concerning Lady Beatrice and Sir Arthur. It is abject fear."

"And I have offered them no hope of freedom from that, have I. First because I was so besotted and bewitched and then because I was so caught up in my own misery." Julian felt utterly disgusted with himself. "Melvin worked in the stables at Colinsmoor," he added softly. "I was told that he quit, went to find his fortune in the Colonies."

"I believe it is called America now," Leopold said and smiled briefly before growing serious again. "Melvin is undoubtedly dead. He probably found out something and they knew he would warn you. Unfortunately, we cannot find this pit Chloe heard of or anyone to speak of it. They do not speak openly of Melvin, either."

"The midwife also disappeared after the babies were exchanged," said Chloe.

"Are any of the rest of my family in danger?" asked Julian.

"Your mother and sisters are safe enough," Leopold replied. "They are not a threat to what your wife and uncle want. Your younger brother Nigel is being protected. Not so difficult as he is with our army in Canada. I sent word to a relative there once this deadly game began, and your brother is constantly guarded. However, I recently got word that he tires of the military and foreign climes. He is considering selling out and coming back home, something he will do when and if he gets news of your death. That

makes it even more imperative that we cease this
waiting and act."

"You seem sure your relative can protect Nigel,
yet, if my uncle believes I am dead—"

"Do not worry. My relative can still protect him
and will continue to do so even if your brother de-
cides to sell out and journey home. Once he is
here, we can watch out for him if my relative de-
cides to return to Canada. This particular Vaughn,
a cousin, has a true skill for sensing who is a threat."
Leopold shrugged when Julian looked skeptical.
"'Tis the truth. Trust me. Even someone who is
simply in a foul humor will have difficulty approaching your brother."

Julian did not argue but was not fully reassured,
either. Within a few moments he was too weary to
participate in the conversation even though it concerned keeping him alive. Soon the Wherlockes politely withdrew but Edgar lingered at his bedside.
Julian gave his old friend a tired smile.

"You *can* trust them, you know," Edgar said.

"I would be a low churl if I did not," Julian said.
"Not only do I owe them for the life of my child as
well as my own, but they have watched o'er my
family whilst I wallowed in drink and whores."

Edgar patted Julian on his uninjured shoulder.
"Do not flay yourself with guilt. Such betrayal as you
have suffered can make a man crazed."

"It made me a useless, self-pitying fool. S'blood,
but I am done with that. As Leopold said, 'tis time
to end this game."

"Yes, for that child's sake if naught else. A
bright lad." Edgar rubbed a hand over his slightly

prominent chin. "Anthony might call Miss Wher-locke Cohee, but, well, it will be difficult to part them, I fear."

"I know." Julian barely smothered a yawn. "It will also be difficult to explain how it is I suddenly have an heir."

"Not when we defeat your enemies and the truth comes out. It will, you know. For the boy's sake, it must."

"True. The scandal will sorely hurt my mother and sisters. And now, they will grieve for me, believing I am dead."

"Better that than you, Nigel, and that child dying. Rest. You will need all of your strength for the fight that lies ahead. Soon Leopold and I will present you with all the man and I have discovered about Beatrice and your uncle."

"God help me, how could I have been such an idiot, such a blind fool?"

"Beatrice's allure is the sort that utterly bewitches a man, blinding him to the evil in her heart. Even I felt it. And no, I do not believe your uncle is so blinded. In truth, I believe he and Beatrice are a mating of like souls." Edgar winked, his blue eyes bright with amusement as he stood up and headed out the door. "Soon they will get what they so richly deserve—swallowed by the Pitahell Monster."

Julian was surprised to find himself smiling as he carefully shifted his body into a more comfortable position. He realized he had not really lied to his son when he had told the boy he had been lost. In many ways it was the cold, ugly truth. Grief, bruised pride, and a deep sense of humiliation had taken him to a very dark place, but he was free of that now. He bore scars, wounds he feared would never heal, but he was ready to face his troubles now. He had a son to protect, a child to raise, and that gave him a sense of purpose he had not felt in a long, long time. As sleep dragged him into its folds, he wondered why the image of an impudent woman with inky blue eyes lingered in his thoughts.

Chapter 3

"Damn them," Julian muttered as he let the last of the papers Leopold had given him fall into his lap and slumped against the pillows. After a full night of sleep he had thought himself strong enough to face even more hard, ugly truths, but he was not so sure of that now. "Do you think it was all planned from the very beginning? That I was naught but a pawn from the start?"

"That is a possibility," replied Leo as he straightened up a little in the chair he had set next to Julian's bed. "I am sorry to get so personal, but was your wife a virgin?"

"I think not." Julian felt himself blush faintly. "I was not vastly experienced when I married and had never bedded down with a virgin. Would probably never have done so even if the opportunity had been there. I saw no glory in dishonoring some foolish, naïve innocent. As for Beatrice, things I have learned since make me believe she feigned all of her innocence. A woman at one particular brothel entertained me with the tale of how she made quite an impressive amount of money by pretending to be a virgin until she was past an age where it was believable. The tale of how she enacted that lie again and again reminded me very strongly of Beatrice on our wedding night. I was sorely tempted to ask the woman if she had ever taught her tricks to a lady, to my wife, but I could not. S'blood, but I really did not wish to hear her answer," he added softly.

"Of course you did not. Eminently understandable."

"Oh? Eminently cowardly might be more accurate."

"Perhaps, but a cowardice most men would share. Betrayal had already sent you crawling through brothels. You did not need to hear of yet another one. In your place, *I* would not have wished to hear the answer, either. However, that does make me think my suspicions are correct, that your uncle chose Beatrice, that he wanted an ally as close to you as possible. Who better than a lover or a wife?"

"Who better indeed? These papers show that they also seek to put me in debtor's prison."

"Which neatly answers the question of *why*, does it not?" Leo said as he stood up and stretched before idly pacing the length of the room.

"I suspect it does."

"From what I have seen and learned through careful investigation and observation, most of your lands and investments are intact and are carefully tended. It appears the pair does realize that they need to do at least that much to keep their purses full of your money. Other lands you own are not faring quite so well." Leo shrugged. "They have no interest in them and so they bleed them dry and invest nothing in them. Since the rumor that you are dead is spreading fast and wide now, there have already been whispers seeping about saying that certain unentailed properties will soon enter the market."

Leo waited patiently as Julian indulged in a hearty, creative bout of cursing, then said, "There is no proof that you are dead, Julian, so it will be very difficult to dispense with your property too quickly."

"And Nigel is my heir, not my uncle. I also changed my will, leaving my wife a very small annuity. I thought of leaving her nothing at all but decided that would raise too many questions, the answers to which would be embarrassing for my family."

"But before that, she had a healthy widow's portion, I suspect."

"She did and it included some property, but that property could not be sold without the new earl's full approval."

"Who is in Canada. So, if your uncle could show that you gave him the right to act in your stead or made him the executor of your will . . ."

"I never did such a thing, never gave him any rights or power at all. Of course, that does not mean that he could not produce some claim that he had them." Julian grimaced. "What would a little forgery matter to such a man?"

"True. He could also dispute your will as it was made in the heat of anger or any other excuse he can think of. So we must conjure up some way to put a spoke in his wheel."

"Such as what?" Julian was beginning to think that Leopold Wherlocke had a very devious mind.

"Such as debts accrued during the year you were, well, not quite yourself."

"You mean whilst I acted the drunken debauchee," Julian drawled, still feeling the pinch of shame and embarrassment over his behavior of the last year. "Unfortunately, I do not believe I have any outstanding debts, certainly not of the sort that could be used to grab fistfuls of any property I own."

Leo sat on the end of the bed and leaned against the thick bedpost. "Nay, you do not, but that does not mean we cannot produce a few. Do you think your uncle and your wife know of every little thing you have done over the past year?"

Julian thought about that possibility for a few moments and then shook his head. "No, I think not. They have obviously kept a watch on what I was doing, and where, or hired someone else to do it so that they could plan their attempts to kill me, but I can think of several times when they would have had a good chance of succeeding yet nothing happened. And I did gamble and there were some losses, but nothing too severe."

"Then I believe it might be wise to conjure up a few sizeable debts, ones that could be produced quickly if the sale of certain properties looked imminent. Think of which properties you would truly regret losing and write a chit deeding it or its profits over to me or Edgar or both of us."

"You have an astonishingly devious mind," Julian said, unable to hold the thought back any longer.

"Thank you."

"I will give some hard thought to which properties I truly do not wish to lose and then see to it that you and Edgar have the proper papers to hold up any attempt to sell them for a very long time."

"Let us pray that we will not need a very long time to clean up this treacherous mess. Now, what about that will?"

"As I said, I made a new one when I realized Beatrice had betrayed me, but I cannot be certain if it still exists. About six months ago, during one of my more sober days, I had a meeting with my solicitor and I got the strongest feeling that he had been corrupted. I told myself Beatrice's betrayal was just making me too suspicious."

Leo nodded. "Possibly, but probably not true in this matter. A copy?"

"There is one at Kenwood House, but if my solicitor does not stand behind it, it may not be worth very much. In it I left much of what was not entailed to Edgar, my sister, or my mother." Julian grimaced. "Even if the copy has been found, Arthur could try to do as you have suggested—declare me incompetent at the time it was written."

"It could still serve to slow down any sales or gross thievery. It would tie their hands with all sorts of convoluted legalities. In truth, it could tie their hands in ways they have never been tied before."

"Of course. I have heard a few men bemoan such legal tangles from time to time. Yet, I would have thought my uncle clever enough to foresee all that. And Beatrice cannot believe she will be my uncle's countess now that I am dead. Nigel is my heir, and Arthur and Beatrice cannot marry anyway. Even if my uncle was not married already, he is too close a relative to me to marry my widow, is he not?"

Leo shrugged. "So he proves your marriage is not valid. Most women would shy away from the scandal that would cause but not, I think, your wife."

"Sadly true, and neither she nor my uncle would care that such a thing would mark my son as a bastard."

"Seeing as they were willing to let the child die—nay. And, remember, they think the boy is long dead."

Julian tensed. "If Arthur plans to marry Beatrice, then my aunt Mildred may be in danger."

"Quite possibly," agreed Leo, "but not to worry. I have someone watching over her and your little cousins."

Staring at Leo in growing wonder, Julian asked, "Someone similar to the relative you have watching over my brother in Canada?"

"In some ways, but better and far more suitable. A mature woman who now acts as a companion to your aunt and a governess to the girls."

"How much protection can a mature woman be?"

"A lot, and her two hulking sons are always close at hand." Leo smiled. "Your aunt needed some new footmen, you see."

"And they all have, er, gifts?"

Leo smiled faintly. "I know you find it all very difficult to believe, but, aye, they all have gifts, ones that will make it nearly impossible for your uncle to hurt your aunt."

"I do not mean to insult you by doubting your word," Julian said and then grimaced, knowing his doubt was indeed an insult, for it implied that Leo was a liar.

"Doubt causes me no injuries. If I had not grown up with such gifts, if they did not infect my entire family like some strange plague, I am not sure I would easily believe in such things, either."

"Are you given to having visions, too?"

"Not as Chloe does. I am not even sure you could call what I have *the sight.*" Leo shrugged again. "I simply, and often abruptly, just *know* things. Sad to say, I usually just know dark things, dangerous things. What I am very good at is knowing that someone is lying—by word, deed, or appearance."

"By damn, but that must be helpful." Julian puzzled over the sadness that briefly swept over Leo's face.

"It is, but it is also a curse in its own way. We all lie, do we not? I have come to accept that; can even see that it is necessary at times. Due to the work I do for our government, king and country, I have also become very proficient in the art of lying. As a small, sickly, homely child, however—"

"You, sir, were never a homely child."

Leo nodded in silent thanks for the compliment, but continued, "I *was*, if only because I was so sickly, and we all know that what one looks like as a child does not always carry through to an adult. Add to that a mother who found such *gifts* increasingly alarming and, let us just say, it was difficult. On the other hand, I can know when a woman's beauty is more false than true, more artifice than nature," Leo drawled and smiled.

"That is a gift many men would like to have." Julian sighed, thinking of all the grief such a gift might have saved him.

"Unless, of course, it tells you that the woman who is telling you what a great lover you are is lying through her pretty teeth."

"God forbid. Did that—no, forget I asked."

"I will. Back to the matter at hand. I believe your aunt and cousins need not worry us. If it is your uncle's plan to rid himself of his wife once he is the earl, then she is safe unless you and Nigel die. The title and estates would not go to the sons of your sisters?"

Julian slowly shook his head. "No, it follows only through the males. Since my father is dead, if Nigel and I die without issue, that leaves no male in my father's line, so it jumps over to my uncle and his line. After that there are only cousins, some quite distant. Arthur is the first Kenwood in written memory who has not bred a son, only daughters."

"Which might mean the man would then look for a new wife."

"Only if he cares about passing down the heritage to a son. These papers imply that he is only interested in the wealth of the estates and titles." Julian rubbed a hand over the back of his neck. "By what I can see written here, once Nigel and I are gone, Arthur will try even harder to wring every coin he can out of the estate. Whoever comes after him will find little of value left."

"And that is why we now make plans to try and put some very strong restraints on him."

"That we can do, and now I can even see how. What might not be so easy is how to prove that he and Beatrice tried to kill my son and me. You have little here and none of it would hold up very well against my uncle's skill with words or deception, nor against the connections he has made over the years. Not friends, but confederates, and some unwilling ones."

"Ah, blackmail." Leo nodded. "I did learn that he is very skilled at discovering those secrets one wishes well buried and wields them well. I have extracted a few from his grasp, but the sort of threat he holds over some of the men, and women, is not one easily fixed or uncovered."

Julian stared at Leo in surprise. "How do you know he has secrets he can use?"

"I work for the Home Office, if you recall." Leopold grinned. "The men I work for are very good at ferreting out secrets, and they do not like anyone to be able to get a tight grip on one of the people they use. I gained a lot of my information on your uncle through my work for them. Not all of his gains are from your pockets. We suspect he sold information to the Americans and is now offering his services to the French."

For a moment Julian felt strongly inclined to *succumb* again, but he fought off the light-headed feeling brought on by the extreme shock of learning a traitor had tainted the Kenwood bloodlines. His line was well dotted with rogues, debauchers, pirates, and a host of other not so proud figures, but never a traitor. The Kenwoods had all been loyal to England. They might have fought on opposite sides in the wars over who would rule Her, cheated Her, stolen from Her, and criticized Her, but none had ever betrayed Her to an enemy. There had been an unbroken line of loyalty to country in the Kenwood family right from the raw beginnings of the family. Julian did not want to think that his uncle had stepped over that line, broken it, and brought such deep dishonor to the family name.

"Are you certain?" he asked Leo.

"As certain as we can be without the hard proof that could put the man on the gallows," replied Leopold. "The Home Office feels that if we can hang him for other crimes, such as killing you—"

"But at the end of this game, if we win, I will not be dead."

"Nay, but others are, and the many attempts upon your life are enough to hang the man or banish him from the country. The men I work for would prefer a more final end to this, however."

"So would I. If Arthur was still alive at the end of this, I would always feel as if I had a knife at my back."

"As would I."

"Do you think my uncle contributed much to the loss of the Colonies?"

"Nay. We never could have won that war, and a lot of us knew it from the first warnings in the air. Everything from the impossible logistics of supplying men, even getting our forces over there, to the vastness of the land, the tenacity of the people, worked against us. Some like to blame the French for the loss, but their aid to the rebels was not enough to credit them with the victory and, personally, I think it demeans all the Colonials who fought and died for what they believed in. Again, we would have lost that battle anyway. I thought it a mistake from the very beginning."

"In truth, so did I. That does not ease the bite of

shame that comes from knowing my uncle was a traitor, however."

"I did not think it would. I just wanted to pontificate." Leo shared a brief grin with Julian but quickly grew serious again. "Your uncle's treachery against England does not need to become common knowledge."

"There is comfort in that. How many know that Arthur might be a traitor?"

"Very few, and they are utterly trustworthy. If the problem were solved in some other way, they would destroy all of their records concerning your uncle's traitorous activities. They do not want to stain the good name of Kenwood. Your father was well loved and greatly respected, as was your grandfather."

Julian nodded and slumped against the pillows. He was exhausted and he knew some of it was because of the shock he had suffered over the news that his uncle was a traitor. Leopold might have said that there was not enough hard proof to hang Arthur for that crime, but the men at the Home Office would not even be hinting at it if they were not certain. They were just waiting to find enough to convince the courts since they knew they would need a lot of proof to convict a Kenwood of treason.

"If Arthur is decried as a traitor, it will destroy my aunt. Not only does she come from a long line of honorable military men, but she will lose everything, and the stain of it will cling to her daughters far longer than it will to any of the rest of us."

"Which is why the Home Office hopes that his crimes against his own country never come to light. Your aunt is well liked and her family's service to the country highly respected. Indeed, a number of my superiors' wives are amongst her very good friends." Leopold smiled faintly. "One or two share most news with their wives, respecting their intelligence and their integrity, and it was made very clear that your aunt and her daughters did not deserve to suffer for Arthur's crimes. Trust me in this, even though efforts are being made to uncover the full truth about his traitorous activities, it is mostly to cut away his contacts and leave him unable to continue to betray the country. The hope is strong that some other way will be found to be rid of the man, and soon."

"Do your superiors know that I am alive?"

"My direct superior and his own superior are the only ones who know. Sad to say, we believe your uncle has a grip on a few of our men. We are working hard to find out who they are. After all, even if all they do is work to hinder us in finding out the truth about Arthur, they are a weak link and the Home Office cannot afford to have any weak links. There are some dark rumblings in France, and who knows where they will lead us."

"'Tis a shame my uncle did not use his obvious talent for ferreting out secrets for the good of England."

"I fear working for king and country does not often make a man rich."

"And wealth is my uncle's god." Julian sighed. "I fear I may be pushed to spill the blood of my own uncle ere this trial is done."

"Let us hope that necessary chore will be done by another. However, better that than the deaths of you, Nigel, and Anthony. And, mayhap, your aunt. Better that well-justified stain upon your hands than the unfair one upon the name of Kenwood."

"Very true. And that is a truth I will hold fast to, for it will keep me from hesitating if I am faced with that choice."

A sharp rap at the door ended the conversation, and Julian was relieved. The talking and the news that Arthur might well be a traitor had sapped his strength. He knew it was cowardly, but he wanted the conversation to end before he was told any more bad news.

The clock on the mantel told him who was at the door. It was time for another visit from his son. Julian was a little disturbed to discover that he was keenly anticipating another visit from Chloe as well. That interest had to be buried and buried deeply. He might have cut all ties to his wife, but, by law, he was still a married man. Instinct told him that Chloe was not a woman one had an idle flirtation with. She was a woman who would drag emotion into it, and he was done with romance.

Leopold opened the door and Julian felt his battered heart actually skip at the sight of Chloe. She held Anthony's hand and led him to the bed. The sight of his son and Chloe together looked right. Too right. As they stood by the bed smiling at him the words *mine* and *family* pounded in his head. He staunchly silenced the refrain. Family implied marriage and, once he was free of Beatrice, he had no intention of ever marrying again. He had his heir. He needed no wife. A part of him scoffed at that and he frowned. It was obvious that he needed to work on strengthening his convictions.

"Do you have pain?" asked Chloe, trying to guess at the cause of the ominous look that suddenly darkened Julian's face. "I can fetch you some tea to ease it."

Julian forced himself to smile. "No. I am well enough. Just caught fast in thinking on even more bad news."

"Ah." She glanced at Leo. "It should probably be handed out in very small doses for just a while longer."

"No," Julian said before Leo could reply. "As you have all told me, there is no more time to play this game. And, concerning your herbal tea, I would appreciate some after I dine tonight. It does help me sleep undisturbed by aches and pains and that is the best medicine, is it not?" He smiled at Anthony. "And how are you?"

Anthony climbed up onto the bed to sit beside him and then proceeded to tell Julian about every single thing he had done since opening his eyes that morning. Chloe added a few words now and then to aid clarity. Julian felt the pain of his uncle's treachery fade away beneath the balm of his child's happy chatter. He struggled to ignore that part of him that also found peace and contentment in Chloe's presence. If nothing else, he did not wish to reveal any interest in Chloe in front of her far too astute and watchful cousin.

"You have had a very busy day," he said to Anthony, idly and fruitlessly trying to tame the child's wild curls with his fingers.

"Aye, I have." Anthony nodded vigorously, his curls bouncing. "I gots more to do."

"*Have* more to do," corrected Chloe, "and you can do it all after your nap."

A stubborn look settled on the child's angelic face. "Nay. Not tired."

Even though he was amused by the boy's use of the country-bred *aye* and *nay*, Julian hid it and nudged his son toward Chloe. "Then just rest and think for a while."

Anthony gave a heavy sigh and slid off the bed. "If I must."

It was hard not to laugh at the child's martyred tone. The way Chloe rolled her eyes severely tried Julian's control as well. As soon as they were gone, however, he slumped back against his pillows. Renewed anger over how Beatrice and Arthur had tried to kill his son flooded him. He closed his eyes and cursed. It would take a very long time to forget just how close he had come to never knowing his child, and all because of his uncle's greed. When he finally opened his eyes again, it was to find Leo sprawled in the chair at his bedside, studying him.

"Aye, it *is* hard to think of how close the boy came to dying before he had even begun to live," said Leo.

"Very hard." Julian reached for the tankard of cider on the table by his bed and took a long drink in an attempt to clear a sudden lump in his throat. "S'truth, whenever I think on it, I believe I could kill my wife with my bare hands if she was in reach. My uncle, too. The fury the thought stirs within me is hot, and, I fear, nearly blind."

"Then douse it. What must be done now must be done logically, meticulously, and coldly."

Julian slowly nodded. "Agreed." He could see a smiling Anthony in his mind's eye as clearly as if the boy still sat beside him. "There is far too much at risk to fail."

Chapter 4

"Just what do you think you are doing?"

Julian clung to the chair he stood next to and looked at Chloe. Her eyes were dark with annoyance and she was scowling at him, her soft, full mouth turned down and slightly taut. He had the wisdom not to tell her she was beautiful when she was angry, the flush of temper upon her soft cheeks flattering. Chloe would probably hit him over the head with the loaded tray for uttering such tripe.

A little unsettled by how well he knew this woman, he answered, hoping conversation would silence his wayward thoughts. "I thought I would have my dinner at this table tonight instead of in my bed."

He decided to pretend not to see how she rolled her eyes as she placed his dinner tray on the table. Instead he concentrated on sitting down without revealing how unsteady and weak he was. After a week in bed, his wounds were healing and he had decided it was time to regain the strength he had lost. Once out of bed it had not taken many unassisted steps for him to know that he had a lot of work to do before he could consider himself back in fighting trim. He just hoped that when he achieved that goal he would be able to do more than just hide in the house and listen to reports of what his enemies were doing now.

When Chloe sat down across from him and helped herself to a tankard of cider, he frowned. "Do you plan to join me for dinner?" The thought was far more attractive to him than it ought to be. "I see no plate for you."

"I have already dined," she replied. "I just thought it might be wise to sit here so that I can aid you in returning to your bed." She smiled faintly, then had a sip of cider when he grunted. "One more week and you will be nearly as good as new."

Pausing in his enjoyment of an excellently cooked and seasoned slice of beef, he eyed her a little warily. "And you know this for certain, do you?"

"You mean, did I *see* it?"

He sighed. "Yes. Well? Did you?"

"Vaguely. I had no dream, asleep or awake. I just know. At times that is all it is. Just a knowing, an absolute conviction. I *know* that, in one week, you will be healed. Although I would not suggest that you immediately rush out to slay your enemies."

"That is not the best way to deal with these particular foes, is it."

"Nay, I fear not. If they were not who they are, were not so highly born and bred, you could probably do as you pleased. Your word on their crimes against you would be enough to justify the punishment you dealt. Not particularly fair, but—" She shrugged.

He forced himself not to stare at how that movement made her breasts shift enticingly beneath the bodice of her dark blue gown. "But true. Instead, I must become a spy, a gatherer of information, and a deceiver."

"Better a short time of playing that game than a long time in a grave."

He grinned at her. "Well said."

Julian fixed his attention on his meal but found it difficult to become completely unaware of Chloe. Even the tempting aromas of a fine meal could not fully obscure her own soft and alluring scent. The attraction he had for her was refusing to be smothered, pushed aside, or ignored. It kept growing. Each time he heard her soft, husky voice, or her laugh, or looked into her wide, inky blue eyes, he felt it grip him even tighter than before.

Listing all the reasons he should not think of Chloe Wherlocke as any more than a friend did not help dim that attraction. Each time he reminded himself that he was married, a little voice whispered that he would not be for very much longer. He owed her and Leo his life and his son's life. She was an innocent, something he was certain of despite the way she ignored the rules of propriety by so often coming into his bedchamber unchaperoned. She thought she could see the future and that her whole family had such gifts. Chloe Wherlocke was the sort of a woman a man married, and he had no intention of marrying again. All good sound reasons, he mused when he finished his silent litany, but a part of him continued to fight to ignore such logic, and that part was winning. Hands down.

Pushing aside his now empty plate, he set the bowl of stewed, spiced apples in front of him. Chloe handed him the small pot of sweet clotted cream and he emptied it over the apples. When he caught her smiling at him, he cocked one brow in question even as he dug into his rich dessert.

"Anthony also loves to have a few stewed apples with his clotted cream," she murmured and laughed when he narrowed his eyes at her but kept right on eating.

Julian felt inordinately pleased by that information about his son. He took a minute to finish his sweet and clean his mouth and fingers before speaking. It was not just good manners that prompted his hesitation to speak. The mere thought of how the child he had been deprived of for three years showed signs of having even one of his quirks or qualities caused an uncomfortable lump to form in his throat. He needed a minute to regain his calm.

"The boy reveals excellent taste," he drawled and sipped his wine in a vain effort to cool his blood when she laughed again. Her laugh had a way of going straight to his groin. "He seems a clever lad."

"Oh, aye, he is."

The look on her face told Julian just how deeply Chloe Wherlocke loved his son. "You have taken very good care of my son," he said quietly, his voice carrying an odd combination of gratitude and a possessiveness he could not fully repress.

Chloe smiled, beating back the pain she felt over the knowledge that she would soon lose Anthony. "Aye, I have, m'lord, but it has also been my pleasure." She stood up and began placing his empty dishes back on the tray. "I love that child, have loved him since the moment I first held him. But I have never forgotten that he is not mine, that he is not even my sister's child despite what we have told others. Not for one single moment. He is *your* child, the future Earl of Colinsmoor. You need not worry that I shall try to keep him tied to my apron strings. Try not to fall on your face as you return to your bed," she added as she left the room.

The telltale sharp click of the door shutting behind Chloe told Julian that she had heard the possessive tone of his voice and probably none of the gratitude. He cursed as he cautiously made his way back to his bed, refusing to acknowledge that he could have used her help. After all she had done, it was churlish of him to feel the jealousy he did whenever he saw how close she and little Anthony were. It was also foolish. Anthony had known the Wherlockes since his birth, but had only known his father for a matter of days, and that was not Chloe's fault. He needed to get control of that unreasonable jealousy.

A knock came at the door as he wearily settled himself in bed, slumping back against a bank of thick pillows. Bidding the person to enter, Julian knew his smile of welcome was a little weak as he greeted Edgar. His body felt as if he had climbed a mountain instead of simply walking around the room a few times. The revival food had given him had proved to be very short-lived.

"Perhaps this should wait until tomorrow," Edgar said, frowning at Julian. "You look pale, tired."

"No, come in. Sit down. I just pushed myself a little too hard in my first unassisted walk. It will pass."

Edgar nodded and pulled a chair close to the bed. "Getting restless?" he asked as he sat down.

"Very. I am straining at the bit to get my strength back so that I can do more in my defense than talk."

"Understandable. Still, you do not want to push too hard or you will just lengthen your recovery."

"I know." Julian suddenly noticed that Edgar was dressed in some of his finest clothes. "Going somewhere?"

"The Paxtons are having a gathering. We are going to see if your uncle and wife appear. They were seen at the Gremonts' just last night."

"Obviously my wife does not intend to mourn me for very long."

"Seems she is telling anyone who will listen that she has considered you dead to her since the day you left her to take to drinking and whoring. Although she does not say *whoring*. Uses some very prim words I cannot recall just now."

"Clever. Makes herself the victim. Is it working?"

"With some, but not many." Edgar cleared his throat and tugged at the lace on his cuffs before mumbling, "Too many know how she was no saint before you left her. Too many angry wives, I think."

"Quite possibly. Who is the *we* going to the Paxtons?"

"Myself, Leo, and Chloe. I came early so that I could have time to speak to you while Chloe finishes dressing."

Julian suddenly realized that Chloe's hair had been done up in a style that had left fat ringlets brushing her slim shoulders. He had had the passing thought that he preferred her hair in a more untamed style. The fact that a woman had sat across from him while he had eaten his dinner and he had never once told her that her new hairstyle looked nice on her astounded him. He had been well trained in such courteous flatteries. It was apparent that he had become a little too sunk in his own misery. To then let her see his jealousy concerning Anthony's attachment to her had probably only added to the fuel of the fire started by his lack of attention. He had obviously drowned all of his charm and courtesy in the copious amount of liquor he had consumed in the last year. It was a wonder she had not slapped him upside the head with the tray and slammed the door on her way out.

"Is this all part of gathering information on my uncle and Beatrice?" Julian found himself wondering if Edgar had a romantic interest in Chloe and was surprised at how much he disliked that possibility.

Edgar nodded. "Last eve, my godmother overheard Arthur and Beatrice discussing your death."

"In public?"

"I am certain they thought they were private, but it smells like a mistake to me. Careless."

"Extremely careless. Considering that my uncle deals in secrets, one would think he would be well aware of how easily someone can overhear something you wish to keep secret. Exactly what did she hear?"

"Your uncle is not certain they should trust in the news of your untimely demise. He reminded Beatrice that he had received no word of your death."

"Very carefully said, damn his eyes."

"He is a clever rogue, no doubt about it. Beatrice, however, is not so clever. Cunning, manipulative, and amoral, but not clever. She said that you were dead even if they had not seen the hand. Suggested that you and their man might have killed each other. After all, if you were still alive, they would have known by now. My godmother said Arthur spat out a few words she could never repeat and told Beatrice to guard her words. It is not the sort of thing that can get a man of your uncle's ilk dragged to the gallows, but at least it confirms his guilt to us."

Julian slowly nodded. "It also shows us who is the weakest link."

"Are you surprised?"

"No. If naught else, Beatrice is supremely arrogant. Worse, she is impulsive, can act and speak without thought. My uncle plans his every move and word. Beatrice just charges ahead. She also believes her beauty will save her from any consequences no matter how vile the crime.

"I admit that I am still shocked by what she tried to do to our son." He held up his hand to silence what Edgar began to say. "Not that she would deny me an heir. Even in my blindness, I realized she was not pleased when she got with child, but I thought she was afraid. Too many women die in childbirth. I also knew she was vain and undoubtedly feared having children might tarnish her beauty. What I still find so difficult to understand is how any woman could set her child out to die. That is what she did when she had Anthony placed in the arms of a dying woman in an isolated cottage on the moors."

"I was not as blinded as you were, but even I find that difficult to understand. Children are cast aside, but usually by the poor, and often because they simply cannot afford another mouth to feed. That certainly was not Beatrice's concern. God's tears, if she did not want a child because she did not like children, she still had no reason to do it. She could have handed the boy over to a nurse and never looked back. To me, it is simply more proof that she and Arthur have planned your death from the start. Therefore, you could have no heirs." He frowned. "Are you certain there were no other attempts upon your life before the ones of this last year?"

Julian thought back over his short marriage and then grimaced. "I once wondered if Beatrice's many attempts to set me upon the dueling field were actually attempts to get me killed. She had an unerring skill for picking men who were deadly upon the dueling field and, often, very eager to duel. After that first duel, I made it clear that I would fight no more over her long-lost honor, and that may have ruined a plan to have me killed in a way that raised no questions."

"A good plan. It might have worked."

A soft rap on the door ended the conversation. Julian was stunned when Chloe stepped into the room. Over the last week he had considered her everything from adorable to pretty. Dressed in an elegant, dark blue silk gown, her hair done in the latest style, she was beautiful. As he pulled free of his shock, he found himself pleased that the muslin tucked into the low neckline of the gown was very modest. He should not care how much of herself she displayed to others, but he did. Neither did he like the idea of her going out for an evening without him at her side. It was glaringly obvious that he was utterly failing in all his attempts to kill his attraction to her.

To his surprise, he found himself a little dismayed by this more stylish and fashionable Chloe. He preferred the one who dressed in comfortable, modest muslins and cottons, her hair only partly tamed. Then he saw her grimace and start to reach for her hair.

"Oh, no, you will not go scratching and ruin all Maude's hard work," said Edgar as he leapt from his seat and rushed to her side. "Try to keep this hair just as it is for at least the start of the evening."

Chloe's sigh was that of a martyr and Julian grinned. Here was the Chloe he recognized. "Have trouble keeping it tamed, do you?"

"I challenge you men to try and smile through the torture of having your hair twisted and pinned up into an unnatural lump," she said and then looked at Edgar. "Leo and I are ready to leave, but we can wait if you need more time to speak to Julian."

"No. Said all I needed to," replied Edgar.

Julian wished them both a good evening and then sighed when they were gone. He hated being stuck in a bed while others hunted down his enemies. Thinking of how Chloe would soon be smiling and dancing with men eager to savor her charms only soured his mood more. He had no right to feel that way as he was still a married man, but that stern reminder did not kill the feeling.

"Only a week to wait," he told himself. "One more week and I can join in this game." *And maybe even steal a dance with Chloe,* he thought with a faint smile as he closed his eyes.

Chloe stood behind a set of heavy drapes in a tiny library. The Paxtons were obviously not the book-ish sort, she mused as she vainly tried to scratch an itch at her waist. Unfortunately, the heavy material of the dress and the corset she wore beneath it were making it impossible. She truly hated coming to these affairs, she decided. If she heard one more man speak of the great hunt he had attended or one more woman slander another with honey-sweet words, she would scream. The only thing that kept her from doing so was the knowledge that it would hurt Leo in many ways. It would also make it diffi-cult for her to hostess his occasional dinners and gatherings, and she liked doing that. His friends did not treat her as if she were some lack-witted doll whose only purpose upon this earth was to smile and look pretty. Sadly, none of those people had at-tended this gathering, nor had any of her relatives besides Leo.

Making herself comfortable on the narrow bench beneath the window, Chloe savored the cool air the heavy curtains blocked from the room. Her thoughts immediately turned to Julian and a smile curved her lips when she recalled how he had looked at her tonight. That one hot look from his beautiful green eyes had given her the confidence needed to face this interminable evening.

He was far too attractive for any woman's peace of mind, she decided. Chloe had to admit that it

was not just his fine looks that stirred something
strong and hot within her, however. She had the
sinking feeling she was coming to care for the man,
and that way lurked disaster. He was a married
man, and the fact that his wife was trying to kill
him, had betrayed him again and again, and that
the marriage was nothing but names on a paper,
did not change that. He was also far above the
touch of a penniless, cast-off daughter of a knight.
She suspected the man held some very poor opinions of women, too. Unfair, but understandable.
She suspected that if a man had done to her what
Beatrice had done to him, she, too, would find it
hard to trust any man again. Sad to say, that knowledge and all the good sense she could muster did
not halt what appeared to be a rapidly growing infatuation.

The sound of a door opening and shutting startled Chloe out of her thoughts. Her moment of
solitude was over. Even as she started to get up, two
men began to speak and she went very still. The
name mentioned by one of the men was enough to
make her sit back down and pray that she would
remain unseen.

"You ask too much, Arthur," said a man with a
low, trembling voice.

"Rubbish. I but ask you to do a small favor for a
friend, Conrad."

"You are no friend of mine."

"No? Is it not a true measure of friendship to
keep a man's secrets? And I do keep your secrets,
Conrad. Or do you no longer care if that sweet girl

you are betrothed to finds out about your lover? How is young George, by the way?"

"Bastard."

"Tsk. Name-calling is so beneath you."

"What you are asking me to do could get me hanged."

"So could what you are doing with young George."

There was a long heavy silence, broken only by the harsh breathing of one of the men. Chloe assumed it was Conrad. Arthur's voice had remained cool throughout the exchange. She wished they would say exactly what was going to be done.

"This is the last thing I will do for you, Arthur. The very last."

A moment later, the door slammed. Chloe stood up, intending to step out of her hiding place, when she realized she had only heard one set of footsteps. A chill went through her. She was alone in a room with Arthur Kenwood, a man who thought nothing of murdering his own nephew, even his own great-nephew. Chloe had no doubt that she would be in danger if he found out she had overheard him and Conrad. She was eyeing the window to see if she could easily, and silently, open it and run when someone else entered the room.

"I just saw that fool Conrad. Did he agree to help us?"

This had to be Beatrice, Chloe thought. She fought the temptation to ease open the drapes just enough to peek out at the woman. She had only seen Julian's wife a few times, either from a distance or in a crowd, and was not exactly sure what she looked like. Her curiosity was pushing her to risk discovery just so that she could see what kind of woman could do all the things Beatrice had done, but she beat it into silence. She would wait to get a look at the woman when it was a lot safer to do so. Chloe reluctantly admitted that a large part of her curiosity was born of a keen need to see what kind of woman could make Julian Kenwood plunge himself into a year of debauchery.

"Very unwillingly," replied Arthur. "After this, I fear he may be more trouble than he is worth. He becomes more angry than afraid."

"Ah. Dangerous. So be it. No one will really miss the fool."

"Except, perhaps, for young George."

Soft laughter trailed behind the couple as they left the room. Chloe did not move for several moments, frightened that one or the other might return. Finally, she eased the drape aside enough to peer into the room. Seeing that no one was there, she stepped out from behind the drape and wondered what to do next.

The first thing she needed to do was find Leo. He would know who Conrad was or, at the very least, know how to find out that information. Once they knew who the man was, they would have some idea of what he was being forced to do for Arthur. Despite her lingering fear, Chloe felt rather pleased that she was the one who had some helpful information this time.

She reached for the latch on the door only to see it move. Chloe yanked her hand back and frantically tried to think of some excuse for being in the library. Discovery meant that two very dangerous people might learn that she had been in the room, possibly even at the same time they were. She was fighting a rising panic when the door opened and Leo stared at her in surprise. Relief swept over Chloe so quickly, she felt a little unsteady, but Leo caught her around the waist and helped her to a seat.

"Are you ill?" he asked even as he lightly touched her forehead and cheeks for signs of a fever.

"Nay. I was afraid I was about to be caught lurking in here, and the relief I felt when I saw you briefly overwhelmed me."

"Who did you fear would discover you?"

"Arthur and Beatrice. They were in here only a short time ago. So short a time ago that I am surprised you did not meet them on your way here."

"Nay, I did not see them. Just where were you?" He glanced toward the large desk set near the far wall.

"Not under there. I was behind the drapes."

Leo ran a hand over his tightly queued hair and stared at her, his concern for her actually making him grow a little pale. "God's tears, Chloe. They could easily have found you."

She nodded and wrapped her arms around herself as a chill of lingering fear rippled over her. "I know. When someone came into the room I began to think on how I could gracefully step into view without causing myself a great deal of embarrassment. Then the two men began talking and I realized one of them was Arthur Kenwood. I stood as still as a statue and hardly dared to breathe."

"Who was the other man?"

"Conrad. That was the only name spoken." She told him everything else she had heard. "Do you have any idea who Conrad is?"

"I have an idea, or two, but I will need to look closely at the matter."

She sighed, disappointed that there would not be a quick resolution. "I was hoping you would know, for I am sure it would tell us what he is going to do for Arthur. The man is in danger, as well, and not just from the consequences of doing what Arthur asked of him."

Leo nodded, stood up, and tugged Chloe to her feet. "Aye, Arthur must see that he is losing his hold on the man, and he cannot allow that to happen."

"Leo? You do not think all that *young* George talk meant that Conrad abuses boys, do you?"

"I hope not. I would sorely regret saving the man's life if that is so. Yet, we need to thwart as many of Arthur's plots as we can."

"Conrad could also be a worthy witness."

"Not if he abuses boys. Sad to say, not even if his lover is a willing adult and just a little younger than Conrad."

"How unfair."

"True, but I fear that will be a long time achanging. And this is not something I should be discussing with an unwed young woman. Now, since you were lurking behind drapes, I will assume you have had enough of this gathering."

"More than enough."

"Then we will gather Edgar and leave. I doubt I have much time to find Conrad and I should like to get started."

"Should we tell Julian about this?" she asked as they started out of the room.

"It is not worth disturbing his sleep tonight. Morning will be soon enough and, if I am lucky, we will know who Conrad is and what Arthur wants."

Chapter 5

Julian was just climbing back into bed when someone rapped on the door. Assuming that it was either Todd or Wynn with his breakfast, he bid them enter as he settled himself more comfortably in bed. He was surprised when Chloe walked in, especially when he saw that there were two plates on the tray she carried.

"You mean to join me for breakfast?" he asked.

"Well, you need to eat and so do I," she answered. "Leo is out, Anthony is walking in the park with Dilys, and I need to talk to you about something we discovered whilst at the Paxtons'. Do you wish to have your meal here or in the bed?"

"At the table," he replied as he climbed out of bed.

Chloe watched as he walked over to the table. His steps were a little slow, but steady, and a vast improvement over the day before. He was improving rapidly. She found her gaze fixed upon his bare feet, long, slender feet with surprisingly long toes. The sight made her all too aware of the fact that beneath the heavy wool robe he wore Julian was probably naked.

At best he wore no more than a thin linen nightshirt. The mere thought of how much more of him she would see if she slipped off his robe made Chloe suddenly feel very warm. Since she had never before been interested in what a man looked like without his clothes, she was puzzled by her reaction. She forced her thoughts to sitting down at the table so that he would also sit and began to set out their food.

"So, what did you discover at the Paxtons'?" Julian asked after a few moments had passed while they both ate, devouring the food that tasted better when hot.

"Aside from bad conversation and even worse food?" she murmured as she spread a thick coat of honey over her bread.

"That was no great discovery. The Paxtons are well known for both."

"And yet they continue to have gatherings and a lot of people continue to attend."

"One must be seen."

"Of course. Well, a great many were *seen* at the Paxtons last night. So many that I felt a need to get away from them all. When a room is filled to bursting with people, not only does one become very warm, but one quickly discovers how few people bathe with any regularity."

Julian laughed and nodded. "A lot of people still consider regular bathing bad for one's health. Now, tell me why you are hesitating to tell me what you have discovered. That is why you are sharing this meal with me, is it not? To tell me what you discovered? Or have you changed your mind?"

Chloe found it a little disturbing that he could so

easily guess that she was avoiding something. She really dreaded telling him even more news that revealed the betrayal and treachery of his wife and his uncle. Julian had accepted the truth about them, but that did not mean he was ready to hear more ugliness. She wished she had left this discussion to Leo, but he was busy trying to thwart Arthur's newest plot and she had agreed to be the one to tell Julian this latest news. It was time to cease being so cowardly and just spit it out.

She clasped her hands in her lap and recited every word she had overheard and how she had come to be where she was when she overheard the conversation. In fact, she related the events of the evening from the moment she had walked away from Lord Tennant and his boasts about how many birds he had shot out of the Scottish sky to the moment Leo had found her in the Paxtons' library. Chloe was relieved that Julian just kept eating as she talked and hoped that meant he was not taking this latest news too hard.

"Did Leo find out who this Conrad is?" asked Julian when she was done. "I have a few suspects, but I am curious as to who he thinks it might be."

"He did not tell me who he thought it was. Leo is always very reluctant to voice any suspicion he has. He left me here last evening and immediately disappeared with Edgar. I saw him briefly about two hours ago. He said he would speak to you later. He hopes later will be at the noon meal. Who do you think it is?"

"Sir Conrad Bartleby." Julian took a sip of the rich coffee the Wherlockes served and decided he might be growing to like the brew a little too much. "This talk of a lover called George does not seem right, however."

"*Young* George," she muttered, still troubled by that repeated designation.

"The implications of that seem even less right concerning the man I am thinking of. He is a much-respected doctor." Julian sighed. "Unfortunately, a lot of things Conrad does could make people readily believe Arthur's slander. Yet, if Conrad has nothing to hide, why would he do what Arthur asked of him?"

"Because until now, Conrad could not think of anything worse than the truth becoming common knowledge."

The sound of Leo's voice startled Chloe, for she had not heard him enter the room. She was pleased to see that Julian looked equally surprised. "Whatever could be worse than being thought of as a man who abuses young boys?" she asked as Leo stole her empty cup and poured himself some coffee from the pot on the table.

"Not much, actually. He was still trying to think of some way to escape the noose Arthur had slipped around his neck when Arthur tightened it. When I started out for Conrad's home this morning, Conrad was already deciding that he could no longer keep the secret, not if it meant betraying all he believed in and being marked as a lover of young boys."

"Leo, what is the secret?" Chloe demanded a little impatiently.

"This can go no further," Leo said and both Chloe and Julian nodded. "Young George is Conrad's sister's bastard. His sister was only thirteen when she was raped by her own uncle, by Conrad's uncle. Fortunately, the man is not blood related, only an uncle through marriage. His sister went to Ireland to stay with an aunt while she carried the babe that resulted from the rape. She has since married and begun a family there. She does not even want to see George."

"How sad for the boy," whispered Chloe. "Yet I do not understand why Conrad would hold fast to the secret of a bastard child at the risk of his own honor and life. And just how did you find this out so quickly?"

"As I said, Conrad had already decided he had to do something, and even as I was leaving to go see him, he was coming to see me. We met within a few steps of the house and returned here to my office. Together we have devised a plausible explanation for George, one that will cause only a faint and fleeting *tsk, tsk*. In truth, Conrad had already prepared most of the story that will be told."

"Which will enrage Arthur," said Julian. "He does not like to lose."

"That is why Conrad is, at this very moment, preparing himself and George for a long visit to my estates in Yorkshire," said Leo.

"Just what did Arthur want him to do?"

"Conrad works for the Home Office, which is but one of the reasons why he thought of coming to me with his troubles. It is only occasional work, but he holds a place of trust. Arthur wanted him to get him some information. It appears that your uncle may well be actively dabbling in treason yet again."

Julian cursed, and then absently mumbled an

apology to Chloe. "Considering the ill wind blowing through France at the moment, I am sure there will soon be all manner of opportunities for the man."

"The opportunities are always there, my good man. Every government collects as much information as they can on every other government."

"On that cheerful thought, I will leave you gentlemen to hammer out this latest tangle," said Chloe as she stood, placed all the plates back on the tray, and asked, "More coffee? I could have some sent up to you."

"Nay, we are fine," Leo replied after exchanging a glance with Julian. The moment Chloe left, Leo took her seat. "As I said, Conrad is well respected at the Home Office, and his medical skills have given him access to some very private information on some very important people."

"And my uncle wanted some of that private information so that he could sink his talons into yet another poor fool." Julian cursed a little more clearly and freely now that Chloe was not in the room. "Has Arthur smeared Conrad's good name yet?"

"Nay, and he will not be able to do so now. Word is already spreading, in the form of a delicious tidbit of gossip, that Conrad has taken George to the country and that the boy is Conrad's own bastard child."

"Will that not cause him trouble with his newly betrothed bride?"

"Conrad has already spoken with the woman and—would you believe?—she was the one who told him to claim the child as his own. She told him that whispers of some indiscretion he had years ago would not trouble or shame her and that the tragedy that had befallen his sister had to be kept quiet. She told him that what little embarrassment she might suffer, what little gossip she might hear, was nothing in comparison to what his sister had already suffered and would suffer all over again if the truth were known. A good woman."

"It would seem so."

Julian could not fully hide his doubt that such a creature existed, yet he could find no gain in such a solution for the woman. Then he thought of Chloe, of all she had done for him and his son without asking anything in return, and felt some of his bitter mistrust of women shake a little on its foundation. He knew it was grossly unfair to think all women were like Beatrice once one dug beneath their outer softness and beauty, but that knowledge did not do much to dim the mistrust that had lodged itself so deeply into his heart. It was easier to think of Chloe as some miraculous exception to the rule.

"Did Conrad say what else he had been forced to do for Arthur? From what Chloe overheard, there was the strong implication that he had done other things."

"He had been forced to do a few things, but he found ways to work around that. The man was truly stunned by Arthur's threats and by his requests. Conrad did his best to do as he was told, yet not do it. One thing asked of him was to dose your aunt so that your uncle could begin a rumor that she was weak in her mind." Leo smiled. "Conrad and my kinsmen have done just enough to make Arthur believe his plan for your aunt is going forward. As he told me, the moment he realized who the footmen at your aunt's were, he knew I was on watch. That was another reason why he chose to seek me out today. Conrad is not a man who lies well or has a mind for deceit, so it took him some time to plot an escape from Arthur's grasp, one that would hurt the least number of people."

"He will be safe at your estate?"

"Very. He will also make a very good witness for us when and if the time comes that we need one. Even better he knows when to be silent."

"Thank God. At last we make a step forward." Julian suddenly realized how those words might sound like criticism to a man who had spent the last three years trying to catch Arthur Kenwood in his own web of lies. "I beg your pardon. You have worked so hard for me, for a man you did not even know, and I—"

"Have spoken naught but the truth. *Finally* we have a witness, one who will talk and one who will be believed." Leo shrugged. "Such work as I do is often very slow and sometimes very dull."

"But that work helps our country. And that work led us here."

"True, and now I pray that work, and all we struggle to achieve now, will put an end to your uncle's treason as well as his plots against you."

Chloe smiled at the young man who tossed a ball for Anthony. Her cousin Modred did not leave his ducal seat very often. It was both a pleasure and a surprise to see him in London. Since she rarely managed a trip to the family seat in Elderwood, their visits were too few. After Dilys took Anthony inside for his afternoon rest, Chloe patted the open space on the bench she sat on, and Modred did not hesitate to accept her silent invitation.

"It is so good to see you," she said. "Are you staying in London long?"

"Nay. You know that I can only bear it for a few days. This is my last day here and then I return to the shelter and peace of Elderwood."

"It was better this time, though. Was it not?"

"You mean, did I end up curled in a corner and weeping? Nay." He laughed softly when Chloe lightly punched him on the arm. "It slowly, ever so slowly, grows better. Dob's lessons are helping. It takes a great deal of strength to keep my walls up and strong, but I am gaining that strength. I do not believe that even if I learn how to completely shut out the world, I will ever like this place, however."

"I am not so very fond of it myself." Chloe grimaced. "The noise and the smell can wear upon one's spirit." She studied Modred for a moment, thinking yet again what an extraordinarily beautiful man he was and yet how terribly lonely his gift made him. "I doubt I shall ever return here once this trouble with the Kenwoods is settled."

"Because when it is settled, you will lose that little boy."

That hard truth felt like a stab to the heart, and her eyes stung with the tears she refused to shed. "He was never mine to keep, Modred."

Modred put his arm around her and Chloe leaned against him. She tried to find comfort in his silent sympathy, but there was little to be found. Every step closer to making Arthur and Beatrice pay for their many crimes was one step closer to losing Anthony. That knowledge caused a hurt she doubted she would ever be free of.

"Lord Kenwood has named Leo and me Anthony's godparents," she said. "I will still be able to see the boy from time to time, still have some part in his life."

"And you will see Lord Kenwood as well. Will that not be difficult for you?"

Chloe pulled back a little and scowled at her cousin. "I thought you said you could not hear my thoughts or feel what I feel. You said I had a very thick wall you could not breach."

"Sometimes even the thickest walls develop a little crack in them. A passing breach in its defense. You still have a very strong wall, but I do sense that it is not just Anthony whom you will miss when this is over."

"Lord Kenwood is too high a reach for me, cousin. I am penniless and have been cast out by my own family."

"Not all of us. Just your fool of a mother. That is one thing I meant to speak to you about. She has lost both of your brothers for that cold, heartless action. They were unhappy over the way she treated your sister, but your sister did break all the rules of society and they were torn. They were not torn over what was done with you and demanded your mother take back her harsh command. When she did not, they left her. Sad to say, I am not sure she regrets it, especially since they have left her in that fine house and still support her. I begin to think it is past time our family ceases to house and feed the ones who desert us."

Chloe took his hand in hers, knowing he thought of his own mother, who had left him the very day he had first told her what she was thinking, or as near to it as made no difference. Vaughns and Wherlockes were cursed in love, she mused. There were far too few people who could accept their gifts, even fewer who could accept how those gifts traveled through the bloodlines into the children they bore.

"I do not think Julian fears what Leo and I can do, but neither is he sure he believes in it all. But no matter, for he sees me only as the woman who saved his son, mayhap saved him, and helps him in his fight against his enemies."

"Oh? Then why is he standing at his window watching us—do not look—and stinking of anger and jealousy?"

It was very hard not to look to see if she could see what Modred felt. "Are you certain?"

"Very. He does not like me sitting here with you, touching you." Modred frowned. "He does not like feeling jealous, which is what is stirring most of that anger."

"Because I am beneath him."

"Fool. I suspect it is because he has been so cruelly betrayed by his own wife, a woman he thought himself in love with. That can leave a man wary, mistrustful."

"Which is not very encouraging. You can feel all of that? Is he such an open book to you?"

"Nay, but, as with you, strong emotion can cause a

crack in the wall." Modred smiled faintly. "I suspect Leo just told him who I am, for that crack has been tightly sealed up. What do you plan to do about that insight, small as it is?"

"I have no idea, but you will be one of the first I tell if I ever come up with a plan."

"Oh? And who will be the first?"

"Me."

She laughed with him and then urged him into the house for something to eat and drink before he left. Chloe pushed down the strong urge to rush up to see Julian. There would be time for that later, and she needed to think before she saw him again. What Modred had told her had sparked hope inside her. She needed time to decide if she should nurse it to full life or extinguish it completely.

Julian moved to look out the window as Leo explained more thoroughly what Arthur's plans for his wife were and how they could continue to keep those plans from being completed. They had both taken a rest from plots and plans soon after Chloe had left them in the morning, but lunch had brought a new round of them. He was just feeling a swell of pity for his aunt when he saw Chloe sitting on a garden bench with a well-dressed and far too handsome young man. He felt the ugly sting of jealousy slap him when the young man embraced Chloe and she did nothing to push him away. There was a chance that she was not so very different from Beatrice after all, he thought angrily, and the disappointment he felt only made him angrier. So did the jealousy that gnawed at him, for he refused to ever again allow his emotions to get tangled up over a woman. Unfortunately, his emotions did not seem to be paying attention to what he wanted.

"I think you need to get your cousin a proper chaperone." Julian inwardly cursed when Leo looked at him with faint surprise, for it was obvious that he had not kept all of his anger out of his voice.

Leo moved to look out the window, stared at Chloe and the young man for a moment, and grinned. Julian folded his arms over his chest to dim the urge to shake some sense into the man. He did not think the fact that Chloe was alone in the garden and wrapped in some man's arms was anything to grin about.

"That is just our cousin Modred," said Leo.

The name startled Julian out of his anger even as the words *our cousin* began to soothe him. He ignored the little voice that reminded him that cousins could still be lovers. His instincts told him that such things would rarely happen within the Wherlocke clan. If nothing else, he doubted they wanted too many matches where both parents had *gifts*.

"Someone actually cursed their son with the name Modred?"

Leo laughed and nodded. "His mother was a fanciful woman." He quickly grew very serious as he continued to stare down at Chloe and the young man.

"I hope he made her pay for that fancy as he grew."

"Ah, no chance to do so, I fear. She walked away from him and his father not long after he turned two. That was when her *darling boy* looked her right in the eye and told her what she was thinking, almost word for word."

"You would have me believe that he can read what is inside a person's mind?"

Leo shrugged. "Not everyone's, and not always clearly, but enough so that places like London are a pure torture for him. He rarely visits, keeps himself tucked away in Elderwood. Mostly he feels what people feel, and we both know how ugly some feelings can be."

Julian dragged his hand through his hair and stared at Leo. He trusted the man, owed him more than he could ever repay, but he was beginning to think the man was beyond eccentric. Surely no man as intelligent as Leopold could really believe such things?

"I do not call you a liar, but . . ." Julian stuttered to a halt when Leo held up his hand, afraid that he had seriously offended the man.

"Even I found it difficult to believe for a long time, but I fear it is true. Modred's gift has become the one every Wherlocke and Vaughn dreads. I have no explanation for it, no true understanding of it; I just know that it is. It has been proven to me so many times that I cannot continue to doubt. And it is that curse that makes our Modred a recluse, a man who rarely leaves Elderwood."

"Elderwood? He lives at a ducal seat?"

"He *is* the duke, has been since the age of nine. I would appreciate it if you talked to no one about his gift. It is one that, if known of and believed in by others, could put him in great danger."

"I doubt anyone would believe me even if I sank so low as to betray this confidence."

"Probably not, but Modred already has the reputation of being a recluse. He does not need to be marked as some madman as well, or seen as a threat that needs to be eradicated." Leo sighed. "Or even more frightening, taken by some enemy to be used against the country or the family or some other criminal venture."

"If he has such a gift, I am surprised he has not already gone mad. And I say *if* only because I have seen no proof. It is a lot easier to accept the gifts you and Chloe have than one that allows a man to see straight into a person's mind and heart." He frowned. "And if he can do that, I am astonished that you allow him near you. You hold far too many secrets for this country."

Leo shook his head and moved to pour them both some wine. "We do not allow or disallow. Our cousin visits us on the rare occasion he leaves Elderwood because he cannot see into our hearts or minds. He claims we have very thick walls. Many of our family do. But I am sure you can see what harm could be done if word got out about what he can do."

Julian grimaced as he accepted the drink Leo handed him and then sat down on his bed. "As you have said, the consequences would be dire. One can only pity him if he truly has such a gift. As you said, some feelings can be very ugly. So can some thoughts."

"And that pity would cut him to the bone. But enough about poor Modred. He returns to Elderwood now, and we have enemies to defeat."

Julian was more than willing to cease talking about the duke if only because he feared insulting Leopold with his continuing disbelief. It surprised him that he actually meant what he had said about accepting the gifts Leo and Chloe claimed to have. Doubt still simmered in his heart, but it was not as strong as it had been at the beginning. Alongside his increasing belief in their abilities was a lessening of his unease concerning such gifts. He was sure that he could not feel so accepting or at ease around the young duke, however.

When Leo handed him a few papers, Julian attempted to read them but his thoughts kept straying. In his mind's eye he could see Chloe held in a man's arms, but it was not the duke who held her. It was he. That alarmed him, but he could not shake or ignore the image. He wanted it to be true too badly to do so. And that, he thought as he forced himself to concentrate on the job at hand, was dangerous. It appeared that he was walking a path that could lead him straight to everything he had sworn to avoid, and yet he could not seem to get off it.

Chapter 6

Chloe smiled to herself as she entered the house. She and Maude had had a very successful day at the shops. Even better, it was such a successful day that she doubted they would have to go shopping again for quite a while. That thought made her so happy she almost skipped up the stairs.

Once she and Maude had put away the fabrics and other items they had bought, Chloe shooed her maid out of the room. She quickly changed into a softer, more comfortable gown and loosened her tightly pinned-up hair. Deciding she would retreat to the library and do some work on the household accounts, she headed out of her room.

A familiar childish giggle caught her attention as she passed by the door of the room Julian was in. It had been two days since she had spent more than a few minutes in his presence at a time. She had needed time to consider the ramifications of what Modred had told her and if there was anything she could or should do about it. The fact that she had had no vision concerning what she should do about

Julian and her growing feelings for the man was probably for the best. She did not want to be guided by anything more than her own wits and emotions. It was time to test her resolve to stand back and see if she could sense any hint of an attraction on Julian's part. Checking on what Anthony was doing in his father's bedchamber was as good an excuse as any to spend a little time in Julian's presence.

She rapped on the door and only hesitated a moment when his deep voice called out for her to enter. The sight that greeted her stole her breath away, although she did her best to hide that reaction. Julian was sprawled on his bed with Anthony tucked up at his side. Both of them looked as though they had indulged in a little tussling, for their hair was mussed and the flush of laughter still stained both their cheeks.

What startled her most was that Julian was dressed. It was in an almost scandalously casual way, but he looked heart-wrenchingly handsome in his flowing, partly laced-up white shirt and snug black breeches and hose. His golden brown hair hung a few inches below his broad shoulders and she felt her fingers tingle with the need to touch the thick waves. Chloe could see a little of his muscular, smooth chest beneath the open neck of the shirt and she ached to touch that skin, to see if it felt as warm and enticing as it looked. It was obvious that even time away from the man had not dimmed her attraction to him in the least. The fact that he did not have any shoes or boots on made the moment feel strangely intimate.

Forcing her attention onto Anthony, she smiled at the little boy, trying not to be jealous of how comfortably he was settled in his father's strong arms. That was where he belonged, and she had to learn to accept that. Chloe knew that Anthony would always care for her and that she would never lose him completely. She had to find comfort in that. She was just finding it very hard to do so.

"Have you been keeping your papa company?" she asked as she moved toward the bed.

"Aye," replied the little boy as he scrambled off the bed and hurried over to wrap himself around her legs. "I was telling him stories."

"Your best ones, I hope."

"My vewy best ones."

"Well, I do hate to be the bearer of bad news, but I believe it is time for you to go and clean up for your tea and for a rest."

Chloe had to bite the inside of her cheek to stop herself from laughing when Anthony shuffled out of the room as if he was headed to the gallows. When she turned to look at Julian as she shut the door behind the little boy, she lost that control the moment she saw the grin on his face. They both started laughing at the same time, although she noticed that Julian winced a time or two, proving that his injuries were still a little tender.

"The boy has a talent for theatrics," Julian said as he sat up and moved to the edge of the bed, bringing him close to Chloe.

He had missed Chloe's visits even though he knew he should not have. Julian knew he should have used the time to push her out of his mind, but, instead, he had spent far too much time thinking about her and wondering why she was not visiting him as often as she had before. Just hearing her laugh had brought back all the wanting he had thought he had begun to cure himself of. He stood up and stepped close to her, drawn by the way a thick lock of her hair had tumbled forward, freed of the binding she had tied it back with. Even as a voice in his head told him that he should step back, that he should not touch her even in passing, Julian reached forward and gently pushed that lock of hair behind her ear. And a very pretty ear it was, too, he thought.

Forcing himself to look up from her lush mouth, he met her gaze and felt himself become lost in the rich depths of her inky blue eyes. Julian began to lower his mouth to hers, ignoring the loud warnings in his mind. For too long he had wondered what she would taste like and he could no longer resist the temptation she presented. The way her eyes widened told him that she knew what he was about to do but she made no move to stop him. He was both disappointed and exhilarated by that.

Chloe knew Julian was about to kiss her. She also knew she ought to push him away, to sternly remind him that he was a married man and then walk away as fast as she could. Instead she leaned toward him, hungry for the touch of his mouth. She had never been kissed and she knew she wanted him to be the first even if, once the kiss ended, the reality of their situation made them both retreat.

The moment his lips touched hers, Chloe knew she was in trouble. As he brushed his mouth over hers, he slid the fingers of one hand into her hair and she shivered from the strength of the desire that roared to life within her. It was wicked to kiss a married man, but she was going to do it. Cautiously, afraid the slightest move on her part might make him come to his senses and pull away, she placed her hands upon his chest. He released a soft moan and increased the press of his lips against hers. And then, quite suddenly, the kiss was no longer a simple, brief taste, just a naughty satisfying of curiosity.

Her senses reeled as he nipped her bottom lip and, when she gasped from the heat that roused, he slipped his tongue into her mouth. Chloe was startled by the invasion for barely a heartbeat before the stroking seduction of his tongue robbed her of the last of her tepid resistance. She wrapped her arms around his neck and gave herself over to the heady delight of his kiss. She did not think that anything had ever felt as good or tasted as sweet.

When Julian abruptly pulled away, she heard herself make a soft, inarticulate sound of protest. She opened her eyes to look at him and found him staring at her in horror. A stab of pain nearly made her gasp but then she noticed that he looked a little flushed and he was breathing as hard as she was. It was not distaste that had made him stop but good sense. Chloe inwardly sighed, disappointed that he had found the good sense she had so readily cast aside.

"S'blood, but you are so damnably innocent," he muttered as he grabbed her by the hand and dragged her to the door.

Chloe suddenly found herself out in the hall, the door to Julian's bedchamber shut behind her. She shook her head as she struggled to regain her wits. When she ran her tongue over her lips, she could still taste him and felt something clench low in her belly. He was right to stop what they had been doing, but she wished he had not regained his senses so easily.

Absently fixing her hair, she started down the stairs. That kiss had accomplished more than making her heart race and her wits leak out of her ears. It had made a decision for her. After two and twenty years of having no interest in a man, she was now deeply interested, and she would see where that might lead her no matter what the consequences.

She was so lost in her thoughts about how she might make Julian cast aside his scruples that she almost walked into Wynn, who stood at the bottom of the stairs. "Were you looking for me?" she asked him.

"You have a visitor."

The man spoke in such a tone of doom that Chloe felt a shiver of alarm. Everything about Wynn implied that some enemy had breached the walls of Leo's home. What troubled her was that the only enemies she could think of were Arthur Kenwood and Lady Beatrice. There was no reason for either of them to come to Leo's residence, however. She was sure that Leo would have warned her if he had had even the smallest suspicion that the murderous pair had discovered his meddling in their affairs.

"Who?" she asked, pleased that she did not sound as uneasy as she felt.

"Lady Evelyn Kenwood, the dowager countess of Colinsmoor."

"Oh my God," she whispered in shock. "Does Lord Kenwood know?" Even as she asked the question, she knew the answer. Julian would not have been playing with Anthony and then kissing her if he had known his mother was in the house.

"Nay. The countess only just arrived. I put her in the blue salon."

"Lord Wherlocke?"

"Gone out, miss. T'ain't sure when he will be back."

Chloe looked toward the small room where disaster now lurked in the form of Julian's mother. She did not think the woman suspected that Julian was still alive and hiding upstairs, but Chloe could think of no other reason why the woman would be waiting in Leo's blue salon. Yet, if the woman did know the truth, Chloe doubted she would be sitting quietly in the parlor.

"I best go see what she wants. Did you offer her a drink? Something to eat?"

Wynn nodded. "Gertie took in some tea and cakes. I was going to get his lordship down here when I saw you." He shrugged his wide shoulders. "I know the man is supposed to be dead, but I thought he might have some idea of what I should do."

"Do not tell him. I think Leo wants to continue the ruse a while longer. This could be something completely benign, a request for help with some charity or the like. Just stay here and I will go and see if I can find out anything."

Chloe approached the door of the room where the dowager countess waited, trying to untie the knot of unease tightening in her belly. Since she did not know why the woman was here, she could not even plan what to say to her. Closing her eyes, she tried to see what she was about to face, what the outcome of this confrontation might be, but there was nothing. It was clear that her gift was going to leave her to stumble around on her own. It was doing that with alarming frequency since Julian had been brought into the house.

She stepped into the room and tried to return the smile the elegant woman on the settee gave her. All she could think of for a moment was that now she knew where Julian got his incredible green eyes. That and the fact that she had just been kissing the son this poor woman thought dead. Shaking free of her wild thoughts, Chloe curtsied to the woman.

"M'lady," she said. "I am Chloe Wherlocke, Lord Wherlocke's cousin. I am afraid he is out and may not return for some while. Mayhap I can be of help?"

"Mayhap you can," Lady Evelyn said. "Please, join me. I have but a few questions concerning my son Nigel."

"I fear I have never met the man, m'lady," Chloe said as she sat down, pushing down the fear that something had happened to Julian's brother.

"I wondered, but my questions concern the person who has become his aide-de-camp. Do you know him? Bened Vaughn?"

"Ah, aye, I do. He is a cousin of ours. I am not sure what you wish me to tell you about him, though. He is a good soldier."

"So Nigel has told me in the few letters we have received from him. Nigel also implied that, when he sold out, he wished to bring the man back with him. Now that Nigel is to become the earl"—for a moment Lady Evelyn's voice wavered and grief twisted her features—"he will be returning to England soon and bringing the man with him."

Chloe clutched her hands tightly together. She desperately wanted to comfort the woman, wanted to ease the terrible grief she had just glimpsed in Lady Evelyn's face. Worse, she wanted to tell her the truth immediately. In all of their planning, she had never really considered what Julian's mother would suffer. It was not wrong to keep all of their attention fixed firmly upon keeping Julian and Anthony alive, but that did not ease Chloe's sudden guilt over the pain that plan had caused this woman.

"Bened is a good man, m'lady," she said quietly. "I know him, although I confess that I do not know him that well, as I was but a child when he joined the army. However, about all I can think of that may be considered a fault in the man is that he is very somber."

Lady Evelyn smiled. "That is probably a very good thing, for Nigel can be very high-spirited and, I fear, a little reckless."

"Well, no one would ever accuse Bened of being reckless."

Before Chloe could say anything else, Wynn peered into the room and signaled that he needed to speak to her. Assuring Lady Evelyn that she would return in a few moments, Chloe hurried out of the room. The look of worry on Wynn's broad face caused Chloe's stomach to drop into her slippers. She should have known that such a pleasant, successful morning at the shops would carry a price. It was turning into a very high one, however.

"What is wrong now?" she asked the man.

"We cannot find the wee lad."

"Dilys?"

"She thought the boy was settled down in his bed, but he slipped away right fast. She has been looking everywhere."

Chloe bit back a curse. "He has to be round here somewhere. He was in with his father only moments ago."

"The boy is quick."

And it might have been a lot longer than she realized, for there was no denying that kissing Julian had scattered her wits. "Still, how far could he have gone? I will look upstairs and the rest of you can search down here and in the garden."

Knowing that she could not leave Lady Evelyn alone for long, Chloe raced up the stairs. Even as she searched the rooms, she cursed herself for ever having played hide-and-seek with the child. She knew that was what Anthony was doing right now, and there were far too many ways for a child to slip from room to room in Leo's passage-ridden house. When she found him, she would do her best to make him understand that such games could not be played unless everyone was told first.

It did not take long for Chloe to grow concerned. She had no sense that Anthony was in any real danger, but she had to acknowledge that her gift had been far too quiet of late. Anthony had not even slipped back into his father's room. She did her best not to reveal her growing worry to Julian as she searched his room, but she could tell by the look on his face that he had not been fooled by her glib explanations. It had been even harder to get him to stay put and not join in the search, but that could not be allowed. The guest she had threatened him with would probably recognize him even if all she heard was his voice, although she could not tell him that.

A brief conference with the others who were searching for Anthony revealed that there was only one room that had not yet been searched—the one holding the dowager countess of Colinsmoor. Although she told herself not to be concerned, Chloe had a sinking feeling in her heart. There were ways the boy could have slipped by everyone and gotten into the blue salon. She started toward the room, all the while praying that all she would be doing in a moment was claiming a small household crisis and sending Lady Evelyn on her way.

Julian frowned at the door as it closed behind Chloe. When she had first returned to his room, he had feared she wanted to talk about the kiss, and that was the last thing he wanted to do. He was still reeling over how that kiss had nearly knocked him back on his heels. For a woman who clearly had little or no experience in the art of kissing, Chloe Wherlocke packed all the punch of the headiest, richest brandy. She tasted better, too.

It had been the greatest of follies to kiss her. Julian mentally flayed himself for being so weak as to give in to the temptation. He and Chloe were often forced into unchaperoned proximity due to the situation they were in, one caused by his enemies. It was wrong to take advantage of that, wrong in so many ways he did not even bother to count them. He had to find some way to resist the allure of the woman. Reminding himself that he was a married man was not working and he suspected it was because, in his heart, he had long considered his marriage over. The law thought otherwise, as did society. There had to be a way to kill his attraction to her, but it was hard to think of one when the taste of her was still on his lips—her sweet, far too tempting taste.

He started to pace as he tried to think why she should be searching for Anthony, shaking all thought of Chloe and kisses from his mind. The boy had obviously gone missing, and that worried him. Yet Anthony had been with him not very long ago, so he could not think that the boy had gone very far. Under normal circumstances, he would just shrug it aside as a naughty little boy playing a game, but he and his son had some very deadly enemies. His offer to help look had been rejected because there was a guest downstairs who might recognize him.

Cursing the fact that he could not go and help search, Julian poured himself a tankard of wine and drank deeply. He would give them an hour to find Anthony. If, after that hour, no one had found the child, then this game of hiding from the sight of everyone would be over. He would not huddle in this room keeping himself safe while his son was in danger. Keeping a close eye on the clock on the mantel, he continued to pace and prayed that the next news he heard was that a naughty Anthony was being dutifully punished for scaring everyone.

* * *

Evelyn dabbed at her watery eyes with a lacy handkerchief. Simply mentioning her lost son in passing had nearly been enough to shatter all her control and bring her to her knees. She suspected it would be a long time before the pain of Julian's loss would lessen to anything close to bearable, even if his body was found so that she could give him a proper burial.

"You cwying, lady? Wanna sweet? Makes you feel bedda."

Startled out of her dark thoughts by that sweet, high child's voice, Evelyn looked at the little boy standing before her. He held one of the tea cakes out to her, a frown of concern on his cherubic and cake-smeared face. She started to smile at him and then looked into his big eyes. His big verdant green eyes, eyes just like hers, just like Julian's. Even the shape of them and the ridiculously long lashes were the same. Evelyn had to take several deep, slow breaths to keep from swooning.

It was impossible, she told herself as she struggled to calm her pounding heart. Unfortunately, the more she looked at the boy, the more she felt sure she was looking at Julian's son. The boy looked exactly like Julian had at that age.

She yanked her glove off her right hand and felt her own forehead, afraid that she had suddenly been afflicted by a raging fever. This had to be some illusion caused by a fevered brain. Perhaps grief had her thinking she could see her son, see him when he was still sweet and innocent of all the hurt and evil in the world.

"Want me to get Cohee?"

Not sure who Cohee was, Evelyn shook her head and tentatively reached out to touch his thick golden curls. Even the boy's hair reminded her of Julian. "How old are you, child?"

"Three. I am a man," he said and puffed out his thin chest. "I have pwetty hair."

"That you do," she said and smiled, but thought only that he had hair just like Julian had as a child. "Does it grow into big, fat curls?"

"Aye. But Leo keeps it cut so I look like a man. Not a girl."

"Very wise. Are you Lord Wherlocke's son?"

The little boy shook his head. "Nay. He just lubs me like Cohee does." He leaned a little closer. "I am hiding."

"Do they know you are hiding?"

"Nay. They are looking. Want this sweet?"

She cautiously took the slightly battered cake and ate a little of it. The smile the boy gave her made her heart ache. Everything about him made her think of Julian, and she was beginning to feel certain that it was not because she was still so mired in grief. If she recalled the gossip she had heard correctly, this boy was a cousin to Lord Wherlocke, an orphan whose mother had married beneath her. Suddenly that explanation seemed suspicious.

"What is your name?" she asked.

"Anthony," he said, pronouncing it very carefully.

"Anthony what?"

He shrugged. "I gots lots of names but I just need one."

"Well then, Anthony, I am Lady Evelyn Kenwood,

the dowager countess of Colinsmoor." She watched closely as his eyes widened and then narrowed in what could only be called suspicion, a look that sat ill upon his sweet face.

"Do you know the Pitahell Monster? He lives dere."

"At Colinsmoor?" When he nodded, she frowned. "I am not sure what that is, but I never saw it. I no longer live there, not since my son brought his wife home five years ago. Why do you think a monster lives there?" *And who would have told you about Colinsmoor,* she wanted to ask but knew that she had to step carefully with such a young child.

"Cohee. She said it swallowed my mama because she did bad things and that be why I never see her. It did not eat my papa."

"And who is your father?"

The boy shrugged and grabbed a cake, shoving a lot of it in his mouth. It was obviously a question he had been told not to answer. Evelyn was not surprised to see her hand shaking. The only thing that kept her from immediately believing that she was looking at her grandson, at Julian's child, was the boy's age. Julian would have still been in enthrallment to Beatrice at the time this child had to have been conceived. She did not believe Julian would ever break his marriage vows, and certainly not when he still foolishly believed his marriage was one of mutual love.

"There is no need to tell me if you do not wish to. It is just that you remind me very much of my son Julian when he was a little boy," she said softly as she touched his hair again. "The same hair. The same eyes. I was just wondering if we were, mayhap, related in some way."

She felt a pinch of shame for using such trickery on a young child, but Evelyn allowed a tear to slip from her eye. As she thought, he grew distressed, not liking to see her cry. Evelyn just hoped that what she got from him now was information and not another badly mangled little cake. Even if this child was bastard born, if he was Julian's son, she intended to make him part of her family. If nothing else, it would mean that she had not completely lost her son, that a small part of him still remained on this earth.

With a small, gooey hand, Anthony patted her on the arm. "Do not cry," he said, the distinct hint of command in his childish voice. "I know I looks like Papa. But I have to keep a secret. Secrets are important. If I tell you, it will not be a secret anymore, and that will be bad."

The last sentence sounded as if the child was repeating, almost word for word, what someone had told him. "I will not tell anyone. I swear it. But I am so curious as we have the same eyes. Can you not see?"

Anthony leaned so close his little nose almost touched hers. "Aye. They looks just like mine and Papa's. I have to keep the secret. Papa was bad hurt and I do not want him hurt again. Me and Cohee have to keep him safe."

"I would never hurt him, Anthony. Is your papa's name Julian?" Just the way the boy stared at her with narrowed eyes and pressed his lips tightly together was answer enough, but Evelyn really needed to hear him say it. "Please. I really need to know, as I lost my Julian and my heart hurts."

Anthony patted her on the arm again. "He is not lost. He is just hiding. Like me."

"Why is he hiding?" she asked, afraid her heart was pounding so fast it would beat itself right out of her chest.

"Because the Pitahell Monster wants him. The monster is bad and it sent men to stick a knife in my papa. Two times. I can count, see?" He held up one, then two fingers. "Two."

Evelyn was just taking slow, deep breaths again to keep herself from swooning when the door opened. She turned with the boy to look at the young woman standing there. For a moment the look of dismay and fear was clear to see on her pretty face. Evelyn could see how such a woman could tempt Julian, yet she did not feel that this woman was the sort to indulge in some sordid affair. There was a look of innocence about her. It was a puzzle she intended to solve just as soon as the woman answered one very important question.

"What the bloody hell are you doing with my grandson?"

Chapter 7

"Julian, we have a problem," Chloe announced as she burst into his room without knocking.

"Anthony?"

Seeing how pale he had suddenly gone, Chloe grimaced. Her mind had been so fixed upon Lady Evelyn and Anthony meeting that she had completely forgotten that Julian still thought Anthony was missing. She moved to his side and rubbed his arm, idly wondering why she thought such a gesture might soothe a man terrified about losing his son. The confrontation she had just had with Lady Evelyn had obviously left her utterly witless just at a time when she needed her wits sharp.

"Anthony is just fine. Truly," she said.

Julian closed his eyes for a moment and struggled to push away the terror that had briefly grabbed him by the throat. "You found him."

"Aye. I did. He was in the blue salon." She took a deep breath and blurted out, "With your mother."

"What?" He stared at her in speechless shock for

a moment before asking, "My mother is here? Down in the blue salon?" Chloe nodded. "Why?"

"She wished to speak to us about our cousin Bened Vaughn, the man who guards your brother, although she does not know that Bened is Nigel's guard and not really just his aide-de-camp. She does not know anything about what has been going on, does she? How could she? She was just sitting in the blue salon when I came downstairs after . . ." She blushed as she remembered what she had been doing just before she had gone to meet Lady Evelyn. "Well, just after I put away the things I had bought from the shops and spoken to you and you threw me out. Then Anthony went missing and I had to leave her to look for him, but he obviously got into the blue salon somehow and—"

Her rambling was brought to an abrupt halt when Julian suddenly yanked her into his arms and kissed her. Chloe forgot all about Lady Evelyn and Anthony and saying *oh bugger* before fleeing the blue salon and flung her arms around his neck. This time she tentatively used her tongue as he did his and she heard him groan, a low, soft, nearly feral noise. A little dazed when he pulled away, she felt a blush heat her cheeks, as she suddenly feared that she had been too daring, too forward.

"Enough of that," Julian said and hastily cleared the husky tone of desire run rampant from his voice.

"*You* kissed *me.*"

"I know. I was scolding myself. I kissed you for two reasons. The first was that you were babbling."

As the memory of why she was in Julian's

bedchamber abruptly returned, Chloe mumbled a curse. "I know. I babble when I am nervous, and the fact that your mother has met Anthony made me very nervous. What was the second reason?"

"I wanted to." And he would surely go to hell for that, he thought. "Help me don my boots. I need to go and speak with my mother."

"Are you sure you should do that?" she asked as she moved to help him tug on his boots.

"If she has met Anthony, she has obviously seen how much he resembles me as a child. She asked you about that, did she not?" Chloe nodded and the blush that tinted her cheeks made him curious, but he pushed that interest aside. "Did you give her any reasonable explanation for that?"

"Nay. She did not say it aloud but there was a look upon her face that told me she thinks Anthony is your bastard child. Even though she only knows us in passing, I suspect she knows we claim Anthony is my sister's child, orphaned, and the get of a very bad, unequal match. She might even think he is mine. I fear that when she asked what I was doing with her grandson, especially when she cursed—"

"My mother cursed?"

Even though she could feel the heat of a blush on her face, Chloe answered, "She said, *What the bloody hell are you doing with my grandson?*"

Julian did not know whether to be shocked or amused. "And what did you say?"

"I fear I also fell to cursing. I said, *Oh, bugger!* and then that I would fetch Leo, and I ran. I did stop in my cowardly flight long enough to tell Wynn to find Leo and get him here quick." She watched as he laced up his shirt and reached for his waistcoat. "Let me help," she said even as she moved to do so. "I have a feeling this is going to be a very long day, and you do not want to start the ordeal already aching because you strained your wounds. Are you very certain we should tell your mother the truth?"

"I do not believe we have much choice." Julian was pleased that, with her help, donning his waistcoat and coat caused only a small pain in his shoulder and side.

"But if we let her think Anthony is my sister's bastard—"

"No. I will not allow your sister's name to be stained by a rumor like that."

"Julian, sad to say, my sister's name is rather stained already. She married a fisherman."

"That does not matter. I have heard some of what is said, and it is never forgotten that it was a love match, unequal though it was, and that eases the taint in many eyes, whether they believe in such things or not. You set a bastard child in her arms and she loses even that."

"Then my bastard child."

"Do not be ridiculous."

He was actually pleased to see her eyes narrow in a show of temper over his pompous tone. She had looked too pale and frantic for his comfort. He also wanted her to never repeat the words she had just said. They had stirred an image in his mind that he would be a long time shaking free of, one of Chloe rounded with his child. Julian knew that some of the attraction of that image was his knowledge that she would love and care for his child; unlike the woman he had married.

Julian wondered exactly what he should tell his mother, aside from begging her forgiveness for any grief he had caused her. He suspected that once she understood how his life had depended upon secrecy, she would forgive him for the deception. It was the truth about Arthur and Beatrice and all they had done, all they planned to do, which might need to be softened. Then again, his mother had said the words *bloody hell*, he thought, and almost grinned. Perhaps she did not need any cosseting.

"Chloe, telling her such things will not make any difference. She will not keep Anthony a secret; will not even attempt to hide him. Not simply because she thinks he is a bastard. She has never believed such treatment of children begot outside of marriage was fair or just. And if she lets the world know about Anthony, then my uncle and wife will know about him. Once Beatrice and Arthur learn about Anthony, then he will be in danger."

"Not if they think he is a bastard, too."

"They will know that he is not. Despite what my disgraceful behavior over the last year might have led you to believe, I am not a man of wide experience. I had little before my marriage and I was faithful to my wife for the first years of our marriage, right up until I discovered she was never faithful to me, did not even try to be. In truth, I was never unfaithful to her until this last year, even after I had doubts that the child we buried was actually mine.

"My uncle will know that I have no bastards, certainly not one who would be Anthony's age. The moment he knows of Anthony, he and Beatrice will know that their attempt to leave my heir to die in some isolated cottage on the moors failed. And even worse, once he has that knowledge it will not take him long to find out or figure out your part in all of this. Then you, too, will be in danger." He grabbed her by the hand, tried to ignore how good that simple touch felt, and led her out of his bedchamber. "My mother needs to know the truth."

Chloe sighed as they paused in front of the door to the blue salon. "Aye, I suppose she does, and not just for Anthony's sake. She grieves hard, Julian." She was not surprised when he had to look away for a moment to compose himself. "Should I go in first and try to prepare her for this?"

"I am not sure there is a way to prepare her for the son she thought dead to walk into a room in all his sartorial splendor."

It was hard, but Chloe made no response to that touch of nonsense, only rolled her eyes. "Is your mother the sort to swoon?"

"Never seen her do so before, but who can say? This might well be the time that she does. After all, I never heard her curse before, either, and it is clear that she does it very well. As do you."

"I was shocked. So was she. Now, I think you should allow me to go in a few steps ahead of you, mayhap even a few minutes before you so that I may keep her from falling wrongly and hurting herself if she does swoon."

Julian nodded and stepped to the side so that he could not be seen when Chloe opened the door. He found that he was eager to see his mother. Over the last year, dreading both her sympathy and her disapproval, he had avoided her. He had reached the point where he even made a conscious effort never to be in some place where she or any other member of his immediate family might be.

Pure embarrassment and shame had been the reason for that avoidance, he admitted to himself. Even in his worst drunken haze, he had been aware of the fact that he was behaving badly and that he was undoubtedly breaking his mother's heart. Julian suspected he would have eventually pulled himself out of the quagmire he had sunken into in time simply because of the grief he was causing that good woman.

What he was going to have to tell her now would also grieve her. His mother had never liked Beatrice and it had caused a slight rift between them, but he doubted she would have ever thought the woman her son had married could be as evil as she was. Fortunately, his mother had never much liked Arthur, either. It was the depth of the crimes against the Kenwoods and the insult to the family name that would hurt her. And, he mused, as he heard his son's voice, the mere thought that her husband's brother and her daughter-in-law would try to murder Anthony would cut her to the bone, just as it had him.

She needed to know the truth, needed to know it all, he thought as he heard his mother spit out a surprisingly pithy curse. There were obviously a few things he did not know about his mother. She could well be a lot stronger than he had ever realized. Deciding he had given the women enough time alone, he stepped into the room and quietly shut the door behind him.

Julian stood for a moment and just studied his mother. He could see a few new lines on her shocked face and felt the pang of guilt. When all the color drained out of her face, he hurried toward her, certain that she was about to faint. Even as he reached for her, she flung herself into his arms. To his utter horror she began to cry.

He looked to Chloe for some help, but she just watched them with an odd, slightly glassy-eyed look on her face. Anthony stood staring at him and looking as if he was about to cry as well. Julian patted his mother's back, uttered what he hoped were soothing, if nonsensical, words, and prayed that the storm of tears would soon end. He felt like the very worst, most ungrateful of sons for making her cry, but he knew there had been little choice.

Chloe watched Lady Evelyn fling herself into Julian's arms and felt an odd chill go down her back. Suddenly what she was seeing was not Lady Evelyn crying all over her son's waistcoat, but Lady Evelyn kissing another man. The man was tall, elegant looking, and gray haired. His clothes were clean and neat but not of the best materials. They were not in the blue salon in Leo's house but on a strip of rocky beach, the moonlit waves lapping very close to their feet. It was obviously a lover's rendezvous.

Then Chloe blinked and the scene disappeared. She saw Julian handing a large handkerchief to his mother, who no longer clung to him as if he would disappear. Chloe was not sure whether she had just seen something that was to come or something that was already begun, but it appeared that the elegant Lady Evelyn had or would have a new love. And, she realized, the man would not be equal in birth and title to Lady Evelyn. Why her gift thought she needed to know that when there were so many other more immediate things she needed to have the answers to, matters of life and death, she did not know.

The moment Lady Evelyn sat down, Chloe moved to the drinks table and poured both Julian and his mother a brandy. When she served the drinks to them, she watched in an amazement that matched Julian's as Lady Evelyn tossed the drink back as if it was the weakest of wines. Julian looked so shocked, Chloe was beginning to think that, like many men, he had not noticed or known everything about his mother. From what little she had learned of men, they were very good at seeing the women in their lives as they thought they should be and not as they really were.

"Why did you let me believe you were dead?" his mother asked, her voice revealing no hint of the fact that she had just poured some very strong liquor down her throat.

"Because I was badly wounded," Julian said. "Too wounded to protect myself and anyone my enemies might hurt as they tried to get to me. Also, I do not believe we can fully trust all the people who work at Colinsmoor. Or at the dower house." He had not wanted his mother to move there as, unlike most dower houses, it was nearly a day's ride from Colinsmoor manor, but she had insisted. Now it appeared that that might have been the best thing for her to do, for it had meant that Arthur and Beatrice did not see her or his sisters as a threat.

"Someone betrays us to your enemies?"

Chloe thought the woman sounded as if she was ready to grab a sword and cut the traitor into little pieces. As she continued to watch Julian and his mother, Chloe also watched Anthony. She reached out and lightly tapped his hand when he reached for another cake. The mess on his face told her he had already had more than enough sweets.

"Mother, Uncle Arthur is the one who tried to have me killed." Julian carefully explained all he and Leo believed Arthur had done. He began to relax a little when all he saw was shock and a growing anger on his mother's face. "It gets worse," he warned when he finished listing all of Arthur's crimes.

"What can be worse than your father's brother trying to kill you? And where was that wife of yours whilst all this went on? With one of her lovers?"

Julian winced. "You could say that. Beatrice is with Arthur. They are lovers and, I believe, have been for a very long time. Lord Wherlocke believes that Arthur chose Beatrice to seduce me to get someone as close to me as possible. I would not be surprised if part of that plan was to make you wish to put some distance between yourself and my wife."

"Poor Mildred," Lady Evelyn murmured. "Is she in danger? After all, if he is to get the title by destroying my sons, he may wish to step into his new role with a new wife."

"Aunt Mildred is protected. It is to my shame that I was not the one to do so. Lord Wherlocke took care of the matter a long time ago. The Wherlockes are the reason I am not dead in some stinking alley in London. They saved my life."

"Is that why your son is here?" Lady Evelyn looked at Anthony and then back at Julian. "And do not tell me that child is not your son. I have eyes. He is you just as you were as a boy. Who is his mother?"

Julian looked at Chloe. "Perhaps Wynn could take Anthony and get the cake cleaned off his face."

"I was list'nen," said Anthony.

"I know," said Chloe, "but sometimes we big people need to say things that little boys should not hear." She probably should have taken him out of the room before Julian had begun the full sordid tale of what had happened to him.

"Will he be back?" asked Lady Evelyn as Chloe walked Anthony to the door.

"We can call for him as soon as we finish talking."

Evelyn looked at her son. She still clung to his hand, unable to let go for fear it was all a dream. For a year she had watched him try to kill himself with drink and prostitutes, but she had always held out the hope that he would pull himself out of that mire. Now it appeared that he had been pulled out of it by the Wherlockes. Worse, she blamed Arthur for driving Julian to such despair that he had sunk into that year of debauchery in the first place.

She watched Chloe Wherlocke as the young woman sent Anthony off with the large manservant. Chloe was a pretty woman, but her attire was that of a country girl. When Chloe sat down on the small settee across from her and Julian, Evelyn realized that this small, pretty woman was obviously part of all these secrets.

"Who is Anthony's mother?" she asked, forcing herself not to look at Chloe Wherlocke.

"Beatrice," Julian answered.

He took a deep breath and told his mother all about the attempt to kill Anthony. When she grew pale, he put his arm around her. He had known that this would be the hardest truth for her to bear, nearly as hard as it was for him.

"I never liked that woman, but I never would have thought her capable of such evil," Lady Evelyn said in a hoarse whisper.

"Neither would I, but there is no denying the truth. Anthony is my son. He even has the birthmark. Arthur and Beatrice could not allow my son to live, could they?" He shook his head. "I still curse myself for a fool who allowed himself to be so beguiled by a woman like Beatrice."

Lady Evelyn patted his knee. "You are not alone in that folly, dear. Men have been making idiots of themselves over beautiful women since time began."

"Somehow that does not make me feel a great deal better," he drawled, and scowled at a grinning Chloe, who just grinned wider.

"So Anthony is your heir. And if Arthur and Beatrice learn that he survived, he will be in great danger." Her eyes widened. "And Nigel is in danger, too."

"Nigel is being watched."

"Bened Vaughn."

"Aye," said Chloe. "Leo had our cousin go and

stay with him. Some of our other relations are also watching over Arthur's wife and daughters."

"But why?" Lady Evelyn asked. "Why would your family do this? We are neither kin nor close friends."

"Anthony was given into my care."

Julian was a little surprised when his mother just nodded as if those few words explained everything. Perhaps to women like his mother and Chloe, it did. He had a feeling that he could have even told his mother about Chloe's visions and she would have accepted that as well. It was for the best that he had left out that part of the tale, however, as he suspected the Wherlockes preferred such things kept as secret as possible.

"So what happens now that I know?" asked his mother.

"I would ask that you continue to keep the secret for a while longer," said Leo as he walked into the room and then graciously introduced himself to Lady Evelyn.

"You believe that is for the best?" Lady Evelyn asked as Leo sat down beside Chloe.

"For a little while longer. Your son is nearly healed and I believe the secret should hold until he is back to his full strength."

"I can see the sense of that, but I wish to come to know my grandson."

"Perhaps we can come up with some reason why you and Chloe are now visiting. Charity work, perhaps. The visits must be here, however. Until we can be certain that Julian is strong and we can adequately protect Anthony, the boy needs to remain hidden from Arthur."

"And my daughters? Julian's sisters have sorely grieved, and I would like to relieve them of that. They can be trusted to keep such a secret, and I often take them with me when I do my charity work."

"If you are absolutely certain they will tell no one, not even their maids, then, aye, tell them. But you must be absolutely certain. And if you tell them, you must do so where no one in your employ might overhear."

"I can do that." She looked at Julian. "They can be trusted to keep this secret."

Julian thought about it for only a moment and then nodded. "I know. But Leo is right. You must be very careful where you tell them. We can be certain of none of our servants."

Lady Evelyn shook her head. "I just cannot believe that our people would betray us."

"They are afraid, m'lady," said Chloe. "People who do not do as Arthur and Beatrice want end up dead. What poor tenant or servant would feel that they could go against them? The fact that we have papers to prove who Anthony is proves that a few have some courage, but as the man who left them said—he had a wife and five little ones. I think they are all under siege. And many of the servants at Colinsmoor would have relatives at your other properties, would they not?"

"Yes, they would." She looked at Julian. "It is not really just you, Nigel, and that little boy who need saving, is it?"

"No," Julian agreed. "I think Chloe put it well when she said our people are all under siege. And from all I have learned and all that has happened to me, to Anthony, I believe my wife and uncle are deadly. Deadly and cruel."

For a while they discussed what was being done and Leo again stressed the need for secrecy. Then Chloe brought Anthony back in to properly meet his grandmother. The way Lady Evelyn was with the child told Chloe that she would be a loving grandmother. She felt both happy for Anthony and sad for herself. The more love and attention he got from his rightful family, the less he would need her. The knowledge was a two-edged sword. She wanted his new home to be a happy one, but a happy home with Julian and his family meant that she would be pushed even further out of his life.

By the time Lady Evelyn left, Chloe was feeling very sorry for herself. She had tried to comfort herself with the thought that, as Anthony's godmother, she would have a place in his life. However, it was beginning to look as if he would never have a reason to turn to her once he settled in with the Kenwoods. She suspected Julian's sisters would welcome him as lovingly as Lady Evelyn had.

By late that evening, Chloe had worked herself into what even she had to admit was a deep well of self-pity. Leaving the men to make plans for when Julian would finally let the world, and his enemies, know that he survived the attack on him, she wandered out into the garden. Breathing deeply of the scents of roses and honeysuckle, she struggled to shake free of the dark mood.

She had thought that she had always understood that she would lose Anthony, that he had never been hers to keep. It was apparent that she had failed in that. Chloe realized that, deep in her heart, she had always felt as if Anthony was her child. Worse, she had somehow managed to mix him up with her grief for her sister and her sister's lost child. It was not fair to make Anthony carry the weight of relieving that grief. She had to let him go, and she feared it was going to rip out her heart to do so.

Letting Julian go was not going to be any easier, she thought, and sighed. Two kisses and she was besotted with the man. If that did not make her a complete fool, she did not know what would. The brief plan she had had to enjoy what he made her feel for as long as he was with them was even more foolish. She was no woman of the world, no gay widow, who could take a lover and then send him on his way with a smile. It would destroy her to hold him and then have to let him go, to watch him with other women after he left.

"I am such an idiot," she mumbled.

"Now why would you berate yourself so?"

The sound of Julian's voice so close made her start so that she nearly fell off the bench she was sitting on. He caught her by the arm and steadied her even as he sat down beside her. Chloe took a deep breath to steady herself only to silently curse as she breathed in his scent. The fact that even how he smelled could make her go weak in the knees only confirmed her opinion that she was already far too infatuated with the man to save herself from all hurt when he left.

"Are you and Leo done with all your plotting?" she asked.

Deciding he would let her change the subject, Julian nodded. "I will not be hiding out in my bed-chamber for very much longer. Finally I will be able to help, to do something to free myself and my family from this danger and not just sit by while others do it."

"That has been eating at you, aye?"

He smiled faintly. "Aye. I have my pride, after all. I think it has been battered enough over the past few years."

"I suppose it has. Your mother already loves Anthony."

Hearing the sigh in her voice, Julian put his arm around her. "Yes, she does, and so will my sisters. You need not fear that. You will always have a place in his life."

"I know. I am just feeling a bit sorry for myself. I will shake it off."

She turned her head to look at him and found their faces alarmingly close. The way he looked at her mouth told her he was thinking about kissing her again. A voice told her to pull away, that she would only sink deeper into infatuation with the man if she kept letting him kiss her, but she stayed right where she was. As he lowered his mouth toward hers, she felt only anticipation.

"Miss Chloe," called Dilys from the door. "Anthony wondered if you could come and read him a story, as he is too excited to go to sleep."

Chloe stared at Julian's mouth for a full moment, feeling a strange mix of relieved and disappointed, before she answered, "I will be right there."

"It might be best," murmured Julian as he helped her to her feet.

"Sometimes what is for the best is damnably annoying," Chloe muttered as she hurried away.

Julian laughed and shook his head. He had to face up to the fact that he had no willpower when it came to Chloe Wherlocke. If he did not acquire some soon, he might just find himself with a new wife within days of being rid of the old one. As he walked back into the house, he realized that the thought did not disturb him as much as he thought it ought to.

Chapter 8

It was astounding the difference three days could make, Julian thought as he donned his own waistcoat and felt barely a twinge in his shoulder or his side. The stitching had been removed two days ago and, with the help of some herbal salve Chloe had given him, the itching often accompanying such healing wounds had never truly tormented him. He was, all in all, one very lucky man. Julian just prayed that he stayed lucky. In a very short time, he would be putting that luck to a hard test as he stepped out of hiding.

He frowned as he checked his appearance in a lavishly framed mirror. When he stepped out it appeared that Chloe would be stepping out with him. It made his blood run cold. Arthur was not a stupid man. Once he knew Julian was alive and once he caught sight of the boy Julian would soon publicly claim as his son, he would soon figure out what and who was responsible for the failure of his plans. Julian knew that at that moment both Chloe and Anthony would be in as much danger as he was. Anthony because he was the heir and Chloe because she had the audacity to interfere. The only one who might not be adding to the danger in his life was Leo, because Julian doubted Arthur would seek the death of a man who was so important to the Home Office, not unless his own life was finally at risk.

Looking forward to eating his first dinner at a proper table and with company, Julian shook aside his fears for the moment. The denouement could not be avoided. The only thing he could do was try his utmost to protect the ones who might be caught in the crossfire between him and his uncle.

Stepping into the dining room, Julian had to smile at his mother and Chloe. They had one interest in common that had immediately made them compatriots—Anthony. Even in the short time they had visited in the last few days, Julian suspected they had found others. To him, his son was a bright, wondrous miracle, but Julian did not think Anthony could account for all the talking the women did when they were together.

He was pleased that his mother and sisters recognized the importance of Chloe and Leo in Anthony's life. There had been no simple show of gratitude followed by the complete taking charge of his son, but a blending. He hoped that would be enough to take some of the sadness out of Chloe's eyes.

They were halfway through the meal when Leo announced, "I believe we shall all go to the Winglingtons' ball on Saturday."

Julian felt an immediate surge of anticipation, something that was not dimmed much by the looks of horror on his mother's and Chloe's faces. "That is the night I make my debut, is it?"

"Aye," said Leo. "They move to grasp hold of as many of your assets as possible. Even the protections we have initiated might not help much. I begin to think your uncle made sure he had allies in the right place so that he could expedite matters when the time was right."

"I cannot believe that all of this is about nothing more than greed," said Lady Evelyn.

"Greed is behind many an ill deed, Mother. The more I have thought on it all, the more I realize that my uncle has always suffered from the sin of greed. My wife also. She, however, may be evil, possessing more faults that I could list, but she did not start this. Nor, I think, will Arthur allow her to finish it."

"You believe Arthur will kill her."

"My uncle does not share well, and Beatrice will most assuredly demand her share."

Lady Evelyn shook her head. "I tell you no secret when I say I never liked Beatrice, but never, not once, did I think she was capable of what she has done." She grimaced. "If nothing else, I thought the woman one of those who only knew how to use her beauty to her advantage. A heartless, and perhaps, witless seducer, one filled with vanity and greed and little else."

"I wish I had had the same clarity of vision. As for Beatrice planning any of this, I doubt she went beyond the point of agreeing that she wanted it all. Still, although she is not a particularly intelligent woman, she is cunning, especially when it comes to her comfort and her life. Arthur chose her because of those skills, and he chose well. I am but shamed by how long it took me to see exactly what she is."

Patting his hand, Lady Evelyn said, "You have seen the truth now, and that is what matters. That and the fact that you never let her taint you with all that is wrong in her. I am just so very sorry that you had to suffer."

"The longer I stayed away from her, the more I realized that it was mostly my pride that suffered." He looked at Leo. "Is there any more to the plan than my simply appearing in public, alive and well? Have we a tale that must be told to explain it all?"

"Just that you needed to recover from your wounds in a safe place, somewhere where the ones who are trying so hard to kill you could not find you," replied Leo. "By letting the world think you were dead, we prevented the further threat of your enemies hunting you down."

"The truth save for the names of my enemies. Very clever."

"I do try," murmured Leo and grinned when everyone laughed, but he quickly grew serious again. "I have always found that giving out as much of the truth as possible is best. It worries one's enemies and arouses the curiosity of others, ones who might well go searching for the truth themselves. And they will naturally share whatever they discover with others."

"And what of Anthony?"

"We shall try our best to keep him hidden, but there is always the chance that he will be found out. Try not to worry about the boy. He will be very well guarded. The best thing you can do for him is to take away the sword that hangs over his neck."

As soon as the dinner ended, his mother left, not wishing to arouse too much suspicion by lingering at the Wherlockes' for too long or too often. Julian was glad his sisters had not come to dine with them, for their constant company would definitely raise a few eyebrows. They did help his mother with her charity work, but not too consistently, as both of them were just entering society, still young and considered far too innocent for much of the work his mother did.

After a short conversation and a brandy in the blue salon, Leo also left. Julian had to wonder what the man did at night, but did not ask. He was sure it was not a continuous round of debauchery, and anything else probably had to remain secret. It amused him, and dismayed him just a little, that Leo had left Julian alone in the blue salon with Chloe without any hesitation. The man did that a lot and Julian hated himself for abusing the trust Leo had in him.

Julian sat next to Chloe even though he knew he should keep his distance. "Are you worried about my debut?"

"Very much so," she replied without hesitation.

"I am completely healed, or near enough so that it makes no difference."

"The matter of your health is not a very large part of my concern. Your enemies are." She smiled faintly. "I know you must do this, that nothing can be solved by simply staying out of their reach, but that does not mean I have to like opening our doors and letting them peer inside. I much preferred it when they thought they were successful in killing off two heirs to the earldom."

"In truth, so did I." He exchanged a grin with her. "It must be done. Leo has gathered all the information he can, but nothing exceeds the value of a direct confrontation. No matter what we tell the world, Arthur and Beatrice will know that we are aware of all their plots and what they have done. Oh, they will think they still have a few secrets, but not enough, not as they had before I was stabbed in that alley."

"I rather agree with your mother. It is so hard to believe that greed alone would make people do this, cause them to kill three members of their closest kin. Plus who knows how many others on the way to achieving that bloody goal."

"With Beatrice it probably is just greed. Even before I gave up on my marriage, I had begun to notice that there was a coldness in her, a hardness. My uncle? Well, I think his reasons are many. There is definitely greed involved, but I think there is also a long-simmering resentment over the fact that he was not born to be the earl."

"That was hardly your fault."

"It is my fault that I continue to stand in the way of him obtaining what he believes should always have been his. Do not try to understand it, or him. There are far too many younger sons who suffer that envy or resentment, although few of them resort to murder to end what they see as a great unfairness."

Julian could not help himself; he began to toy with one of the fat curls her maid had twisted Chloe's hair into. Ever since the night in the garden when she had been called away before he could kiss her, he had taken every, and any chance he could grasp to kiss her, to touch her. His whole body ached for more, far more, every time he was near her.

She enthralled him, intrigued him, and aroused him. Every time she was within reach he wanted to touch her, *needed* to touch her. It worried him. His mind told him he could trust this woman with his life, that she had proven herself over and over again. Yet his battered pride kept him wary. He did not want to feel this way about any woman, especially not one who could prove to be a quick road to marriage. Despite that, he kept coming back to her, kept wanting her.

He leaned closer and whispered in her ear, "You should slap me. I grow too bold."

"Actually, I believe I should kick you right off this settee and pour the last of the wine over your head."

Chloe felt a shiver of pure, raw desire go through her as he laughed softly and his warm breath caressed her ear. She really was a fool to allow him to continue what was clearly a seduction. After the way he had spent the last year, it should be easy to keep her distance from the man, to be reasonably wary of his every sweet word and soft touch. In many ways, she did question the sincerity of his desire, but not enough to save herself. The best she could manage was to hope that he was not using her simply because there was no other woman in reach.

"A little violent, but it would certainly prove effective." He kissed the hollow beneath her ear. "I am still married."

"Who are you reminding of that fact? Me? Or

yourself?" Chloe decided that, if any man had a right to forget his wife, it was Julian.

"Both of us."

"I, m'lord, have never forgotten that. Not once."

"Yet, you do not push me away." He turned her so that she faced him and held her face in his hands, stroking the softness of her cheeks with his thumbs.

"Nay, although even a few stolen kisses are wrong by all the rules we try to live by. I tell myself that all the time but," she felt herself blush and continued in a whisper, "I rather like your kisses. Not that I have anything to compare them to."

"And that pleases me far more than it should. It also should make me leap up and flee this room, for you are clearly far more innocent than most misses your age. However, it seems that all it makes me want to do is to steal another."

Before she could approve or disapprove of his plan, Julian was kissing her. She wrapped her arms around his neck and sank into the wonder of it. Chloe savored the way his lips and tongue stirred a heat inside her, one that traveled rapidly from her lips to her toes and warmed all the places in between. She savored the taste of him, the crisp male scent that was his alone, and the way her small soft body fit against his large, hard one with such perfection. She even savored the way his touch and his kisses silenced the voice in her head that told her she should not be doing this. This was what she wanted and, maybe, for once in her life, she really would just reach out and take what she wanted.

Julian could not believe how sharp the bite of hunger was but he could not deny it, either. Chloe, with her innocent kisses and unfettered passion, did things to his body, mind, and heart that he had never experienced before. Not even Beatrice with all her wiles had made him so crazed with need so quickly. And crazed he most certainly was, for even thinking of his murderous wife did not make him hesitate in slipping his hand inside the bodice of Chloe's simple blue gown. The way she trembled in his arms as he stroked her full breast, the way her breath caught in her throat and her nipple hardened to a tempting point with just the light brush of his fingertip ensured that nothing would make him stop now.

"Is this how you repay the debt you claim you owe us? By seducing the woman who saved your son?"

Except that, Julian thought as Chloe squeaked and pulled away from him. The sound of Leo's voice was like a splash of icy cold water. His questions were like a knife to the heart. Shame reddened his cheeks as he turned to look at the man he had begun to consider as good and true a friend as Edgar. The cold steel in the man's voice and his tightly clenched fists told Julian that Leo was fighting the urge to beat him bloody. Julian knew that he would not have shown such restraint if he had caught some man pawing one of his sisters.

Chloe looked from her cousin to Julian and back again. If they were dogs, their hackles would be up and their teeth bared in snarls. She was not sure what she could do to soothe the violently troubled waters between the men, but she had to do something. After all, she was as much to blame for what Leo had seen as Julian was.

"It was just a kiss, Leo," she said in what she prayed was a mature, calm voice and then winced when Leo fixed his glare upon her.

"A kiss does not include fondling a woman's breasts," Leo snapped.

Despite the heat of the blush flowing over her cheeks and throat, Chloe frowned at Leo. "I do believe I know that. I also know that I am a grown woman and what I allow or do not allow is my business, not yours. Any folly I stumble into is also my business alone."

"You are an unmarried woman under my protection. Whatever folly you attempt to commit *is* my business."

Shaking free of his surprise over the fact that Chloe was not sitting quietly, blushes covering her pretty cheeks, and awaiting her fate as decided by men, Julian looked at the two cousins. It was plainly evident that they were about to get into a heated argument. Although it was tempting to let them brangle for a while, giving him time to collect his thoughts before Leo's fury was turned back on him, Julian resisted. He could not allow these people who had done so much for him have a falling-out simply because he could not control his lusts.

"As soon as this trouble is over and I am free of my wife, I will marry Chloe," he said.

He waited for a feeling of being trapped to sweep over him, choking him, but it did not happen. Julian realized that he felt very calm about stepping out of one marriage and straight into another. It would be easy to think of all the reasons why he did not want to get married again, but his mind refused to follow that path. Instead, all he could think of were the many advantages there would be to having Chloe as his wife, including giving his son a mother who loved him. First, however, he had to make the two people staring at him in shock understand that he meant what he said.

"That would be acceptable," said Leo.

"Pardon, cousin, but I do not believe he was asking *you* to marry him," Chloe said, outrage weighting her every word. "S'blood, he did not even ask me!"

"This is not a proposal, Chloe, but a statement of fact," said Julian, finding a perverse pleasure in her fury.

"I should have some say in this," she began, only to make an odd little squawk when Leo strode over to her, grabbed her by the arm, and started to drag her to the door. "Are you, even for one tiny heartbeat of a moment, thinking of tossing me out of this room?"

"Aye, I am," said Leo and he pushed her out the door, shut it, and latched it.

Chloe stared at the locked door in utter disbelief. "You let me in right now, Leopold Wherlocke!"

"This is men's business, Chloe."

She kicked the door and ignored the sharp pain in her toes. "Well, when you are done planning my future for me, do not forget to tell me what it is. Then *I* shall tell you exactly what *I* think! Pithily!"

Resisting the urge to kick the door again, Chloe strode off to her bedchamber. There might be a few things she could find there that she would not miss after she threw them at Leo's and Julian's heads, she thought. She was all the way inside her room before her temper cooled enough for her to start thinking of anything aside from causing those two men as much physical hurt as possible.

It was all her fault, she thought. If she could just have controlled the fierce infatuation she had for Julian, she would not be facing this trouble now. Chloe had to wonder how anyone controlled desire when it felt so extraordinarily good. It was a wonder people were not indulging themselves in their desires every day and night.

"Considering where I found Julian, they probably are," she muttered.

The thought of marriage to Julian brought both delight and despair. Chloe would like nothing more than to be his wife, but not this way. She wanted more from him than the fact that he wished to bed her, and there had not been much sign of any deeper feelings from the man. He would also feel trapped, and that could be a curse upon any marriage.

One thought kept her from panicking completely. If she married Julian, then she would truly be Anthony's mother. Chloe quickly shook the thought from her head. She would not allow that to tempt her into accepting something she should not. For a marriage to work, especially to a Wherlocke, there had to be more behind it than reckless desire.

The only way she would agree to marry Julian would be if he revealed some feeling for her beyond a need to bed her. Julian would have to prove to her that he felt something, no matter how mild, beside desire. Her reputation was of no matter to her, for she was not truly accepted by the society he called home anyway. She was penniless, cast out of her family by her own mother, and one of the very eccentric Wherlockes. It was only Leo's presence at her side that kept her from being shunned completely. Julian could do so much better then her.

A forced marriage born of some chivalric need to protect her good name and no more could not happen. Chloe knew both her cousin and Julian would not understand what troubled her about it. She also doubted they would listen to her qualms. There was only one thing she needed to think about right now while the men planned her fate. She needed to plan how to avoid it.

Julian joined Leo in staring at the door an angry Chloe had kicked, waiting to see if she had any more to say. He suspected she would rebuke them both soon—pithily. It was hard to believe, but that one shouted word had almost made him laugh. When there was no other sound for a few minutes, he turned his attention back to Leo, who was scowling at him. Julian sighed and sat down, knowing he had no excuse to offer for what he had tried to do with Chloe.

"Have you changed your mind?" asked Leo. "Are you about to say you do not wish to marry my cousin?"

"No, I will marry her as soon as I am free of Beatrice. On that I swear." Julian decided that now the decision was made, he could clearly see just how many advantages there were to marrying Chloe, ones far beyond the need to get her into his bed. "I realize that I have abused your trust in me."

"Only as pertains to my cousin." Leo cursed and moved to pour them both a brandy. "I should have seen it. Now that I think on it, it was right there before my eyes. Ha, it was right there in Chloe's eyes." He handed Julian a brandy. "Yours as well, but that did not worry me all that much. Chloe is a pretty little thing, and you were not dead. It would have worried me if I had thought more on the way Chloe often looked at you. Leaving the two of you alone as often as I did was asking for trouble."

"I should have had more control," Julian muttered and then looked at Leo in surprise when the man laughed.

"When the attraction is equal and the woman has the strange idea that she can act with the freedom of a man? Aye, you should have, but I cannot put this all on your shoulders. Nay, I do not blame you for all of this. Some, but not all. I should have behaved like the guardian I thought myself and I should have paid far more attention to what was brewing right beneath my nose. You *will* treat her well."

Although it had been a command and not a question, Julian nodded. "I honor the vows I take, even the marriage ones. What happened with Beatrice..." He paused as he struggled for words.

"Bah, I have no worries that you will act as the debauchee once married. Chloe will never behave as Beatrice did. And I do not consider you married even though the law says you are. The law and the church. That marriage is long dead, and it is just a matter of when you see the knot untied legally and finally. As to that, it can be as soon as you wish, as I have found two men who can swear that your wife was their lover before she married you. Embarrassing for you, but a perfect way to get the marriage made null and void."

"I believe I can tolerate a little more embarrassment as concerns Beatrice. And I doubt I am the only man who was fooled into thinking the woman he bedded was an innocent. In fact, that whore who played the virgin so many times proved to me that it can be a hard thing to detect for a certainty. What is it?" he asked when Leo suddenly scowled into his drink.

"Virginity," Leo muttered and then cursed. "I hate to say this, but I think we need to prove that Chloe still has hers."

"I did not take it. We—"

"I know. I was thinking of Anthony. She has had him in her care for three years. The world and its mother think Anthony is her sister's child, and a few do whisper that he might be Chloe's. If you wed her, that is the rumor that might grow and it might give someone an opportunity to question his legitimacy."

Julian cursed. "And even if it cannot be proven that Chloe is his mother, the rumor will never fade. It will dog both Chloe and Anthony for the rest of their lives. It is also the sort of thing Arthur will immediately try to do. But we cannot go about announcing to one and all that Chloe is a virgin."

"We do not need to. We just need to have it documented that she is one and that she has never borne a child *before* you remove that thin bit of proof."

"I will—"

"Not touch her? You are betrothed now. You have given your word that you will marry her as soon as you are able. You are both attracted to each other. Are you a saint then to ignore all those things and hold fast to a vow of celibacy until wed? I sure as bloody hell would not be."

"*I* know I am betrothed but I am not sure Chloe believes she is."

"That will pass. You need to let her know that it is not just because you want her in your bed." Leo held up his hand when Julian started to speak. "I do not ask that you whisper sweet words of undying love unless you discover that you feel them, but you must convince her that you feel more than lust. We come from a long line of families that suffer in bad marriages. The only ones that work are the ones that are not arranged, the ones where there are more than bloodlines, lust, and gain tying them together. If there is not, then our *gifts* become curses that leave children without mothers or fathers."

"Ah, yes, her gift. I find that does not trouble me. I may not fully believe in such things, but it truly does not trouble me and I do not fear it. I most certainly would never turn my back on whatever children we might be blessed with just because they had one of those gifts."

"Considering what we are dealing with now, it might be a good idea if you try harder to believe in Chloe's gift. Just swear that if she gives you a warning, you heed it. If you wish to ride in one direction and she tells you to go in another, do it. She is unerringly right in her warnings and whether you wish to call it a gift or just simple intuition, heed it."

"That I can do. If naught else, there really is no other explanation for how she found me in that alley just when I needed help."

"But there will be no more of those, er, alleys, will there?"

"I told you—I hold to vows given, even marriage ones. In truth, I find myself questioning the honor of any wedded man who claims to hold true to his word yet has a string of mistresses. This year past . . ." He shook his head. "I can only claim some sort of insanity."

"Understandable. S'blood, the fact that you held to your vows for as long as you did says a great deal of good about you. Most men would never have done so, not after his wife had taken her first lover. Certainly not after she had borne him a child that he felt was not his. Believe me in this, if I considered you still married and not just tied by law to someone who wants you dead, I would not be taking this so well."

"You mean you would have ensured that my fine, elegant nose was no longer such a handsome thing?"

Leo grinned. "Among other things." He sighed and glanced at the door. "Now we must decide who is going to tell Chloe that she must be examined."

Julian also looked at the door and his heart sank. Making Chloe submit to an examination to prove her purity was not going to make a good start to their lives together. "It needs to be made clear that it is only for Anthony's sake, to safeguard his rights as my heir."

"Aye, for Anthony's sake she just might do it without killing us first."

Chapter 9

Chloe stared at her hands as the carriage eased its way through the crowded street toward the Winglingtons' elegant townhouse. She was still too embarrassed by the exam she had undergone mere hours ago to look at Leo and Julian, who sprawled elegantly on the seat opposite her. Although she fully understood the need for proof of her virginity and that she had never borne a child, even agreed with the need for such proof, she hated the fact that both men knew what she had endured that afternoon.

She sighed and looked out the window even though there was little of any interest to look at. It had been humiliating in many ways to be examined so intimately, the state of her innocence legally recorded by two physicians and a midwife, affidavits for other men to read if the need arose. Throughout the ordeal she had continued to remind herself that it was being done for Anthony's sake. That had not helped all that much, but it had ensured that she did not flee the room.

And now she had to go to a ball, smile and chat

as if all was right with her world. Worse, there was a very good chance that she would see Lady Beatrice Kenwood, the woman who still held a legal claim to Julian. How often did a woman meet her betrothed's wife? she mused. Not that she had yet agreed to the betrothal. Chloe wondered if she had ever had such a trying day. Only those last, heartbreaking hours at her dying sister's bedside could be considered worse than what she had endured and still had to endure.

Glancing covertly at her two escorts, she surprised herself with an urge to smile. Both men looked as embarrassed as she felt. It had not occurred to her that the men who had ordered the exam could possibly feel as uncomfortable about the whole business as she did. Strangely, their obvious discomfort eased her own. It also reassured her that they had only done what they felt was absolutely necessary to protect Anthony's place as Julian's heir. That eased the lingering fear that Julian himself questioned her innocence and had demanded proof of it before he married her.

The one good thing about the whole mortifying business was that it had taken her mind off the Winglingtons' ball. She heartily disliked such events, but this one was going to be a lot worse than any other she had ever attended. Julian was about to reveal to the world that he was still very much alive. Chloe had no doubt that that would set Arthur and Beatrice after him again. The only question remaining about the result of this plan was just how soon Julian's enemies would start hunting him again.

It was also going to be a little awkward to be escorted to a ball by a married man. The fact that Leo was with them would be the only thing that might diminish the strength of the gossip that would ensue. Tonight all the attention and the talk would concern Julian's miraculous rise from the dead, but Chloe knew that protection would not last long. Soon someone would recall that she had entered the ballroom on his arm, and the conjecture about her place in his life would begin. She dreaded it.

When the carriage pulled to a stop, it was Julian who helped her down from the carriage. Chloe was still not sure that his escorting her into the ball was particularly wise, but he had insisted upon it. Aside from the gossip it would cause, it stank too much of a challenge tossed right at Arthur Kenwood's feet and a well-aimed slap in Lady Beatrice's beautiful face. Chloe did not feel afraid, for she knew that Leo and Julian would keep her safe, but she did not wish to become of too great an interest to Julian's wife or his uncle. Then she sighed, for she knew there was no escaping that fate. She was a part of all this and even if she had remained at home, Arthur would soon discover just how big a part she had played.

Beneath her hand she felt the tension in Julian's arm increase as they greeted their host and hostess. The plump Lady Winglington nearly swooned, but the thought of what a social triumph the night would become because of Julian's surprise resurrection quickly put some steel in her backbone. When Julian was announced, the abrupt silence in the room lasted for barely a moment. The noise that followed told Chloe it was going to be a very long night filled with questions and rumors. She hoped that noise had kept everyone from hearing her name, but feared she would never be that fortunate.

Julian looked toward where Chloe stood with his mother and his sister Phillipa. He had yet to find the words to speak to her concerning the ordeal she had endured to ensure Anthony's inheritance. To his surprise, it had proven to be an ordeal for him as well. Several times he had had to force himself to just sit and wait, to swallow the strong urge to race up to her bedchamber and rescue her from the embarrassment she had to have been suffering. His only comfort during that time had been that Leo had looked to be suffering as much as he was.

It would be easy to just ignore the whole matter, to pretend it had not happened, but he knew that would be a mistake. Julian had no doubt that, at some point, Chloe must have wondered if he had asked for the exam in order to assure himself that she was pure. That was not a doubt he wanted to let fester. Especially since Chloe had yet to openly agree to marry him. He and Leo considered the betrothal all settled, but it would be nice if Chloe actually voiced her agreement to the arrangement.

"It is good to see you well. Are you fully recovered?"

That deep, smooth voice made every muscle in Julian's body tense with the need to strike out. He turned to face his uncle. Arthur Kenwood was a handsome man, only fifteen years older than him. The man was fit and strong, had all his hair and a full set of teeth. He needed no padding at his shoulders or his calves to make his elegant clothes fit to perfection. In the man's steel gray eyes Julian only saw questions and a touch of the hurt his uncle tried to make everyone believe he felt.

Clinging to his uncle's arm and dabbing at perfectly formed tears with a dainty lace handkerchief was Beatrice, his traitorous wife. Julian ached to do violence to the woman who had left his son to die, and he hated her for that. He had never touched a woman in anger, and he had no intention of allowing Beatrice to make him mar that record. He had always considered a man who hit women to be weak, no more than a cowardly bully, and he would never stoop to that low behavior.

The interest of everyone in the ballroom both irritated and amused him. Even before he had sunk into debauchery, the world and its mother had known what a cuckold he was. They were undoubtedly awaiting some scandalous argument. He did not intend to give them one, but he had no doubt that Beatrice and Arthur would try their best to give the curious crowd a fine show.

"How could you leave us to grieve for you, Julian?" asked Beatrice in a choked voice, as if the strength of her hurt made it difficult to speak.

"Grieve? Somehow I find it difficult to envision you suffering from such an emotion," he said and nearly smiled when her beautiful hazel eyes began to glitter with fury.

Here was the Beatrice he had come to know. The cold, selfish virago hidden beneath the beauty was getting harder for her to hide. That could only work in their favor.

"Of a certain I grieved," she said, her voice no

longer so soft or trembling. "Despite the humiliations you have heaped upon me this last year, you are still my husband."

He glanced at the low-cut gown of soft green silk she was wearing, a color she knew complemented her eyes, and just quirked one eyebrow. "Ah, so I am. Mayhap it is I who should grieve," he murmured and then looked at his uncle. "And am I to kindly thank you for comforting my distraught widow? But wait, you were already comforting her for being deserted by her cruel, uncaring husband, were you not?"

"You should not jest so, nephew," Arthur said without even glancing at Beatrice when she hissed in fury. "Show a little consideration for your family, if you do not mind."

"No, I do not mind at all, and I have great consideration for them. My mother and sisters understand why I needed to recover from my wounds in secrecy. They have forgiven me for the deception. Now, if you would both excuse me?" Julian started to turn away but then hesitated for a moment before looking back at his uncle and his wife. "I forgot. I believe I will soon return to Colinsmoor. It would be best, I believe, if you, uncle, and you, Beatrice, were no longer there. Or at Kenwood House. S'truth, I want you and any of your people gone from all my properties aside from the one I have deeded over to Beatrice. A tiny cottage in Kent, I believe. And I shall have my new solicitor send men to be sure that you leave with only what you came with."

"You cannot throw me out of our home," snapped

Beatrice, casting aside all attempts to act anything but what she was, furious. "What will the world think if you cast your wife out into the street?"

"That I have finally come to my senses? Do not distress yourself, Beatrice. I have no doubt that you will land softly."

Julian walked away before he said anything more. At the moment the sympathy of the crowd was on his side. His uncle and his wife had not made many friends. But Julian knew that if he spat out the fury churning inside him, that sympathy could wane. Even those who suspected that Arthur and Beatrice had had a hand in his near murder and the need to hide as he healed would frown upon his spitting out accusations and threats at a ball. The fact that he had just thrown both of them out of his house would be readily accepted, for Beatrice had made her unfaithfulness to him common knowledge. That constant humiliation had been one of the things that had driven him into the stews.

He caught sight of Edgar standing near the doors to the rear garden. Edgar patted the left front of his blue brocade coat and Julian almost smiled. He knew that beneath that hand, just inside that elegant coat, was a fine silver flask filled with excellent brandy. A drink was just what he needed to rinse the bitterness from his mouth and mind. Julian followed his friend out into the torchlit garden.

"I think I expected a lot more fire when you finally confronted them," said Edgar as he handed Julian his flask.

"Neither of them wanted that." Julian grimaced and took a deep drink before returning the flask to

Edgar. "Beatrice could easily have indulged in a fine tantrum, but I believe my uncle keeps her on a tight leash. Dear Uncle Arthur does not wish too much attention drawn to him or to any ill feelings that exist between us. I am not sure why he should concern himself. The whole of society knows he is my wife's lover and has been for a long while. None of them expects us to behave like loving relatives."

"True, but appearances must be maintained."

"It will be interesting to find out what gossip makes the rounds now that I have thrown them both out of my house."

"They may well leave the ball early so that they can return to Colinsmoor posthaste and rob you blind."

"They will find that difficult, for there is a large group of burly men waiting there for their return. We got word this morning that the servants have been very helpful in indicating just what belongs to both of them. They may well find all their baggage already packed and set in the drive."

Edgar laughed but then grew serious. "Arthur will be enraged."

"I know. I but hope that that rage will cause him to make a serious error."

"Is your plan to catch him trying to kill you? He has not been caught yet and he does not try to do it by his own hand, either."

Julian shrugged. "Nothing else we have done has been enough to catch him and charge him with any crime. That leaves us nowhere to go but to push his back to the wall."

"All-out war?"

"Yes." He frowned. "I just worry about how far

he will carry it. We have a lot of men to protect everyone, but Arthur is very good at turning men to his side. Yet, what other choice is there? This must be ended."

"Indeed it must." Edgar handed him the flask again. "So, has the fair Chloe said she will marry you yet?"

Julian cursed and took another drink. "No. And after what she had to endure today, she may never do so."

"Distasteful as the business was, she is smart enough to know it was necessary. Chloe would never have agreed to it if she had thought otherwise. You are going to have to dig up whatever charm you used to possess and woo the woman, Julian."

"It was wooing her that got us into this betrothal."

"No, it was lust. A shared lusting, I am sure, for you would never have been able to compromise her unless she wanted you to. That might be enough for many women, especially when an earl is the prize, but not for Chloe."

"I am not going to offer her words of love that I do not feel," Julian snapped, even though he knew Edgar was right, that he was going to have to do some wooing.

"No one asked you to. But you like her, do you not? And you trust her."

"Yes, and I am not scared of her gift or that our children will have one. That is not what a woman looks for when a man woos her, however."

"It will do for Chloe if you make it clear and make her believe it. I have known her for years, and I be-lieve she is not some foolish romantic. She has been thoroughly compromised and knows marriage is the result of that. What she does not want is to marry a man whose only interest in her is to get her into bed. I am sure Leo has told you of how badly so many of the marriages end in their family. Chloe knows it, too, and she needs more than lust or she will do her damnedest to get out of this betrothal. Since you can tell no one about it, as you are still tied to Beatrice, that gives Chloe plenty of opportunity to find her way out of it, too."

Julian nodded, handed Edgar back his flask, and idly brushed down his silver brocade coat. "Then I shall go a-wooing. I can convince her that I like her and trust her for I do. I also have one ace up my sleeve."

"And what is that?"

"If she marries me, she does not have to lose Anthony."

"You would use your son to pull her into marriage?"

"In a heartbeat," Julian replied and had to wonder at his own determination to get a wife when he had so adamantly claimed he did not want one.

Lady Evelyn watched her son walk away from Arthur and Beatrice and join his friend Edgar. She then looked at the pair who was trying to kill her son and shivered. Knowing them as well as she did, she could see their hatred beneath their polite masks. It was evident that Julian had done as he had threatened and told them to get out of Colinsmoor.

"I think, until now, I had not really accepted that

my husband's brother and my son's wife truly want my son dead," she murmured.

"It is hard to believe," agreed Chloe. "When one considers their reasons for it, one can easily think of many who share the same feelings, yet those people do not indulge in murder. And it is important that we end their reign because of the attempt to kill Julian, for that is the only way to keep the other crimes Arthur is guilty of becoming public knowledge."

"I know. I would hate for that stain to touch the Kenwood name, yet I do not like Julian being presented like some sacrificial lamb to protect us all from that."

Chloe patted the hand that Lady Evelyn had clenched by her side. "It is more than that, is it not? He protects the name and the honor of all those who have gone before. And treason," she whispered, "is a crime that will mark the Kenwoods for generations."

"Here comes Lady Marston. Oh, bugger." Lady Evelyn smiled. "Is that not what you said? It has a nice feel to it."

"It does. I thought as much when I heard it in the stables once. However, it is a wretchedly coarse curse."

"I know. I made a point of finding out what it meant. Ah, well met, Lady Marston," Lady Evelyn greeted the rotund older woman who stopped before them. "Allow me to introduce my companion, Miss Chloe Wherlocke."

"Came in with your son," the woman said, raising her lorgnette to look Chloe over. "A Wherlocke, eh? You look like Helena Cummings. Knew the gel years ago."

"She is my mother. She married Sir George Wherlocke, who died seven years ago," replied Chloe.

"Ah, heard that. Horse tossed him."

"That it did." And Chloe had tried to warn him, but he had refused to listen. She still wondered at times if he had ignored her because he simply did not care if he lived or died, and for that she blamed her mother. "He was a good man."

"He was. Married the wrong woman, though. No disrespect, but Helena was a whiny brat who was spoiled beyond all good sense and never gave a thought to anyone but herself."

Chloe simply nodded. Such a statement really could not be answered. She did wonder how the woman could say no disrespect and then rip a person's character to shreds. If she had loved her mother, Chloe suspected she could have thought of some way to defend her. She was saddened by the knowledge that she could not bring herself to do so.

"Why did you arrive with Lord Kenwood?"

"Mirabelle," Lady Evelyn murmured in protest, but the woman ignored her and kept her small dark eyes fixed upon Chloe.

"I came in with my cousin and guardian, Lord Sir Leopold Wherlocke, as well, m'lady."

"Sauce." She looked at Lady Evelyn. "Glad to have the boy up and walking about, eh?"

"Immeasurably," replied Lady Evelyn. "I also hope to keep him that way."

"Best get someone to shoot that uncle of his as well as that whore the fool boy married, then."

Chloe joined Lady Evelyn in gaping at Lady Marston, who left as abruptly as she had arrived. "Well, at least we know that some people already suspect Arthur and Beatrice," she said after a moment. "Do you think Lady Marston has shared her opinion with anyone else?"

"With great regularity," replied Lady Evelyn. "I just hope the people she shares it with actually believe her. I also wonder how she knows."

"She might not know; she might just feel certain. Does not matter. Even one very opinionated woman stating the fact will only help our cause."

When Phillipa returned from her dance with an obviously besotted young viscount, Chloe excused herself to go to the lady's retiring room. She prayed it was not too crowded, for she was growing very weary of crowds. The ball had satisfied her on one matter. At the moment the gossip was almost all against Beatrice and Arthur. She was surprised that the two had lingered as long as they had, for the murmurs about them were growing too loud for anyone to ignore.

Chloe was just thinking that she ought to try to edge closer to the pair so that she could get a good look at the infamous Beatrice when she entered the lady's retiring room and came face-to-face with the woman. She immediately wished she had remained ignorant of exactly how beautiful Beatrice was. Taller than her and far more voluptuous, Lady Beatrice had all most men claimed they craved in a woman. Hazel eyes containing a strong hint of green, a full bow-shaped mouth, and thick golden curls. Seeing the white expanse of the woman's impressive bosom,

Chloe fought the urge to look down at her own smaller one modestly covered with a fichu.

"You are the woman who came in with my husband."

Startled by the abrupt confrontation, Chloe glanced around and grimaced. The room was not crowded but it was not deserted, either. Three women were in it adjusting their hair or their gowns. This was not the place to get into an argument with Beatrice. If nothing else, Chloe was afraid she would say too much if the woman made her angry.

"I arrived with Lord Wherlocke, my cousin and guardian. Your husband"—the words tasted foul on her tongue—"was simply accompanying us."

"You came in on his arm."

"He was the one standing the closest to the carriage when I began my descent."

It was clear from the look on the woman's face that she had made up her mind about Chloe's place in her husband's life and nothing would change it. After all her infidelities, Chloe thought it the height of hypocrisy for Lady Beatrice to look so outraged by the fact that her husband had escorted another woman into a ballroom. She supposed it was part of the show the woman liked to put on—that of a wife deserted and continuously humiliated by her husband's infidelities. A quick glance at the avidly listening women told her that Beatrice was a fool if she thought anyone believed her pose.

"I know it was you and your cousin who hid him from me," snapped Beatrice. "How dare you keep a husband from his loving wife?"

"Loving wife? Ah, well, I suppose you could be

called that, as you are rumored to be very loving, just not always with your own husband."

Beatrice slapped her, the loud crack of her hand against Chloe's cheek silencing their giggling audience. It took all of Chloe's willpower not to curl up her fist and slam it into Beatrice's pretty little nose. She stared at the woman and suddenly felt a familiar chill down her spine. Instead of Beatrice's pretty face, flushed with fury, she saw a skull. The skull still wore the luxurious hairstyle that Beatrice did and even had Beatrice's body, but it was still a skull. There was a thick rope around the woman's neck.

"Why are you staring at me like that?" demanded Beatrice, her voice growing a little shrill. "Are you simple?"

Chloe started to free herself of the vision even as Beatrice raised her hand to strike her again. Then a hand in a lacy black glove grabbed Beatrice's wrist. Chloe looked to see Lady Marston standing next to Beatrice and scowling down at the woman.

"You three"—she tilted her head toward the other women making her elaborate hairstyle wobble on her head—"get out." The three women scurried out of the room and Lady Marston looked at Chloe. "Hit you, did she?"

"I have every right to strike her, as she is trying to steal my husband away from me," said Beatrice as she unsuccessfully tried to free her wrist from Lady Marston's grasp.

Lady Marston snorted in a very manly way. "Gadzooks, gel, you cannot believe you are fooling anyone, can you? Are you really that witless?" She pushed Beatrice toward the door. "Get out. There might even be a man or two out there you have not yet spread your legs for."

Although Beatrice made a soft growling sound of pure fury, she left. Chloe moved to the bowl of rose-scented water left on a marble table and gently bathed her cheek. One look in the ornate mirror hung over the table told her it would bruise, and she sighed.

"She clipped you good. Why did you let her?"

"I did not see it coming."

"Did not seem inclined to retaliate, either, eh?"

"I would have broken her little pert nose if I had, and that would have shifted the scandalous tale onto me. I believe I will let her keep the weight of it." She glanced at Lady Marston and said, "I will be out of here in a moment if you require privacy."

"Did not come in here for that. Knew the bitch was in here, so followed you in."

"Oh. Well, thank you kindly for interceding on my behalf."

"No bother. What did you see?"

"I beg your pardon?"

"Come, gel, I know about you Wherlockes and Vaughns. You got gifts. I also recognized that look on your face as you stood there doing nothing to stop that bitch from hitting you a second time. What were you seeing?"

"Lady Marston, do you have some, well, anger toward Beatrice, a personal grievance or the like?"

"Other than I cannot stand a whore who pretends to be some fine lady, no. Do you mean did she bed my husband?" Lady Marston laughed, a hearty, deep laugh. "No, gel, my Harold loves horses more than women. He had interest enough to give me seven fine children, and so it was enough for me. Now, tell me what you were seeing."

Chloe sighed. "So that you might have some tale to tell at some future gathering?"

"No," she said almost gently. "I do know when to keep silent. As I said, I know about you, even friends with a few. Father was, too. Very useful in the military."

Knowing the woman would not give up until Chloe told her what she had seen, she looked the woman right in the eye and said, "I saw a skull with Lady Beatrice's hair and body attached. Lady Beatrice is going to die soon. She also had a thick rope around her neck, so it may be that she will die that way."

"Ah, that is why you were so pale. Not a pretty sight. Gratifying, but not pretty."

"Are you certain you have no personal grievance against the woman?"

"Just that the Kenwoods are good people aside from that Arthur. They do not deserve what the man and that whore are trying to do." Lady Marston smiled. "And my dear friend Mildred Kenwood needs to be free of the burden of the both of them."

Yet again Chloe found herself gaping after the woman as Lady Marston strode out of the retiring room. Shaking herself free of the shock, she glanced at herself in the mirror again. The print of Lady Beatrice's hand was very clear to see on her face, but Chloe smiled faintly. It would make a very good reason for someone to take her home.

Chapter 10

"Beatrice should never have touched you."

Chloe eyed Julian, who sat far too close to her in the carriage, his glare fixed upon her reddened cheek. Much to her relief, he and Leo had immediately agreed to take her home. However, they had not gone far when Leo had halted the carriage and slipped away into the night. Chloe wished she could ask him what he was doing, but she knew her cousin would not be able to tell her much, so it seemed pointless to question him. However, Leo's desertion had left her alone with Julian and she was finding that—disturbing. Julian's fury over the fact that his wife had struck her was oddly arousing.

"She just slapped me, Julian," she said. "She is trying to kill you and tried to kill Anthony. I think that makes this red mark upon my cheek a very small matter indeed."

He lightly thumped his fist against his thigh. "Her attention turned to you far more quickly than I had anticipated. This is not good."

"We knew they would look my way eventually. It

just happened tonight instead of later in the week. You had to have expected some sort of reaction when you threw them out of Colinsmoor."

He nodded and wrapped his arm around her shoulders, ignoring how she tensed beneath his grasp. When he had first seen the mark upon Chloe's cheek, a mark left by the wife he was eager to rid himself of, Julian had become enraged. If not for the fact that Chloe had looked a little wan and Leo was urging them to leave, he would have taken the time to hunt Beatrice down and make her pay for striking Chloe. He knew, however, that there was not much he could have done. Worse than that, he would have only added to the attention that had become fixed upon Chloe. She was right to say that, as of now, she was seen as the wronged party and that could only work in their favor.

"Word of that banishment spread very quickly even though I had not noticed anyone listening to the conversation I had with Arthur and Beatrice. It could be that Beatrice made her anger about that a little too loud and too public." He lightly ran his hand up and down her arm, biting back a sound of satisfaction when she softened and leaned against him. "And the tale of the confrontation between you and Beatrice in the lady's retiring room also spread quickly. Beatrice did not act wisely there. There were witnesses and they quickly told the tale to anyone who would listen. Why did you not strike her back?"

"That would not have been wise of me. Best to stand there and look like an innocent victim of a virago." She sighed. "And if I had hit her back, I would have knocked her flat or broken her nose. Then all sympathy for me would have been lost."

"Knocked her flat?" He picked up her small hand and studied it. "With this little thing?"

"I have two brothers. I learned how to fight at a very young age."

"Tormented you, did they?"

"A little, but mostly it was that they played rough and if I wished to play with them, I had to learn how to play rough as well. When I knocked the squire's son down at the age of fourteen, I decided I had learned my lessons well. Although I was never able to knock down my brothers," she muttered, still a little disappointed by that.

"Why did you knock the squire's son down?"

"Because he was sixteen and spotty and thought I would wish to kiss him. I did not."

"As a man who was once sixteen and spotty, I should feel sorry for the fool, but I think I should like to knock him down myself."

"Best not. He is married now and his wife could knock us both down with no trouble."

Julian laughed and rubbed his cheek against the top of her head, enjoying the feel of her silky hair against his skin. "I saw Lady Marston before we left." He felt Chloe tense again.

"Oh?" Chloe silently cursed, certain that Lady Marston had decided the vision Chloe had had did not need to be kept secret from Julian. "Did she greet you with what appears to be an innate bluntness?"

"As always. Since the day I married Beatrice, Lady Marston has felt it her duty to tell me I made a grave mistake in judgment. This time she suggested I shoot both my uncle and, as she has always referred to Beatrice, that whore."

"She told your mother the same thing."

"Lady Marston also said that I should ask you what you saw. She said she was sure I would enjoy it."

"Humph. She said she would keep it a secret."

"Then she will. She obviously felt that I would do so as well. So what did you see? What was your vision about, as I assume that was what her ladyship referred to. A vision."

"Are you certain you wish to hear about it? It was not a pleasant one. I am not sure why Lady Marston thought you would enjoy it."

"Tell me, Chloe. Should I not know what Lady Marston does?"

She pulled away from him but he kept his arm wrapped firmly around her shoulders, so she did not get far. "I was staring at Beatrice after she slapped me when it came to me. That is one reason why I did not hit her back. I saw Beatrice, but not Beatrice. I could see her hair, her gowned body, and even the hand she had raised to hit me again. But her head was not as it should be. It was a skull. Around her throat was not the rope of pearls she was wearing but a real rope. A hempen noose. Beatrice is soon to die."

He held her close and began to stroke her arm again. "You do not think there could be some other explanation for what you saw?" It was a chilling sight for a young woman to see, but Julian had the strong feeling that she had seen others just as dark.

"Nay. I have seen such things before. Just before my father was thrown from his horse and killed, I saw him in his saddle, his riding clothes clean and fine, and then, suddenly, his head became a skull. It was also sitting oddly upon his shoulders. Afterward I understood why. He broke his neck and he died. I told him not to go riding, told him I had seen that it would be dangerous for him to do so, but he rode out anyway."

"S'blood, Chloe, do you often have such dark visions?"

"Sad to say, the dark ones outweigh the good ones. Warnings are probably more powerful than glad tidings."

Julian thought about that and decided that it made a strange sort of sense. "Do you think your vision of Beatrice means that she will hang?" It was a punishment Beatrice had undoubtedly earned, but he would rather not have to tell his son that his mother had been hanged.

"I would think it does. Other deaths matched the things I saw in my visions. Yet, despite committing crimes she must know are hanging offenses, Beatrice revealed no concern about punishment."

"Beatrice believes her beauty will save her from all consequences of her actions."

"She is very beautiful," Chloe whispered, able to see all too clearly how the woman had been able to enthrall Julian.

"In her face and form, yes. Beneath that she is ugly. Never forget that that beautiful woman set her own child in the arms of a dying woman living on the desolate moors and never gave another thought to the child." He grimaced. "As if you ever could, for that was a time of grief for you. But that is the true Beatrice. Cold and deadly. That is what I saw when I finally had the blinders taken from my eyes. And that was before I learned the whole truth, a truth that revealed just how deeply ugly she really is." He kissed Chloe's cheek. "You are far more beautiful. Your beauty goes to the heart."

Chloe had no chance to respond to what she considered was a ridiculous piece of flattery, for the carriage came to a halt in front of Leo's home. She allowed Julian to help her out of the carriage and then tried to hurry into the house ahead of him, but he was far too quick for her. Instinct told her that she had just lost all chance of escaping his attention for the evening. It was cowardly to even considering hiding in her room, but that did not make the thought any less tempting.

She inwardly sighed with resignation when she heard him order Wynn to bring them some wine before he led her into the blue salon. Chloe had to wonder if Julian had chosen the room purposely. Leo did have another salon, after all. They did not have to sit in this one.

"Sit, Chloe. We need to talk," he said even as he pulled her down onto the settee beside him as if he did not trust her to obey him.

That was probably wise of him, Chloe thought, and nearly grinned. Her good humor was fleeting, however. She had a sinking feeling she knew what he was going to talk about. There were not that many topics he would look so serious about, and since they talked freely about Arthur and Beatrice, that left only her exam and the marriage he and Leo were planning on. As Wynn served them some wine and then left, Chloe tried to prepare herself for what could well be a very uncomfortable conversation.

"First I would like to beg your forgiveness for what you had to suffer through earlier today," he said, staring into his wine, for he felt awkward looking at her while he spoke on the intimate exam she had had to endure. "I did not do it just to prove to myself that you were pure. You do know that, do you not?"

"I know that. It was for Anthony. There must be proof that he is not my child, or someone could try to steal what is his rightful place as your heir. It is the only reason I allowed it to be done. For him." She was not about to tell him that she had wondered if he had needed to reassure himself of her innocence. It had only been a passing doubt, and telling him about it would do no good, could only insult him.

He cleared his throat with a sip of wine. It surprised him, after all the sin he had indulged in for the last year, that he found it so awkward to speak about her exam. Julian supposed it was because it had been such an intimate thing and he knew she was a complete innocent. He had been well trained to be careful in how he spoke to a virginal miss, and some lessons could not be shaken off.

"And now we must speak about the marriage," he said and sighed when she grimaced. "I will be a good husband to you."

"I never thought you would be a bad one," she said.

"Then why have you refused to say yes?"

"Why should I offer an answer when I was never asked a question?"

"Ah, you wish to be proposed to." He took her hand in his and kissed her palm, pleased when she shivered slightly. "Marry me, Chloe."

"That is still not a proposal."

"Chloe, you were prepared to give me your innocence. Right here on this settee. If Leo had not interrupted us, that exam you had this afternoon would have been a waste of time. It was not well done of me, but I did it, and—"

"Now you must pay the consequences?" she snapped.

Julian sighed and dragged his hand through his hair, ruining his queue. "I do not think of marrying you as a consequence. I will be honest and say that I had thought to never marry again. Can you blame me for that thought?"

"Nay. I daresay I would feel much the same if I had suffered like you. Although it is no compliment to be thought of in the same breath as Beatrice."

"I know you are nothing like Beatrice. For one thing, you make me smile and she never did. Neither did I need to get her in my arms simply because she is in the same room with me. I do not know how to explain this to one who is so innocent, but you enflame me with just a look. I knew I should leave you alone, that you are a virgin miss and that I am still married in the eyes of the law and the church, but I could not."

That was a very flattering thing to hear, but Chloe struggled not to let it turn her head. "Desire is not a good reason to get married. Marriage is forever. Desire fades. I am the penniless daughter of a knight and my own mother cast me off. I live on

Leo's charity. You, m'lord, could do so much better than that in a wife."

"No, I could not. And do not belittle the importance of passion, Chloe. It is important in a marriage. And there is more. I trust you."

"In everything?"

"What do you mean?"

"You have suffered the sting of an unfaithful wife. Do you trust me to be faithful to my vows, or will you always be watching for me to betray you as she did?"

Julian stared at her for a moment. He thought about her question, even imagined a few incidents that could look suspicious, yet he found he did not immediately feel threatened by them. At some point during his stay at the Wherlockes', he had come to trust Chloe in every way. It surprised him, but he was glad of it. Not only did he know such constant doubt and mistrust would sour a marriage, but it would also sour him.

"No, I will not. I said I trust you and I do. I know you will hold as firmly to your vows as I will."

Chloe breathed a sigh of relief, but she was still not sure what he offered was enough. She feared she was being foolishly greedy. Julian was the man she wanted, but she had thought they would just have an affair. That would be a disaster in the end and she knew it, but she was not sure she should step into a marriage simply because they both wanted to fall into a bed.

"Chloe, I also like you. We enjoy each other's company. We can talk about so many things, so there will be no long, silent meals with me at one end of the table and you at the other. And, Chloe, you love my son."

"Ah, aye, I do. And with you comes Anthony, is that what you are saying?"

"What I am saying is that no matter what my thoughts on marriage were, I feel that at some time I would have begun looking for a mother for him. I can think of none better than you, none I would trust to love him as he deserves to be loved."

"So what you offer me is passion, liking, trust, good company, and Anthony."

He just stared at her and she sighed. It was a lot more than she had thought she was getting from him, and she really could not say what else she wanted. Yet it was such a big step to take. Marriage was forever. Could she marry a man who did not speak of love? And did she even love him? Did it even matter?

"What about my gift? My visions? My family that is riddled with such gifts?"

"I cannot promise to believe in all of them, but they do not frighten me."

"And if we have children?"

"I am hoping that we will and if they, too, have gifts, I will still love them. And you have family enough to help them learn how to deal with whatever gift they are born with." He took both of her hands in his. "I know you fear that I will flee as so many in your family have done, leaving wives, husbands, and children. I swear I will not do that. It is not something I can prove to you now, is it. You will just have to trust in my word."

She stared at her hands in his and then at his

face. He was so handsome he made her heart hurt. Chloe suddenly knew that if she did not at least try to make a strong marriage with him, she would regret it to her dying day.

"Then I will marry you."

When he pulled her into his arms and kissed her, Chloe decided that there was one good reason to marry him. She did not believe any other man could ever make her feel the way he did. Her whole body ached for him.

She cried out in surprise when he lifted her into his arms and strode toward the door. "What are you doing?"

"I plan to show you the importance of passion," he said.

"Now? What about Leo? What if he comes home?" she asked as he carried her up the stairs to his bed-chamber.

"I do not believe you need to worry about him."

Chloe had no chance to argue that. Julian carried her into his room, kicking the door shut behind them, and tumbled her down onto his bed. He kissed her and she quickly forgot what she wanted to argue about. Curling her arms around his neck, she kissed him back with all the passion that was burning through her veins. It was as if every feeling he had stirred inside her with every kiss and every touch had remained lurking inside her and was now flooding her whole body. Chloe knew she would never tire of kissing this man.

She tensed a little when she realized he was not only caressing her, he was removing her clothes. No man had ever seen her naked. Even during that humiliating exam, her modesty had been protected as much as was possible. She forced a sudden attack of shyness aside and began to undo the buttons on his coat and waistcoat. If she was going to be exposed, then so was he.

Julian needed to see her naked. It was a need that demanded to be fed, but he tried to be careful as he stripped her of her clothes. He could see her blushing and he did not want to frighten her with the ferocity of his hunger for her. He paused when he got her stripped to her shift and, keeping his gaze fixed upon her lithe body, he stood up and began to shed his own clothes. It was only then that he noticed she had been trying to get his clothes off as well. He certainly had not undone his coat or waistcoat.

It proved to be highly arousing to take his clothes off before her. The way she watched him, her cheeks flushed and her breathing rapid, fired his blood as much as it flattered him. Julian did not think he had ever been so enflamed simply by the way a woman looked at him. He hesitated only briefly when it came to remove the last of his clothing. She was a virgin, after all. Then he shrugged and decided it was best to begin as he meant them to continue. He intended to spend a lot of time naked with Chloe.

Chloe stared at him when he was finally fully naked. He was beautiful, she thought. Dressed he was handsome and elegant, a true gentleman of society. Naked he was somehow more manly, more primal. She reached out to touch the erection that jutted out from a thick nest of golden brown hair and he groaned.

Even as she started to withdraw her hand, afraid she had done something wrong, he joined her on the bed and finished stripping her of her clothing. Chloe shivered with pleasure at every brush of his fingers against her skin as he unlaced her shift and pulled it off over her head. When he sat back on his heels and stared at her, however, all the warmth of desire began to slip away. She was all too aware of the fact that she did not have the lush curves Beatrice did.

Julian ran his hands down her sides, savoring the feel of her soft, warm skin beneath his hands. Her skin was unmarred, her body slender yet holding all the womanly curves any man could desire. He wanted to bury himself deep within her immediately, but he knew he had to go slowly. The very last thing he wanted to do was give her pain. A little was probably unavoidable but he was determined to make it as little as possible.

He slid his hands up her rib cage and covered her breasts. Her nipples hardened and pressed against his palms, begging for his kiss. With a soft groan, he bent his head and granted their wish. The soft cry that escaped Chloe and the way she clutched at his shoulders pleased him more than he could ever say. There was a deep well of passion in Chloe Wherlocke, and he intended to wallow in it.

When Julian's mouth covered the tip of her breast and he drew her aching nipple deep into his mouth, Chloe felt all of her desire rush back. She clutched at his shoulders, wanting to hold him close even though he showed no sign of leaving her. When he moved his mouth to her other breast the cool air dried the warm dampness he left

behind, and she gasped at how good it felt. The way
he suckled her made an ache begin low in her belly,
need throbbing there with every draw of his mouth.

Chloe slowly moved her hands over his broad
back, trailing her fingers down his spine, and back
up again. He growled softly and she heard his pleasure in the sound. That proof that he enjoyed her
touch as much as she did his encouraged her. The
heat of his skin seeped into her blood and en-
hanced the passion that was burning inside of her.
In her curiosity about the body that was giving her
so much pleasure, she smoothed her hands over his
taut buttocks. He shifted against her and the feel of
the hard length of him rubbing against her womanhood sent a blaze of fire right through her.

She murmured in disappointment when he began
to kiss his way down to her stomach, for she could no
longer reach all the way down his back. He slid his
hand over her thigh and stroked the place where she
now ached almost beyond bearing. His touch was
both shocking and soothing, but all too soon his
touch was not enough. Instead of shying away from
such intimacy, Chloe opened to it. When he slid a
finger inside her, she tensed for just a brief moment,
the humiliating memories of the earlier exam trying
to break through the haze of desire in her mind.
Then he kissed her again and the chilling effect of
those memories vanished.

Julian slid another finger inside Chloe, and the
wet heat surrounding his fingers had him gritting
his teeth against the need to unite their bodies. He
wanted to be buried to the hilt inside, but he had
to ready her as much as possible. The way her body

wept for him told him he could have what he craved soon. All he needed was patience. That was hard to grasp when her small, soft hands moved over him with an increasing boldness.

"Julian," Chloe whispered, hardly recognizing the soft husky voice as her own. "I need." She could not think of what else to say, or even if there was more to say to make herself clear. "I need."

"I know. I but try to ease my way so that I do not hurt you too much."

"This hurts."

He understood exactly what she meant, for he was feeling the same way. As gently as he could, he eased into her. When he met with the shield of her innocence, he kissed her and pushed through it. A strangled noise escaped her and her nails dug into his back, but she did not retreat from his invasion. Julian grit his teeth and went still, struggling to remain that way as he kissed and caressed her to restore the passion the pain had dimmed. He was just wondering how much longer he would be able to endure being so still while the tight heat of her made his body ache to thrust when she moved against him.

Chloe tried to shift even closer to Julian. At first she had felt as if he had stretched her too wide. She had expected the brief pain but not the feeling that she was too full. Then her body softened around the intrusion and she felt her desire return to its previous ferocity. What had felt odd now felt wonderful, but she knew instinctively that it could feel even better. She shifted again, moving against him, and it felt as if he was driven even deeper inside her. That felt so good that Chloe moved yet again, wrapping her legs around his waist.

She gasped when he suddenly began to move, thrusting into her and withdrawing just enough to thrust again. Strange as the movement seemed, her body was rejoicing in it. Chloe found herself quickly meeting and matching his rhythm. A part of her could hear herself panting, hear Julian murmuring soft words against her skin, but all of her attention was fixed upon the way they moved together, the way his body was joined to hers, and the way each stroke of his body inside hers made the heat of her desire begin to pool down low in her belly.

Then it exploded, sending ripples of sharp fire throughout her body. Chloe heard herself cry out his name as she tried to hold him as close to her as possible. Julian's movements briefly became fierce, his body ramming into hers, and then he tensed and warmth filled her at the point where they were most deeply joined. His seed, she thought, and felt herself shatter yet again. When he collapsed on top of her, she held him close, enjoying the way his body trembled just like hers did.

Chloe felt as if every bone and muscle in her body had melted away. She muttered a protest when Julian moved but could not seem to even open her eyes to see where he was going. Then she felt a cool, damp cloth move over her privates and she squeaked in shock. When she tried to grab something to pull over her naked body, she was prevented from doing so by Julian. Chloe just grimaced and kept her eyes closed tightly until he rejoined her in the bed.

Julian had to grin at the way Chloe had her eyes

closed, like a small child who was trying to hide. He pulled her into his arms and kissed her, idly undoing her badly mussed hairstyle and wondering how he could have forgotten to take it down. He usually liked to take a woman's hair down, but with Chloe, his need had been too strong for such niceties, such idle seductions. He was thankful he had retained enough of his senses to make her first time more about pleasure than pain.

And she had felt pleasure, he thought with what he knew was a cocky grin. The passion Chloe revealed was more than any man would need. He admitted to himself that he had had a doubt or two. Some gently bred women could love the kisses and caresses that began a wooing, but loathe the messy business of making love. Chloe did not hesitate to take her full enjoyment. The fact that she had found her pleasure not once but twice during her first time told him that she allowed no maidenly fears or doubts to dim her desire or her pleasure. It was going to be a joy to show her all the ways that could bring back that pleasure.

"I concede," she said as she snuggled up against him, openly appreciating his body in a way that could easily make him vain, he thought with a smile.

"Concede to what?" he asked as he combed his fingers through her thick hair.

"Passion is very important in a marriage." She smiled against his chest when he chuckled. "I should probably slip away to my own bedchamber." She felt his arms tighten around her.

"Nay. You shall stay here." Julian realized that he

was not just reluctant to have her leave and make him sleep alone; he loathed the very thought of it.

"But we cannot allow Leo to find us like this."

"We are betrothed." He wondered how to tell her about Leo's attitude concerning such intimacies and then decided the truth was best. "He expects this. Even said he could never be saint enough to resist, so how could he expect me to. Leo considers us as good as married."

"Oh." Chloe felt a brief twinge of embarrassment but then pushed it aside as she realized she could stay right here and return to his arms whenever she wanted. Her thoughts quickly went to all they could do while she was in his bed. "Julian? Do people do what we did more than once a night?"

Julian laughed, more with joy than amusement, as he pushed her onto her back.

Chapter 11

A cold, damp wind slipped down the back of Julian's coat and he shivered. Huddled in the shadows with an eerily motionless Leo was not Julian's idea of fighting his enemies. Swords, pistols at dawn, fists. That was fighting. This was lurking. This was spying. Julian decided that he did not like spying.

"Cold?" asked Leo in a barely audible whisper.

"Not any longer. All that bone-rattling shivering I just indulged in has warmed me up."

A quick flash of white teeth was all that told Julian he had managed to amuse Leo. That was good. What would be even better was if he was back in his bed curled up around Chloe and amusing himself. Julian knew he could not express that desire to Leo. The man seemed content to allow Julian and Chloe to act as they pleased now that Chloe had become his betrothed. However, Julian doubted that Leo wanted to hear any details about exactly what did please him and Chloe.

Just thinking about how Chloe had felt in his arms last night made him ache to hold her again.

Despite her innocence Chloe had been the best lover he had ever had. Her response to his every kiss and caress was quick and hot. She had shattered in his arms, her sweet cry of release still echoing in his mind. It was as if they had been made for each other, and that was both a dangerous and a frightening thought.

"Here they come."

Although he wanted to ask Leo how he could speak so softly, Julian remained silent and pressed deeper into the shadows enclosing the passage between two elegant homes. He stared at the townhouse across the street, the front of it illuminated by a pair of lanterns hanging on each side of the front door. He watched as his uncle and Beatrice climbed out of an elegant carriage Julian was certain had once rested in the stables of his own townhouse. A well-dressed butler let them inside, and the moment the door closed behind them, Julian looked at Leo.

"Is that it?" he asked. "Have I stood here risking the loss of important parts of my body to the cold just to watch Arthur and Beatrice walk into a house?"

"Inside that house is one of France's best spies."

"Oh." Julian had to admit he was intrigued now. "So how do we prove that my uncle is working with that spy, betraying his own country? Again. We cannot see or hear anything from here."

"We will move closer in a moment, although it probably will not help us much. Simone would have made sure she was well guarded against such an intrusion."

"Simone? The spy is a woman?"

Leo nodded. "And she is the best spy I have ever come up against, and I have been at this for seven years. I always thought that she was Arthur's lover, but then he turned to Beatrice."

"Mayhap he just added Beatrice." He grimaced when even in the thick shadows he could see the surprised question in Leo's quirked brow. "Yes, she has provided entertainment for more than one man at a time." He scowled toward the house they watched as dark memories swamped him for a moment and suddenly realized that they did not sting as sharply as they had before. "Beatrice is what some men claim they want—an adventurous lover who will do most anything once."

"And you decided that adventurous was not what you wanted?"

"Not when it included any man Beatrice thought exceptionally handsome or rich or young or a thousand and one other qualities. Adventurous with me, yes. Adventurous with any and every male within fifty miles of home, sometimes two at a time, no. There is also a coldness in Beatrice, one that goes bone deep, despite that sensual greed that can make a man act the fool. At first I made all manner of excuses for it or told myself I was imagining it all."

"What was it that changed your mind?"

"After we had an argument where I flatly refused to pay another one of her gambling debts, she said she was going out. I watched her call for her mount and then shove the stable boy aside when he brought it to her. The boy fell and struck his head upon the steps. Beatrice glanced down at him and then just shrugged. She mounted her horse and rode off, leaving the boy sprawled on the steps, blood pooling around his head. That was when I stopped lying to myself, stopped trying to make excuses for her. It was as if I woke up from some feverish dream and found myself locked into a nightmare."

"And the boy?"

"He was fine. His head hurt for a while and he has a scar just at his hairline, but he is otherwise fine. His father was Melvin," he added in a whisper.

Leo cursed softly and lightly patted Julian on the back. "We will find out where he is buried soon and give him a proper burial, one his family can attend. The best we can do for him now is make sure that his killers are punished."

"Speak quietly," Simone snapped when Beatrice began to loudly repeat some gossip, brandy making her boisterous and mean. "We are being watched." She ignored the glare Beatrice sent her way.

Arthur frowned. "Are you certain?"

"Of course I am. Do you think I have stayed alive all these years by being foolish or blind? Your nephew and that annoying bastard Leopold are tucked in between two houses just across the street. One of my men saw them there."

"Then get rid of them," said Beatrice. "If you have men who can get close enough to see where they are hiding, then you can get men close enough to them to cut their throats."

"You wish me to order my men to kill an earl and a baron directly across the street from where I live?"

"I am certain you know of many places where the bodies can be hidden."

Arthur stared at the window, tempted to move to it and see if he could find his nephew in the shadows. The boy was proving to be a royal thorn in his side. His plan had been perfect, Beatrice one of his best weapons, and yet Julian still lived. Arthur had seen how blindly besotted Julian had been with Beatrice and Beatrice had certainly done her part, yet Julian had survived or avoided every accident they had planned out for him.

When his nephew had stated that under no circumstances would he fight in defense of his wife's honor ever again, Arthur had known that Beatrice had lost her value as a weapon. It was then that he had begun to look to outsiders to do what needed to be done, and they too had failed. Even though he was often drunk and roaming about the stews where murder was common, Julian had managed to evade death again and again. Arthur had begun to have dreams where he just walked up to Julian and shot the arrogant little bastard in the head. That would be a huge mistake, but at least it would end this interminable game.

He took a deep breath to calm the fury that surged through him every time he thought of Julian, of how the man thwarted Arthur's carefully laid plans at every turn. The fact that the fool had not even realized someone wanted him dead until recently only added to Arthur's burning rage. Someone that blind should not be allowed to live. Now, however, it was going to be even more difficult to be rid of his nephew, or nephews, for Nigel could not be allowed to take the helm of Colinsmoor, either. Not only did Arthur no longer have Colinsmoor to rule over and access to its riches to fund his plans, but he had been cast out like some impoverished relative who had overstayed his welcome. All of society now watched him and Beatrice with suspicion. Worse, there were secrets hidden at Colinsmoor that he had had no time to collect or destroy, proof of things he had done that could get him hanged a hundred times over.

The sound of the two women arguing and exchanging insults finally pulled Arthur from his dark thoughts. Simone spoke in a cold, too-sweet voice that Beatrice, if she were not so stupid, should have known was a deadly warning and one she would be wise to heed. Beatrice was cold, could order someone's death without a qualm and had done so many times, but Simone could do her killing herself, quickly and silently. Although it appeared that Beatrice was becoming more a liability than an asset, he was not ready to be rid of her yet. She could still have uses, if only through her sexual greed and her beauty.

"Enough," he said in a cold, hard voice and both women immediately grew silent and looked at him. "This arguing amongst ourselves only aides our enemies." Tight-lipped, Simone nodded her agreement, but Beatrice pouted. "Since Leopold Wherlocke is with the Home Office, we have to assume that Julian has gained himself some powerful allies."

"And that someone has begun to realize your interests are in more than becoming the earl," said Simone. "I did not think of that, for I have had to deal with Leopold before."

"Perhaps I should—" began Beatrice.

"No," said Simone. "Wherlocke is not seducible. Better than you have tried. And Julian is obviously united with Leopold, so that man now knows more about you than is good. It would only give him more strength against you."

Arthur could see that Beatrice took that as a personal insult, and he inwardly sighed. He would try to rein her in just once more, and if she continued to put them all at risk with her recklessness, he would have to make her disappear. For a moment he considered the idea that she might well serve him one last favor. If he gave it some thought, he might be able to make her death look like murder with the finger of guilt pointing straight at Julian. It was a thought that eased some of his growing anger.

"If you would excuse me," Beatrice said icily as she stood up and brushed down her skirts. "I require a moment of privacy."

Simone cursed the moment the door shut behind Beatrice. "She has become dangerous, Arthur. To you and to me."

"I will take care of her. She was a useful tool and she may yet have a purpose, but I am no sentimental fool. I watch my back most carefully."

"I know. While she is gone, let us discuss this information you said you could obtain for me. Have your recent troubles caused that plan to fail?"

For a few moments, they discussed the information he had promised her. She wanted it badly, having already told her superiors about it. Arthur had to soothe her with assurances that he had not been defeated, only delayed. It was not the truth.

The man he had thought would get him what he needed had disappeared, and none of the ones searching for him had yet found a clue as to where he had gone. The man's fiancée would probably know, but grabbing hold of her so that they could pry the truth out of her would be a risky venture.

"There," said Beatrice with an irritating cheer as she rejoined them, "all is taken care of."

Before Arthur could ask what she meant, the sound of swords clashing reached their ears and he joined Simone in glaring at Beatrice, but it was Simone who spoke. "What have you done, you stupid whore?"

"How dare you," began Beatrice.

"I dare." Simone pulled a knife from some hidden pocket in her voluminous skirts and started toward Beatrice. "You have put us all at risk, but do not worry about how that may harm you. You will be too dead to notice."

Arthur stepped between the two women even though he was tempted to let Simone kill Beatrice. "Not now." He turned to look at Beatrice, who obviously had enough wits to understand that he had not given Simone a resounding no. "Answer the question, woman. What have you done?"

"I sent some men out to rid us of those two fools. That Leopold is a danger to all of us, and you want Julian dead. This will give us what we all want."

"This will give us nothing but trouble," snapped Simone, but she sheathed her knife. "Did you leave your carriage in front, Arthur?"

"No. I sent it round to the back."

"I will join you in a moment and we will go

somewhere else. If we are very lucky, those two men will end their lives out there and we will have been seen so far away from here we could never be accused of the crime," she said as she strode out of the room.

"Arthur," began Beatrice.

"Shut up and move. We have to get away from here before too many people are drawn to the fight and we are seen."

Arthur strode out of the room not particularly caring if Beatrice came with him or not. Everything was falling to pieces around him. He knew it was not all Beatrice's fault, but he would have to give some hard thought to her uses or complete lack thereof, especially since Simone was so sure that Beatrice would not be able to seduce Wherlocke. It was time to decide if and when he would strike where he knew for certain Julian had a weakness. If he was judging the relationship between Julian and the little Wherlocke woman correctly, he might be able to do that without even leaving the city.

Julian was about to point out to Leo that they were fighting a losing battle in their attempts to see or hear anything that was going on inside the house they crept around when he saw a movement to his right. He pushed Leo to the side and drew his sword just in time to counter the thrust of an attacker's sword. Behind him he could hear that Leo had quickly drawn his own sword and was also engaged in a battle.

The two men who had attacked them were excellent swordsmen, but they could not breach the small fortress Julian and Leo made by standing back to back and wielding their swords with a skill that matched, perhaps even exceeded, theirs. Julian was beginning to think the victory would only come when one of them grew too exhausted to fight anymore when he felt Leo jerk behind him.

"You hurt?" he asked without once taking his attention off the man trying to skewer him.

"A scratch. Curse it, they are fleeing," he muttered.

Julian suddenly heard the sound of a carriage pulling away from behind the house. "Going to try and make it look as if they were somewhere else when two lords of the realm were brutally murdered on their doorstep."

"Exactly."

Not sure whether it was the thought that he was about to kill two lords of the realm or the realization that he was being deserted to take all the blame for it, but the man facing Julian hesitated. Julian saw the brief distraction of his opponent and took quick advantage of it. In two quick moves, he disarmed the man and thrust his sword through his heart. He turned to help Leo only to see that his opponent had made the same mistake. Unlike Julian, however, Leo disarmed his foe and then stabbed him through the shoulder. When the man stumbled back and started to turn to flee, Leo kicked him in the face and the man fell to the ground like a stone.

Julian stared down at the man and then looked at Leo. The move he had made had been swift and graceful. "A good kick."

"Learned it from a Frenchman."

"An enemy taught you that?"

"Actually, he is only partly French and a relative. And at the moment, the French are not exactly our enemies. Aside from that, he is one of ours." Leo winced as he crouched down to tie the man's hands behind his back with his own cravat. "I will need your help in carrying this fellow back to the carriage."

"Because of your scratch?" Julian wished it were not so dark, for he had the feeling that Leo's wound was more than a scratch. "Allow me," he drawled and picked up the man, putting him over his shoulder. "I hope we can get to the carriage without being seen. This will be a little difficult to explain."

"Someone tried to rob us and we are taking him to the authorities."

"You are obviously accustomed to coming up with a tale to explain such strange things. I see. Sorry I killed my opponent. Just thought of staying alive and not of how the man might be a useful source of information."

"One is all we need. The only thing I am sorry for is that your uncle and Simone have fled and will undoubtedly be able to show that they were elsewhere when we were cruelly attacked just outside their home. I am not sure the fact that we have one of their men will even make them falter in their plans. Simone trusts no one and we have discovered that not one of her men appears to know everything. A piece here and there, but not enough to charge and try her. It does not help that she is the mistress of several very important men."

"Several? Ambitious woman. Beautiful, is she?"

"Very."

"Has she tried to seduce you?" he asked, something in Leo's tone making him curious.

"Once. I laughed at her and for that, more than anything else, she would like to see me dead. I do not think she ordered that attack on us, however."

"It was her men and her house. Although I suppose the men could have been Arthur's."

"I do not think your uncle would be fool enough to order an attack on you right outside of the house of a woman he is well known to be involved with. This was foolish and ill thought out. Does that seem like your uncle?"

"No. It sounds like Beatrice."

"That is what I was thinking. It would explain the swift leave-taking. Simone and Arthur seek to distance themselves from this. It will be investigated, but I am certain they will provide dozens of witnesses to say they were nowhere near the house when we were attacked. Beatrice may have just made a very serious mistake."

"Do you think Arthur will be rid of her now?"

"If not him, then Simone."

It was nearly dawn by the time they were able to return to Leo's home. Leo quickly retired to his bedchamber. His wound had not been serious but had required stitching, and Julian suspected the man was also suffering from a loss of blood. He knew all too well how that could rob a man of all his strength. Julian stepped into his bedchamber and felt his weariness immediately vanish when he saw Chloe curled up in his bed.

He quickly shed his clothes and washed up before crawling into bed beside her. When he pulled her into his arms, she stirred and then looked at him with sleep-heavy eyes. Julian thought that she had never looked lovelier. He kissed her, and even though it was only a gentle kiss, he felt his desire for her stir to life.

"It is acceptable that I waited here for you then, is it?" she asked as she cuddled up next to his warm body.

"Very acceptable." He suddenly realized that her soft touches were not caresses, that she was actually searching for a wound. "I am not hurt. We were attacked and Leo suffered a small wound to his shoulder, but we are both hale." He told her what happened.

"Leo is right, that does sound very impetuous, ill thought out and risky. Not at all like your uncle. Or Simone."

"Leo has told you about Simone?"

"He felt the need to warn me about her because he feared she might try to get to him through me. I have seen her once or twice on the arm of a man who should know to be more careful in choosing his lovers. She is stunningly beautiful."

"So he said. He believes Beatrice sent the men out to kill us. He also believes that either Arthur or, most certainly, Simone will make her pay dearly for that error in judgment."

"You mean they will kill her."

"Yes. Leo really believes that she signed her own death warrant with this act."

Chloe raised herself up to look at him although

it was hard to clearly see his expression in the light of one candle set by the bed. Yet there was something in the tone of his voice that troubled her. She was certain he did not love Beatrice, but he sounded as if the thought of her death bothered him in some way.

"You are reluctant to see her killed?" she asked.

"No. Her death does not bother me and, strangely enough, that lack of feeling is what troubles me. S'blood, I was married to the woman." He gave her a brief kiss to silence her when she began to speak. "I know that I still am, but only on paper. As I have said before, in my heart, and mind, my marriage ended a long time ago. As for someone killing her, well, she chose the path she is walking and the people she is walking it with. In a way, I think she was walking toward her death from the moment she joined forces with my uncle. There is just a small part of me that feels I should warn her in some way, not just sit here knowing someone wants her dead and waiting for the culprit to do the deed."

"Could it be that your unease comes from the fact that you wish to be freed of your marriage and her death would do that?"

Julian stared at her for a moment and then kissed her again, this time with a lot more heat. "I believe that is exactly it."

"I have wrestled with the same problem. I saw her death and yet I have made no effort to warn her. It took me a while to see that although I shall benefit from her death, I am not the one planning it and I am not the one who will do it. I also know that, even if I could get to her and warn her, she would not heed any warning of mine. As you have said, Beatrice thinks her beauty will keep her safe from all harm."

He slid his hands beneath her nightgown and gently squeezed her nicely rounded, taut bottom. "Nor would she believe me. And when all is said and done, she has a lot of blood on her hands."

Chloe could not stop herself from asking, "Your concern is not because you still have feelings for her, is it?"

"I feel nothing for the woman. Even my rage at her has eased except as concerns what she tried to do to Anthony." He kissed her throat as he slid his hands up her slender back. "However, I have a few feelings stirring for you right now."

She rubbed her thigh against his erection and smiled. "So I have noticed. Are you not too weary?"

"To share a bit of the passion we have been blessed with? No. I think I will have to be long dead before that happens."

"Perhaps you could make no more jests about being dead until this trouble is at an end," she said as fear briefly clutched at her heart.

"Worried about me?" he asked.

"As I should be. Someone wants you dead and has been trying to accomplish that for a long time."

Julian was touched by the fear for him he could see in her eyes. He pushed her onto her back and kissed her. When her arms slipped around his neck and she pressed her lithe body against his, all his weariness faded away. He could still feel the thrill of battling for his life rushing through his veins, and that soon turned to pure desire. In a few swift movements he removed her nightgown and tossed it aside. When their bodies were flesh to flesh, he groaned with a mixture of desire and contentment.

As he made slow, gentle love to her, he forgot all his worries, forgot that his life was still in danger, and just thought about how good she tasted and how soft her skin was. She was a balm for his soul, and he knew he ought to think more on why that was. But then Chloe slid her soft little hand down his belly and curled her fingers around his erection. Her touch pushed the last of his ability to think away. His lovemaking quickly grew fiercer, greedier, but Chloe kept pace with him every step of the way. When he emptied his seed inside her and she cried out in release, he could almost see it taking root and her body rounding with his child.

This time when Julian washed them both clean, Chloe barely blinked. His lovemaking had again left her boneless with satisfaction. When he returned to the bed, she flopped over onto him with her head against his chest and knew that she would soon be asleep. Listening to his heartbeat was one of the most comforting things she had ever enjoyed.

"Is it not sad that there are so few ways to prove someone is guilty of a crime?" she asked and barely smothered a yawn.

"It is, and not just because it can be difficult to make ones like my uncle pay for their crimes, but I fear a lot of innocent people pay as well. If you cannot prove someone is guilty, then how can you prove that someone is innocent?"

"Oh. That is even sadder. There has to be something, Julian. There just has to be. He will soon know that Anthony is alive, and I want the man gone. Now that he is out of Colinsmoor perhaps there will be something there, proof of some crime that will allow us to safely accuse him and see him hanged."

"That is what I am hoping for." He kissed the top of her head. "Sleep, Chloe. There is a lot we must do in the coming weeks."

Julian grinned when her answer was little more than a grunt. After years of seeking out women of style, elegant well-trained ladies conversant in all the various arts of womanhood, he realized that one of the many things he appreciated about Chloe was her lack of artifice. Chloe hid very little about herself, played no coy games, and that made him feel more comfortable in her presence than he had ever felt with any other woman.

The more time he and Chloe spent together, the more he realized that they made a good match. There was a lot more to them than a passion that was hard to deny, although he was not sure what he would call it. Julian smiled as he closed his eyes. There was no real need to study it all as if it was a great mystery. They would be married soon and that was all that mattered, the fact that he would have Chloe in his bed for the rest of his life.

Chapter 12

"Good catch, Anthony," said Julian, laughing as his son did a strange little hopping dance while still clutching the ball in his hands.

"Are we going to return to Leo's now?"

Julian looked at Chloe, who sat on a nearby bench surveying the park as if she expected an armed man was lurking behind each one. If there was, then Leo's men were lurking right behind them. He understood her fear, however, for he felt it, too. A week had passed since he and Leo had been attacked, and nothing else had happened. Chloe did not completely agree, but he and Leo felt certain that attack had been an ill-planned lashing out in retaliation for being thrown out of Colinsmoor and all other Kenwood properties owned by the earl. She certainly did not agree that it was time to introduce Anthony to the world, but he and Leo were going ahead with their plans anyway.

"Not yet," he replied, but gently, even though it was the tenth time she had asked the question in the two hours they had been at the park. "Just a little longer."

Seeing that Leo was now playing with Anthony and teaching him how to kick a ball, Julian sat down next to Chloe. "As soon as Lady Marston meets him, we will all return home. I swear it. She should be along soon. She always walks her dog here at this time of the day."

Chloe wanted to scream. Sitting on the bench while Julian let everyone he met know that Anthony was alive, thus letting Arthur and Beatrice know, was driving her mad. She knew it had to be done. She also knew Leo had placed a near army of his men all around the park. None of that mattered to her fear. All she could think of was that Arthur would soon know he had yet another heir to kill.

She looked at Anthony kicking a ball around with Leo. The boy had a lot of grace for such a small child and was revealing a skill at the game. The park was lovely, people wandering through it alone, with a companion or a dog, or with children. The sun was shining and it was actually pleasantly warm. On any other day she would be thoroughly enjoying herself in what was a touch of the countryside in the midst of a huge noisy and dirty city. But all she could think about was that Anthony's time of hiding safely in Leo's house had come to an end.

"The announcement about Anthony will be in the paper tomorrow," she said.

Julian took her hand in his and kissed her knuckles. "Chloe, I am afraid, too, but it is best if we let as many people as possible know the truth, or as much of it as we are able to tell. It is going to stir up a storm of gossip and interest. That will be a strong shield for Anthony to hide behind. Arthur will know that if anything happens to Anthony, all eyes will start turning in his direction. That is the last thing he wants to happen."

"I know," she whispered and took a deep breath to calm herself. "I truly do know that. It is just that sometimes my fear for Anthony pushes it all out of my mind."

What Chloe really wanted to do was throw herself into Julian's arms and try to soothe her fears with his warmth and his strength. However, despite how they had been acting the married couple at Leo's house, out in public they had to behave with the utmost propriety. Even his kissing her hand was probably enough to stir up a few whispers. She hated the distance they were forced to impose upon themselves whenever they stepped outside Leo's door.

The way she had to constantly fight her need to touch him did not make her very happy, either. She was becoming far too dependent upon him, perhaps even too clinging. It actually hurt a little to be unable to touch him whenever she wished, to lean against him if she felt like it, or even to be completely at ease with him.

Bloody hell, I am in love with the rogue.

Chloe was so shocked by that revelation that she nearly fell off the bench. All the time she had been calling it an infatuation, she had been deceiving herself, fighting hard to ignore the truth that was staring her in the face. Why that truth should slap her in the face right now, she did not know. Obviously her mind had simply grown tired of the game.

The fact that her gift had not warned her about what she was stepping into when she first kissed him was just another puzzle she had no answer to.

"Did you just see something again?"

That already familiar sharp voice pulled Chloe out of her thoughts and she looked up into Lady Marston's eyes. She had not even noticed that Julian had stood up to greet the woman. Chloe quickly rose to her feet and curtsied to the baroness.

"Nay, m'lady," she replied. "I was just thinking."

"Ah, not a vision, then. Just a revelation." Before Chloe could ask what the woman meant by that, Lady Marston turned and stared at Anthony, who was skipping up to greet them "Humph. Where have you been hiding him?" Lady Marston demanded of Julian. "By-blow, eh? Well, your mother will never agree to hiding the lad away like some dirty secret. She will be giving you the sharp side of her tongue, and you deserve it."

"Not a by-blow, m'lady," Julian said as he picked Anthony up in his arms. "My son by Lady Kenwood. Legitimate. All the officials that are needed, and then some, have reviewed the papers I have and have heartily agreed. This is Anthony Peter Chadwick Kenwood, my heir and my miracle. The notice will be in the paper on the morrow."

"Who is buried in the family plot, then?"

"Someone else."

Lady Marston stared at Anthony for a moment and then, in a surprisingly gentle move, stroked Anthony's cheek with her finger. "A handsome lad."

"I have pretty hair," said Anthony and grinned when Lady Marston laughed.

"That you do, laddie. That you do." She looked at Julian again. "Letting the world know, eh? What tale are you putting about? The truth or a hint of it?"

Julian put Anthony back down on the ground and the boy ran back to Leo. "I have given the truth to the authorities, although I have little proof. It is still but my word, and although that is accepted, there is more needed before any punishment can be meted out. Everyone treads cautiously when the gentry are involved."

"Annoying. There are far too many who should have been hanged or tossed into the gaol just running about the country."

Deciding there was no need to remark upon that opinion, Julian continued, "The world will also be told the truth—that my son was stolen from me and I have only just gotten him back through the aid and the kindness of the Wherlockes."

"Well said." She stared toward Anthony, who was kicking a ball around. "Keep him close. Keep all the heirs close."

"Do you know something, Lady Marston?" asked Chloe.

"I just know what I know. Keep the heirs close together. Safety in numbers." Lady Marston started walking away, her fat little dog wheezing and panting as it struggled to keep up with her long strides. "And keep that boy's hair cut. It is too damned pretty."

Chloe laughed. Both Leo and Julian glared after the rapidly disappearing Lady Marston as if she had just uttered the foulest of blasphemies. Chloe had no doubt that Lady Marston had known exactly how the two men would react to her parting words.

"Do you think Lady Marston knows something?" Chloe asked Julian as they all walked back to Leo's home. "She keeps speaking as if she does. Mayhap she has Wherlocke blood."

"You could always check your bloodlines, but the fact is that Lady Marston is from a long line of military men," he replied. "I think she would have been an excellent officer if she had been born a son. I believe she simply sees the plot against us quickly and clearly, that she has a true skill for deducing who the enemy is."

"Military," Chloe murmured and then nodded. "That explains a lot."

"Such as how she speaks her mind so bluntly?"

"Aye, and especially why no one seems to argue with her when she does."

"Beatrice tried once." Julian grinned when Leo laughed and shook his head in disbelief. "Fortunately that confrontation occurred after I had already begun to see the truth about Beatrice, or I might have tried to defend her and made myself a very bad enemy."

Chloe thought about that for a moment. "Nay, I do not think that would have happened. It would have been the loyal thing to do, and Lady Marston admires loyalty. Lady Marston would have simply and bluntly told you to open your eyes and then walked away."

"That is probably exactly what she would have done."

"Did we accomplish what you intended to today?"

she asked as they stepped inside, where Dilys waited for Anthony and quickly took the boy off to be cleaned up for his tea.

"The word of my son's tragic disappearance and miraculous return to home and hearth will be spreading far and wide as fast as people can move from one event to another. I doubt there will be many left who have not heard the tale by dinnertime."

"Oh, Leo?" she called out to her cousin, who was headed to his office.

Leo turned and gave her an absent smile, revealing that his mind was already on other things. "Something I can do for you, cousin?"

"You told Julian that you had men who could attest to the fact that Beatrice was, well, not pure when she married him and that that would allow him make his marriage null and void? Correct?" She knew it was, for Julian himself had told her, but spoke more to spark Leo's memory than to question what had been said.

"Aye. It would be embarrassing for Julian, but it would work."

"I think it might be more than embarrassing. I think that if the marriage is annulled, then Anthony's legitimacy is gone as well. I could be wrong, but it might be wise to look into that."

Julian cursed and ran his hand through his hair, nearly undoing his queue. "He does not need to look into it. You are right. I cannot get an annulment without making Anthony a bastard. After all, if my marriage is no longer valid, is said to have never been valid, then Anthony's legitimacy is also no longer valid."

"I wonder how I did not know that?" muttered Leo.

"You probably do not know anyone who has had it done or even considered it. I happen to know a few men who are trapped in abysmal marriages, and they once said that they will stay trapped, for divorce is almost impossible to get and is a scandal one rarely overcomes and annulments make your children bastards. I cannot get an annulment."

"How do you know about that?" Leo asked Chloe.

"Overheard something about it in the lady's retiring room last evening at the Hinkleys'."

"Ah, of course, the place where all the most important information is uncovered."

"Do not be so contemptuous." Chloe started toward the stairs. "You would be surprised what is spoken of in those rooms. A good female spy could find out all sorts of interesting things."

Julian watched the way Leo scowled at his cousin until she was out of his sight. "I believe she may be right about that, too. As for the annulment, I suspect whatever solicitor I chose would have quickly informed me of the risk to Anthony."

"I do not like not knowing things. Especially things that are such common knowledge they are spoken of in the ladies' retiring rooms. Meet me in my office in two hours?"

Julian barely finished nodding before Leo had turned and continued on his way to his office. It was tempting to follow the man and demand to know what was weighing so heavily on his mind, but

he suspected Leo would not tell him unless it was
directly related to his own troubles. The man was a
very good spy for England. He was also as good a
friend to Julian as Edgar was, so he decided to just
leave the man to his work and not pester to know
things he was not supposed to know.

Instead, he thought, and grinned, he was going
to go and pester Chloe. Now that Anthony's survival
had been revealed to the world, life could grow very
hectic. And very dangerous, Julian thought, his
good humor fading a little.

For a moment Julian's confidence in the plan he
and Leo had contrived wavered badly. Had he put
his son in danger? Far more than the boy was in already? He quickly shook that doubt away. There
was no choice. As a secret Anthony was a lot easier
to dispose of than if the whole world knew of his
existence. What he had told Chloe, that being
widely known about and of great interest because
of the tales being told, it would be very hard for
Arthur or Beatrice to do anything to the boy without attracting suspicion to themselves, was absolutely true. At least that was the plan, and it was a
good one, he told himself firmly as he entered
Chloe's bedchamber.

He grinned when he found Chloe had already
stripped to her shift and let down her hair. Even as
she eyed him with suspicion, he shut the door
behind him and latched it. They had just spent several hours in each other's company without being
able to even touch in any way other than the most
fleeting and proper. He had risked gossip when he
had simply held her hand for a moment and kissed

it. Julian realized that he now ached to make up for the enforced distance.

"Julian, it is the middle of the day," she said as he approached her with an easily recognizable gleam in his eye.

"Passion knows no time restrictions," he said as he pulled her into his arms.

"How very convenient for you."

"It is, is it not?" He laughed and carried her to their bed.

Our bed. Julian found he savored the words, that they felt right in his mouth. For the first time he understood some of what his parents had shared. As he had grown into an adolescent, he had realized that his parents slept together all the time. He had suffered the occasional twinge of embarrassment over the fact that his parents shared a bedchamber, as if there were not enough rooms in Colinsmoor to house all of them. He had even worried that his friends would find out. Then, as a man, when Beatrice stoutly demanded her own bedchamber, he had accepted that, assuming his parents had just been a little eccentric.

Now he understood them. Sharing a bed with your spouse ensured a continued closeness, and not just the one that came from a shared passion. They talked, were completely private for perhaps the only time during the day, and could share memories or news or even secrets. Waking to your spouse every morning only strengthened the bond. This time, he thought as he lowered Chloe to the bed, he would have a real marriage, a strong one, one where he and his wife actually shared a life.

"You suddenly look very serious," Chloe said as he dropped down beside her and pulled her into his arms. "Changed your mind?"

"Not at all." He proved his words by kissing her with all the desire that was already rushing through him. "I was just wondering on the sleeping habits of married couples."

"Ah, so it is a nap you are after. Well, I am feeling a mite tired myself."

"You can take a nap—after."

Chloe soon lost herself to the passion he could stir within her. She even forgot that it was the middle of the day and the sun was shining brightly into the bedchamber. Julian's kisses and caresses wiped all rational thought from her mind and made her a creature of need, of heat, of blind desire. She cried out in welcome when he entered her. Their lovemaking became fast and furious after that, both of them greedily reaching for that sublime culmination. She called out his name when her release swept over her with such force she bowed up in his arms. Julian quickly joined her, thrusting home so hard that she bumped her head against the carved headboard of the bed. When he slumped into her arms with a groan, she closed her eyes and savored the weight of his body for a few moments.

As her mind began to clear of the haze of spent passion, Chloe opened her eyes and gasped. The bed was aglow with the rays of the sun shining through the window. She shoved a still limp Julian off her and yanked up the blanket to cover herself. When she looked at him, at how he was sprawled on his back unabashedly naked, she threw part of the blanket over his groin. It was a very handsome groin, even with his manhood lying as limp as its master in a thatch of curls still damp from their lovemaking, but she still covered it up. It was too distracting and she had no intention of spending the rest of the day in bed.

Julian glanced down at the blanket draped over his groin and then looked at Chloe. She was clutching the blanket to her as if she feared some crowd would walk by at any moment and peer in the window. Her face was covered in a blush. It might have been too soon to make love in the broad light of the afternoon. Chloe was still very modest. Then he turned on his side and kissed her on the cheek. She would lose some of that modesty as time passed, but he decided he liked it. It never interfered with their lovemaking or dimmed her passion.

"I feel much better now," he said. "Thank you."

Chloe frowned at him. "You were feeling badly?" Although she was concerned about him, Chloe was deeply flattered that making love with her could make him feel better no matter what was troubling him. A little voice in her head whispered that it could be that any man would feel better after making love to a woman, but she ignored it.

"I was doubting my plans." He wrapped his arm around her waist and tugged her against his chest. "I fear for Anthony. I am furious that Arthur and Beatrice are still walking about free, that my word is not enough to bring them to justice simply because they are of the gentry. Leo's people could grab Arthur simply on his word alone and question him hard, but they do not wish the taint of treason to touch the Kenwoods. It is frustrating."

"Very." She lightly kissed his chest and then rested her cheek against it, listening contentedly to the sound of his heart beating.

"The event at Mother's on the morrow should finish spreading the news of Anthony's existence." He smiled when Chloe groaned. "There is something else I must consider."

She lifted her head to look at him. "You sound so serious. What is it?"

"Divorce."

Chloe winced. Divorce was rare. It was difficult to get, and the scandal it caused could result in near banishment from society. The gossip surrounding the discovery of an heir to Colinsmoor would seem like no more than irritating whispers compared to what a divorce would stir up.

"You probably have more than enough to get that. It is not an easy thing to get and you might find that marrying again is difficult."

"I will look into that. I cannot remain married to Beatrice, and I want to marry you. The only other choice to gain freedom from her is her death, and although she makes my blood run cold and I think she is well deserving of the ultimate punishment, I cannot bring myself to wish for her death."

"Of course not. No matter how badly she treated you and Anthony and all the other wrongs she has done, she was your wife. You exchanged vows before God. She was the one who chose not to honor them. You will find a way. You just have to be patient."

He took her chin in his hand and kissed her. "Pa-

tience is becoming very hard to hold on to. I do not
like the secrecy you and I must hold fast to."

"I am not very fond of it, either, but there is
no choice."

"No, sad to say, there is not." He glanced at the
clock on the mantel and then stretched. "I must go.
Leo wishes to meet with me in an hour and I have
some papers I need to look over." He kissed her
again and got out of bed.

Chloe remained huddled beneath the blanket
and watched him dress. The man was not shackled
by modesty, she thought, and almost smiled. It was
both pleasant and strange to share a room with a
man, to watch him dress and shave and all the
other things men did. It made her feel close to him.

Of course, now she wanted and needed far more
than this compatibility they seemed to share. She
wanted Julian to love her. The thought almost made
her laugh. He was so far above her touch, a man
of title and wealth as well as a man many women
wanted. Chloe doubted a little, unimportant, pass-
ably pretty woman like her could win the heart of a
man like him. She had his passion and his trust, and
she knew he liked her. Somehow she would have to
learn to make that enough. She would also have to
learn not to grieve over the fact that the man she
loved did not love her.

Julian entered Leo's office and almost grinned.
The man had papers and books scattered all over the
place. Leo was an intelligent man, possibly the most
intelligent man he had ever met, but he obviously

did not know anything about organization. Julian walked up to the desk, carefully removed a large book from the chair facing Leo, and then sat down.

"Here I am as ordered, sir," he drawled.

"How terribly amusing." Leo dragged his hand through his hair, which had long ago escaped its tidy queue.

The look on Leo's face made Julian immediately grow more serious. "What is the trouble? Not that we do not already have enough."

"No real added troubles. I am just sick to death of playing these games with Arthur. I know the man has betrayed his country, know for a fact that he has killed people, and know for a fact that he plans to kill all the heirs to your earldom and take the title for himself. Yet I cannot get the man in gaol or hanged. We need proof, the fools in power keep saying. Even the men I answer to, who also know for certain that Arthur is guilty of all we accuse him of, hesitate."

"It is because my uncle is gentry, born to a name that has long been loyal and helpful to the crown. And there is that little matter of treason that we are all trying to keep secret. It is much the same with Beatrice. She was no more than a soldier's daughter when I met her, but the soldier came from a very important family. The younger son of a younger son. We also battle the fact that both Arthur and Beatrice have recruited a lot of important allies. It will happen, though. We will get them and we will get them soon."

"Did Chloe see that?"

"No. I just look at the odds. They are losing their

aces one after another. They have to fall soon. And now that I have sobered up enough to kick them out of my homes, we are free to search for that irrefutable proof that is being asked of us."

"Well, my men have not found anything yet, but it is early days. You do not think Arthur is clever enough to have destroyed all evidence of his crimes, do you?"

"He would try, but the way he is so fond of blackmailing people into working on his behalf would require that he have some proof of something. Not everyone is going to do as he says just because he threatens them. And that is another tool we are robbing him of. The more that gossip and rumor tarnish him, the less power he has to destroy people."

Leo sat back in his chair and scratched his chin. "True. But that is not really what I wished to talk to you about."

Julian nodded. "You wish to talk about Chloe."

"About how to free you of Beatrice, actually. It looks as if the only way, aside from her conveniently skipping off to her Maker, is divorce, and if we think catching Arthur at his sins is hard, getting a divorce will make it look like a stroll in the park."

"I know. There is time yet to come up with a solution."

"Uh, there should be, but, well, are you being cautious in your times with Chloe?"

"What do you mean? I am taking great care not to stir up any rumor about our relationship. Do you think I should move out? Return to my own place?"

Leo shook his head. "Nay. And as far as rumor and gossip goes, there has always been some about me and Chloe. She is my cousin and I claim myself her guardian, but we are not so far apart in age. Cousins is not a close enough relationship to give her an immediate gleam of respectability. I was referring more to, well, are you being careful not to breed a child."

Julian stared at Leo. "Well, no, for we are to be married and for all our difficulties in bringing my enemies to justice, I feel sure it will happen soon. As I said, the odds are in our favor. I will not hesitate to marry Chloe once I am free of Beatrice. Even if that does not happen for a few months, there is no desperate concern. There is little chance Chloe would get with child too quickly."

"Actually, there is. A very good chance." Leo cleared his throat. "The Wherlockes and Vaughns may have trouble holding their marriages together, but they breed well."

"They breed well?"

"Like rabbits."

"Bugger."

Chapter 13

"Must we go?"

Julian grinned down at Chloe, who was buried so deeply beneath the bedcovers that he had barely understood what she had said. It had been a week since they had first made love, and Chloe had still not once left his bed to sleep in her own. The more he had thought about the sharing of a bed, the more he realized that Beatrice had always kept to her own bed, not out of propriety but because she enjoyed the way he had had to come to her like some supplicant. He knew he would no longer enjoy being in a bed all by himself, and that had nothing to do with making love. Having Chloe at his side all through the night suited him just fine.

"We have to," he said and slapped her on the bottom, knowing she would feel very little beneath all those covers. "Get up."

"I know we have to go, but that does not mean I have to like it," she grumbled as she sat up, careful to keep the covers tucked up over her breasts. When she looked at the clock on the mantel, she gasped.

"I cannot believe I have slept so late." When she saw the arrogant, very male look upon Julian's face, she stared at him with eyes narrowed in warning. "Say nothing."

"You are no fun."

"I am a lot of fun. Just not in the morning."

"It is already afternoon."

"Go away."

"This is my bedchamber." He laughed at the look she gave him, dropped a kiss on her mouth, and started toward the door. "We leave in two hours. Mother has already collected Anthony. She wanted a short visit with him before all her guests began to arrive."

Chloe sighed, took one last longing look at the bed she sat in, and then got up. After donning her nightgown, which had somehow ended up dangling from the tall bedpost, she slipped through the dressing room that connected her bedchamber to Julian's. When he had first arrived, the door on her side of the little room had remained firmly and securely locked. Now it was rarely even closed. In many ways they were already acting like a married couple.

Surprised to find her bath already set out, Chloe rang for Maude. Julian must have seen to having her bath prepared, she decided as she stripped off her nightgown and climbed in. Maude arrived to help her, laying out what Chloe should wear as she finished her bath. The smell of the food Maude had brought in with her kept tempting Chloe despite how much she liked to linger in her bath until the water grew cool. She finally gave in to that temptation and she was soon partly dressed and eating while Maude arranged her hair in an appropriate style for a late-afternoon visit with a dowager countess. It was going to be a long day, and Chloe knew she would need the strength a good meal would bring her.

Once she was ready and Maude had left to tell Julian that Chloe would be down in a few moments, Chloe studied herself in the mirror. She had spent a lot of time dressed in her finery with her hair tortured into some elaborate style since Julian had let the world see that he was alive. It was, she realized, only a small taste of what she would have to endure as a countess. There would always be some ball, musicale, tea, or salon she would have to attend simply because it was expected of her to do so. Chloe wondered if Julian had given much thought to that part of the marriage he wanted them to enter into. Her own poor background plus the rumors about the Wherlockes and the Vaughns could make taking on the duties of a countess a little difficult. There might not be as many invitations as Julian expected or needed to maintain his place in the gentry.

Sighing because even that fear was not enough to make her step away from marrying Julian, Chloe made her way down the stairs. Julian had given his word that he would marry her and, on that word, had taken her innocence. Knowing him as she did, Chloe knew nothing would keep him from exchanging wedding vows with her. At least she did not have to worry about his mother accepting her into the family. Lady Evelyn had made Chloe's welcome clear and, even though they had not told the woman about their betrothal, Chloe had the feeling she already knew, or suspected, there was one.

"You look beautiful," Julian said as he met Chloe at the foot of the stairway and took her hand in his to escort her to the carriage.

She blushed and he nearly grinned. Chloe always looked a little flustered when he complimented her. It was an endearing trait but he feared it meant that she did not completely believe in his flattery. If he did nothing else for Chloe, Julian was determined to make her see that she was a beautiful woman, in face, in form, and in soul. He would do it because she deserved that confidence, had earned it, and because he knew she would never suffer from vanity. Chloe was too sensible and fair-minded to succumb to that sin.

"I am still not certain I fully understand why we are having this gathering, although I would never deny your mother the pleasure she seems to feel about it," said Chloe as she got into the carriage. "We have already told a lot of people about Anthony. He does not really need what feels very much like a formal introduction to society. He is just three years old." Knowing it would wrinkle her gown, which could cause a few unwelcome remarks, Chloe resisted the urge to snuggle up against Julian when he sat down beside her.

"True, it *is* unusual," Julian said as he signaled the driver to start on their way. "Yet is it not also unusual for an earl's heir, one thought dead at birth, to suddenly appear?"

"There is that," she murmured and idly fiddled with the ties at the neck of her cape. "Your mother said she felt all the speculation and gossip this is causing is best dealt within one clean slash rather than a slow, torturous bloodletting."

"I had never realized that my mother could be so gruesome," he drawled and laughed when her small elbow nudged him in the side. "She is right. That is the best way to do it. Truly. It is why I had that notice with its short explanation posted in the papers and then paraded my son and myself all around the park."

"Stopping to speak to nearly everyone there and introduce him."

"Exactly. Mother's gathering this afternoon will be very busy as everyone and their mother comes to look at this *rescued* child of an earl. The fact that he looks so much like me only adds to the allure of the tale. Mother has even hung the portrait of me done at that age in a very prominent place, God save me."

Chloe laughed. "Did you have pretty hair, too?"

"Hush, impudent wench. It is the lacy child's clothes that trouble me more." He grinned when she laughed again. "The announcement in the paper, signed by three lords of the realm and two well-respected solicitors, should be enough to quiet most of the gossip that could rise concerning his legitimacy, but a good look at the boy and my mother's adamant belief in his right to be called my heir should quiet the rest. Considering who poor Anthony has been cursed with as a mother, it is best to make certain that there are no other slurs that might be used against him."

"Do you think he will always suffer for Beatrice's crimes?"

"Most will forget, and once the whole truth is out they will know that she had nothing to do with him, so could not have tainted him with any of her ways. But there are always some who like to sniff out a person's weaknesses so that they might make themselves feel more important. Anthony will have to learn how to deal with such people. They are always about, I fear. I believe that when he is of an age to fully understand what she did, he will have a harder time learning that it had nothing to do with who he is."

"Aye, I fear you may be right. It will be a hard blow when it comes, no matter what his life has been until then." Chloe sighed as they pulled to a halt before the large townhouse his mother and sisters called home. "I just hope I can hold to the tales already told. Everything within me wishes to tell everyone what truly happened, not just hint at it. I want everyone to know what monsters Beatrice and Arthur are."

"The ones who need to know have been told, and the rest will learn the whole sordid truth, or most of it, when this is over. I could openly accuse Beatrice right now and demand a trial, but I want to be absolutely certain that she pays for what she did to our child, that an accusation becomes a conviction. Right now I do not have enough to have the accusation hold firm against Arthur and Beatrice's skills at influencing or threatening people into doing what they want." Julian kissed Chloe just before the carriage door was opened. "You will do fine."

Chloe was not so certain of that but followed him into his mother's house. It was not that she feared she would forget the carefully chosen tales told about Anthony and the equally carefully selected reasons for why Julian was still living with Leo. The latter one was a lot easier than the first, as there was not much twisting of the truth. Part of her, however, had a very strong urge to simply tell anyone who asked too many questions that they were being intrusive and it was none of their bloody business. Not the way a future countess should behave, she warned herself as Lady Evelyn greeted them.

All too soon the people began to arrive. Chloe did not think the last ball she had attended had drawn so many people. Lady Marston had arrived a few minutes early, settled herself in a comfortable chair, and watched the parade of people with an amused eye. Blunt as she was, Chloe decided she liked the woman. The way Anthony kept returning to talk to Lady Marston told her that he liked her, too. The way she acted with the boy told Chloe that there was a softness beneath that blunt exterior. Other people were not so kind and looked at Anthony as if he were an exhibit at some strange museum.

When one man dressed in eye-watering colors looked Anthony over through a fancy monocle, she had had enough. Chloe was just about to go and say something when Lady Evelyn came up to her. Although she knew it was for the best that she was halted from doing anything that might cause a scandal, Chloe was still disappointed that she could not go and stomp that foolish monocle under her foot.

"That is Lord Bertram Handley," Lady Evelyn

said, her eyes bright with amusement. "He is a fool and is obviously completely devoid of any fashion sense, but he is the biggest gossip in the town."

"And that is a good thing?" Chloe asked.

"In this matter, yes. He is just the sort we need. He will speak of this everywhere and by the look on his face, he has decided that Anthony is indeed the heir to Colinsmoor."

"How kind of him."

Lady Evelyn laughed. "There, Lady Marston has said what you wanted to or something very close to it. He does not look any better when he tries to puff up in offended dignity, does he?"

Chloe grinned. "Worse. One has to wonder who his valet is." She glanced at the huge portrait that hung over a massive fireplace. "I must remember to tell Julian that he, too, had very pretty hair when he was a boy."

Slapping a hand over her mouth, Lady Evelyn quickly smothered her hearty laugh and nodded. "Anthony has been sure to tell every woman here. I think the boy is a born flirt."

"He is." She looked to where Anthony was offering Lady Marston a rather battered little cake. "He likes Lady Marston." Chloe had to smile when Lady Marston accepted the cake with great dignity and began to eat it.

"She is a good woman and she adores children. All her children adore her. I always thought she deserved a much better husband than the horse-mad fool she married, but she seems quite content."

"He gave her those children who adore her."

"Very true. One wit said that she carried a child

seven times and had seven children. She never lost one because God was terrified that she would come after Him and demand He give it back." Lady Evelyn grinned when Chloe laughed. "She is blunt and a bit odd, but she has a very good heart. I have also learned to never ignore her opinion of someone, no matter how bluntly put."

Chloe slowly nodded, thinking of the advice Lady Marston had given Julian in the park. "Aye, she has excellent insight. It must have been difficult when she made no secret of her opinion of Beatrice."

"It did not trouble me, for I agreed with her. Fortunately, a confrontation between her, Julian, and Beatrice did not occur until Julian had already begun to see what she was." Lady Evelyn shook her head. "He made a very bad choice there. I am glad he is making a better one this time."

Chloe stared at the small, gloved hand that patted her arm and then looked at Lady Evelyn. The woman's look told Chloe there was no point in even arguing the assumption. She was curious as to why the woman had come to that conclusion, however.

"He is still married," she felt obliged to say.

"Not for long. I dread the scandal of a divorce, but if that is what is needed to shake free of that harpy, then I will endure the scandal. I was a little afraid she would show herself here. She has to know what is being said about her. Julian has not openly accused her of anything, but no one else is inclined to be so cautious. It would be just like that woman to come here and try to play the poor mother whose child was stolen from her and whose husband maligns her by letting people think it was her doing. I would not be surprised if some of the people who came here did so hoping that she would."

"I suspect Arthur holds her back." Chloe bit back the tale of the attack on Leo and Julian that had driven their enemies into hiding, for she was not sure Julian had told his mother about it.

"True. He will need to plan a response to the gossip making the rounds."

"I am not sure what one can say but I suspect he will try to turn it round. Ah, Lady Marston is trying to get our attention."

Even as Chloe and Lady Evelyn moved toward the woman, Julian reached her side. He picked up a very sleepy Anthony, who settled himself comfortably in his strong arms. Chloe could see how everyone looked at the two together and suspected it was the final proof for many of them. No one with eyes could deny that the pair was father and son. No matter how much she had disliked the event, Chloe had to admit that it had done what was intended. Anthony was accepted by society as Julian's legitimate heir. His future was secured. For that she could not regret the time spent politely answering rude questions.

"I believe one little boy has had a busy day," said Lady Evelyn as she smoothed the curls off Anthony's forehead.

"Lots of cakes, too," mumbled Anthony.

Julian laughed softly. "I had best take him home." He glanced at the clock on the mantel. "It is close to his bedtime anyway."

"No, Julian. Let him stay here. I will return him the moment he is up and dressed in the morning. I have the nursery all prepared for him and someone to help care for him."

After a brief, gentle argument, Julian agreed and took Anthony up to the nursery. Lady Evelyn excused herself from her guests for a moment to go with him. Chloe knew she had to stand back this time or risk stirring up some unwanted gossip, but one glance at Lady Marston told her that that woman knew how disappointed she was not to be able to give Anthony his kiss good night.

"He will be all yours again soon enough, gel, and with no fear that some mincing gossip will slander you for it," said Lady Marston.

Chloe did not argue or agree, just smiled at Lady Marston and asked, "Do you happen to know if there is a Wherlocke or a Vaughn dangling from your family tree?"

Lady Marston just laughed as she stood up. "Got to be on my way now. Give my regards to Lady Evelyn." She patted Chloe on the cheek. "You will be good for the boy, gel. Very good."

Either Julian had said something to his mother or Lady Evelyn and Lady Marston had simply decided that Chloe Wherlocke was the one Julian should marry next. As with many women of that age, they felt their decision about such a matter was the final one. They always claimed the value of wisdom and experience over youthful passion. It was almost a shame that they would be proved correct even if Chloe was not sure that their optimism about the outcome of that marriage was right. She was not about to argue over the acceptance of two lionesses of society, however. Their acceptance of her would certainly make her life easier when she did marry Julian. Chloe stoutly ignored the knot of fear that returned each time she thought of the marriage.

Julian returned and saved her from the attentions of a young man who obviously shared Lord Handley's valet. It took them a while to gather Leo and make their farewells as everyone seemed to need to say just one more thing. When they finally climbed into the carriage, Chloe flopped into her seat and sighed.

"It was a bit of a trial," agreed Julian when, as soon as the carriage was on its way, he moved to sit next to Chloe. "But, for all that, I believe its purpose was served admirably." He looked out the window and scowled. "The street is blocked. We shall have to return home by the longer route."

"It matters not," Chloe said. "Just as long as you do not make me look or talk to any more people who share Lord Handley's valet." She grinned when both men laughed.

"The man does make one's eyes hurt," agreed Leo.

"Your mother and Lady Marston are matchmaking," Chloe said and grinned at the horrified look on Julian's face.

"I shall have to tell my mother about our plans to marry as soon as I am free. Who was she trying to make a match for? Or Lady Marston?"

"For both of us." She laughed and shook her head. "They both told me that they approve of your next choice—me."

"Damn. One has to wonder if it is just matchmaking or if they know. I do not believe we have given ourselves away."

"Nay, I do not believe we have, either."

"Mayhap they just decided you are the one they want and I had better do as they say. It almost galls one that we will have to prove them right."

"I had the same thought." She looked out the window and frowned. "Where are we going?"

"The long way round," replied Leo. "Once a street is as clogged as the one in front of Lady Evelyn's, even this long route will take less time and effort."

Chloe absently nodded but she could not pull her eyes away from the window. She tensed and grabbed Julian by the hand. "Go left. Now. Go left."

Julian hesitated just enough that Leo beat him in giving the order to their driver. Chloe was shaking, and that had grabbed his attention. Even though he wanted to comfort her, he joined Leo in preparing their pistols. He was now glad that he had given in to his mother's wishes and left Anthony at her home.

"Did you see something?" he asked her as he peered out the window, cursing the dark and the poor lighting.

"Not *see*," she replied. "Just know. There was danger awaiting us in the direction we were going."

Leo cursed. "It may be that the road was blocked apurpose to drive us into a trap."

Before Julian could agree, a shot rang out. He pushed Chloe to the floor of the carriage as it sped up. He tried to see who pursued them but only shadowy forms of men on horseback were visible behind them. They had definitely been sent into a trap. Although they were still in danger, they had a chance to get away now. Leo had been right to warn him to never hesitate when Chloe gave him some abrupt warning.

The carriage bounced along the road and it was not easy to keep himself in his seat. One man actually road up alongside the carriage and Julian shot him before he hurt the driver. Julian knew the driver had been the man's target, for a driverless carriage rolling along at top speed was a death trap.

"It appears that bringing Anthony to the fore certainly did cause our enemies to react," said Leo.

"Aye, but which enemy? Beatrice or Arthur?" asked Chloe as she tried to press herself close to the floor to ease the hard bouncing she was suffering.

"This time they may be in accord," said Julian and then he cursed.

Something smashed through the window on one side of the carriage and barely missed Leo as it smashed its way out the other side. Julian heard Chloe whisper a curse. She had courage, he thought. Most ladies of his acquaintance would be screaming or crying, but she held fast. She also stayed where she had been told to even though he knew it had to be uncomfortable down there.

A shout from the front of the carriage caused Julian's heart to leap up into his throat. The carriage swerved sharply and he feared they would be overturned, but it righted itself. Leo shot out the shattered window and a scream told Julian he had found his target. He was a little surprised when Leo pulled another pistol out from beneath the seat and handed Chloe his used one for reloading. She sat up with her back against a seat and rapidly did just that. Since he had only one pistol, Julian had reloaded his own, but he cursed himself for not bringing two.

"Leo!" cried Chloe in alarm when her cousin stuck his head out the window.

"Todd's been hit," he said as he yanked his head back inside.

"If you keep sticking your head out there you will be, too. He is still driving the carriage, so it cannot be too bad, can it?"

"He is losing blood, so he is losing strength, and there are still three men on our heels."

"I can get up there," said Julian as he began to shed his coat.

"There are people shooting at us!" protested Chloe. "And you could fall into the road."

"I have climbed out into the driver's seat of a racing carriage before," Julian said. "In my reckless youth. My drunken friend was driving when the drink he had consumed finally caught up with him. I was a bit more sober so I went out and took over. Just keep up a steady fire," he said as he set his pistol next to Leo.

Before she could try again to talk him out of what he was doing, Julian was swinging himself out of the window. It was a tight fit but that did not slow him down much. Chloe was terrified for him, afraid she would soon see him fall, but she was given no time to give in to that fear. Leo was shooting and handing her each empty pistol to reload as fast as possible. The noise made her head hurt and the smell of pistol smoke was choking, but Chloe kept loading pistols and praying. When the carriage began to move much more smoothly, she nearly fainted from relief.

"Safe?" yelled Leo.

"Safe enough," Julian yelled back. "Todd is bleeding badly but will be fine if we can get back home. Ah."

She could hear him and Todd talking although she could not hear what was being said. Chloe could not stop the squeal of surprise that escaped her when the carriage suddenly took a sharp turn. She barely saved the ammunition for the pistols from spilling all over the floor. When Leo stuck his head out of the window again, she thought she would scream, fearing she would see him shot right before her eyes. But to her surprise, he turned toward Julian.

"They have fallen back," he said and pulled back into the carriage.

A moment later Chloe got up on her knees and could see why the men chasing them had fallen back. They were entering the better sections of London again, the areas where there were watchmen and far too many people who would not hesitate to tell the authorities what they had seen. Their pursuers were no longer free to chase and murder someone with no fear of being caught. After another moment she eased her battered body back up onto the carriage seat, careful to avoid the glass shards scattered over it.

"Well done, cousin," Leo said as he collected the pistols and shot.

"My brothers taught me well," she managed to say.

The moment the carriage pulled up in front of Julian's home, Chloe scrambled out. She needed to see that he was unharmed with her own eyes. He climbed down as Wynn hurried out of the house. Leo moved to help Wynn get Todd back into the house and Chloe threw herself into Julian's arms. It was weak and she risked the neighbors seeing the embrace, but she had to hear his heart. It was all that would ease the fear still clutching her by the throat.

Julian put his arm around Chloe's shoulders as the stable hands hurried out to take care of the carriage. Even though she did not ease her hold on him, he managed to get them both inside the house. He immediately took her to the blue salon where he knew there was some brandy. After forcing her to take the drink he poured her, he poured himself one. The liquor burned down his throat and soon warmed him enough that he could shake off the chill of fear.

The only thing he had been able to think of as he had climbed out of the carriage and into the driver's box was that Chloe was in danger. This time Arthur and Beatrice had put Chloe in danger. Julian suspected his deep need to get her to safety was why he had managed something that he admitted scared him half to death. He urged her into a seat and sat beside her, wrapping his arm around her shoulders and holding her close.

"I cannot believe you climbed out and up to the driver's box," she muttered and took another drink.

"Todd was not going to be able to hold the reins much longer. Someone had to do it," he said. "I was the one who had done it before." He laughed softly. "I had forgotten how damned terrifying it was, too."

"I am glad I was not alone in being terrified, then."

Before he could say anything, Leo strode into the room. The man went straight for the brandy and drank nearly half of what he poured himself before he sat down across from them. He looked more furious than afraid but, in the work he did for the government, perhaps being shot at was not so unusual.

"How is Todd?" asked Chloe.

"He will be fine. It is not a mortal wound, just hurts and bled a lot, weakening him," replied Leo. "How are you, Chloe?"

"I expect I shall have some bruises but no more."

"I will admit that this was unexpected. We shall need to take guards with us wherever we go from now on. Whether it is Arthur or Beatrice does not matter. We can not be caught off guard like that again."

"Agreed," said Julian. "Which is why I have just come up with a plan."

"And this plan is?"

"In two days we leave for Colinsmoor."

Leo said nothing for a moment and then nodded. "A good plan. There are too many places for your enemies' hirelings to hide in this city. In the country any stranger is immediately seen and spoken about. I will make some plans for the securing of the area," he said even as he stood up and left the room.

Chloe looked up at Julian. "Colinsmoor?"

"Yes," Julian said and kissed the tip of her nose. "We have done all we can here to make life a misery for my enemies. Time to return home."

"And search for the proof you want?"

"That is certainly one good reason to go there,

but it will also be a great deal safer for you and Anthony. Leo was right about that."

Chloe touched her snifter to Julian's and they made a soft chiming sound. "To Colinsmoor. I think I will enjoy returning to the country."

Chapter 14

"Look! Horse!"

Chloe kept a firm grip on the back of Anthony's coat to ensure that the boy did not tumble out of the window he was so avidly staring out of. "Aye, it is a horse." A hearty stallion, she thought, and prayed that Anthony did not notice the rather startling appendage on the beast. "Ah, look there, Anthony. There are some sheep."

Pleased when the child's attention was immediately drawn to a small herd of sheep peacefully grazing on the hillside, no rude appendages visible, Chloe sighed and glanced at the two men seated across from her. Both Leo and Julian were grinning like fools. They obviously knew exactly why she had quickly diverted the child's attention. Her scowl did nothing to dim their amusement.

"Did you hear anything about where Beatrice and Arthur may have disappeared to before we left town?" she asked.

Julian laughed softly and shook his head, amused by her attempts to ignore a stallion that had obviously scented a mare in heat, but then he grew serious. "No. They have gone to ground. If that attack on us was Beatrice's idea, I believe the next word we have of her will be that she is"—he glanced at Anthony— "gone. Arthur will hate having to hide, to stay away from all his usual haunts. He is a man who has a great love for all the pleasures society offers. I would not be surprised if he has begun to feel that all his grand plans are crumbling about his ears, and he will be looking for someone to pay for those failures."

Although Chloe was glad to leave the city, she had to ask, "And you still believe we should be going to Colinsmoor? You do not think he will follow us there?"

"He might, but he found us often enough in a crowded city, did he not? At least here in the country he cannot hide so easily. It is too open and too many would recognize him and send us warning." He glanced out the window and started to say something about wanting Anthony to come to know his heritage only to see a group of men preparing to breed a mare with the barely restrained stallion. "Divert Anthony's attention again. Quickly."

"Oh! Cohee, look! More horses!" Anthony reached up to put his little hands over Chloe's when she covered his eyes. "I cannot see. I wanna see what the horses were doing."

"They were wrestling," Chloe said, removing her hands from his eyes the moment the men and the horses were no longer in view.

"Wrestlin'? Like me and Papa do in the garden?" asked Anthony.

"Uh, nay. The horses were doing a sort of animal wrestling. It is not something people do."

When Anthony just nodded and returned to looking out the window, Chloe looked at the men. They both had a hand over their mouths and their shoulders shook with the laughter they valiantly tried to smother. *Men can be such children*, she thought with disgust, and turned her attention back to the same scenery that so fascinated Anthony.

It was beautiful countryside they were passing through, she mused, realizing how little of it she had seen or appreciated when she had been in the area three years ago. Then suddenly the beauty was gone. She was seeing the city again. When she realized she was staring at Lady Evelyn's elegant townhouse, Chloe felt an icy finger scrape down her spine. Then she was inside the house and the vision began to flow past her eyes at an increasing speed. A blood-soaked settee. A pale hand lying limply on a bed. Items knocked to the floor. A broken vase, its pieces scattered next to the twisted form of a young woman. When the face of that young woman passed through her mind, Chloe screamed and everything went black.

Strong arms wrapped around her and Chloe began to hear things. Anthony was crying and she could hear Leo trying to calm the child. Julian was ordering her to open her eyes. Nay, not just her eyes, she mused. Her *damn* eyes. She almost smiled. Then remnants of her vision wafted through her mind and she gasped even as she opened her eyes. Looking around, she was reassured that she was safe inside the carriage with Anthony, Leo, and Julian.

"I am fine, Anthony," she quickly reassured the child. "It was just a bad dream."

"You scareded me," Anthony said as he climbed up onto her lap.

"I am sorry, Anthony, but, truly, I am fine. Listen to my heart," she said quietly as she rubbed his back. It was not until Dilys appeared at the door of the carriage that Chloe realized their little caravan had stopped. "Oh, I am so sorry. I had not meant to cause so much trouble."

"Nay, you did not cause trouble," said Leo. "It never hurts to let the horses pause for a moment now and again." He leaned forward and ruffled Anthony's hair. "Hey-ho, lad, Dilys is here. Why not go with her so that Chloe can rest a bit after having such a bad dream?"

Chloe was reluctant to let the boy leave. It had been a long time since she had held him close as he slept, something she knew he would soon do, and his weight in her arms was a comfort. After kissing his cheek and reassuring him that she was fine, she handed him into the care of Dilys. She had to tell the men what she had seen. Although she could not tell them exactly when the danger would strike out at Lady Evelyn and her daughters, she knew the women needed to be taken out of the city right away. Since the rest of them were traveling to Colinsmoor, she decided that Lady Evelyn and her daughters would probably be safest with them.

"What did you see?" demanded Leo the moment Dilys and Anthony were gone and the carriage had begun moving again.

"Mayhap it should wait until she is calmer," said

Julian, for he could feel the fine tremors of fear rippling through her body as he held her close.

"Nay, it cannot wait," Chloe said, and straightened up in her seat, pulling away from Julian just enough to look straight into his eyes. "I think Arthur has gone mad. Or it might be Beatrice who has allowed fury to rob her of all reason."

"Why would you say that?" asked Julian, alarmed by how white she was. He could almost smell her fear.

"You must go and bring your mother and sisters here, Julian. Bring them now. They need to be taken away from London."

A cold fist tightened around Julian's heart, and that was when he realized that he believed in Chloe's gift. He had no doubt in his mind that his family was in imminent danger. "Tell me what you saw."

After taking a deep breath to steady herself, Chloe told him everything she had seen and watched all the color drain out of his face. She knew she would remember other details later, whether she wished to or not, but they could not wait. One thing her vision had made horrifyingly clear was that someone intended to turn Lady Evelyn's lovely home into a charnel house.

"An act of blind, mindless fury," murmured Leo, yanking on the boots he had shed so that he could be more comfortable in the carriage. "This is a strike at all that you hold dear, Julian."

"Which means it could be either Arthur or Beatrice. Either is fully capable of such brutality." Julian was surprised he could speak so calmly when everything inside him shook with fear. "Your vision did not happen to show you *when* this would happen, did it?" he asked Chloe who looked as terrified as he felt.

She shook her head. "Only where. Do you think he has heard that he is, more or less, already convicted of murder and treason? That you and Leo now hunt him and can kill him without fearing punishment?"

"It is quite possible," replied Leo. "Ready, Julian?"

"Yes. Chloe." Julian lost the ability to speak when he saw how glassy her eyes had gone. "Another one? S'blood, Leo, can she bear them coming so often?"

"I have no idea. If it is any comfort, I have never heard of any of our other relatives with such a gift going mad or the like."

"No, it is not much comfort. Chloe," he urged when she groaned softly.

Chloe slowly opened her eyes and stared up at Julian's too pale face. "You must bring your aunt and cousins here, too. Safety in numbers, Lady Marston said."

"But Aunt Mildred lives in a direction quite opposite from London, where my mother and sisters are."

"They are not safe, either. He is clearing the fields. If he cannot have what he wants, no one else will."

"I will go after your aunt and the girls, Julian," Leo said. "I have men there who can help, and they will be needed at Colinsmoor."

"But if we both hie off after the others, that will leave Chloe and Anthony alone," Julian said. "He has to be planning to come after them as well."

"They will be guarded and guarded well. My men have already cleared away the ones who were faithful to your wife and not just terrified into doing as she asked."

"Go, Julian. I will be safe."

"And have you seen that, too?"

"Nay, I just know it. Go and save the rest of your family."

He gave her a brief, hard kiss and, the moment Leo ordered the carriage stopped, leapt out. Leo was right behind him. Chloe watched as each man gathered a horse and one man to ride with them. She sent a prayer with them, one that asked that they were successful in saving Lady Evelyn and Lady Mildred and their daughters.

The rest of the ride to Colinsmoor was peaceful. Chloe wished she could have enjoyed it. Instead her mind clung to her worry about Leo and Julian and the ones they had gone to save. Things had become so much worse than they had been. Either Arthur or Beatrice had clearly gone mad. No longer was this a matter of protecting the heirs until proof could be found to end Arthur's deadly game. Now it was about the survival of all the Kenwoods.

When the manor house came into view Chloe could not stop herself from gaping. She had only seen a brief glimpse of it from a distance when she had stayed with Laurel. Never had she thought it would be so huge or so beautiful. A flutter of unease struck her in the belly. How could she ever be mistress to such grandeur?

The carriages rolled to a halt before the big doors of the mansion, and one of the waiting footmen hurried over to put down the steps and open the carriage door. Chloe reluctantly stepped out, her gaze

fixed upon the place she was expected to call home.
Feeling a little helpless and lost, she looked toward
the man who held the carriage door open, only to
see another man walking toward the horses, and she
gaped.

"Jake?" she whispered, recognizing the man who
had left the papers with Anthony, the ones that had
helped them prove he was Julian's son.

The man stopped and turned to look at her.
"Miss? Do you know me?"

She moved closer to him. The man looked suddenly pale and she realized that the fear Beatrice
and Arthur had bred in these people had not left
them yet. "I was in the cottage on the moors, hiding
in a niche by the fireplace." She caught him by the
arm when he stumbled back, his face twisted in
fear. "Nay, do not fear. I will not harm you, nor will
the earl."

"But what I did—" he began.

"You had no choice. That is understood. But I do
believe you and I have to talk."

Julian leapt down from his horse and ran up to
the door of his mother's townhouse, praying that she
would be at home. He was filthy and sweaty, but he
had no care for his appearance. Fear for the safety of
his family controlled him. He did not think he had
ever ridden to London with such speed and lack of
care for his mount. When the door was opened, he
shoved past the butler and strode into the hall.

"Mother!" he bellowed.

Before he could take a breath to call out again,

Lady Evelyn rushed to the top of the stairs and looked down at him in open-mouthed shock. "Julian? What are you doing here? You were on your way to Colinsmoor. What has happened?" she asked as she hurried down the stairs and then she suddenly stopped only a few steps from the bottom. "Anthony?"

"He is fine. Chloe is fine. But you and the girls need to pack and come with me." He grabbed her by the arm and started to take her back up the stairs.

"Julian, you have to tell me what is wrong. I cannot just leave. I have plans, invitations I have accepted," she babbled, only to stop speaking when Julian dragged her into her bedchamber and ordered her maid to start packing her belongings. "What are you doing?"

"Getting you and the girls out of here. You are coming to Colinsmoor." He looked at the maid. "Jane, get someone to pack up the girls' things, enough for a few days. The rest can be sent down later. Then get back here and do the same for my mother." He then tugged his mother along with him as he strode into her sitting room.

Lady Evelyn sank into a chair near the fireplace and watched her son pour himself a large drink of wine. For a brief moment she feared he had taken to drink again and this madness was a result of that. Then she saw that he was covered in the dust of a long journey. His hair had been pulled free of its queue and he smelled of sweat and horses. There was a look on his face that told her he was consumed by some fear.

"What is it, Julian? You are frightening me."

A little calmer, Julian sat down in the seat next to

her. "There is something I have not told you about Chloe. You have heard the rumors about the Wherlockes, have you not?"

"Foolish things about them and the Vaughns. Tales of witchcraft and how they can see spirits and the like. Nothing worth repeating."

"Well, it is not all foolishness. This is to be kept secret," he said and she nodded. "A lot of them do have some strange, er, skills. Chloe has visions."

"Visions?" Lady Evelyn frowned. "You mean she sees the future as some gypsies claim they can?"

"I suspect they claim a gift they do not have. Chloe really has the gift. Have you never wondered how she managed to save Anthony? How did she come to be there when her sister needed her, when my son needed her? She saw it. She never would have gotten word that she was needed in time to help in any other way." When his mother said nothing, just stared at him, he told her of other ways Chloe's gift had aided and protected him. "She truly has visions. I doubted at first, but no longer. If you could see her when she is gripped by one, you would believe it, too."

"How miraculous, but what does that have to do with you rushing in here like a madman and demanding we all go to Colinsmoor?"

"She saw you and the girls murdered." He quickly rose and poured her some wine when she paled. "Here," he said as he handed her the drink, "steady yourself. I do not mean to upset you, but I do not have time for delicacy. There is more. Leo has gone to get Aunt Mildred and the girls because Chloe said they, too, were in danger."

"And you trust in what she has told you? You are certain we need to flee?"

"I have just nearly ridden my horse to death to get here as swiftly as I could. Yes, I believe it. Even if I did not have full confidence in what she says she has seen, I would still do as she asked. Arthur or Beatrice have acted with a recklessness of late that hints at madness. But I do believe in what she says she has seen. Since she cannot tell me when this will happen, I must insist that you come with me now."

Lady Evelyn finished off her wine in a very unladylike hurry and then stood up. "Then we will go with you. You go and clean up while I see that we have packed enough to last us until the rest of our things can be sent on." She pulled him to his feet and started to push him toward the room he had once used. "I believe there are some clothes stored in your old room. Some of yours, some of your father's, and even some of Nigel's. There will be something you can use. I will tell my companion to send our regrets to all the people we have agreed to visit and have the carriage brought round."

The next thing Julian knew he was standing in his old bedchamber and several footmen were rushing around preparing a bath for him. He could hear people hurrying around outside and occasionally heard his mother and sisters. Shaking his head in surprise over how quickly his mother had fallen in with his demands and how few questions she had asked concerning his claim that Chloe had visions, he stripped off his filthy clothes and climbed into the tub.

He lingered in the heated water just long enough

to ease the aches caused by his mad ride and then began to dress in some of Nigel's clothes. By the time he stepped out of his room, ready to leave, he saw his mother hurrying toward the stairs attired in her traveling clothes. He hurried to catch up with her.

"Ah, Julian, you do look a great deal better," she said when he reached her side at the foot of the stairs. "Everything is already strapped to the carriages and the girls are tucked in one along with my maid. I assumed you would ride with me in the other. I called for two carriages because it is so late I know we will probably sleep a little, and that requires room."

"You are a wonder," he said and kissed her on the cheek before leading her to the carriage. "I imagine the girls are not very pleased with this sudden journey."

"No, they are not," Lady Evelyn said as he helped her into the carriage and then climbed in to sit on the seat across from her.

When the carriage started to move, Julian felt the tight knot of fear that had gripped him so many hours ago begin to loosen. "I am sorry for that, but it is necessary. You will be safer at Colinsmoor, with us and the men we have gathered there."

"Julian, about these visions you say Chloe has. I do think some people know things that we cannot, but—" She fell silent when he held up his hand.

"I swear to you, they are real. Frighteningly so." He shook his head. "When she first told me that it was a vision that led her to join her sister and be ready to help my son when Beatrice left him to die,

I did not believe it. I do believe it now. It is just not something I can talk you into believing. It is something you have to live with for a while, to see how they come to her, before you can believe."

"Very well. A part of me does believe in it all, but I hope I will not insult her or hurt her feelings if my belief is not wholehearted."

"No. As she and her cousin say, a lack of belief, or doubt, does not trouble them. It is the fear that does. And fear is also dangerous, so that is why they keep the truth about the gifts so many of their family has to themselves."

Lady Evelyn stared at Julian in surprise. "Lord Sir Leopold has visions, too?"

"No." Julian explained what Leo could do. "I am not sure I will believe all the gifts they claim in their family, but I do believe in Leo and Chloe."

"And so you should. You would not be alive without them and neither would Anthony. Who do you think planned to," she hesitated and then took a deep breath before saying, "kill me and the girls?"

"Either Arthur or Beatrice." He shrugged. "Mayhap both. As I said, they have grown reckless, striking out in ways they never have done before. Each attack against me was obviously carefully planned so that no suspicion would turn their way. Now? Now they just attack. That they do when everyone is now watching them with suspicion only adds to my belief that they, or one of them, has lost control and is acting out of fury. That would be much like Beatrice, but it could also be Arthur in a fury. He must see that his plans to be earl are going awry faster than he can fix the problem or protect himself from blame."

"I have never liked Arthur," Lady Evelyn said quietly, "but I never thought him a danger. I hope Lord Sir Leopold finds Mildred and her girls safe."

"So do I, Mama. Aunt Mildred is as innocent as the rest of us. She and her daughters do not deserve to suffer for my uncle's ambition."

"It will be very late before we get to Colinsmoor," she said and quickly covered a yawn with her hand.

"Rest, Mama. You will need your strength to get the girls settled once we are there."

"Have you seen the place since you walked away from Beatrice?"

"No. In truth, I have not seen it since long before I left my wife. Beatrice preferred London. We rarely spent much time at Colinsmoor when we were married. The reports I have gotten from the men Leo sent there imply that it is in good shape but that work needs to be done. Uncle obviously did not wish to waste his coin on it for all he seems to covet the title."

Lady Evelyn closed her eyes. "I think Lady Marston is right. Shoot them both."

Julian laughed softly and then stared out the window as his mother dozed on the other seat. He was calmer now but he would not relax completely until he got his family tucked safely behind the thick walls of Colinsmoor. The final confrontation with his enemies was coming; he could feel it. He just wished he could find out which one of them was going to hunt him down.

* * *

Chloe sighed as strong, lightly calloused hands stroked her breasts. "Is that you, Julian?" She laughed when one of those hands slapped her hip.

"Wretched brat." He brushed a kiss over her mouth. "You felt sure we would all arrive safely?" he asked as he tugged her nightgown off and tossed it aside.

"Aye and nay. I stayed awake long enough to see your aunt and cousins settled, but Leo sent me to bed when he caught me sleeping on the bench in the hall. I was simply too tired to argue. Did your mother protest too much?"

"Not much. After all, the threat was not just to her, was it? I am afraid my sisters are not very happy, but they know when to just do what their mother tells them and not waste their breath arguing with her."

Chloe stroked his back, trailing her fingers up and down his spine. "She did not believe the source of the warning, did she?"

"She is doubtful, but not so doubtful that she would risk staying in London."

"That is good enough."

"This is good, too," he murmured as he encircled her breasts with soft kisses and heated strokes of his tongue.

"After all that riding back and forth to London, are you sure you are not too exhausted for this play?" she teased.

He shifted so that his erection pressed against the soft curls at the juncture of her slim thighs. "Does this feel as if I am too exhausted?"

"Nay, it feels very nice." She tugged at his hair until he lifted his head and then she kissed him.

"However, now that so many of your family are gathered around us, are you certain we ought to be indulging ourselves like this?"

"We will be discreet, but I am not giving this up."

She opened her mouth to argue but he kissed away her protests. Chloe gave herself over to his love-making. She had been afraid for him right up until the time Leo had told her to go to bed. Although she had had no further visions, she had known that he was on his way home and would soon return to her side. The taste of that fear still lingered, however, and she was more than willing to wash it away with the passion he could stir to life inside her.

By the time he finished kissing and nipping at her breasts, she was squirming beneath him, her need strong and greedy. She sighed with pleasure as his warm mouth trailed down to her stomach and his clever fingers teased and stroked her womanhood until she ached. Her passion abruptly hesitated when she felt the warmth of his mouth replace his fingers, however, shock pushing aside the need that had possessed her.

"Julian?" she squeaked and tried to move away from him.

"Hush," he said and gripped her by the hips to hold her in place as he kissed her and licked her. "You will like this."

Chloe wanted to argue with that command but her passion was already returning, flowing through her hotter and stronger than before. She closed her eyes and let herself be swept away by the magic of his intimate kiss. When she was sure she was going to shatter into small aching pieces if he did not join with her, she tugged at his shoulders. He slowly kissed his way back up her body and when his mouth touched her, he thrust inside her.

He rode her hard and Chloe reveled in it. She wrapped her arms and legs around him and hung on tight as he drove them both to the release they craved. Her body still trembling from the strength of her release, she barely flinched when, a few moments after, he cleaned them both off. He crawled back into bed and pulled her into his arms. Chloe rested her head on his chest and could hear his heart begin to slow its frantic beat.

Embarrassment over the intimacy they had just shared tried to creep over her, but she pushed it aside. Despite his year of debauchery, she doubted Julian was given to strange or forbidden practices in the bedchamber. Chloe was determined not to shy away from anything that brought them both that sweet pleasure they could find together.

"Rest, Julian," she said and kissed his chest. "I can still feel the hint of concern in you. Put it aside for now. You will need your strength in the days to come."

"True, if only because my house is now overrun with females." He grunted and then chuckled sleepily when she pinched his waist.

Chloe peeked at him a moment later and saw that he was asleep. She settled herself against his chest again and closed her eyes. She had forgotten to tell him about Jake, but there would be time for that when he woke. Chloe's last clear thought was that she was glad his family was safe with them now, but she hoped their presence would not rob her of the pleasure of sharing Julian's bed.

Chapter 15

The branch creaked under the weight of the gently swaying body. Chloe could see it so clearly she was surprised that the tree in front of her held nothing on its branches. She wrapped her arms around herself in a vain attempt to still the shivers rippling through her. It was too late to save Beatrice. What she saw now was more a knowing than a vision. Whatever or whoever sent her the dark, chilling visions just wanted her to know where to find the body this time. She was not meant to save the woman.

"Chloe, dear, are you ill?" asked Lady Evelyn as she stepped up beside Chloe and lightly rubbed her back. "You look so pale."

"Do you know if there is a large oak tree around here?" she asked Lady Evelyn instead of answering the question about her health. "One with big fat roots that run partly above the earth and trap two pale rocks within them? It sits upon a small hill and I think there is a small rose planted at its feet. Is there something like that around here somewhere?"

"Oh, my, you have had another one of those dreadful visions, have you not? Another warning?"

Seeing how frightened Lady Evelyn looked, Chloe took the older woman's hands between hers. The doubt the woman had felt about Chloe's gift had rapidly disappeared when a day after arriving at Colinsmoor her servants had arrived with her baggage and a tale of someone breaking into her home. There had been a battle between the intruders and the servants that had left two of her footmen badly injured. Chloe had seen belief in the woman's eyes after that. It was a shame that only two days after that she was going to have to reveal more proof to her.

"It had naught to do with you or your daughters or anyone here," she reassured the woman. "And it was not truly a vision, only a knowing." That was mostly the truth even though she did not usually have a moment of knowing something complete with an image. "I fear I just saw Beatrice hanging from a tree."

Lady Evelyn sighed with relief and then shook her head, her expression one of remorse. "I should not feel good about that. It was just that I was so relieved that you had not seen some dark fate for me and mine again." She grimaced. "I never liked Beatrice or trusted her. I certainly will not pretend a grief I do not feel. Yet—" She hesitated.

"Yet she gave us Anthony," Chloe said quietly, finally releasing the woman's hands.

"And tried to kill him. No." She held up a hand when Chloe started to speak. "You are right. It was Beatrice's body, her womb, that birthed that bright little boy. All her other crimes aside, one must be grateful for that one good thing that came of her short, misspent life."

"So, do you know where that tree might be?"

"Yes. It is about an hour's ride from here, mayhap less. Since I am most often a passenger not a rider, I am not good with the distances from one place to the next. It was Julian's favorite place when he was a boy. When Beatrice was with child Julian confided in me that he hoped to be able to show his son his favorite place someday. When he thought his son dead, he planted a rose there. I am surprised it has survived."

"Oh, that is rather sweet." Then a horrible thought struck Chloe. "Nay, please do not tell me that he has taken Anthony there today?"

"No, no. Be at ease. Anthony was playing some game with the girls in the long gallery when I last saw him. That was but a few moments before I came out here and found you."

Chloe slumped a little in relief. The mere thought that Anthony might see something so horrible had terrified her. What made it truly chilling was that someday he would have to be told that that woman hanging from a tree had been his mother. It was one of the things many people would say she should never tell him, but she would not keep it a secret from him. Too many people would know and could accidentally tell him, if nothing else.

Shaking off that moment of fear, she asked, "Do you know where Julian and Leo might be, then?"

"In Julian's office," replied Lady Evelyn. "They

returned from their search for signs of Arthur just a little while ago."

"Since they have not spoken to me, I have to assume that they did not find Beatrice's body. There would have been a small uproar since they would have brought the body here." She sighed. "I had best go tell them that I think I know where at least one sign of Arthur's presence is." When she realized Lady Evelyn was walking beside her as she started back to the house, she said, "You do not need to come with me, m'lady. I did not mean to ruin your walk in the garden."

"S'truth, talk of Beatrice's body hanging from a tree did briefly dim the beauty of the garden, but I do not flee that. No, I have a sudden need to see my family, my girls, and my darling grandson. All of them. Even poor Mildred."

"Is Mildred unwell?" Chloe had seen little of Julian's aunt and wondered if the woman was one of those who felt it was almost a lady's duty to be weak and ailing at all times. Somehow she doubted it, but there seemed no other reason for the woman to spend so much time in her room.

"No, just sad. She has to know that all this will end with Arthur's death. It will pass, for she lost her love for her husband a long time ago."

"Oh. Well, that loss and the understanding that there will never be a chance to make it right may be what has made her so unhappy."

"True, but I think it is time for speaking bluntly to the woman. She is usually much stronger than this. Cheerful even. This is so unlike her."

"Is it possible that she somehow thinks she bears

some blame for all of this? That mayhap she feels she should have seen what Arthur was doing and warned someone?" When Lady Evelyn just stared at her, Chloe felt a blush creep over her cheeks. "It was just a thought."

Lady Evelyn kissed her on the cheek. "And an excellent one. That sounds very much like Mildred. Now I know what to say to pull her out of this melancholia."

Chloe watched as Lady Evelyn hurried up the stairs with the energy and grace of a much younger woman. She thought of the vision she had had of the lady embracing a man on a beach and smiled. It was going to be interesting to see just what sort of man caught the woman's attention.

Straightening her shoulders she went in search of Julian. She was feeling uneasy, for it seemed as if her visions were coming from Arthur's twisted mind. It terrified her to think that she might have become tied to him in some strange way. If that was true, then they needed to find Arthur not simply to stop him from killing anyone else but to preserve her sanity. She could not endure many more of these visions of death, not when they came so frequently and clearly.

"The man is near at hand. I know it," said Julian as he poured himself a brandy. "I swear I can almost smell the bastard." He handed a drink to Leo and took a sip of his own.

Leo took a drink and then nodded. "I know exactly what you mean. It is no longer just you and

Anthony in danger, either. I still think that Arthur now plans to eradicate your whole family. And his own. From what that fellow Jake said when we talked to him, Arthur and Beatrice had become far worse in the last few weeks before you banished them than they had ever been before. He felt sure that the only thing that kept him and the other servants from being killed was that the pair spent so much time in London. Others share his opinion."

"It has all fallen apart on him, all his plans turning to dust, and now he strikes out in pure fury. We are dealing with a madman now and not just some coldhearted bastard who wanted to be earl and was willing to kill off a few heirs to gain the title and the wealth that came with it. I just know it in my gut. I also do not like how Chloe is having one dark vision after another. It is almost as if my uncle is sending them to her, and that is a damned frightening thought."

"It will be over soon."

"Are you certain of that?"

"As certain as one can be of anything. He is losing or has lost all of his allies, the ones who were just fooled into following his lead and the ones who were being threatened into helping him. Simone has disappeared again and is rumored to be back in France, so he has lost all the aid and money she could give him. I think he had promised her something and could not get it. Perhaps the information he wanted the good doctor to get for him. That means he has not only lost her help but could well have someone hunting him down to make him pay for that failure. The people she works for do not tolerate failure. You still live and so does Anthony. He has lost the prestige he had gained through deceit or, again, blackmail. He has also lost the running of this place and the money that put into his pocket. Arthur could now be thinking of killing as many of you as possible before he just disappears."

"I should have just shot him when I discovered he was cuckolding me instead of going off to sulk in the stews as I did. No one would have faulted me for that, and then this trouble would not be haunting us now."

"You would have been banished from England no matter how justified anyone thought you were. That justification would simply have saved you from hanging. And then you would have been of little use to your family or your tenants."

Julian took another sip of the brandy. "Or to my son."

"Exactly. Now, what we need," Leo began and then frowned when there was a knock on the door. When he bade the person enter he was a little surprised when Chloe came in. "Is there a problem, cousin?"

"Ah, aye, I believe so," she replied as she walked up to stand at Julian's side. "Do you recall where your favorite tree is?"

Although it seemed an odd question for her to ask, Julian nodded. "I have not been to it for a while. It might have been taken down by a storm for all I know. It was very old."

"It still stands."

"Have you been to see it?"

"In a manner of speaking. I did not have a vision but I did have a strong knowing." She swallowed hard as the memory of what she had seen turned her stomach a little. "I saw it clearly. Worse, I saw what was in it."

Julian set down his drink and took her into his arms. "You have seen something dark again. Was it Arthur?"

"It had to have been his doing, but it is not him. I fear Beatrice is now hanging from your favorite tree." She nodded when he stared at her in shock. "She is dead and I suspect your uncle did it. That would mean he is close at hand just as you have suspected."

Julian cursed and then sighed as he stared at the body of his late wife. If one did not see the contortion of her face, she would look almost peaceful as her body swayed gently in the breeze. Hanging was a gruesome way to die, quite often no more than a slow strangulation, and Beatrice's once lovely face revealed every torturous moment.

"We had better cut her down," he said as he dismounted.

"I can do it, m'lord," said Jake, who had ridden with them, a spare horse trailing behind him. "I can get up in that tree easy as you like and cut her down."

"Thank you. I would appreciate it."

As he stood watching the thin man nimbly scramble up the tree, Julian sensed Leo coming to stand at his side. "Not a pretty way to die."

"Nay," agreed Leo. "Are you upset?"

"Upset," Julian said slowly, tasting the word. "No. I just do not like to see her dead. In truth, I would much rather have had her alive so that she could turn on Arthur and help us send him to the gallows."

"Which is something he would never allow. He killed her not because she erred, but because she was now a threat to him."

"She knew too much. So did Simone."

"Simone would not be fool enough to stay long enough for Arthur to see her as a threat. In truth, she may have seen it coming and that is why we now hear rumors of her being in France. She is clever enough to have seen how it was all falling apart and so she slipped away before she was trapped and killed by the debris."

"Very nicely put," Julian said as Jake laid Beatrice out on the ground.

"How kind."

"Thank you, Jake. Can you fetch the blanket from my saddle? I do not believe the women back at the house should see this." When Julian saw how Leo frowned at the body, he asked, "Do you see something there that tells you who did it?"

"Nay. I was just wondering on all the cruel ways it could have been done. By the look on her face and the blood on her wrists where the rope rubbed them raw, I think she was not even unconscious when he hung her up there. I was just trying to decide if he then walked away or if he stood here and watched as she vainly struggled against her bonds as she died."

"Why would you wish to know the rather gruesome details?"

"Because the how could tell us just how dangerously insane your uncle may have become." Leo crouched by the body as a frowning Jake stood by with the blanket. "Aye, she was fighting as she strangled to death." He looked around and noted how empty the land was. "I do not believe he picked this spot just because he knew it was one of our favorites, either. By killing her out here, he did not need to gag her. No one would hear her die."

"So he could listen to her die?" Julian asked softly, a little horrified by that thought.

Leo moved out of the way so that Jake could wrap the body in the blanket. He brushed off his pants as he replied, "Quite possibly. What do you think, Jake?"

Jake looked terrified for a moment and then stiffened his stance. "I think he could have done it just like that, m'lord. He was very angry those last few days he stayed here. He did not yell or the like, but you just knew that the anger was bubbling inside of him. And there were a few times when the way he looked at her ladyship were right nasty. That were different."

"Thank you, Jake," said Julian. "Secure her body to the horse and we will return to the manor." He looked at Leo. "So my uncle is undoubtedly rabid now."

"I think you guessed that when Chloe told you of her vision in the carriage," he said softly so that Jake would not hear him. "It might have been Beatrice who was going to do that, but the note I received today said that the one man they caught implicated your uncle. As the rogue said, the woman was right cheerful over the plan but the man was cold and precise."

"You told me nothing of this note."

"I was planning to when Chloe told us about Beatrice."

"And just how does one adequately protect oneself from a madman?"

"Just as you have done. You gather everyone in one place, a place that is not easily crept up on, and you surround it with big, well-armed guards."

Those words were not as comforting as Julian had hoped for.

Chloe sighed as she watched the men dismount before the house, a blanket-shrouded form draped over the fourth horse. She did not need to see the body to know it was not a pretty sight. She had already seen most of it in her vision. Chloe just wished her visions would show her the one committing the crime instead of just the crime. However, with Beatrice dead, there was really only one person who could be guilty of her death, and any other crime that happened in the area.

"I am sorry, Julian," she said as he stepped up to her.

"For what?"

He clenched his hand against the urge to stroke her cheek. They were still trying to keep their affair secret, but it was hard to keep a distance from her all day. Glancing at Beatrice's body being carried into the house, he realized he was free, and then felt guilty. It might be true that Beatrice had earned a hanging a long time ago, but it should not have been done as it was. And if his uncle was trying to send him some sort of message, he should not have bothered. Hanging his wife from his favorite tree told him nothing he did not already know—that his uncle was a killer and just might be a madman as well.

"For what has happened to Beatrice."

"Do not grieve over her. She was the one who brought herself to this death with her greed and her vanity. All I am sorry for is that if she died because she was ready to set free a few of Arthur's secrets, we have missed a great opportunity to get some important information on him. Nay, she killed whatever it was that I felt for her a very long time ago. But, as the mother of my child, I mean to give her a decent burial."

"Your mother and Mildred have already said that they will clean the body up for burial. I thought I might help them but they said I should see that you and Leo have all you need."

As they stepped into the house Julian saw his mother leading the men into a room down the hall from his office. "It is not a pretty sight."

"I told them that, but they informed me that they have prepared bodies for burial before and while they may not have been hanged men or women, they were gruesome in their own way." Chloe could not fully repress a shiver. "I confess that I was just as glad to be turned away. I have never dressed the dead before. Well, save for my sister, and she just looked as if she was sleeping."

"As soon as it is safe we will fetch your sister home," he said quietly.

Chloe swallowed a sudden surge of tears. "Thank you, Julian." She took a deep breath to push away that grief. "As soon as I saw you riding up I had the cook prepare some simple food. You missed your lunch. But perhaps you are not in the mood for it just now."

"Hardhearted as it may sound, I am hungry."

"So am I," said Leo as he joined them.

"It will be served in the breakfast room."

After checking to be sure only Leo could see them, Julian kissed her on the check and then strode off toward his bedchamber to wash up. He performed his ablutions quickly and hurried back downstairs, meeting his pale mother just outside the breakfast room. Without a word, he pulled her into his arms and lightly patted her back.

"It was bad," she said and, after a moment of enjoying his attempt to comfort her, pulled away. "We can bury her as soon as you wish. I could fetch the vicar to say a word or two."

"If that is what you want to do. I am not sure what one can say over the grave of a woman who has harmed as many people as Beatrice has."

"Not much, true enough, but we should do this all as properly as possible."

"Agreed. Let me know when the vicar can come and then we will have a brief service. Send one of the footmen to ask someone to dig the grave in the family plot. I will not put her in the crypt with the rest of the Kenwoods."

"I do not wish her to be put there either, so do not look so guilty."

He watched her hurry away to prepare a small service for Beatrice and then shook his head. Beatrice was being treated far better than she deserved, but he could not bring himself to refuse to give her a proper burial. Whatever punishment she was due for her crimes was no longer his to mete out. When he stepped into the breakfast room, the tempting scents of food pushed all thought of Beatrice from his mind. A moment later Leo strode in and he joined the man in devouring much of what had been put out for them.

It was almost dusk when he found himself standing beside Beatrice's grave while the vicar droned on about sinners and redemption. Except for the verbosity of the vicar, it was a quick and silent service. Julian threw a handful of dirt on Beatrice's grave and then left the three stable hands to finish burying her. He would put up a simple headstone later.

Julian glanced down at his mother, who walked on his left side while Chloe strolled along on his right. "Mother, there is something I have to tell you," he said, knowing it was a poor time to mention his marrying Chloe even as he knew he needed to get the vows said as soon as possible. He could still hear Leo saying *like rabbits*.

Lady Evelyn patted his arm. "Yes, I know, dearest, but at least wait a few days. No one liked Beatrice and all are well aware of her sins, but marrying the day after her funeral would be a little rash. Maybe by Saturday."

"Three days' wait is better?"

"Much better."

She hurried away before he could say anything, so he turned to look at Chloe. She was staring at him and looking a little shocked. Julian was certain she knew he had no lingering feelings for Beatrice, so was not sure why marrying so soon after the woman's death should trouble her.

"I told you I would marry you as soon as I was free," he said, hoping he did not sound as defensive as he thought he did.

"I cannot believe you would do so but days after burying her," said Chloe, although she knew she should not be so surprised or even shocked. Beatrice had not been a wife to Julian for a very long time.

"Actually, what I cannot believe is how my mother knew what I was going to say before I even said it."

"I told you that she and Lady Marston both spoke as if we were already engaged."

"Ah, so you did. Well, that explains why she was not shocked at what I wanted to do. She has been anticipating it."

"Julian, marrying me within days of burying Beatrice will cause a great scandal."

"Nonsense. It is not as if one is required to wait by any law I know of, and the world and its mother knows she was no wife to me."

"I still think we should wait a while before we have a very quiet ceremony."

"No. We will not wait. I am very tired of pretending that we are no more than acquaintances every time anyone save for your cousin is around. I am also very tired of either you or I having to slip from bedchamber to bedchamber as if we are conducting some illicit affair. We will be married on Saturday."

"You are ordering me to marry you?"

"Yes, I believe I am." Seeing that she was about to release a stream of undoubtedly scathing words, he grabbed her by her arms and gave her a little shake. "Just calm down."

Chloe did not feel inclined to calm down. "You cannot order me to get married."

"Then I shall ask you nicely. Chloe, we have been lovers for weeks."

"Not that many."

"Enough. I have made no attempt to pull back or pull out. I have spilled my seed into you every time we have made love. You could already be carrying my child."

She ignored the little tickle of delight over the idea that she might already be carrying his child and frowned at him. "It can take months, even years, to conceive a child."

"Your cousin informed me that I might not wish to delay our marriage for too long after I was free to marry again because the Vaughns and the Wherlockes are all very fertile."

"Not that fertile," she said even as her traitorous mind started adding up the multitude of cousins she had.

"Like rabbits," he said. "Chloe, you know I want to marry you and that it would not be simply because I fear I may have gotten you with child. However, I would rather endure what little scandal might be stirred up by a hasty wedding than have the whole world counting on their pudgy little fingers and figuring out our child was born fat and happy after only seven months, or less." He kissed her on the tip of her nose. "Now you can argue or sulk or do whatever else you want to make your disagreement with my arrangements clear, or you can help my mother arrange the celebration I know she is already planning. Whichever you decide, we *will* be getting married on Saturday."

Chloe stared at him as he strode into the house and then cursed. She went around the side of the house and into the garden. Sitting on a bench, one that did not face the tree that had inspired the vision of Beatrice's hanging body, she crossed her arms over her chest and glared at a small bush weighted down with fat white roses.

It took a while before she would admit what was really troubling her. She was afraid. Now that the actual wedding was drawing near, all the reasons why she should not marry Julian swamped her mind. On Saturday she would become Julian's wife—and a countess.

She was so unsuited to become a countess, she thought. As far as Chloe could see there was no way she could escape that fate, either. She had agreed to the betrothal. Julian was almost eager to get married, if only so he had to cease creeping around in his own home. And Lady Evelyn was probably already writing up the menu for the wedding breakfast.

For a brief moment she saw a chance to put it all off. They needed a license. Then she cursed. Chloe knew that either Leo or Julian would have thought of that, and she had no doubt that it was all prepared and just waiting for the time it would be needed.

"You do not look like a woman who is about to marry," said Leo as he sat down beside her. "It is rather late to be having doubts now. Horse out of the barn and all that."

"You told him we breed like rabbits."

"We do." He gave her a sympathetic smile. "You know as well as I that you could already be carrying a child. Your choice could be as simple as a scandal now or a scandal later."

"Leo, I will be a countess."

He draped his arm around her shoulders and kissed her cheek. "And you will be a very good one. You have had all the same lessons and training as Lady Evelyn would have had. You have been running my home for three years and, by damn, I will miss that. You have cared for the sick, worked on charities, attended all manner of social events, and raised a child. Now, I admit the latter is not often listed as a qualification, but it is a good one."

"You make it all sound so easy," she mumbled.

"And you make it all seem so much harder than it is. He is an earl, Chloe, not a royal duke. He is also, at heart, a man of the country, not the city. Cease worrying about how wrong you are for the role of his countess and start thinking about all the good you can do as the countess of Colinsmoor."

"I suppose there are things I can do. There is no need to talk me into the marriage, Leo. I agreed and, even if I think this is being done too soon, I will not go back on my word." She shook off his arm and stood up. "I know I have made my bed and now I must sleep in it—literally. I just thought there would be more time to get used to the idea of being called *my lady*."

He stood up, hooked his arm through hers and started to walk back to the house. "You will be fine, Chloe. I would have thought your visions would have told you so."

"Nay. It is as if they do not wish to invade my privacy," she drawled.

He grinned as he led her inside. "Go decide what dress you will wear on your wedding day, what flowers you might carry, and even what little cakes will be served to whatever guests may appear. That should keep you too busy to fret over this."

When he started to walk away, Chloe had to fight the urge to kick him in the backside. She started up to her bedchamber. The truth was that she could argue for the next three days and yet still end up at the altar beside Julian, resentment bubbling inside of her, or she could accept her fate. There was always the passion to consider. And, she thought as Lady Evelyn caught up with her and started to drag her off to the sewing room chattering about laces and corsets every step of the way, there were also those two simple words of warning to consider—*like rabbits*.

Chapter 16

"This was not the way I wished to spend my wedding day," grumbled Julian as he and Leo rode toward the section of his land that was a strange mixture of marsh and rock. Jake had sent word that he and a ditch-digging crew had found something important, but Julian could not see what of any importance could be found on this desolate piece of land.

"It is hours before you wed. Your mother very cleverly arranged it so that you marry just before the noon hour, thus we can all stumble out of the church, our ears and backside numbed by that word-loving vicar, and head for the table with all the food."

"What a romantic you are, Leo."

"I do my best. She is nervous, you know," Leo said quietly. "She fears she will make a terrible countess. Perhaps you should have spoken to her about that."

"I would have if my mother had not made sure Chloe was guarded every moment of the day and night."

Leo laughed. "She is trying to keep you respectable."

Julian thought his mother was trying to make him suffer, but did not say so. He had been stunned to find that Chloe was not in her bedchamber the night after they buried Beatrice, even more stunned to find out she was not in his, either. At first he had feared that someone had taken her, even that his uncle had somehow stolen her away. He was pleased he had not made too great an uproar because his mother had cheerfully told him that Chloe had been moved to the bedchamber next to hers. The master bedchambers were being readied for after the wedding. Worse, he had been stuck in a small room right next to his aunt. It was clear that a guard had been posted to make sure he and Chloe did no roaming in the night.

"It is a little late for that. And I have no idea why Chloe should think she would make a bad countess. She has been acting the hostess of your home for three years and she is a gently reared woman. Has had all the same teaching and training as my mother."

"That is what I told her. Do not worry. She will not stand you up at the altar. Just do not make any criticism until she has settled in a bit. It will cut her to the heart. Once she is the countess for a while she will see that she can manage it well enough. Look, that is Jake."

Julian spurred his horse to a slightly faster pace and rode up to where Jake stood with two other burly men. None of them looked well, all three being surprisingly pale for such muscular and fit men. They all stood in front of a large depression in the ground but he could not see past them enough to see what was in that hollow.

"You sent word that you have found something, Jake?" he asked.

"Aye, m'lord, that we did." Jake stepped aside a little. "I am thinking we just found us The Pit."

Cursing softly, Julian dismounted and one of the men quickly stepped forward to take the reins of his horse. Another did the same for Leo's horse when he, too, dismounted. Julian cautiously walked to the edge of the pit and realized it was a lot deeper, and steeper sided, than he had anticipated. At the bottom were the remains of several people. He was sure that Jake was right in his assumption. They had found the infamous pit.

"Do you know how many are down there?" Julian asked.

"We think it be five, m'lord," replied Jake. "We counted feet. Got ten. So, five people." Although he did not move any closer to the edge, Jake did lean forward so that he could peer down into it. "I think that one near the far end, to the right, be Melvin. I recognize them boots. And one of the ones in the middle is Gordon, the butcher's eldest lad. He went missing about two months past. They could not believe he would leave them but then decided he had trotted off to London. Too many of the young ones do and they never come back. I recognize that coat, as he was right proud of it. I can guess at the others just by recalling who is missing and mayhap, if we get closer, see something that I recognize."

"Why would they kill the butcher's lad?"

"He done said no to the lady. Had himself a sweetheart, he did, and he was going to be amarrying her in a month. He was not going to be betraying her in

any way. That made m'lady furious." Jake nodded
down at the rotting remains of five men. "This is
what he got for being a good, honorable lad who
did not want to be no whore's toy. Beggin' your
pardon, m'lord."

Julian rubbed a hand over his hair and sighed.
"No need, Jake. Let us see if we can get the bodies
out of there. Once we know who is in there, as best
as we can leastwise, we can tell their families and
give them a proper burial."

"We can do it, m'lord. You got a wedding to be
at, eh?"

"Not for a few more hours, and since my mother
has locked my bride away for safekeeping, I might
as well keep busy." He found the strength to smile
when the men chuckled, but it was fleeting.
"Damnation. I think the two of them were as mad
as hatters."

"They certainly were not right in the head near
the end, no doubting that."

Julian and Leo worked alongside the three other
men to bring out the gruesome trophies of his uncle
and late wife's reign over Colinsmoor. Guilt was a
heavy stone in Julian's chest. This was but one horrible example of what his people had suffered while
he was sunk in drink and whores. Chloe was worried
that she would not make a good countess, yet he, a
man born to the role, had made a poor earl.

By the time they had dragged up the bodies, Julian
was covered in dirt and sick at heart. Jake and his
friends had identified four of the bodies from recognizable bits of clothing, and were fairly certain they
knew who the fifth one was. Julian looked at the body

marked as Gordon, the butcher's son, a young man in his prime, in love, and murdered by Beatrice because he had told her no. Melvin had been killed because he had tried to do right and tell his lord what was happening. The others had all died for much the same reason, self-preservation or stung vanity. It did not bear thinking about or he would disgrace himself by weeping like a babe.

He had brought this trouble to his people, good honest people whose families had worked for the Kenwoods for generations. Julian did not like to think of all the times he had left Beatrice to handle matters while he went into London to pursue a thriving career in government. He cringed as he thought of the year he had left Beatrice and Arthur in complete control while he had swallowed enough drink to fill the Thames and wallowed in whores. Gordon had been murdered during that time. He had put a knife at the throat of the people of Colinsmoor and then walked away.

Instructing the men to take the bodies to Colinsmoor and contact their families, he hurried back home. He would see that the bodies were buried well with a nice headstone although he doubted that would assuage the grief of those who had lost someone or ease his guilt. Julian cursed himself over and over for a blind fool as he rode.

"It is not your fault," said Leo.

"No? I am the earl, the owner of these lands. I might be able to excuse myself for being blind in the first few years, but not at the end. I was wallowing in self-pity while my uncle and my wife treated these people like serfs. It is bad enough that I let them rob me blind, but this? How could I not have seen it if I had just paid a little attention to something other than myself."

"We all pay attention to ourselves, Julian. It is the nature of the beast. And, forgive me, but even at your most wretched, I cannot blame you for not seeing that your uncle and the woman you married were any more than adulterers and thieves. I feel certain that if Melvin had reached you, you would have listened to him and done something."

Julian wanted to believe that, but seeing those bodies had shaken his confidence in himself. He needed to find the other half of the treacherous pair that had murdered his people and kept the others too afraid to fight or even hope. They all looked to him now to fix things, and he did not deserve their trust.

He struggled to shake off his sadness and guilt as they reined in in front of his home. It was difficult when he could see the small signs of neglect, knowing from the ledgers he had gone through that the money for repairs had gone straight into the pockets of Beatrice and Arthur. He paused just as he opened the door and looked at Leo.

"Beatrice was wearing no jewelry," he said.

"What?" Leo looked at Julian as if he thought he might be going a little mad.

"Beatrice could never have enough jewels, yet there was not even a locket on her body."

Leo cursed. "He stole it all. Has undoubtedly pawned it."

"Or will soon. Beatrice had not been dead for long. The carrion crows had not even pecked at her yet."

"As soon as you and Chloe are wed, I will start looking into that matter. Do you have any listing of what jewels she might have had?"

"I have one in my office. When you are ready to look it over, let me know and I can have it for you in minutes. Now"—he took a deep breath and forced aside all thoughts of Beatrice, Arthur, and how badly he had failed the people of Colinsmoor—"it is time for me to be married."

Chloe winced as she was stuffed into her wedding gown. She did not understand why the dresses were all made for a corseted figure. She hated corsets. There should be gowns for people like her who detested corsets.

"I hope I do not have to take a deep breath today," she murmured as Lady Evelyn's maid laced her up. "It might embarrass Julian if I fall over at the altar gasping for air."

"Hush," said Lady Evelyn, a laugh clear to hear in her voice. "You look beautiful and you will be all grace and beauty as you kneel by Julian at the altar."

"From your lips to God's ears."

Lady Evelyn stood back and studied Chloe for a moment. "Do you not want to marry Julian?"

"M'lady, I love the fool," she said bluntly. "If you tell him, I may have to show you all my brothers taught me about playing rough, however." She exchanged a brief grin with the woman. "I am just afraid. Afraid that he will never care for me as I do for him. Afraid I shall turn bitter if he does not.

And afraid that I shall be such a bad countess that I shall shame him."

"Foolish, all of it. I can help you whenever you have a question about being a countess." She laughed when Chloe looked at her in shock. "Did not think of that, did you?"

"Nay, so now I shall worry that I am too stupid to be his wife."

Lady Evelyn ignored that and said, "As for the love? Well, that is hard to comfort you on. I do not know what is in my son's heart. I will say that despite all the trouble that has plagued the two of you, he is happier than he has been in years. He laughs. He smiles. He makes foolish manly jests. He barely drinks at all. I can promise you that he was ill pleased when I moved you out of his reach for a few days. He pouted as only a man can do. I think you are already an important part of his life. What you make of that is your business." She gently slipped a rose into Chloe's hair. "And you are the woman who saved his son and has loved that boy, raised him, and always waited for the time when his father could come and claim him. I do not mean that you should use the great debt he owes you to try and hold him to you; I just point out that he already has enormous respect for you, and that is no small thing. Even better, he trusts you. I can see it."

"Aye, he told me he did."

"After the hell that Beatrice put him through, that is probably of more worth to him at the moment than something called love."

Chloe slowly nodded as she acknowledged the truth of that. When one had been deeply and repeatedly betrayed, someone who could be trusted was more important than anything else. She began to feel a little less uneasy about the step she was taking. She would still like to have him speak of love, but she could wait. She had the foundation. It was time to marry the fool and build the house.

"Well then, I am ready."

"Good, for I believe I just saw him walk toward the chapel," Lady Mildred said from her place by the window before turning and looking Chloe over. "And you do look beautiful, child."

"Lady Evelyn has worked hard."

"You have a natural beauty. Subtle. It will last and, even more important, if it fades a little as the years pass, you have the deeper beauty that is needed to hold a man to your side. Well, a man like Julian at least. Some men never learn the importance of it and always want more or something new."

"Sometimes, m'lady, people are just bad and no one and nothing can change it."

Lady Mildred gave her a kiss on the cheek. "I think I am beginning to understand that sad fact. I but pray that badness does not infect any of my girls."

"I doubt it. They were raised by you, were they not."

She smiled. "Oh, child, how can you think you will be a poor countess." She hooked her arm through Chloe's and waved to Lady Evelyn to open the door. "Let us go show Julian what a prize he is getting."

Chloe fought back the nervousness and fear that tried to swamp her as she made her way to the little stone chapel at the end of the garden. Lady Evelyn had given her some very wise advice and she intended to heed it. One thing she was sure of, and that was that Julian would honor the vows he took today. All she had to do was make sure that he never regretted it.

When she reached the inside of the chapel, she had to smile. Anthony stood near the altar carefully holding a little pillow with matching rings on it. The pews were nearly filled between the Kenwoods and the men who worked for Leo, most of who were her kinsmen. Leo looked very handsome as he stood beside Julian, ready to be both Julian's man and the man who gave her into Julian's keeping. As she reached the altar, she smiled at Julian's sisters and cousins, who had all insisted upon being her handmaidens.

Then she looked at Julian and felt the bite of panic. There was a darkness in his eyes, something that looked very much like grief. Did he now realize that he still loved Beatrice?

"Julian?" she whispered as she leaned toward him, unable to stop looking into his eyes as if she could read the answer to her fears there.

Julian knew she had seen the grief and shame he could not bury as deeply as he would like to. It astonished him that she could know him so well. When he saw the fear that darkened her eyes to almost black, he bent down and kissed her on the cheek.

"Hush, my little seer. What you see has naught to do with you or this marriage. It has to do with all that happened at Colinsmoor while Beatrice and Arthur ruled here."

"What—"

"No. It is dark and unpleasant and I refuse to allow it to intrude on our wedding day."

Chloe nodded and soon found herself kneeling beside Julian as they exchanged their vows. He spoke in a clear, firm voice, revealing no hesitation about binding himself to her for life. She did her best to sound as confident as he did. When he kissed her, she felt a tenderness in the caress that she had never felt before, and her lingering fear faded away.

The food and drink were joyfully consumed by the guests and Chloe felt her spirits lighten as she wove through the crowd, speaking with each one and accepting their congratulations. She thought it a little amusing that her relatives were all male and, except for Anthony, Julian's were all females. Knowing what incorrigible flirts her kinsmen could be, she was pleased to see that both Lady Mildred and Lady Evelyn were keeping a very close eye on their daughters. She was just walking up to Leo when Anthony ran up to her and hugged her legs.

"You are looking very handsome today, young man," she said as she stroked his curly hair. "Very manly."

"That is what Papa and Leo said. You are my mama now."

Chloe could not repress the wide smile that spread over her face. "Aye, I am."

Anthony nodded. "That is what Papa told me, so I comed over to hug my new mama."

Julian appeared and picked Anthony up. "Where are my thanks for getting you such a beautiful mama?"

"Thank you, Papa."

"My pleasure." Julian grinned and winked at

Chloe. "Ah, I see that Greta has brought out some very fine cakes."

"Cakes?" Anthony squirmed to get free even as his father set him down. "I needs to get some or the girls will eatem all."

"Ah, obviously there are a few gentlemanly manners we need to teach the boy," he drawled as Anthony reached the table the cakes were on and nudged his way to it through the girls. "Although I can hardly blame him. Greta makes some very good cakes."

"I will wander over and make the *oink* noise and that might slow him down," said Leo. He paused by her side and kissed her cheek. "You make a very lovely bride, cousin. I was almost sorry to hand my burden over to this rogue."

Chloe gasped in outrage when she felt a distinct pinch on her bottom and she glared at her cousin's back. Then she had to smile because she knew he had just made the *oink* noise. Anthony looked at the cake he held in each hand and slowly put one back on the table. The girls were nearly helpless with laughter.

"Did he just pinch your bottom?" Julian asked, leaning close to her ear to speak so that no one could overhear him.

"Aye, he did, and I will make him pay for that sometime soon. That and calling me a burden."

"Ah, well, now you are my burden." He laughed when she made a noise that sounded very much like a growl. "Exactly what is the *oink* noise?"

"Just what you think it is. It is a piglet sound. If you make it when Anthony is being particularly greedy, it slows him down. He put one cake back, did he not?"

"And you do not believe he will go back for it later?"

"Of course he will, but later is better. If he stuffed all he wanted in his little face at one time, he would make himself sick."

She leaned against him when she realized she could do so now. They were married. Even better, this was their wedding day, and even the most pious could not object to a little show of affection on such a day.

Julian breathed deeply of her scent, a faint touch of lavender and beautiful, clean skin. His whole body tightened with need for her. He had missed her in his bed, had even had some trouble getting to sleep because she was not curled up in his arms. It was probably a weakness but he could not make himself care.

"We can slip away soon," he said and brushed a kiss over the hollow by her ear.

Chloe felt herself blush, which she thought was foolish. They had been lovers for weeks before this and had only spent a few nights apart. However, this would be their first time as husband and wife. There would be no concern about being caught together or remembering to get back to the right bed before any of the servants saw them. The only concern she had was that the moment she and Julian left the room, everyone would know what they were going to do.

"And just where are we to slip away to?"

"Well, there is a suite of rooms in the back that

has been cleaned. It is to be our bower. A very nice bower it is, too. Food will be brought to the little sitting room while we are all cozy in our bed and a bath will be waiting for you if you want one."

"I do not think we can slip away quietly or unnoticed."

"It is all family here, Chloe. And with my mother and Lady Mildred here, there will be none of those risqué remarks people like to hurl at a newly wedded couple."

"I hope you are right."

He was not right, and Chloe had to laugh, for two of the worst offenders were his mother and his aunt. They were careful in what they said because their daughters were in the room but the men, Chloe, and Julian knew just what they were saying. Still laughing about it and Julian's discomfort, which still tinted his cheeks a very nice rose, Chloe broke free of his hold and skipped into their suite.

"It is lovely, Julian," she said as she peered into the bedchambers on either side of the large sitting room. Huge windows looked out onto the garden. She caught a quick glimpse of it before Julian closed the curtains.

"And very private, away from the rest of the family and the kitchens." He grinned as he slid his arms around her waist. "Not so far that the food will be cold by the time it reaches us, however. We will go on a proper wedding journey when Arthur is caught. But for now, we can pretend this is our little cottage by the sea."

"Not by the sea," she said and kissed him under the chin. "The lakes."

"Even better. I admit that I prefer the lakes, and I have a small property there that I believe you will love."

She almost told him that she would love any place as long as he was with her, but she hastily bit the words back. Chloe did not want to make him feel uncomfortable or pushed into a corner. It was going to be difficult because her love for him seemed to fill every corner of her heart, but she had to go slowly.

"Now let me see if I can get you out of all this finery."

It did not take him long and Chloe pushed aside the small pinch of jealousy she felt as she considered where he had gained his experience in removing a woman's clothing. He was a man of thirty who had been married before, she sternly reminded herself. Men struggled to get as much experience as they could from the moment their voice grew lower and a few spindly hairs appeared on their chests. Her randy brothers had proved that often enough.

As he nudged her toward the bed, he stripped her down to her shift and undid her hair. Chloe was busy herself, stripping him of his coat, waistcoat, and shirt. She was just about to undo his trousers when he gently pushed her down onto the bed. Throwing aside all modesty, she sprawled on her back and watched him shed the last of his clothes.

Julian Kenwood was a well-built man, she decided. He was gloriously male from his broad shoulders right down to his long, narrow feet and every lovely taut, muscular inch in between. Her gaze settled on his manhood, erect and growing larger right before her eyes.

She suddenly thought of the way he had used his mouth and tongue so intimately on her, on how it made her crazed, and she sat up. Reaching out, she wrapped her hand around his erection and stroked him very gently. He groaned softly and clutched at her shoulders. Taking that as a sign of approval, she leaned forward and kissed the broad tip that glistened slightly.

"Chloe," he said in a choked voice, "are you sure you want to do that?"

"You do not like it?" she asked and then slowly ran her tongue along his length, knowing by the way he shuddered that he liked it very much.

"Women do not like to do it." Julian was astonished that he could still talk, as his blood was running so hot it should have boiled his brain.

"Well, let us just see if I am one of those women." She used his reactions to learn what he liked as she made love to him with her mouth. His obvious pleasure fed her own until she thought she would have to drag him onto the bed and leap on him. She took him into her mouth and gently sucked and his whole body rocked toward her, so she did it again. A moment later she found herself flat on her back and watched her shift go sailing out over the room.

"I cannot wait," he growled and reached down to test her readiness with his fingers.

Finding her hot and wet nearly had him spilling his seed on her belly. He bent down to kiss her even as he thrust inside her. Chloe cried out his name and wrapped her slender, strong legs around his waist. The last clear thought he had was that he had finally found the adventurous lover he had always wanted.

Some wonderful person had put a bowl of water and several cloths right on a table next to the bed, Julian noticed, so that he did not even have to try to walk after he finally rolled his weak and sated body off his new wife. He had to smile when Chloe barely twitched as he cleaned her off and then himself. He blindly tossed the used cloth in the direction of the table, reached for a flatteringly limp Chloe, and pulled her into his arms. He decided he really liked the way she curled up against him, kissed his chest, and then idly rubbed her cheek against it before settling down.

He was married again and he actually felt happy. Then he recalled what he had found that morning and he sighed. Chloe proved yet again how well she sensed his moods by lightly stroking his chest.

"We found the pit," he said abruptly and was not surprised when she hugged him and kissed his chin. "Five men were in it. Well, four men and one who was barely a man. All killed because they knew too much and were honorable men who would tell me, or because Beatrice wanted them and they did not succumb to her charms."

Chloe lifted herself just enough to brush her mouth over his. "It is not your fault," she said.

"I am their lord. I should have been watching out for them. I left her here time and time again to manage things while I was off playing lord of the manor at the House of Lords."

"Where you are expected to go from time to time. And every man leaves his wife to manage his home when he has to go to work. Julian, no one, no matter how suspicious their nature, would ever have thought such things were being done while he was away."

"But I found out the truth about my uncle and my wife and I just left."

"You found out they were betraying you. That does not suggest that they were murdering people and throwing them into an unmarked grave. It took you a long time to accept that they were trying to kill you. Nay, Julian, this was not your fault. We have buried one of those beasts and soon we will bury the other. That is what you must do now that you have learned the depths of their depravity. You find justice."

She could see him struggling to heed what she said and understood how hard it was for him to do so. His feeling of responsibility for the people of Colinsmoor ran deep and it would be a while before he could break free of a guilt he did not deserve to suffer. But, she thought, at least he had listened to her.

"You need to stop thinking about it." She slid her hand down his stomach and stroked his manhood, feeling it immediately rise up to welcome her touch.

"That certainly might help to clear my head," he said, and ran his hands down her back until he could gently squeeze her backside.

"Well, is that not what a wife is for? To clear the troubled thoughts from her husband's head? To soothe his worries?"

"Do you expect me to argue with you when you are doing exactly what I want?"

Chloe laughed and kissed him. She knew the guilt he felt would return, but she hoped it would lessen with time and thought. For now she would do her best to keep him so dazed with passion that he forgot his own name. That was what wedding nights were for.

Chapter 17

"Fools. Look at them down there smiling at each other and acting as if all is right with the world." Arthur slipped around the tree so that he could get a better look at the small group gathered in the graveyard by the chapel. "Told you we should have buried those bodies better and deeper, Beatrice. They have gone and buried them in Kenwood land. Right near you, which I have to admit is a clever twist. They are burying that girl whose babe you took now. From what little I could learn, she was the new countess's sister. Made a mistake there."

Arthur thought about his dead lover and sighed. He missed her from time to time, which amazed him. She had made so many mistakes, ruined all his plans, and he had enjoyed watching her dance at the end of that rope, yet he still found himself talking to her. One of those puzzles of life, he decided, and growled softly when he saw Julian put his arm around his new wife.

How dare he marry again so soon after burying Beatrice. She must be stomping around in hell right now demanding some sort of punishment for him. If she was still alive he would not have been able to take a bride, and the fact that now he could must make dear Beatrice livid. That was something he would do for her, Arthur decided. He had money now that he had sold all of Beatrice's jewels. Not as much as he would have had had the fool woman not left the Kenwood jewels in the safe in the manor, but enough to hire a gang of thieves and cutthroats. They would help him end his brother's line for once and for all.

He straightened and glared down at his wife as she joined the group in the churchyard. Traitorous bitch. She would pay, too. Hiding with the enemy, consorting with them, could not be forgiven. All he had ever asked of the stupid woman was that she give him a son, and she had failed him three times. He would make sure she saw those failures die first, right before her eyes. He wanted her to grieve as he had each time she had pushed yet another cursed daughter out of her useless womb.

They had all failed him, cheated him, and destroyed him. His plans had been perfect and they had thwarted him at every turn. No more. He might not gain the prize he had once sought, but he was a man who could adjust. Now he just wanted them all to pay for his losses. Let the cursed earldom go to some far-flung cousin or, even better, to the crown.

Arthur rubbed at the pain in his head and decided he needed a drink. Drink was the other thing that eased the constant pain. He did not like how it made him act, but it would do until he had rid himself of all the sources of his pain. Slipping back down the hill away from the graveyard and his family of traitors, Arthur made his way to his horse. It was time to go back to the inn, have a few drinks and a meal.

Then, when the pain was eased, he would gather his men and make plans. All he had to do was divert a few of the men guarding Colinsmoor and he and his men could easily get inside the manor. The bastards he was paying to fight for him could loot the place to their heart's content while he took care of all those interfering women. Then he would help himself to the real treasures at Colinsmoor and slip away. With a full purse and a little luck he would be able to avoid Simone's people and start a new life.

"Thank you so much for this, Julian," Chloe said as she wiped the tears from her cheeks with one of the embroidered handkerchiefs Phillipa had given her as a wedding present.

Suddenly she smiled for she realized that, skilled though Phillipa was, there was no way she could have embroidered Chloe's new initials on a dozen lovely handkerchiefs in the few days allowed before the wedding. Sneaky Lady Evelyn, she thought. The woman had plotted and planned to get her and Julian together from the beginning.

"I am pleased it makes you happy," he said, "although you still appear to be crying."

"Happy tears. You have a mother and two sisters, Julian. You must understand what they are." She laughed when he sighed, and decided she would not tell him how his mother and sisters had plotted to get him married. "This is right. This is where Laurel would want to be, her and her baby, not in the crypt."

"Outdoors, under the sky."

"Exactly. And Henry, too."

She looked at the three headstones and sighed with a mixture of grief and happiness. Her sister and her men were all together again. The smooth little marker for the unknown child whose bones they had used was also there and she knew that her sister would love that child, too. She prayed their spirits had found each other wherever they were.

Chloe suddenly tensed. She felt as though two wasps were stinging her right between her shoulder blades. Turning around, she looked behind her but could see nothing.

"Something wrong?" Julian looked in the direction she seemed to be searching in but saw nothing.

"Just an odd feeling. As if something hot was poking me in the back. I just wondered if someone was watching us."

"Good or bad watching."

After considering that for a moment, she said, "Bad. That would explain why it felt as wasps were stinging me." She looked all over the hillside again. "I see no one, however."

"I could send some men out to search the area." Julian had quickly learned to respect Chloe's instincts and decided he would send a few men out to search anyway.

"There is no one there, Julian."

Chloe turned back to the graves and stepped closer. She lightly traced her sister's name with her

fingers and said a silent farewell. Then she turned
back to Julian, grasped his hand, and tugged him
after the others who were already heading back to
the house. Someday she would tell Anthony the
story of Laurel and his birth, when he was old
enough to understand and not be frightened by it.
She deserved to be remembered by the child she
had helped to save. She would also send her brothers a letter to tell them who she had married and
where their other sister was buried. Chloe felt certain that they would wish to visit Laurel's grave and,
she hoped, her as well.

"It is not worth troubling anyone. I see no one
and you see no one. So I must have imagined it or
whoever was looking is now gone."

She was not surprised when he very nicely slipped
away once they were back inside the house. Chloe
knew he was going to go and look. It would make
him feel better and she supposed it was the wise
thing to do. The fact that he heeded her warnings,
trusted in her instincts was such a gift, she would not
complain if he was a little overprotective.

"You happy now, Mama?" asked Anthony as he
skipped up to her.

Chloe could not stop the smile that lifted her lips
if she tried. Hearing Anthony call her Mama was
music to her ears. It had never felt uncomfortable,
had felt right from the first moment he said the
word. Finally she could claim the child openly as
her heart had claimed him three years ago.

"I was happy before, Anthony," she said. "Those
were happy tears." She laughed when he made a

face very similar to his father's. "Do you want to walk in the garden?"

"Can I bring my ball?"

"Of course, but do not expect me to be as good at playing ball as your father or your uncle. I have long skirts that make it hard for me to run about."

"Tuck 'em up like Lady Mildy and Granmere do."

"I just might do that," she said as she took him by the hand and started toward the garden, idly trying to imagine the two older women with their skirts rucked up playing ball with a little boy.

"Someone was here, m'lord," said Jake, who was revealing some real skills as a tracker. "Do ye think it was your uncle?"

Although the question was asked in a calm voice, Julian caught the flash of fear in the man's eyes. He could not blame Jake for fearing Arthur. His uncle was certainly a man to fear, especially now. No one could easily judge what a madman might do. That was what made them so very hard to catch.

He looked up at the wind-contorted tree at the top of the small hill and frowned. Someone had stood there and watched them gather in the grave-yard. It was what Chloe had said she had felt that made that seem ominous. So did the fact that who-ever it was had done his best to remain hidden and hide his tracks as he left. Who else could it have been but Arthur or some hireling of his? The stealth of the whole matter was what troubled him. That and the fact that if it had been Arthur, the man had come far too close to his family without being seen.

The question was, why was the man still lingering around Colinsmoor? Why was he even still in the country? It did not make sense and that disturbed Julian. Arthur was a smart man with a lot of cunning, who knew how to commit all manner of crimes yet not get caught or banished. To stay at the scene of so many of his crimes did not seem smart or cunning.

"It could be, but we cannot know for certain unless we can track him back to wherever he came from," Julian said.

"Damnation, I thought he was gone for good."

"So did I, Jake. So did I. Let us take another look round just to be sure."

It was late when Julian finally returned home. He rushed up the stairs and hurried to prepare for dinner. It was a little disappointing not to find Chloe waiting in their bedchamber for him, but he knew she was spending as much time with his mother as possible. Julian did not think Chloe needed any lessons in how to be a proper countess, but if it made her feel more confident in who she was now, he had no objections.

When he reached the salon where everyone waited to be called into dinner he had to grin. With two older women, one newly married woman, three young women in the process of looking for a husband, and two that were old enough to join them for dinner but too young for an introduction to real society, family meals had become a raucous affair. Leo sat in a chair set near the fireplace and just smiled. If the man could endure this with such calm, Julian suspected he was ice under fire. He made his way toward Leo thinking that the man ought to know what should be done about the mysterious watcher.

After accepting a drink from the footman, Julian said, "Someone was on the hill overlooking the graveyard. They watched the burial of Laurel, her child, and her husband. Jake and I could see that he had been there, see where he walked to his horse, but when we tried to follow the hoofprints they left, the damned things faded away only a few feet from the tree."

"Did you travel along a ways in each direction to see if they turned up again?"

"Yes, and there was nothing. It was as if whoever had been crouched there climbed on some sort of Pegasus beast and flew away."

"Too careful to hide his tracks. Always a bad sign."

"That is what I thought." He told him about what Chloe had felt as it had been the reason he had gone looking in the first place.

"Then it was definitely not a friend up there. But was it Arthur? That is the question, eh? I would think Arthur would be as far away from here as he could be, even out of the country. My people tell me that he sold Beatrice's jewels and walked away with a very heavy purse. It would have been more than enough for most men to sail away into a fine new life. Another question—would Arthur think it was enough? I was also told that some of Simone's people are lurking about also looking for Arthur, and not to kindly thank him for all his help. That would be another reason any sane man would leave, go as far away as he can."

"And here the question becomes—is Arthur still sane? If he ever was."

Leo nodded. "One has to question his sanity when he coldly plans to murder three of his closest family so that he can take the title. It has happened before, however. Cold and unfeeling but not necessarily insane."

"Talking about Arthur again?" asked Chloe as she walked up and curled her arm around Julian's. "Think he was my watcher?"

"There is a chance," said Julian. "It is just that it makes no sense. He was always smart, always cunning, and yet he lingers in the very place where people hunt him down?"

"But you have not been able to catch him yet, thus still smart and still cunning. He also needs money to get away and live somewhere else in the comfort he craves." She looked around the large salon. "A lot of expensive things here, and I wager you have a safe which holds even more. Probably much easier to carry and sell, too."

"Like Beatrice's jewelry," murmured Leo.

"It is possible that Arthur would know how to get into the safe. He would certainly have found where it is with all the time he had to look for it over the last few years. But, Chloe, it is not just us who are looking for him. Simone's people are, too. He promised them something and he did not get it for them. They seek, er, restitution of some sort. They want him dead. We would at least attempt to take him alive so that he can stand trial for the murders he has committed."

Chloe saw Lady Evelyn signal that it was time to go in to dinner and tugged Julian toward the door. Leo escorted Lady Evelyn and walked right behind them. Any more discussion about Arthur would have to wait, for the two older ladies would not allow such harsh topics to be discussed at the table. They did not want their daughters to hear about murders and theft and adultery. Chloe almost grinned, for she was certain the daughters would eat it up with a spoon.

It was not until they retired to the salon with cakes and wine, the daughters all sent to their rooms, that the subject of Arthur was brought up again. Chloe leaned into Julian as Leo told the older women what had happened and what Julian had found and had not found. She watched Lady Mildred and breathed a sigh of relief. There was no grief visible on the woman's narrow face. Mildred did not care about the fate of her husband, but she was worried about the safety and happiness of her daughters.

"Arthur will do whatever he can to get as much money as he can before he leaves," Lady Mildred said bluntly. "He is arrogant enough to think he can elude everyone and come away the victor. I would not be at all surprised if he blames each and every one of us for all of his failures."

She briefly looked so unhappy that Chloe started to move, thinking of comforting her, but Julian tightened his grip around her shoulders and held her back.

"He sees my three daughters as one of my biggest failures."

Realizing the woman's pain was for her daughters, who had never known a father's love, Chloe sent Lady Mildred a sympathetic look. "A man who, when he fails, always finds someone else to blame."

"That is Arthur. He never does anything wrong. I bore only girls, so it was my fault. He did not get the earldom, so it was your father's fault first," she said to Julian, "and then your fault, especially since you had the audacity to breed a son. Another heir. And Anthony is at fault for surviving the hard first years. You, Chloe, are at fault because you took the child to safety instead of just leaving him out there to die. I could go on for days about all the things that have never been Arthur's fault. He will think you owe him all he can steal simply because you stood in his way and he could not get it all."

"So, he will try to rob you and probably kill a few of us. At least we know what he wants. Now we only have to find out where he is and when he will strike," stated Chloe.

"I think that in the morning it might be an idea to begin another search," said Leo.

It was late by the time the men had finished making plans for a search in the morning. Chloe was yawning before she even crawled into bed. She decided the constant fear that Arthur would return and hurt someone she cared about was wearing on her. When Julian crawled in beside her, she curled up next to him and sighed.

Julian could tell that Chloe was really too tired to make love, so he just held her and stroked her back. He was weary as well and he suspected it was for much the same reason she was. The battle was not over but they could not find the enemy.

By the time he had gone over all the possibilities for why Arthur would still be in England, even near Colinsmoor, Chloe was sound asleep and he grinned. He had been a greedy man since their marriage. It was only fair to allow her to have a respite. Then he tensed. He was not sure, but it had been nearly a month since they had first made love, and not once had Chloe turned him away because she had her woman's time.

Staring down at her, he tried to control his rising excitement. Yesterday he had caught her napping in the middle of the day and not a light doze, either, but a good, hard sleep. She was eating a lot more as well. Julian was sure that her breasts were a little bigger, but he had put that down to the fact that she was eating more. Those two things also happened when a woman was with child. He had studied the signs closely when Beatrice had gotten with child and could recite them as well as he once had his alphabet for his grandmother.

Julian tugged Chloe a little closer and pressed a kiss to the top of her head. He would give it another week and then he would quietly ask his mother what she thought, for he was certain that Chloe had no idea. A slow grin curved his mouth as he heard Leo's warning in his mind, only now it sounded like a promise. *Like rabbits.*

* * *

Chloe rinsed out her mouth and then slowly slumped against the wall right near the close-stool in case she had to use it again. It must have been the fish, she thought, and then frowned. She had decided not to eat the fish last night. Her hand on her roiling belly, she tried to think of what she had eaten and as the list grew, she wondered why Leo was not there making the *oink* sound. Obviously making love day and night with her new husband had given her the appetite of a six-foot man.

She weakly responded to a rap on the door and Lady Evelyn slipped inside. The woman's eyes widened and she rushed to Chloe's side. Chloe retained enough sense to slam shut the lid to the close-stool but had the sinking feeling that she had not really hidden the fact that she had been ill. Lady Evelyn placed her palm on Chloe's head and cheeks, and Chloe savored the feel of that cool hand.

"You do not look well at all, dear," the woman said and studied her very intently. "Hmmm, just a moment."

When Chloe heard Lady Evelyn ask a maid to bring her some sweetened tea and lightly buttered toast, Chloe really wanted to refuse it. The mere thought of food had her retching over the close-stool again. This time Lady Evelyn bathed her forehead with a cool cloth as she helped Chloe back to bed. Chloe decided it was rather nice to be coddled.

Once the tea and toast arrived, the sweet Lady Evelyn turned into a tough general and made Chloe drink every drop and eat every bite, but very slowly. By the time she was done, Chloe had to admit that she felt a great deal better. Since the maid had cleaned away the mess she had made in the close-stool, even the room smelled better.

"Thank you for forcing me to eat that," she said as Lady Evelyn moved the tray aside and sat down on the edge of the bed. "I do feel a great deal better. I think I just ate far too much last night. In truth, when I tried to think of what made me sick and began to remember exactly what I had eaten, I was surprised Leo had never come over to me and made the *oink* noise."

"I did notice that you had a very healthy appetite last evening and the evening before."

When Chloe thought on her explanation for that she blushed. "I intend to keep a closer watch on that. Your cook is too good, I think."

"She is excellent. Now, I am going to ask you a few questions, and one or two may seem very personal but I want you to answer them, if you please."

"Of course," Chloe said, but she began to feel a little uneasy.

"When did you last have your courses?"

That was certainly personal, Chloe thought and opened her mouth to answer, but suddenly hesitated. "I must have had them before I got married, yet I do not recall. Odd, it is not something one usually forgets. And I am as regular as clockwork. Perhaps I have just been too nervous, anxious, or some such thing. I have heard that that can affect those things."

"It is one thing that can," Lady Evelyn murmured. "Have you been tired a lot lately?"

Again Chloe thought of why that might be and

blushed. "Some. Fell asleep yesterday afternoon, and I have never done that."

"And Mhave you ever spent the first few moments after waking up with your head over the close-stool?"

"Nay, and I do not understand, for I am never ill."

Lady Evelyn took Chloe's hands in hers and smiled faintly. "There are a lot more questions I could ask, but I do not believe there is any need. Chloe, you have not had your courses recently, and since you do not recall when, I feel sure it is because you have missed a turn. You are eating like a draft horse. You are sleeping a lot. And, final proof, you are turning your stomach inside out within the first few moments after you wake up. You, my dear, are with child."

Chloe just stared at the woman for a moment and went through that list again in her head. "Oh. I thought it was just because Julian is a very demanding husband."

Lady Evelyn giggled. "Well, yes, it is."

Placing her hand on her belly, Chloe felt a sense of wonder spread through her. "Do you really think so?"

"I really think so but it would not hurt to wait, oh, another week or two to see if the symptoms continue or if your courses arrive. Are you pleased?"

"Oh, aye. I am pleased." She suddenly heard Julian telling her what Leo had warned him about concerning the Wherlockes and the Vaughns. "Damn, Leo is right again."

"About what?"

"He told Julian to be careful because Wherlockes and Vaughns are fertile."

"But that is wonderful, dear."

"Not in the way he put it."

"Ah, and how did Leo put it?"

"Like rabbits." When Lady Evelyn burst into giggles like a young girl, Chloe could not help but join in.

Julian rode beside Leo, keeping his gaze fixed upon the ground. It seemed to him that the trail had become suspiciously clear. He glanced up at the sky and realized it was late afternoon and they were hours from Colinsmoor. That realization sharpened his growing unease into fear.

"This is wrong, Leo," he said, reining in to a halt.

"Aye," murmured Leo. "I was just thinking the same thing."

"A trap?" Julian looked all around but saw no one except for two horsemen ambling down the road, and they both wore uniforms so he did not consider them a threat.

"Possible. There is a much worse possibility, however."

Julian paled. "We have been led away from Colinsmoor."

"Aye." Leo frowned toward the two soldiers. "Those men are moving this way fast."

"I find it hard to believe that a trap is two dusty soldiers," Julian said but he pulled his pistol, holding it ready in case the soldiers did the same.

"Julian!"

"By damn," Julian whispered and nearly dropped his pistol as he recognized the voice and a moment later recognized the rider. "Nigel!"

Leo stayed on his horse and neatly caught up the

reins of Julian's when the man leapt to the ground to go and greet his brother. The man with Nigel did the same as that young man also dismounted hurriedly. As the two brothers hugged and slapped each other on the back, Leo nodded to the man who had ridden up beside him. He was big, broad-shouldered and black-haired. Even his skin was dusky but he still had those somewhat eerily silver eyes.

"Greetings, Bened," he said. "Long journey?"

"Bloody long, and I do not ever wish to see the sea again," the man replied in his deep voice, his Welsh accent heavy in each word.

"Hate the bloody ocean myself. Even the short float over to the Continent." He glanced toward Nigel and Julian, whose reunion had calmed down a little. "Any trouble?"

"Two tries. Both failed. Both men dead."

"Good work."

"How has it gone here?"

"A lot busier. Oh, and Chloe is now the Countess of Colinsmoor."

"Well, damn." He glanced toward Julian. "Wife is dead, then."

"Very. We think the uncle hanged her. She was left dangling from a tree on Colinsmoor land." Leo smiled when Julian brought his brother close and introduced him and Nigel then introduced Bened, a little surprised to discover that Leo was the man's cousin.

"I have been being watched, have I not?" asked Nigel.

Before Leo could respond, Bened said, "Aye. Complaining?"

Nigel laughed. "Not at all." He looked at Julian. "So where is this new wife you just told me about? She does not like to ride?"

"Oh, she is a very good rider, but she is at home. I left hours ago and I believe we really need to head back."

"Think it is a trap?"

"Yes, but not, I fear, for us."

Nigel quickly remounted and they all started toward Colinsmoor. "So tell me what has happened and what you think might be happening now."

Julian quickly ran through all the events of the past few weeks and then presented the concern he and Leo had just begun to feel. "There is no trap here, so we can only think that we have been led astray." He reined in when Bened suddenly halted, dismounted, and crouched by the trail they had followed. "What is he doing?" he asked Nigel.

"He always tells me he is reading it," replied Nigel and then shrugged. "Have no idea what that means but he has never led me wrong yet."

Bened remounted and nodded. "Not a trap and it was a lone rider, not too heavy, and simply ambling through here a few hours ago."

Julian cursed and started toward Colinsmoor. He kept his horse at an easy pace, not wishing to exhaust the animal and losing his mount altogether. His only comfort in having been so fooled was that Leo had also been tricked.

"There are men there, Julian," Leo said. "We did not leave them unprotected."

"I know. That is all that is keeping me from

riding this poor horse to death in some crazed effort to get there as fast as possible."

"If he attacks the house, he could hurt Mama, the girls, even his own wife and daughters," said Nigel. "Why would he do that?"

"Because we think he has gone mad. He killed Beatrice, his mistress and ally for several years. The only reason we are not sure that he has already tried once to kill Mama and the girls is because Beatrice was alive then. It could have been her plan. Chloe thinks it is him."

"Then it is," said Bened and shrugged when the Kenwoods looked at him. "Chloe has the knowing."

"And what do you have?" asked Julian.

"When we are still out of sight of your home I will be able to tell you if your enemies are there. Do not need to see them to know."

"Damnation, but that must have been helpful out in that wilderness."

"Very," said Nigel and a shadow crossed his eyes that told Julian his young brother had seen more of the ugliness of war than he had ever planned on. "He can get right up behind them before they even know he is there, but he will know where each and every one of the bastards are. Man could steal the saddle you are sitting on and you would hardly notice."

"Not that good," murmured Bened, and then he looked at Julian. "But I will know where your enemies are and how many of them they are. That might help."

"Let us just hope they are not there and we worry for naught," said Julian, although he did not believe in his own assurances.

"Aye. But do not forget Chloe. She has the knowing."

She did, but even she admitted that it did not work every time she would like it to, thought Julian. He just prayed that, if their enemies were going after Colinsmoor, Chloe's gift was kind enough to give her a warning.

Chapter 18

Chloe woke up with a start and it took her a moment to realize that she had fallen asleep on the settee again. Her heart was pounding and she felt the bitter taste of fear in her mouth. Slowly sitting up, she tried to recall what her dream had been about and then her eyes widened as the images rushed back into her mind and the warning chill she was all too familiar with washed over her.

It had all started out so pleasantly. She had seen Julian and a younger man who looked a great deal like him laughing and slapping each other on the back in that strange way men did. Then everything had begun to grow dark. Shadows crept toward the house. There was blood splashed upon the outer wall of the stable. A young man slumped on the ground not moving. The shadows kept coming closer.

Chloe could feel her heart pounding with fear but she kept forcing the memory of the dream to the forefront of her mind. The shadows burst into the house. They were big, and she sensed evil and anger. Knives flashed. Screams echoed in the halls.

There was blood on the wall. One shadow kept moving toward a small bed and Chloe realized it was in the nursery.

"Anthony," she whispered in terror and leapt to her feet.

As she ran to the nursery, she suddenly understood. The house was about to be attacked. There were armed men outside to protect them, but her dream had shown the shadows right in the house, killing and destroying everything they touched, so she could not be sure that the men guarding them would be enough to save them. Not knowing how much time she had to warn everyone, she banged on the bedchamber doors as she ran past them and yelled for everyone to gather in the front hall. By the time she reached the nursery, Dilys had a sleepy Anthony dressed and in her arms.

"Heard your warning, miss," Dilys said.

"Good girl. Get him to the room in the wine cellar that Julian showed us. I will try to get everyone else rounded up and down there." Chloe took a moment to kiss Anthony's forehead and stroke his head.

"Aye, miss," Dilys said and ran for the stairs while Chloe resumed her search of the house.

"Heavens, child," said Lady Mildred as she stepped out of her bedchamber, her spectacles still perched on her nose. "What is all the noise?"

"We all have to get to the room in the wine cellar," she said. "Where are your daughters?"

"Here, m'lady," said Helena, the oldest of Mildred's three daughters, the two younger ones huddled behind her.

"Down into the hiding room. You remember how to get to it?"

"Yes, m'lady." Helena grasped her mother by the arm. "Come, Mama, we need to hurry."

"But I have not heard a sound."

"You will soon, Lady Mildred," said Chloe. "If anyone is down in the front hall, make sure they understand that they must go with you."

"But do we not have men outside to guard us?"

"Mildred, I think you better do as Chloe asks," said Lady Evelyn as she stepped out of her room. "Are you sure we in the house are in danger?" she asked Chloe.

"Aye, m'lady," she replied. "The shadows came into the house. I went for Anthony first because a shadow was making its way to the nursery."

"He is safe now?"

"Dilys took him right down there."

"What the bloody hell do you mean by this talk of shadows?" demanded Mildred.

Chloe almost smiled at the way all three of Mildred's daughters gasped and stared at their mother in shock. "Perhaps Lady Evelyn can explain. I have to make sure everyone is headed down to that room."

Lady Evelyn nodded. "I will explain it all to you, Mildred, as soon as we get into that room. Chloe?" she called over her shoulder.

"Aye, m'lady?" Chloe answered absently as she peeked into each bedchamber.

"Remember that you might have more than yourself to worry about now."

"Oh." Chloe could not stop herself from putting her hand on her belly. "I will remember."

"Good. Then I shall see you soon."

Chloe marveled at how Lady Evelyn could make an order sound so polite as she watched the women go down the stairs. They paused only to pull Julian's two sisters in with them. Chloe hurried back to checking the bedchambers and then rushed down the servants' stairs. In the kitchen she found two kitchen maids huddled by the stove and shooed them down to the wine cellar.

The girls argued that the cook had told them to stay in the kitchen, and just as Chloe was reminding them that she outranked the cook, shouting and a few shots sounded from outside. Chloe rushed to bar the kitchen door even as she ordered the girls to get into the wine cellar. This was going to be a very close call, she thought as she moved away from the door, and a moment later a shot shattered the glass in the window over the huge sink.

"I do not understand, Evelyn," said Mildred as they made their way down the stairs, servants in front and behind. "I hear nothing and I saw nothing. Everything is quiet out there. Why are we all rushing into that small dark room?"

"Mildred, Chloe, well, knows things," Evelyn tried to explain. "Can you not trust me when I say that if she believes we need to get into that little room, then we really need to get into that little room."

"Because Chloe knows things?"

"She has the sight, Mama," Helena said quietly and her two sisters nodded in agreement.

"The sight? Where did you get that idea?" asked Mildred.

Helena blushed a little. "Because I heard Julian and Lord Sir Leopold speaking of it. The earl believes in it," she added quickly when she saw the doubt on her mother's face.

"There have always been rumors about such things concerning the Wherlockes and the Vaughns. That does not mean it is true."

At that moment two terrified scullery maids came running down the stairs, nearly knocking over the Kenwoods. There were muffled shouts of alarm and then the crash of glass breaking. Lady Evelyn grabbed the arm of one of the scullery maids and then had to lightly slap her to make her stop screaming.

"Where is Lady Kenwood?" she demanded.

"She was in the kitchen and told us to be coming down here right quick. Them men is shooting at us, m'lady. They shot right inta the window in the kitchen."

Lady Evelyn turned to start back up the stairs only to have Mildred grab her by the arm and hold her back. "I have to go find Chloe."

"This house is so huge it is easy to get lost, and you mean to search for her while men are shooting into the house? You will only get yourself shot," Mildred said and pulled Evelyn along with her. "And while we are waiting for her to join us, you can explain this whole thing to me in a far clearer way than just saying Chloe *knows* things."

"Mildred, I am almost sure that she is with child."

Mildred stumbled a little but then straightened and kept on walking. "You will be of no help to her running around up there when you do not even know where she has gone. She is no tenderly raised child and she obviously has a very useful gift. She will find a place to hide if she cannot get down here before whoever those people are break in." Mildred sighed. "I am sorry if I sound hard."

"No, practical, and that is what is needed. Searching for her now would be much akin to trying to find the proverbial needle in the haystack. I could not even call out for her, as that could bring their attention on me or her. So I will come along quietly."

Just as Lady Evelyn stepped into the crowded room and prepared to shut the door, a frantic Dilys pushed her way to the front. "You have to stay here, Dilys. Where is Anthony?"

"I do not know, m'lady," she choked out. "He was right with me and I set him on his feet just as people started to push in here and then he was just gone. I have to find him."

Mildred pushed a stunned Lady Evelyn farther into the room, blocked Dilys's attempt to get out, and shut the door. "Now, we shall be calm and try to think of a sensible way to find that child and Lady Kenwood. Rushing out into the middle of a battle will just get one or both of you killed."

"Mildred, it is Anthony," protested Lady Evelyn. "He is out there where there is shooting and men fighting, and—"

"And he is a smaller target than either of you women. He is also a very clever little boy who has the wit to hide." Several people murmured a hearty agreement and Mildred fleetingly wondered what that little devil had been up to. "We need a plan. No one is rushing out there to do anything unless they can give me a plan."

A lot of people started whispering to each other, but no one immediately stepped forward. Mildred stared at Evelyn's tear-filled eyes and sighed. If none of these younger and stronger people came up with a plan or an offer to enact a good plan, then she and Evelyn would go together to find Anthony and Chloe. It would destroy Julian if he lost either of them even if he was being a blind fool and not seeing what was right in front of him. She nodded in response to Evelyn's pleading look and saw her relax. Mildred just hoped someone came up with a plan, because she really did not wish to go out there even though she loved that little boy and was very fond of Chloe. She had also lost her spectacles on the stairs and her vision was not that keen.

Chloe kept crouched low as she made her way toward the stairs down to the wine cellar. As far as she knew she had managed to herd everyone down-stairs. Now it was time to herd herself down there.

Just as she crawled in front of a linen closet she heard a whimper. Trying very hard to be quiet in case someone was already in the house, Chloe eased open the door. The wide, tear-drenched eyes of an ash-bucket girl stared back at her. The girl could not be much more than ten or she was very small for her age. Chloe realized she needed to meet all the servants and not just those who warranted the stature of being addressed by their last name.

"Do you know who I am?" she asked in a whisper.

The girl wiped her dripping nose on her sleeve and nodded. "You be the new lady, the one what married the earl."

"Good, then you know you should do as I say. Your name?"

"Brindle."

"Do you know how to get down to the wine cellar?"

"Aye, m'lady, but why would I be wanting to go there?"

Obviously someone had neglected to tell the lowest-ranking servants that there was a place they could go to be safe. Chloe made a note to herself that she would find out why they were not told and then personally show every one of the lower servants the room. Since most of them were very young boys or girls, it made her angry that no one was looking out for them.

"Because there is a room there to hide in with a door so heavy and thick even a bullet would not get through. Now, are you alone?"

A dirty little face suddenly appeared over her shoulder. "I be here, too, m'lady."

"And you are?"

"Drew, the boot boy, Mama," said a voice by her shoulder that sent shards of icy fear into her heart.

Julian immediately slowed his mount to a halt at one signal from Leo. "I think I heard a shot," he protested but trusted Leo to know what he was doing. In truth, the other three men were far more experienced in such matters than he was, and he decided he would be wise to follow them no matter how much higher in social rank he was.

"Aye, m'lord, you did that," said Bened in a voice that would make one think they were talking about a bird's call. "There is fighting up ahead." He dismounted. "Be back in but a minute."

The man disappeared into the shadows of early evening so quickly it startled Julian. "Where is he going?"

"To see what we are up against," replied Nigel. "He has been trying to teach me how to move like that but I am not sure I will ever get the trick of it."

"He is good," agreed Leo. "I think my cousin Owain might be better, though."

"How many bloody cousins do you have?" asked Julian.

"I told you—"

"I know—like rabbits."

Julian suddenly thought of the suspicions he had had about Chloe last night and his heart clenched. It was not only his wife down there but quite possibly his *pregnant* wife. His mother, his sisters, his cousins, his aunt, and his son, the son he had only just found. He could lose everything that mattered to him. Fear clutched like a vise around his chest.

"Breathe, Julian," snapped Nigel as he reached over and shook his older brother by the arm. "We will get them all out safely. They went to the room in the wine cellar. I am certain of it. Do you not recall how often Mother made us practice getting to that room from several different ways?"

Before Julian could reply to his brother's assurances, a sound made Nigel draw his pistol and turn, all the while keeping his mount steady. "Who is there?" Nigel demanded.

About a dozen men crept out of the shadows, their hands held out where they could be seen. It took Julian a moment to see that Bened was standing behind them. He looked closer and sighed.

"It is all right," he told Bened. "They are not the ones attacking the house."

"Know that, m'lord," said Bened. "Just wondering if they could be of use or would it be better to send them home."

"We came to help, m'lord," said Jake as he stepped forward. "We heard the shots and then Kip, he is the fourth footman and my nephew, he came running saying that someone was attacking the house. We thought we could help. Some of us have pistols."

Julian did not know whether to laugh or cry. He was well aware of what a poor man's pistol was like, usually some cast-off mended and mended again until the one firing was fortunate it did not blow up in his face. Yet, he was touched. After the way he had failed these men, they were here ready to fight for his family as he had never fought for theirs.

"I think we will know better what we are about to do when Bened tells us what we are facing. Then we can actually make a plan that might help a few of us come out of this alive."

"You have twenty well-armed men down there, most of them still outside. Your men are putting up a good fight but I am thinking they were surprised, for a few are down and I do not think they will all rise again. At least three men have slipped inside already. I heard nothing to say they found anyone in there. By now you would have heard a woman scream, but there has been none of that. The men have encircled the house. A few of your men are on the roof and they are holding the men on the ground down so that they have to crawl if they want to move ahead. If you want to move ahead I can tell you the best place for a man to go, where to stop until I wave you on, and then you move again right up to the house."

"I have to move ahead, Bened. Except for Nigel, my whole family is in there including my son and my wife, who just may be carrying my child."

"Told you. Like rabbits."

Nigel snickered and Julian wondered how these men could be so calm, make jests, and even talk when this siege was going on. He supposed it was because of what they did. Nigel was a soldier and had been for almost ten years. Julian was not exactly sure what Leo did but he suspected the man's work for the government was not all reports and gathering information. Bened was also a soldier, but he had the feeling the man was the embodiment of the stoic soldier.

He, on the other hand, was an earl. It carried a lot of weight in the courts and in society, but in this situation it was next to worthless. The only thing he was sure of was that he had to get to his family and, he hoped his mother and sisters forgave him the thought, but right at that moment that was Chloe and Anthony.

It was at that moment that Julian realized he loved Chloe. He also realized that he had never really loved Beatrice. He had been entranced, seduced, and bewitched, but never really in love. With Chloe it was love and he had no doubt about it, knew it with a certainty that had him wondering why he had taken so long to acknowledge the feeling. Now all he had to do was save Chloe so that he could tell her and, he prayed, pull the same emotion out of her.

"You tell me what you think I, or we, should do, and I will do it."

Bened looked at Nigel, who just idly waved his hand indicating Bened should lead. When had his brother grown up, Julian wondered. When Nigel had first joined the military, he had been cocky and had thought that no one could know anything better than he did or do anything better than he did. He had obviously gained enough maturity to realize the error of his thinking. Shaking free of his straying thoughts and hammering down his emotions, he dismounted and listened to Bened's plans with the others.

Everything moved quickly after that and Julian soon found himself slipping through the shadows, his pistol in his hand and his heart in his throat. On one side of him crept Jake and on the other crept Nigel, a large intimidating knife in his hand that he seemed to know what to do with. He was obviously going to have to get to know his brother all over again.

"There is where we are supposed to go," whispered

Nigel when he signaled to stop and wait for Bened's signal before they went any farther. "Front door, straight in and then divide. You remember the directions for inside the house, Jake?"

"Aye, sir. No need to tell me again, as I been in there."

Even in the dim light of a fading moon Julian could see the blush on the man's face and knew just what Jake had been called to the house to do. He nearly growled, except that he was sure that sound would carry farther than the soft whispers they were using now. "I thought you had a family, a wife and children."

"I do, m'lord, and I sorely love my Tibby, but men what said nay ended up dead. My Tibby told me that she knew I was not wanting to go but she would rather me let that whore play with my jock a time or two than try to find what pit she put my bony arse into."

"Sounds like a wife to me," said Nigel.

"And, sad to say, it sounds like Beatrice to me. I am sorry, Jake, and tell your wife I beg her pardon for not stopping the woman long, long ago."

"My Tibby will be right pleased to think your lordship done begged her pardon. Of course, that will only be after she rips a strip off me with her tongue for telling you."

"Do not trouble yourself. I begin to suspect Beatrice used my lands as her own little stud farm." He grimaced. "I still do not understand how I never saw it."

"Fair face like that hides a lot and the things she did, well, just hard to believe, is all. If it be any comfort, I made sure I was real bad at it and she never called on me again."

Julian could not believe how badly he wanted to laugh. He felt it must be because he was so bone-deep afraid for his family and nervous that he would not be able to do what he needed to do to reach them and keep them safe. Then he saw the signal from Bened he had been waiting for and all three of them began a fast creep toward the house.

"Obviously no one here can think of a plan or has the backbone to enact it," snapped Lady Evelyn, and then she looked at Mildred. "My grandson is but three years old and my new daughter may well be carrying the earl's child. Either get out of my way or come with me."

"You were always a bossy girl," Mildred said calmly as she opened the door.

"I will come with ye, m'lady," said Dilys as she shoved her way to the front of the shamefaced crowd.

Lady Evelyn touched the young girl's face. "No, sweet girl. I could never rest knowing I sent such a young girl out there. You wait here. I will bring Anthony back to you."

"Are we going or not?" asked Mildred.

"Going," replied Evelyn.

"Mother," whispered Helena.

"What is it, dear? I really must go or Evelyn is going to run off and get herself killed."

"Take this."

Both Evelyn and Mildred stared at the large, gleaming knife Helena handed Mildred. Evelyn suddenly grinned and took it away from Mildred. "That is definitely your daughter, Mildred," she said as she hurried out of the door.

Mildred cast a last look at her sweet-faced child and said, "Good girl." Then she hurried after Evelyn as fast as she could without her spectacles. "Wait, Evelyn, we should still try to have a plan."

"My plan is that we whisper," Evelyn said very softly, "and I think we had best stay together. It would be faster to search separately, but neither one of us could defend ourselves against a grown man without help. I also think I need new servants."

"Chloe needs new servants."

"Quite right, and she better find some with some backbone."

"That girl Dilys has some."

"Hush," Evelyn whispered close to Mildred's ear and they slipped into the kitchen. It only took her a moment to see that neither Anthony or Chloe were there. As she turned to leave she caught sight of the huge iron pan the cook used to do her sausages and she grinned. She took it down off the ceiling hook and handed it to Mildred. To her surprise her friend hefted it a few times and then nodded in satisfaction. She was just about to continue on to another room when she heard heavy footsteps coming their way. Evelyn pushed Mildred behind the door while she slipped behind the far side of the huge kitchen oven.

A man came in, a sword at his side and a pistol in his hand. As he turned around looking over the kitchen in disgust as if he were some self-important French chef, Evelyn noted that a pistol was tucked in his waistband and the hilt of another knife stuck out of the top of his boot. Unless they were very clever, Evelyn knew she and Mildred could never defeat such a huge, well-armed man.

She signaled to Mildred that she wanted her to hit him over the head with the pan. Mildred looked at the pan and then at the man's head as if testing for distance. Evelyn shook her head and then made a noise, just a quiet shuffling of feet. It was enough to cause the man to look her way and Evelyn did her best to look afraid. The smile he gave her made it a lot easier to look terrified. He took a step toward her and then Evelyn heard a sound she silently prayed she would never hear again. The man's eyes rolled up in his head and he fell to his knees before toppling face-down on the stone floor. Evelyn winced, deciding the noise his face made as it hit the stone was nearly as bad as the sound of an iron pan hitting a head.

"That were so fine, m'lady," said a scratchy little voice.

Evelyn sniffed, smelled a dirty little boy, and looked behind the oven. She reached in, grabbed a bone-thin arm, and pulled out a filthy boy. At a guess she would say he was seven, but she had the feeling he had not eaten well for a very long time.

"And who are you?" she asked.

"I be Jem, m'lady, and I be the pot boy."

"Why are you not down in the room in the wine cellar?"

"Cook told me to hide up here. T'aint enough room down there for dirty boys." He leaned back a little. "Doan beat me, m'lady. I still got bruises from that last woman and I be liking to heal a mite first. Oh, m'lady, you are looking right fierce."

"You are, Evelyn, dear. Calm down. You are scaring the child," Mildred said in the voice she always used on her daughters when they got their tempers up and could not seem to calm down. "We still have to find Anthony and Chloe."

"You looking for the little earl?" Jem asked and both women nodded. "I seen him go that way toward the big hall a wee bit ago. The new lady came through first and she sent the two scullery maids down to the room."

"Then that big hall is where we shall go," said Evelyn as she stood up, still holding the boy by the arm. "You need to go down into the wine cellar and—bugger—"

"Evelyn!"

"Oh, m'lady, you should not be sayin' that word."

"I like it. I cannot send him down there because those cowards in that room will not open the door for him, I am certain."

"Then he goes with us," said Mildred.

"Why should I do that?" asked Jem.

"Because we have weapons."

"So does I." Tugging Lady Evelyn along with him, Jem reached behind the oven and brought out a thick, short club. "See?"

"Very impressive." Evelyn saw him frown in confusion and smiled. "A proud weapon."

"What about the man's weapons?"

"Oh." Evelyn did not really want to touch the man but decided it was not wise to leave him armed and behind them just in case Mildred had not actually crushed his skull. "Best disarm him, then." She hastily stripped him of his weapons and hid them behind the huge cupboard against the wall, keeping one of the pistols for herself. "Now. Let us go find the little earl—I do like that—and Chloe before they get hurt." She tapped the boy on the head and silently hoped she would not contract lice. "You stay close to us and do just what I say."

"We going to help the little earl?" asked Jem.

"That is my plan. Do you know him?"

"Aye, he gives me food when Cook ain't looking. He gets a real fierce look on his face like you done when he hears that I doan get no more than a scrap or two a day. He be a good lad."

"Yes, he is, and after we rescue him and his mother and all these ruffians are gone, I intend to show my new daughter how a countess disciplines her staff—starting with a fat, greedy pig of a cook."

As Evelyn marched away, Mildred looked at the little boy following her and sighed. Poor little boy was mad in love with the dowager countess. Mildred hurried to keep up, for she had to make sure Evelyn did not get herself killed. Never mind that it would upset Julian, Nigel, and the girls, plus many others—the pot boy would probably die of a broken heart.

Chapter 19

"Anthony!" Chloe cried and grabbed him. "What are you doing out of the room?"

"I had to get Jem. The cook lefted him in the kitchen."

"I saw the cook go into the room."

Anthony nodded vigorously. "But she lefted him in the kitchen."

"What do you mean—she left him behind?" It was the kitchen staff's duty to make sure everyone who worked in the kitchen was led out if there was an emergency. It was a rule that was put in place in case there was a fire, but men trying to get into one's home and shooting out windows was just as big an emergency.

"She said she would never take the filthy brat anywhere."

Chloe briefly admired the way Anthony could sound like so many adults when he was mouthing their own words. She then hoped that Julian knew how to find another cook because if what anything Anthony said was true, the one he had was going to be leaving. She did not care if the woman cooked the best apple tarts in the whole of the country. If Anthony was right, the woman had left a child in the kitchen while men fought all round the house and tried to get inside. She would not allow anyone like that at Colinsmoor.

"If he is still up here, we will get that boy," she promised, thinking on how they would pass near the kitchen on their way to where the Kenwood people all huddled in a too-small room. "What happened to Dilys?"

"I runned away from her when I could not see Jem."

"We shall discuss how naughty that was later, but we have to go now. All of us."

"We be fine right here," said Brindle.

"Nay, you are not. Where would you run to if some man opened the door? These men have guns. You can hear them."

Brindle shrugged her thin shoulders. "Then I will be shot."

There was such resignation in the child's face it took all of Chloe's willpower to fight the urge to pull her into her arms and hug her. Something was very wrong here. Anthony was speaking of a pot boy who was rarely fed, and now she had two very thin children hiding in the closet with the tablecloths and other linen. The two scullery maids had also been left behind to fend for themselves. Chloe could not believe that Julian would ever treat children this way, but she had no more time left to get answers to the many questions now rippling through her mind.

"No more arguing. We go now. We will find the

pot boy, Anthony." She held her hand out to Brindle. "Come along."

"Nay."

Chloe grabbed Brindle by the arm and pulled her out of the linen closet and the boy quickly followed. "You do not get to say nay to a countess, young lady, especially not when she is trying very hard to get you to safety. Hang on," she told Drew.

It was not easy, but Chloe shepherded the children toward the kitchen using a complicated path full of twists and turns. Each time she heard someone moving around, she went in the opposite direction. The kitchen was not that far away from where she needed to take them to safety, but if she kept winding her way through the house it could take a long time to get there. She kept everyone as close to the wall as she could because of the gunfire. Every now and then she could hear glass shatter as a bullet cut through it. Under the arm she had draped around Brindle and Drew she could feel the boy shaking. The men Julian and Leo had placed to guard the house were doing their best and she had the sinking feeling that some would die, but the men attacking the house were getting closer. She could actually hear them shout at each other.

The moment they entered the kitchen, Anthony broke free of her grasp and ran to the oven, peering behind it. The boy did not seem to notice the blood on the floor and she hoped he continued to be blind to it. Brindle glanced down at it and then looked at Chloe with wide, slightly frightened eyes. Chloe did not like to see the girl so frightened, but it was a far better look than the one of complete resignation to whatever fate handed out she had before. She held her finger to her lips and the little girl nodded.

"Jem is gone," Anthony said.

"I am sorry for that, darling boy, but we cannot search the house for him. We have to go to that room. There are four of us to worry about now. We must pray that Jem has found a safe place to hide."

"Mayhap you ought to pray for yourself."

Chloe shoved all three children behind her back even as she turned toward that voice. It was only barely recognizable, as was the man standing before her, a pistol in his hand. It was as feral as he looked. Arthur had definitely been living very rough since that last time she had seen him. His fine clothes were dirty and worn, his hair was dark with dirt and sweat, and his face looked as if he had aged ten years. It was in his eyes that she saw the madness that had gripped him.

"Greetings, Sir Arthur," she said. She clutched her hands in her skirts as any frightened woman might do, but she did it to hide the fact that she was holding her skirts out a little to further hide the children.

"Sir," he snarled and spat on the floor. "I should have been the earl."

"I believe you have made that clear. If not in word then in deed."

"You are the one who saved the brat." His voice carried a harsh accusation and he aimed the pistol right at her. "That was a damn good plan and you ruined it."

To her relief the children started slipping away. Chloe suspected it was the girl Brindle who was trying to get the two younger children out of reach and had the sense to use Arthur's distraction with her to the best advantage. The girl had the look of one who knew how to take responsibility for others. Chloe needed to make sure that Arthur stayed distracted until the children were safely out of his reach.

"You put him in my house. That made him mine, and I chose to let him live."

"I put him there to die, you stupid cow!"

"I am sorry, sir, but I could not allow that to happen."

"We be gone now."

The whispery words were hard to hear, but Chloe caught them and she gave a sigh of relief. To her dismay, the look on Arthur's face told her he had heard them, too. Chloe prayed that the children were already too far away for him to catch. All he would need was one look at Anthony and he would know whose child he was.

"What was that?" he demanded as he stared in the direction Brindle had taken the two boys.

"I have no idea."

"Liar. But then all women are. They are born to the art. At least Beatrice did not try to be something she was not. She was born a whore and she clung to that truth until the day she died."

"You mean the day you killed her, do you not?"

"Figured that out, did you?"

"It was not so hard. No one else had a reason, at least a reason that made any sense. You, however, had a lot of reasons, for she was destroying your plans for Colinsmoor."

"We had everything planned, but that fool Julian

just would not die. And you were there, always there. You saved him when he got stabbed in the alley, I know it. Save the baby, save the man. Busy. Well, you will not be able to save him this time, neither him nor his family. And by family I include that little brat."

"Your own family is here, too. Your wife and your daughters."

"Ah, God save me, that stupid cow. Could not even give me a son, could she. No, she just kept grunting out daughters. I have decided I am going to let her watch me kill the little bitches before I kill her. Make her feel the grief I felt each time she failed to give me my son. And then that fool Julian gets a son off Beatrice. Sweet Jesus, off Beatrice, who had rutted with near half the county and never once got with child.

"Well, he does not deserve a son. Weakling that he is. He could not bring himself to kill his wife even though she cuckolded him from the beginning. Ha, he cannot even be sure the boy is his. Beatrice spread her legs for any man, even the ditch-diggers if she liked the look of them. For all any of you know the brat is the get of some ditch-digger."

"Nay, he is Julian's son. He has the mark."

The fury that contorted Arthur's face was terrifying. Every part of Chloe's body was screaming at her to run but she knew that would only get her shot in the back. She could see her death in his eyes. He wanted to kill her simply because she had told him Anthony really was legitimate. Chloe forced herself not to put her hand over her stomach. If this madman suspected she might be carrying a child for

Julian, she knew he would shoot her dead before she could take her next breath. What had her terrified was that she could see no way out of this trap.

Julian slammed his fist in the face of the man who blocked his way to the wine cellar. He needed to get down there and reassure himself that his family was safe. Nigel covered his back as he shoved the unconscious man aside, but before he could take a step he heard Nigel curse. Slowly, his pistol at the ready, Julian turned around and nearly gaped. Standing only a few feet away were his son and two very thin children.

"Papa!" Anthony cried and ran to him.

Julian shoved his pistol in his waistband and caught his son up in his arms. He looked at the other two children and wondered where Anthony had found the waifs. The girl held tight to the hand of the little boy and watched him and Nigel as if they might turn on her at any moment. Anthony turned in his arms and pointed at the children.

"These are my fwiends, Papa. That is Brindle and that is Dew."

"Drew," the little boy muttered.

"I said that." Anthony took his father's face in his little hands. "You need to go gets Mama. A bad man has her in the kitchen. Brindle saw him."

Julian looked at the little girl again. It was difficult to guess what age she was, but he suspected she was a few years older than Anthony and could probably speak more clearly. There was wisdom in her eyes, one born of a hard life. He needed more information than the fact that a bad man had trapped Chloe in the kitchen. Julian handed Anthony to Nigel.

"That is your uncle Nigel, Anthony," he said as he took a careful step closer to the children, not wanting to frighten them. "He has just come home from far away. He was a soldier." Hearing Nigel and Anthony talking softly, Julian crouched down in front of the children. "Do you know who I am?"

"The earl," the girl replied. "I am Brindle. I empty the ash buckets. This is Drew. He is the boot boy."

Julian wondered why he had never seen them before, as well as why they looked as if they had not had a bath for months and maybe not a decent meal for at least that long. "I need you to tell me if you saw my wife, if you saw the countess."

Brindle nodded. "She is in the kitchen. We went to look for the pot boy but he was already gone. Then the man came behind her and stuck his big pistol right at her."

"She put us all behind her," said the little boy.

"She did that and she nudged me and I knew she wanted me to get the lads away, so I did. She kept her skirts held out a bit so that man would never see us and we crept away while she kept him looking right at her and talking to her and waving that pistol round. You going to go get her and kill that fool?"

"I will do my best. There is only the one man?"

"Just one, but he has a bad look on his face. A real bad look. Makes you feel like you better run real fast afore he starts looking at you with them mad eyes."

Julian stood up and looked at his brother.

"Guard the children. I will make my way to the kitchen and see what is happening there."

"I done just told you what is happening," said Brindle.

He forced himself to smile pleasantly when all he could think of at the moment was getting to Chloe as fast as he could. "I know, but I need to see where he is standing and what he carries for a pistol. It is important that I gather a bit more information or all I may accomplish is getting my wife killed."

"That be what he is going to do anyway," grumbled Brindle. "He got a killing look in his eye. Not just a rutting one."

"She called him Sir Arthur," said Drew. "He looks like the man what used to live here and liked to touch the girls, but dirtier. Go kill him now, because she was nice and I doan want him to be hurting her."

The words the two children said burned into Julian's brain but he had no time to think on this newest revelation—that his uncle abused very young girls. Now he had to go and try to save his wife. Moving silently, he made his way toward the kitchen. The sight that met his gaze nearly made him act foolishly. He wanted to cut his uncle down just for holding a gun on Chloe, for threatening her life, and, if the paleness of her skin was any indication, for frightening her. He did not need Nigel's silent presence at his back to know that would be a bad idea. Arthur still had his pistol aimed straight at Chloe's heart. Julian could not chance that the man might pull the trigger even as he died.

"Nay, he is Julian's son," Chloe said. "He has the mark."

Julian was stunned by the rage that twisted Arthur's once handsome features. Arthur must have thought that Julian was trying to fool everyone, might even have planned some grand denouement. The news that Anthony had the Kenwood birthmark had shattered the last hope that he might yet win this game, or, at the very least, win another seat at the card table.

A movement to the right of Arthur caught Julian's attention briefly. With one eye on his very still wife, he glanced in that direction and saw a filthy boy with a thick short club in his hand. He was staring at Arthur with a wild look of hatred. Suddenly, as if the boy sensed his presence, the boy glanced at Julian and Julian took that moment to slowly shake his head. He could not afford having the child try some grand rescue. Then, silently stepping up behind the boy came his mother and his aunt. Was anyone down in the room that had been so carefully built to keep the family safe, he thought a little wildly.

"I think I will wait until Julian is close enough to watch you die. He had once sworn that he would never take a wife again and yet, here he is, married to you, a filthy Wherlocke."

"Actually, I bathed today," she murmured.

"Are you foolish enough to think I will not kill you simply because you are a woman?"

"Nay, I know that that is your plan. You wish to wipe out the Kenwood line, at least the one you could rule."

Julian heard a very soft shuffle, as if someone had just tried to take a step with fully lifting his foot off the floor. Unfortunately, Arthur heard it too and looked at him. The man's eyes widened and he grabbed Chloe by one arm, dragging her across the thick table that had separated them. The soft cry of pain that escaped Chloe had Julian instinctively raising his pistol and aiming it at Arthur's head. Arthur then pushed her down so that she was lying half on the table on her back. He drew a knife from his belt and held it to Chloe's chest as he set his pistol down out of her reach and then, in a movement too swift to stop, he stabbed her in the upper part of her arm. The way he kept himself crouched near Chloe made it impossible for Julian to get a clear shot at him. Only a soft groan escaped Chloe, and Julian could tell that annoyed Arthur. Before Julian could even correct his aim and take a shot at Arthur, the man had Chloe back on her feet and pinned in his arms, using her slender body as his shield.

"Let her go, Arthur," Julian said, aching to grab her and ease her pain.

"No, I think not. I need to get out of here, and because of her, you are going to let me. Now move aside so I can return her to her cottage myself."

"Why would you take her to a cottage that has been empty for years?"

"Because that is where she should have died years ago. I will not make the mistake of sending fools to do my work for me. I will do it and you can find her body on the moors later. It is only fair. I lost my love when Beatrice died and now you will lose yours. I hope you have your next wife already chosen, for you will soon lose this one."

Chloe was just wondering if, in his madness,

Arthur thought she was the woman who had had the stillborn child, but she was not able to ponder that mystery for long. A noise at the kitchen door grabbed Arthur's attention. Chloe hissed in a breath between her teeth when his sudden movement as he turned sideways caused her wound to scream in pain. He could now keep an eye on the growing crowd encircling the kitchen and on the man who now stood big, and tall, and silent in the doorway. He aimed his pistol right at Bened.

"Greetings, cousin," Chloe said, pleased to hear that there was only a slight hint of the pain tearing through her to be heard in her voice. "Sorry to drag you into our troubles."

"Mine, too, love. As the brother of that earl you married is my friend and soon-to-be partner, and the fact that you are my favorite cousin, it all becomes my trouble as well."

Chloe smiled. Bened was speaking in Welsh. She knew that meant he soon intended to give her some order that might put an end to the problem of Arthur. Bened was her guardian angel, she decided, and nearly laughed. Then she decided that the loss of blood was making her crazed.

"Just let me know what to do before I bleed to death," she said to him in Welsh.

"When I say *down* in English, my little seer, you fall as fast and hard as you can. I need a clear shot at the bastard's head."

"Understood."

"What the hell are you talking about? What is that gibberish you speak?" demanded Arthur, and Chloe could hear the rising panic in his voice. He was cornered and he knew it. *Now would be a good time to help me, Bened*, she thought.

"It is the fine old language of Wales," Bened said in his deep, almost soothing voice as he aimed his pistol at Arthur's head. "I will ask you to leave go of my cousin now, if you please. If you do not, then you will die."

Julian started and would have said something if Nigel had not pinched the back of his neck. He knew Bened had told Chloe something of his plans, but Julian could not see how the man could take his shot without the bullet going through Chloe before it went into Arthur. Yet he could think of nothing to end this, to free her without any further harm.

"Trust him, Julian," whispered Nigel close to his ear. "Bened would never put her in harm's way."

"I have little choice," Justin whispered back.

He glanced quickly over his shoulder when he heard a faint sound and saw Brindle holding a crying Anthony, the boy Drew helping her to keep his son from running into the middle of this mess. He wished the children had left as he had told them to, but he was not surprised by their presence. Anthony was too attached to Chloe to leave her side when she was in danger and too young to know that he could not help, only hinder. He had to be glad that the girl Brindle had the sense to know it.

Julian turned his full attention back on Bened, Chloe, and Arthur, and raised his pistol so he was prepared if a chance came for him to shoot without putting anyone else in danger. Out of the corner of his eyes he watched his mother and his aunt grab the filthy little boy with the club and pull him back until they were sheltered from view and harm by the oven. Using his free hand, Julian signaled Brindle to move back as well and a soft scuffling noise told him she was obeying him. He was going to have to find out who this very adult child was, he mused, watching both Bened and Arthur for some sign of what was to come.

"You shoot me, you fool, and you shoot your cousin." Arthur chuckled and it was a chilling sound. "Why not just wait there and you can watch me cut away a piece of her at a time."

"Down," Bened said.

Chloe dropped to the ground, her sudden added weight making Arthur stumble and let go. She rolled away and heard two shots ring out. Something warm splattered her face and she had the horrible feeling that it was Arthur's blood. A moment later, she was surrounded by people. A wet cloth was swiped over her face and hair, much to her relief, and familiar strong arms encircled her. Just as she turned to look up at Julian she heard a wail.

"Anthony? Oh, God, do not let him see what is left of Arthur," she said.

"Done, cousin," said Bened as he crouched by her side. "Threw him out the back."

"Mama!" Anthony cried as he started toward Chloe and she braced herself for the pain of his arrival in her arms.

Bened caught Anthony before he could throw himself on Chloe. "Your mama is going to be fine, lad." He spoke in a low voice to Anthony until the boy began to calm down and then set him on his feet. Bened clasped Anthony's shoulders. "There are some people hiding down in the wine cellar, aye?"

Anthony nodded. "My cousins and my nurse are down there. But, Mama?" He looked toward Chloe.

"I will be fine, love," she said and forced herself to smile at him. "It is a clean cut and Lady Evelyn knows what to do."

Anthony looked back up at Bened. "Who are you?"

Bened introduced himself and waited patiently while Anthony introduced his friends. "Now I think we need to go and tell those people that everything is safe again." He looked at the other children. "Some help would be appreciated." He looked down at Anthony again. "I need a man I can trust at my side when I let those people free."

Chloe watched as Bened led the four children away. Anthony's fright had disappeared, washed away by the thought that the big man following him needed his help. She hissed in a breath of pain as Lady Evelyn gently tugged away the part of her gown Arthur had stuck his knife into.

"Bened has a way with children," Julian said in a vain attempt to take Chloe's mind off her pain.

"He should, he has twelve siblings."

"Good God."

"Told you. Like rabbits," drawled a familiar voice and Julian just shook his head at Leo's nonsense. He could see by how pale the man had gone that he had been nearly as afraid for Chloe as he himself had.

Chloe knew she was going to lose her grip on consciousness very soon, and so she sought Lady Evelyn's gaze. The moment the woman's eyes met hers, Chloe put her hand over her belly. Lady Evelyn smiled and shook her head before she returned to working on her injured shoulder. Reassured that if she was carrying Julian's child, it was safe for now, Chloe allowed herself to finally slide into the blackness that beckoned her so strongly.

Chapter 20

"I must be better by now. I certainly feel better."

Chloe sighed when Lady Evelyn insisted on testing her forehead and cheeks for any sign of fever, and for what felt to be the hundredth time. She had never been cosseted like this even as a child. Back then she probably would have reveled in the attention. Now, although she loved Lady Evelyn, after a fortnight of it, it was getting a little tiresome.

"And where the bloody hell is my husband?"

"I believe he will be in to see you soon. He is out riding the boundaries of the estate."

"Oh. Pardon. Did not realize I had said that aloud."

Chloe looked at the food on the tray Lady Evelyn set on her lap. At least it was no longer broth, she thought. It was a rather hearty meal of meats and cheeses and thick-crusted bread. Suddenly feeling famished, she began to eat. When she realized a little later that she had eaten everything, she sighed and slumped back on the pillows.

"I am with child," she murmured.

"That you are. Most everyone knows it, but it might be nice to say it aloud to your husband just once."

"True. If he would just wander by here once in a while, I might have a chance to."

"He has had a lot of cleaning up to do, and not just the damage done by all those ruffians Arthur had hired. There are all the wrongs done to the people of Colinsmoor that need to be, well, not righted, as that cannot be done, but assuaged. He has taken Jake on as a steward of the land, as the man is a fount of knowledge about crops and animals. Then there is the hiring of all the new servants."

"I am well enough to help with that and have been for days. I do not need to stay abed. I may need to rest more because I carry a child, but I am certainly hale enough to hire servants."

Lady Evelyn smiled. "Yes, you are. You are, in truth, completely healed. I promised the physician that you would rest for a fortnight, and that time is done. Your wound closed up very nicely and all the stitching has been removed. And, of course, there is no sign that your injury caused any harm to the babe. Not that we can peek inside and see for ourselves, but you are showing no signs of distress."

"That did worry me. How are the children doing?"

"Well, Jem and Drew are doing better, finally settling to learning a little bit, but it is Brindle who is a wonder. That is a thirty-year-old woman trapped in an eight-year-old girl's body." Lady Evelyn shook her head. "Considering the sins Arthur committed while those children were there, I am astonished that they are so normal. Only Brindle seems to have suffered, although Arthur never touched her. She is just not a very joyful child, acts as if the weight of the world is upon her shoulders."

"I think it might have been for a while," Chloe said. "I also think it will take a while before she dares to trust in her change of fortune. Once she knows it is not going to be snatched away she may actually smile now and again."

"Possibly. And I can now answer that question you have been afraid to ask. Julian will suffer no consequences for killing Arthur. Mildred took Arthur's body home and, as she said, dumped it in a hole."

Chloe laughed softly but quickly grew serious. "It was so chilling to listen to him speak of killing his own children, and right in front of their mother, simply because she had not given him a son. Wherever he is, I hope he is being appropriately punished for ever even thinking of such a thing."

"Mildred did have a quiet word with her daughters and thanks be to God, he never soiled them with his perversions. It is why Helena carries a knife, however. She did not like the way he watched her younger sisters the few times he stopped by to act the husband and father."

"It is all being righted," Chloe whispered.

"It is, yes. And that seems to be lifting the weight of guilt from Julian's shoulders. I believe tomorrow the girls and I will return to London and attend a few events before the summer's heat drives all those who can leave to do so."

The arrival of the children for their morning visit ended the pleasant interval of genteel gossip.

Chloe was astonished at the change in Jem, Drew, and Brindle. They all looked remarkably healthy now, a steady regimen of good food working wonders. Anthony was pleased to have other children around even if the very serious Brindle did not act much like a child. By the time they left, Chloe needed a rest. She was healed enough to do most things, but she acknowledged to herself that she still tired easily.

By the afternoon she was sick of her own company and rose to get dressed. Just as she had donned a clean shift, her long-missing husband wandered in her bedchamber. Due to her injury he had not shared her bed yet. Chloe had every intention of changing that. She missed him at her side in the night and was hoping that he might have missed her, too.

"Going somewhere?" he asked her and brushed a kiss over her lips.

"Just getting out of bed and out of this room for a while."

Julian slid his arms around her waist and held her close. For a moment he just stood there enjoying the feel of her in his arms. For those few torturous minutes in the kitchen when he had to see her caught by Arthur and then stabbed, he had feared he would lose her, but that fear was finally easing. Since he ached to prove to himself just how alive she was in the usual way, he had avoided her somewhat during her recovery, but there was no question that she was fully recovered now.

"All healed and strong again?"

"I was never that strong," she teased and ran her

hand up and down his arm. "But, aye, I am officially and completely healed."

"Thank God," he muttered, picked her up, and carried her to the bed.

"I just got out of bed," she protested as he set her down on her back. "I am not at all sleepy."

"Nor am I," he assured her as he began to strip out of his clothes.

Chloe blinked in surprise at the soft growl of his voice. Then her body awoke to the need she always shared with him and heat flowed through her veins. She began to suspect that some of Julian's absence was due to the fact that when he was near her, he needed to touch her. Worse, she might have tried to comply with what he wanted and slowed down her healing.

It took only one kiss to ignite the fire they had kept banked for two very long weeks. Chloe was not sure who tore his clothes off and flung them all around the room, but she suspected it was both of them. Since he was now touching her, skin to skin, she really did not care. They both struggled to outdo each other in the way they touched, stroked, and kissed each other, but it was finally too much to bear. When Julian turned onto his back and demanded that she ride him, Chloe was in such a fever she did not even hesitate to try this new way of making love. She tried to go slow but her body was hammering at her for release. Chloe finally gripped his shoulders, bent down to kiss his mouth, and rode him as hard as she could, slowing down only now and then to regain her lost rhythm.

When her release began to roll through her

body, she suddenly found herself on her back. Julian went up on his knees and lifted her legs up until they rested flat against his chest, and then he thrust himself home. Chloe had to clamp her hands to her mouth to keep herself from screaming out her pleasure as he drove them both to the release they had missed for too long.

It was a while before Chloe found the strength to even open her eyes. Her cheek was against his broad warm chest. Her favorite pillow, she mused with a smile. His lightly calloused hand was moving up and down her back in a caress that was more tender and comforting than sensual. Glancing up at him, she saw the faint, slightly smug smile of satisfaction he wore and decided this was the best time to tell him her news.

"Julian, I am with child," she said, reverently touching her still-flat belly.

"I know."

She propped herself up on her elbows and frowned at him. "I know? That is all you have to say? And how did you know? Did your mother tell you?"

He turned his head and kissed her on the tip of her nose. "No. She would never intrude that way. In truth, I strongly suspected it the night before we were attacked by Arthur."

"Ah, so it is no surprise."

"I can act surprised."

She laughed. "Nay. I certainly was surprised, which was foolish."

"The child you carried was one reason I was so terrified when you fell into Arthur's hands."

"And what was the second reason?"

"Because I love you."

Julian did not know whether to laugh or feel nervous when she just stared at him, her mouth agape and her eyes wide. She looked completely stunned and he was not sure why she should be. To him it was obvious from the moment he allowed the words to slip into his mind. The only thing he was not sure of now was whether or not she returned his feelings.

"Nothing to say?" he finally prompted and to his horror, she burst into tears. "Chloe!" He wrapped his arms around her when she clung to him and cried all over his chest. "Hush, you will make yourself ill, and it is not good for the child for you to get so upset."

"Not upset," she said against his chest. "Happy."

"This is happy? I am sorry, love, but this does not sound happy to me."

Fighting for some control, Chloe finally grasped a thread of it and held on until it grew strong enough to slow the fall of her tears. Her heart was so full it actually ached. She had never imagined he would just lie there and calmly say the words she had wanted to hear for so very long. Chloe had a wish to just sit there and savor the feeling of knowing he loved her, but he was starting to look uneasy and she took mercy on him.

"I love you, too," she whispered against his mouth and found herself the recipient of such a ferocious kiss that she feared they would both return to making love, and she needed to talk.

"I feared you would never give me those words," he said and trailed soft kisses over her cheeks.

"You were afraid? And of me never saying I love you?"

"Yes. I was very precise about what I felt we could share in a marriage, and never let you know that I was finding so many other things we shared, things I needed like the air I breathe."

"Such as what?"

"This."

"This? You mean sharing a bed?" When he nodded she frowned. "Not every married couple shares their bed?"

"No, and you will undoubtedly find that out after you have been in society for a few years. I had always thought that I would not like it, but I cannot think of why I would ever want to be alone in my bed again. Without you in it, it is unbearably cold and empty. Here is where we can be truly private, share secrets and worries and hurts. No, I never wish to have a bed without you in it."

"Then praise my ignorance, for if I had known that married couples in society do not usually share their beds, I would have dutifully gone off to mine every night no matter how much I hated to. Then we would never have known how wonderful this is. This and waking up to you in the morning."

"On that we also agree. I open my eyes and there you are and my day can begin. A smile from you and it begins even better."

She hugged him. "Careful, or you will make me cry again."

"Please, do not. I am only just beginning to dry out." He laughed when she playfully slapped him. "Ah yes, and then there is laughter."

"Laughter is easily come by, Julian."

"Not for me. I found little to laugh about, and

when I did there was a sharp biting edge to it. Occasionally, even a meanness of spirit."

"I cannot imagine the man who would accept three orphaned children in his home, make them part of his family, mean."

He took her chin in his hand and looked right into her eyes. "It was not mean of me to do that, but it was not all kindness and love at first. I was sunk in guilt for all that had been done to the people here. Those children were also victims because I allowed Beatrice and Arthur to run free here. It did not take long, however, for me to care for them as if they were my own."

"They are good children and readily understand that they are being given an excellent chance to be more than a servant for people like us. Your guilt, which I have never thought you should be feeling to begin with, may have opened the door, but it was not guilt that made you play with them, try to make them comfortable, and welcome all their noise now that they are comfortable. That was the goodness in you, the goodness that made me fall in love with you."

That flattery required a kiss, which led to another until they were both breathing heavily and sorely tempted to forgo any more conversation or revelations. Julian combed his fingers through her thick hair as he reminded her, "I was not very good when you found me in that alley."

"Nay, you were not. You were a very wicked man. But you were also doing no more than many men do, and, sad to say, that which many men continue to do even after they are wed. And that is another reason I love you. You believe in marriage, in upholding vows taken. Even when you could not conceive of sharing a bed or speaking of love, you meant to keep your vows to me and that shows a core of honor most men wish they had and most women covet." She smiled when she saw the faint hint of a blush on his cheeks and brushed her fingers over it. "So there *is* a time and place where you are unable to endure flattery."

"Impudent wench," he teased. "I can probably abide that a great deal more than I can the kind that says you are rich, fairly handsome, and titled."

"Oh, you are much more than fairly handsome," she murmured as she kissed his neck. "You take my breath away, but I would still love you even if you spit and scratched your bottom every morning."

Julian sputtered with laughter. "Spit and scratch my bottom? Do you know someone who does this?" Then he narrowed his eyes. "And I am now thinking that you better not know what some other man does when he wakes in the morning."

"I speak of one of my brothers only. And he always did it just to annoy me."

Julian held her close in his arms and idly smoothed his hand over her still-flat belly. "You are well?"

"Very well. I still must be careful of what I eat in the morning, but nothing else troubles me. I am rather hoping for a girl."

"All I want is for both you and the babe to be healthy. But why do you want to have a girl?"

"I was hoping that if I have a girl, you will allow me to call her Laurel, after my sister."

"That would please me."

"Thank you. Oh, Julian, I do love you so much, and I was so afraid that I would never hear those words from you. I knew I felt more than a mere liking when we married, but I decided to settle for what you first offered." She lightly placed her fingers over his lips when he started to speak. "I do not complain. You offered me far more than many women get. But so many marriages in my family crumble into dust that I was afraid anything less than some great love would fail, too."

"Chloe, I think we have a great love."

"Oh, aye, so do I, and do you know one reason why?"

"Because we have both seen each other at our worst."

"I have never seen you at anything that even approaches a worst."

"Nay? Have I not been a whiny little nuisance this last fortnight as I healed from that wound?" she asked, surprised that he did not see how bad a patient she was.

"Chloe, love, everyone hates to be stuck abed like that and ends up short-tempered."

"You were not."

"Oh, I fear I was, but never when you were around. I also had a lot to keep me occupied, and that helps. But I think it might not be wise to try to see who has the greatest faults, for we could inadvertently hurt each other's feelings. What does it matter? As you said"—he grinned—"you would love me even if I spit and scratched my bottom in the morning."

Chloe laughed. She was a little startled when she caught him watching her laugh yet only smiled himself. "Do I have food in my teeth?"

"No, love. I just like the sound of it." He kissed

the blush that flooded her cheeks. "I used to laugh and be foolish but I lost it somewhere. I had not realized how much I missed it until you gave it back to me. I do believe the way you could make me smile and laugh, the way you would tease, was what stirred the seed of love inside me." He leaned back a little and looked at her warily. "Are you going to cry again?"

"Nay, just a moment's weakness. That was the loveliest thing that has ever been said to me. I was just trying to think of what you gave me and what made me start to really fall in love with you, and it does not sound as lovely as that."

"Tell me anyway," he demanded as he rolled her onto her back and sprawled on top of her.

"You will laugh."

"Not at something that you think is serious, not at something you tell me that is straight from the heart."

"I really liked the way you could make me feel so wicked," she whispered against his chest and felt as if her cheeks were on fire from embarrassment.

Julian tilted her face up to his. "Wicked? You say I made you feel wicked?"

"All the time. I had assumed because of your year of debauchery you would be a very wicked man, but that was not the way it was at all."

"Except when I did this?" He kissed the hollow at the base of her ear.

"Aye," she said and shivered when he trailed his hands up and down her back. "I suppose it seems a bit foolish to a man like you who has done so much—"

"And remembers so very little of it. But, love, no man would ever think it is foolish that his wife feels wicked in his arms, and when he kisses her."

"That is good, because I believe I am feeling a little bit wicked right now."

"You have chosen the right man to tend to that."

Chloe squirmed against him, smiling as she felt his ready response. "I know," she said. "My wicked cavalier," she whispered.

Julian brushed his lips over hers and whispered, "My laughter, my joy."

Epilogue

Eight and a half months later

"Why is it taking so long?"

Leo grinned as he watched Julian pace the length of the green salon, Anthony right behind him. "I believe the birth of a child takes a little work and a little time. Chloe did not really get started on it until three hours ago."

"It is a good thing I listened to you." Julian turned sharply and paced in the opposite direction, Anthony mimicking his move. "If I had given into her wish to wait a while, we might be trying to explain a seventh-month baby."

"Little rabbits," Leo said cheerfully.

Julian paused to stare at him. "You enjoy being proven right entirely too much."

"How uncivilized of me."

"Quite right. However, the words are emblazoned upon my mind."

"Very wise. You would not want to have to add too many more bedrooms."

Nigel strode into the room. "Baby born yet?"

"No. I am hoping it will have the courtesy to arrive soon," replied Julian.

"Ah, good of it. Bened and I have plans to go to the Rectonshires' stables and see a mare." Nigel laughed when Julian glared at him. "At least Chloe is not bringing the roof down with her screaming."

Julian frowned up at the ceiling. "You are right. It is too quiet. Something must be wrong." Julian felt his heart clench with fear.

"Nay, Pegeen is with her," Leo said.

"She is such a skilled midwife that women make no sound?"

Leo shrugged. "Most of the women in the family insist that she attend them at their births, and very few of them scream or shout out bloodthirsty threats against their husbands."

"She did seem to be a capable woman," Julian murmured.

"Pegeen is a healer. She has the touch. She is especially good at taking away your pain."

"The military could use someone like that," said Nigel as he poured himself a drink.

"And she has helped them on occasion, but treating too many at a time leaves her dangerously weak. However, no one can help a woman with birthing her child like Pegeen can, and she is kept very busy with our family."

Julian nodded. "A healer. I can accept that."

"Still having trouble with Chloe's choice of Modred as a godfather? He is a duke."

"Not as much trouble as I had before. He told me

the Kenwoods have very strong walls. It is Cassandra
I am not too certain about."

"I have not met Cassandra, but Bened says she is
a strong woman," said Nigel and then he grinned.
"When Bened says that he usually means tart-
tongued and bossy."

Julian was surprised he could do so, but he
laughed. "I chose Edgar and Lady Marston."

"So there will be two strong women as godmoth-
ers. God help you if you have a daughter."

"It does not trouble me. I would want her to be
strong. I have recently come to realize that our
mother is a very strong woman. So is Aunt Mildred.
The only time our aunt stumbled during the ordeal
with Arthur was when she realized how many people
he had killed and how many crimes he had committed. That weighed her down with a monstrous
burden of guilt, for she felt she should have seen the
evil in the man and done something. She shook it
off with the help of Mother and Chloe."

"Good to know, for she did not deserve to suffer
it. And just what is wrong with Modred, aside from
being cursed with that name? I asked Bened, but he
just said that his cousin is a special man."

Julian explained what Modred's gift was and
grinned at the look of horror on Nigel's face. "Do
not look so afraid. As I said, he told me we Kenwoods have very strong walls." Before there was
time for him to say anything, his mother walked in.
"Is Chloe well?"

Lady Evelyn kissed him on the cheek. "Very well.
Go and see your wife and new family."

Julian did not need a second invitation. He

hurried up the stairs, leaving his mother to tend to Anthony and the other curious children. Just as he was about to knock on the door of the master bed-chamber, a plump dark-haired woman opened the door for him, gave him a wink, and left.

"The infamous Pegeen, I presume," he said as he cautiously walked to the bed and looked down.

Julian did not know whether to sit down or fall down. Chloe lay on the bed, her hair spread out prettily on the pillow and a wriggling swaddled baby tucked up in each arm. He stared at her again and then stared at what she held again.

"Two?" he finally managed to croak out.

"Two." Chloe was tired and her body felt as some-one had beaten her up from the inside out, but she felt exhilarated as well. "One boy." She slightly lifted her left arm and Julian noticed there was a blue ribbon tied on the corner of the blanket. "One girl." She slightly lifted her right arm.

He sat down on the bed, his head reeling. "Damna-tion, woman. Two?" He stared down into the sleep-ing faces of his children.

"Laurel, after my sister, and George, after my father." She glanced at him a little uncertainly. "If that still pleases you."

"It does." He suddenly grinned at her. "You cer-tainly solved the problem of how to not disappoint at least one of the other children. The girl wanted a girl and the boys wanted a boy. One of each will keep them all quiet." He kissed her. "I love and thank you for giving me this."

"Ah, nay, thank you. I always feared I would never find the right man and never have children." Chloe winked at him and looked at her children. "Mayhap the Fates are just making certain that I know you are my right man. My wicked cavalier."

He smiled and rubbed his nose against hers. "My joy."

"We are so well suited it is a little embarrassing."

"No, m'dear, we are just perfect and we should glory in it." He laughed with her and reached for his daughter, ready to introduce himself to her. "We will do as Jake's wife has suggested, however, so that you do not wear yourself out having a dozen children."

Chloe just smiled as she watched him look his children over with an adoration he did not even try to hide. She decided it would be best if she kept what she had seen during the birthing all to herself. Julian would worry if she told him that despite the tricks Jake's wife had told her about how to keep a man's seed from taking root too often, they would be having those dozen children. She had seen them with them all, with Anthony grown tall and strong, and the three children they had taken under their wing. And each one of the children she and Julian would create would be blessed with a gift. Recalling how big a smile he had worn on his handsome face as his flock had gathered around him, she decided he would not mind.

Please turn the page
for an exciting sneak peek of
IF HE'S SINFUL,
coming in December 2009!

London—fall, 1788

There was something about having a knife to one's throat that tended to bring a certain clarity to one's opinion of one's life, Penelope decided. She stood very still as the burly, somewhat odiferous, man holding her clumsily adjusted his grip. Suddenly, all of her anger and resentment over being treated as no more than a lowly maid by her step-sister seemed petty, the problem insignificant.

Of course, this could be some form of cosmic retribution for all those times she had wished ill upon her step-sister, she thought as the man hefted her up enough so that her feet were off the ground. One of his two companions bound her ankles in a manner quite similar to the way her wrists had been bound. Her captor began to carry her down a dark alley that smelled about as bad as he did. It had been only a few hours ago that she had watched Clarissa leave for a carriage ride with her soon-to-be-fiancé, Lord Radmoor. Peering out of the cracked window in her tiny attic room she had, indisputably, cherished the spiteful wish that Clarissa would stumble and fall into the foul muck near the carriage wheels. Penelope did think that being dragged away by a knife-wielding ruffian and his two hulking companions was a rather harsh penalty for such a childish wish born of jealousy, however. She had, after all, never wished that Clarissa would die, which Penelope very much feared was going to be her fate.

Penelope sighed, ruefully admitting that she was partially at fault for her current predicament. She had stayed too long with her boys. Even little Paul had urged her not to walk home in the dark. It was embarrassing to think that a little boy of five had more common sense than she did.

A soft cry of pain escaped her, muted by the filthy gag in her mouth, when her captor stumbled and the cold, sharp edge of his knife scored her skin. For a brief moment, the fear she had been fighting to control swelled up inside her so strongly she feared she would be ill. The warmth of her own blood seeping into the neckline of her bodice only added to the fear. It took several moments before she could grasp any shred of calm or courage. The realization that her blood was flowing too slowly for her throat to have been cut helped her push aside her burgeoning panic.

"Ye sure we ain't allowed to have us a taste of this, Jud," asked the largest and most hirsute of her captor's assistants.

"Orders is orders," replied Jud as he steadied his knife against her skin. "A toss with this one will cost ye more'n she be worth."

"None of us'd be telling and the wench ain't going to be able to tell, neither."

"I ain't letting ye risk it. Wench like this'd be fighting ye and that leaves bruises. They'll tell the tale and that bitch Mrs. Cratchitt will tell. She would think it a right fine thing if we lost our pay for this night's work."

"Aye, that old bawd would be thinking she could gain something from it right enough. Still, it be a sad shame I can't be having me a taste afore it be sold off to anyone with a coin or two."

"Get your coin first and then go buy a little if'n ye want it so bad."

"Won't be so clean and new, will it?"

"This one won't be neither if'n that old besom uses her as she uses them others, not by the time ye could afford a toss with her."

She was being taken to a brothel, Penelope realized. Yet again she had to struggle fiercely against becoming blinded by her own fears. She was still alive, she told herself repeatedly, and it looked as if she would stay that way for a while. Penelope fought to find her strength in that knowledge. It did not do any good to think too much on the horrors she might be forced to endure before she could escape or be found. She needed to concentrate on one thing and one thing only—getting free.

It was not easy but Penelope forced herself to keep a close eye on the route they traveled. Darkness and all the twists and turns her captors took made it nearly impossible to make note of any and every possible sign to mark the way out of this dangerous warren she was being taken into. She had to force herself to hold fast to the hope that she could even truly escape, and the need to get back to her boys who had no one else to care for them.

She was carried into the kitchen of a house. Two women and a man were there, but they spared her only the briefest of glances before returning all of their attention to their work. It was not encouraging that they seemed so accustomed to such a sight, so unmoved and uninterested.

As her captor carried her up a dark, narrow stairway, Penelope became aware of the voices and music coming from below, from the front of the building which appeared to be as great a warren as the alleys leading to it. When they reached the hallway and started to walk down it, she could hear the murmur of voices coming from behind all the closed doors. Other sounds drifted out from behind those doors but she tried very hard not to think about what might be causing them.

"There it be, room twenty-two," muttered Jud. "Open the door, Tom."

The large, hirsute man opened the door and Jud carried Penelope into the room. She had just enough time to notice how small the room was before Jud tossed her down onto the bed in the middle of the room. It was a surprisingly clean and comfortable bed. Penelope suspected that, despite its seedy location, she had probably been brought to one of the better bordellos, one that catered to gentlemen of refinement and wealth. She knew, however, that that did not mean she could count on any help.

"Get that old bawd in here, Tom," said Jud. "I wants to be done with this night's work." The moment Tom left, Jud scowled down at Penelope. "Don't suspect you'd be aknowing why that high-and-mighty lady be wanting ye outta the way, would ye?"

Penelope slowly shook her head as a cold suspicion settled in her stomach.

"Don't make no sense to me. Can't be jealousy or the like. Can't be that she thinks you be taking her man or the like, can it. Ye ain't got her fine looks, ain't dressed so fine, neither, and ye ain't got her fine curves. Scrawny, brown mite like ye should be no threat at all to such a fulsome wench. So, why does she want ye gone so bad, eh?"

Scrawny brown mite? Penelope thought, deeply insulted even as she shrugged in reply.

"Why you frettin' o'er it, Jud?" asked the tall, extremely muscular man by his side.

Jud shrugged. "Curious, Mac. Just curious, is all. This don't make no sense to me."

"Don't need to. Money be good. All that matters."

"Aye, mayhap. As I said, just curious. Don't like puzzles."

"Didn't know that."

"Well, it be true. Don't want to be part of something I don't understand. Could mean trouble."

If she was not gagged, Penelope suspected she would be gaping at her captor. He had kidnapped the daughter of a marquis, brought her bound and gagged to a brothel, and was going to leave her to the untender care of a madam, a woman he plainly did not trust or like. Exactly what did the idiot think *trouble* was? If he was caught, he would be tried, convicted, and hanged in a heartbeat. And that would be merciful compared to what her relatives would do to the fool if they found out. How much more *trouble* could he be in?

A hoarse gasp escaped her when he removed her gag. "Water," she whispered, desperate to wash away the foul taste of the rag.

What the man gave her was a tankard of weak ale, but Penelope decided it was probably for the best. If there was any water in this place it was undoubtedly dangerous to drink. She tried not to breathe too deeply as he held her upright and helped her to take a drink. Penelope drank the ale as quickly as she could, however, for she wanted the man to move away from her. Anyone as foul smelling as he was surely had a vast horde of creatures sharing his filth that she would just as soon did not come to visit her.

When the tankard was empty he let her fall back down onto the bed and said, "Now, don't ye go thinking of making no noise, screaming for help or the like. No one here will be heeding it."

Penelope opened her mouth to give him a tart reply and then frowned. The bed might be clean and comfortable but it was not new. A familiar chill swept over her. Even as she thought it a very poor time for her *gift* to display itself, her mind was briefly filled with violent memories that were not her own.

"Someone died in this bed," she said, her voice a little unsteady from the effect of those chilling glimpses into the past.

"What the bleeding hell are ye babbling about?" snapped Jud.

"Someone died in this bed and she did not do so peacefully." Penelope got some small satisfaction from how uneasy her words made her burly captors.

"You be talking nonsense, woman."

"No. I have a gift, you see."

"You can see spirits?" asked Mac, glancing nervously around the room.

"Sometimes. When they wish to reveal themselves to me. This time it was just the memories of what happened here," she lied.

Both men were staring at her with a mixture of fear, curiosity, and suspicion. They thought she was trying to trick them in some way so that they would set her free. Penelope suspected that a part of them probably wondered if she would conjure up a few spirits to help her. Even if she could, she doubted they would be much help or that these men would even see them. They certainly had not noticed the rather gruesome one standing near the bed. It would have sent them fleeing from the room. Despite all she had seen and experienced over the years the sight of the lovely young woman, her white gown soaked in blood, sent a chill down her spine. Penelope wondered why the more gruesome apparitions were almost always the clearest.

The door opened and, before Penelope turned to look, she saw an expression upon the ghost's face that nearly made *her* want to flee the room. Fury and utter loathing twisted the spirit's lovely face until it looked almost demonic. Penelope looked at the ones now entering the room. Tom had returned with a middle-aged woman and two young, scantily clad females. Penelope looked right at the ghost and noticed that all that rage and hate was aimed straight at the middle-aged woman.

Beware.

Penelope almost cursed as the word echoed in her mind. Why did the spirits always whisper such ominous words to her without adding any pertinent information, such as what she should *beware* of, or whom? It was also a very poor time for this sort of distraction. She was a prisoner trapped in a house of ill-repute and was facing either death or what many euphemistically called a fate worse than death. She had no time to deal with blood-soaked specters whispering dire but unspecified warnings. If nothing else, she needed all her wits and strength to keep the hysteria writhing deep inside her tightly caged.

"This is going to cause you a great deal of trouble," Penelope told the older woman, not really surprised when everyone ignored her.

"There she be," said Jud. "Now, give us our money."

"The lady has your money," said the older woman.

"It ain't wise to try and cheat me, Cratchitt. The lady told us you would have it. Now, if the lady ain't paid you that be your problem, not mine. I did as I was ordered and did it quick and right. Get the wench, bring her here, and then collect my pay from you. Done and done. So, hand it over."

Cratchitt did so with an ill grace. Penelope watched Jud carefully count his money. The man had obviously taught himself enough to make sure that he was not cheated. After one long, puzzled look at her, he pocketed his money and then frowned at the woman he called Cratchitt.

"She be all yours now," Jud said, "though I ain't sure what ye be wanting her for. T'ain't much to her."

Penelope was growing very weary of being disparaged by this lice-ridden ruffian. "So speaks the great beau of the walk," she muttered and met his glare with a faint smile.

"She is clean and fresh," said Cratchitt, ignoring that byplay and fixing her cold stare on Penelope. "I have many a gent willing to pay a goodly fee for that alone. There be one man waiting especially for this one, but he will not arrive until the morrow. I have other plans for her tonight. Some very rich gentlemen have arrived and are looking for something special. Unique, they said. They have a friend about to step into the parson's mousetrap and wish to give him a final bachelor treat. She will do nicely for that."

"But don't that other feller want her untouched?"

"As far as he will ever know, she will be. Now, get out. Me and the girls need to wrap this little gift."

The moment Jud and his men were gone, Penelope said, "Do you have any idea of who I am?" She was very proud of the haughty tone she had achieved but it did not impress Mrs. Cratchitt at all.

"Someone who made a rich lady very angry," replied Cratchitt.

"I am Lady Penelope—"

She never finished for Mrs. Cratchitt grasped her by the jaw in a painfully tight hold, forced her mouth open, and started to pour something from a remarkably fine silver flask down her throat. The two younger women held her head steady so that Penelope could not turn away or thrash her head. She knew she did not want this drink inside her but was unable to do anything but helplessly swallow as it was forced into her.

While she was still coughing and gagging from

that abuse, the women untied her. Penelope struggled as best as she could but the women were strong and alarmingly skilled at undressing someone who did not wish to be undressed. As if she did not have trouble enough to deal with, the ghost was drowning her in feelings of fear, despair, and helpless fury. Penelope knew she was swiftly becoming hysterical but could not grasp one single, thin thread of control. That only added to her terror.

Then, slowly, that suffocating panic began to ease. Despite the fact that the women continued their work, stripping her naked, giving her a quick wash with scented water, and dressing her in a lacey, diaphanous gown that should have shocked her right down to her toes, Penelope felt calmer with every breath she took. The potion they had forced her to drink had been some sort of drug. That was the only rational explanation for why she was now lying there actually smiling as these three harpies prepared her for the sacrifice of her virginity.

"There, all sweets and honey now, ain't you, dearie," muttered Cratchitt as she began to let down Penelope's hair.

"You are such an evil bitch," Penelope said pleasantly and smiled. One of the younger women giggled and Cratchitt slapped her hard. "Bully. When my family discovers what you have done to me, you will pay more dearly than even your tiny, nasty mind could ever comprehend."

"Hah! It was your own family what sold you to me, you stupid girl."

"Not that family, you cow. My true parents' family. In fact, I would not be at all surprised if they are already suspicious, sensing my troubles upon the wind."

"You are talking utter nonsense."

Why does everyone say that? Penelope wondered. Enough wit and sense of self-preservation remained in her clouded mind to make her realize that it might not be wise to start talking about all the blood there was on the woman's hands. Even if the woman did not believe Penelope could know anything for a fact, she suspected Mrs. Cratchitt would permanently silence her simply to be on the safe side of the matter. With the drug holding her captive as well as any chain could, Penelope knew she was in no condition to even try to save herself.

When Cratchitt and her minions were finished, she stood back and looked Penelope over very carefully. "Well, well, well. I begin to understand."

"Understand what, you bride of Beelzebub?" asked Penelope and could tell by the way the woman clenched and unclenched her hands that Mrs. Cratchitt desperately wanted to beat her.

"Why the fine lady wants you gone. And, you will pay dearly for your insults, my girl. Very soon." Mrs. Cratchitt collected four bright silk scarves from the large carpetbag she had brought in with her and handed them to the younger women. "Tie her to the bed," she ordered them.

"Your customer may find that a little suspicious," said Penelope as she fruitlessly tried to stop the women from binding her limbs to the four posts of the bed.

"You *are* an innocent, aren't you." Mrs. Cratchitt shook her head and laughed. "No, my customer will only see this as a very special delight indeed. Come along, girls. You have work to do and we best get that man up here to enjoy his gift before that potion begins to wear off."

Penelope stared at the closed door for several moments after everyone had left. Everyone except the ghost, she mused, and finally turned her attention back to the specter now shimmering at the foot of the bed. The young woman looked so sad, so utterly defeated, that Penelope decided the poor ghost had probably just realized the full limitations of being a spirit. Although the memories locked into the bed had told Penelope how the woman had died, it did not tell her when. However, she began to suspect it had been not all that long ago.

"I would like to help you," she said, "but I cannot, not right now. You must see that. If I can get free, I swear I will work hard to give you some peace. Who are you?" she asked, although she knew it was often impossible to get proper, sensible answers from a spirit. "I know how you died. The bed still holds those dark memories and I saw it."

I am Faith and my life was stolen.

The voice was clear and sweet, but weighted with an intense grief, and Penelope was not completely certain if she was hearing it in her head or if the ghost was actually speaking to her. "What is your full name, Faith?"

My name is Faith and I was taken, as you have been. My life was stolen. My love is lost. I was torn from heaven and plunged into hell. Now I lie below.

"Below? Below what? Where?"

Below. I am covered in sin. But, I am not alone.

Penelope cursed when Faith disappeared. She could not help the spirit now but dealing with Faith's spirit had provided her with a much needed diversion. It had helped her concentrate and fight the power of the drug she had been given. Now she was alone with her thoughts and they were becoming increasingly strange. Worse, all of her protections were slowly crumbling away. If she did not find something to fix her mind on soon she would be wide open to every thought, every feeling, and every spirit lurking within the house. Considering what went on in this house that could easily prove a torture beyond bearing.

She did not know whether to laugh or to cry. She was strapped to a bed awaiting some stranger who would use her helpless body to satisfy his manly needs. The potion Mrs. Cratchitt had forced down her throat was rapidly depleting her strength and all her ability to shut out the cacophony of the world, the world of the living as well as that of the dead. Even now she could feel the growing weight of unwelcome emotions, the increasing whispers so few others could hear. The spirits in the house were stirring, sensing the presence of one who could help them touch the world of the living. It was probably not worth worrying about, she decided. Penelope did not know if anything could be worse than what she was already suffering and what was yet to come.

Suddenly the door opened and one of Mrs. Cratchitt's earlier companions led a man into the room. He was blindfolded and dressed as an ancient Roman. Penelope stared at him in shock as he was led up to her bedside, and then she inwardly groaned. She had no trouble recognizing the man despite the blindfold and the costume. Penelope was not at all pleased to discover that things could quite definitely get worse—a great deal worse.

More by Bestselling Author
Hannah Howell

__Highland Sinner	978-0-8217-8001-5	$6.99US/$8.49CAN
__Highland Captive	978-0-8217-8003-9	$6.99US/$8.49CAN
__Wild Roses	978-0-8217-7976-7	$6.99US/$8.49CAN
__Highland Fire	978-0-8217-7429-8	$6.99US/$8.49CAN
__Silver Flame	978-1-4201-0107-2	$6.99US/$8.49CAN
__Highland Wolf	978-0-8217-8000-8	$6.99US/$9.99CAN
__Highland Wedding	978-0-8217-8002-2	$4.99US/$6.99CAN
__Highland Destiny	978-1-4201-0259-8	$4.99US/$6.99CAN
__Only for You	978-0-8217-8151-7	$6.99US/$9.99CAN
__Highland Promise	978-1-4201-0261-1	$4.99US/$6.99CAN
__Highland Vow	978-1-4201-0260-4	$4.99US/$6.99CAN
__Highland Savage	978-0-8217-7999-6	$6.99US/$9.99CAN
__Beauty and the Beast	978-0-8217-8004-6	$4.99US/$6.99CAN
__Unconquered	978-0-8217-8088-6	$4.99US/$6.99CAN
__Highland Barbarian	978-0-8217-7998-9	$6.99US/$9.99CAN
__Highland Conqueror	978-0-8217-8148-7	$6.99US/$9.99CAN
__Conqueror's Kiss	978-0-8217-8005-3	$4.99US/$6.99CAN
__A Stockingful of Joy	978-1-4201-0018-1	$4.99US/$6.99CAN
__Highland Bride	978-0-8217-7995-8	$4.99US/$6.99CAN
__Highland Lover	978-0-8217-7759-6	$6.99US/$9.99CAN
__Highland Warrior	978-0-8217-7985-9	$4.99US/$6.99CAN

Available Wherever Books Are Sold!

Check out our website at
http://www.kensingtonbooks.com